Praise for Maggie Pouncey's

Perfect Reader

"[A] wryly perceptive first novel."
—*The Boston Globe*

"Sparkling, shrewd, and at times hilarious in its parsing of family dynamics, academic competition, the solace of literature, the aggression of the blogosphere, and what it truly means to be a 'perfect reader' and a generous soul."
—*Booklist*

"A novel of . . . sentence-by-sentence pleasures."
—*The Columbus Dispatch*

"Marvelous. . . . Page for page *Perfect Reader* is an assured literary debut."
—*BookPage*

"An absolutely wonderful novel that I hope every one of you who love fine fiction will read." —Ann La Farge, *Hudson Valley News*

"Pouncey's debut is marked by an extraordinary blend of tact, wit, mercy, and intelligence. The father/daughter knot is explored from an entirely fresh perspective, and it ties us in from beginning to end." —Mary Gordon, author of *Circling My Mother*

"Pouncey hones her wry wit in poking fun at small town academia, and readers with an inside view will laugh at its truth. . . . An unusual coming-of-age story. An intelligent and witty debut."
—*Sacramento Book Review*

"A pleasure, an uncommonly smart, character-driven first novel."
—Nancy Pearl, author of *Book Lust*

"Elegantly framed and thoughtfully considered. . . . Pouncey confidently forgoes any gimmicks, her prose tempered and understated and her control of each meaningful scene confident and sure." —*Bookreporter*

"Tender, smart and often wicked, especially on the subject of college towns. . . . Pouncey's first is impressively mature and entertaining." —*Kirkus Reviews* (starred)

"Pouncey imbues her debut novel with lively turns of phrase, perceptive observations about people and society, and a natural tendency to analyze living spaces. . . . A thoughtful person's novel. . . . Assured and smart." —MostlyFiction.com

"Memorable. . . . *Perfect Reader* sows the rich and fertile ground of parental loss." —*Campus Circle*

"*Perfect Reader* is a whale of a gracious, insightful, and thoroughly enjoyable book. . . . Should be on your must-read list." —BookLoons.com

Maggie Pouncey

Perfect Reader

Maggie Pouncey was born in New York City and grew up there and in Amherst, Massachusetts, and New Haven, Connecticut. She received her B.A. and M.F.A. from Columbia University and has taught writing at Columbia, the Bard Prison Initiative, and the New York City nonprofit Girls Write Now. She lives in Brooklyn with her husband and son.

Perfect Reader

Perfect Reader

A Novel

Maggie Pouncey

Anchor Books
A Division of Random House, Inc.
New York

The Library of Congress has cataloged the Pantheon edition as follows:
Pouncey, Maggie.
Perfect reader / Maggie Pouncey.
p. cm.
1. Young women—Fiction. 2. Critics—Fiction. 3. Poets—Fiction.
4. Fathers and daughters—Fiction. 5. Fathers—Death—Fiction.
6. Psychological fiction. I. Title.
PS3616.O8575P47 2010
813'.6—dc22 2009029991

Anchor ISBN: 978-0-307-47480-3

www.anchorbooks.com

Printed in the United States of America
10 9 8 7 6 5 4 3 2 1

For my mother, Susan Rieger, and my father, Peter Pouncey—
my first and favorite storytellers, my great good luck

He's my poet of poets—I know him almost by heart.

—Henry James, *The Aspern Papers*

'You look as if you wished the place in Hell,'
My friend said, 'judging from your face.' 'Oh well,
I suppose it's not the place's fault,' I said.

—Philip Larkin, "I Remember, I Remember"

Contents

Fall

1

Borrowed Houses

IT WAS AFTER HER FATHER'S DEATH Flora returned to Darwin. Returning—with all the criminal associations—to the scene of her growing up had been a task she'd put off, rebuffing her father's invitations. "You don't go home much, do you?" friends would ask. Home—that fuzzy image of innocence, that haven of recognition. The place you long for when adrift.

Her father's voice in her mind's ear paused her: *So all I had to do, Flo, to get you to Darwin was die?* But it did not stop her. She caught a taxi to the bus station, and took the bus to its terminus, a desolate former mill town thirty minutes from Darwin, and then she loaded herself and her body bag of a suitcase into a country cab—more properly called a car, a crumby minivan, with nothing marking it as professional in any way—now bringing her to her father's house.

She did not sublet her apartment in the city; there wasn't time, and the thought of someone else sleeping in her bed and filling her closets made her anxious—an only child, she'd never liked to share. She knew what people did in other people's houses, and did not want it done to her. And who knew how long she'd be gone. But she had taken the time to pack all the things she liked best, leaving the B garments behind. She packed her three favorite pairs of jeans of varying degrees of tightness and wear, a pair of black corduroys, two A-line skirts, one high-slitted denim pencil skirt, and a black silk dress she'd bought several years back upon receiving her first reasonable paycheck, imagining a life of cocktail parties and cigarette holders, and worn once. She packed socks and tights, three delicate wool cardigans, one milky white cable-knit cashmere turtle-neck, five long-sleeved cotton shirts of assorted saturated colors, clogs, her turquoise old-lady slippers, sweatpants and two concert T-shirts she'd had since high school, boots (one pair heeled, one flat), her six sexy pairs of underwear and her four unsexy, old, comforting pairs of underwear, and various scarves and hats. She packed a short, beaded 1920s-style flapper dress—a prime example of her favorite category of clothing: inappropriate for every occasion (and thus equally appropriate for all occasions)—and a pair of pewter-colored four-inch heels of the same category. She packed soap, shampoo, and other ablutions (as if she were traveling to the tundra, where such items could not be procured, and not to New England, where they could, but then they might be inferior), and, in the midst of the vanities, she buried the folder of her father's poems. If I lose this bag, she thought, forcing the zipper across its length, I'll be very sad.

Darwin was three hours from everywhere: Flora was unready to arrive. It was dusk, and quiet, her country cab passing the odd station wagon loping home. Darwin—the one place in America SUVs had not yet colonized. Perhaps they were against the law. Here the indigenous station wagon still reigned supreme over his niche. Here talk of carbon footprint was as routine as talk of gas prices elsewhere. The town of Darwin knew unhappiness—the Darwinians self-satisfied but not content. Thick with academics and their broods—idlers, ruminators, moseyers. Thoughtful people, thinking thoughts. No one hurrying down the few placid streets. Hadn't the Darwinians anything urgent to attend to? Yes, they had not. Poets and the world romanticize being idle—the boon of free time praised, guarded, envied—but anyone who has idled for a living knows the damaging effects it can have on the moods.

The minivan was overheated, stifling. The window wouldn't budge. Flora's hair itched with sweat. She was being cooked alive. She took off her hat, uncoiled her scarf, unbuttoned her coat. She was a child. Her clothes, hidden all day beneath layers—why did one prefer to keep one's coat on in public transit?—announced a complete regression. The faded black sweatshirt, the army green pants with the patched knees and safety-pinned waist, the red sneakers that she dearly loved. "Not a day over sixteen," her father had said of her face. At what age did the compliment of youth expire?

The driver tried talk: "What brings you to Darwin?" He had the overeager voice of one stranger requiring something of another.

"You know," Flora said. "Family." But once she'd said the words, they sounded unkind. The man's face ravaged, ungroomed. It was possible he did not know much of family. A woman in his life would have suggested a haircut weeks ago.

Still, the unkindness hanging in the close air was preferable to chat. She glanced at her cell phone to check the time. It was now "rejecting" text messages—an apt technological gesture—its tiny brain at capacity, and Flora thought with pleasure of her friends agonizing over compassionate abbreviated condolences, only to have them bounce right back to their machines as though repellent.

Her father's house sat at the edge of the town proper, a ten-minute walk from the Darwin College campus. An old farmhouse, it had recently been repainted an excellent taupe. When, exactly? Even through the fouled window of the car, it had never looked prettier, or she hadn't remembered it that way. A pretty house, certainly, but she'd thought of it as resigned and downtrodden in that way peculiar to academics and their surroundings. But her father, it seemed, had even taken up gardening, or else hired someone to work on the historically neglected flower beds circling the house like a moat, the odd stem standing its ground as though it didn't know it was November. The house was a relic from a happier time. The house was showing off. The house was oblivious; it hadn't been informed of recent developments.

She overtipped the driver as an apology for her curtness and he hauled her morbid duffel to the door—newly painted, slate blue. Flora hesitated, as at the door of an acquaintance, where she might not be welcome, or know anyone inside. The house of a sixty-eight-year-old retiree bachelor, a reclusive reader, an academic with no more classes or committees to order his life around. Would it be pathologically unkempt, like the foul apartments of boys she'd dated post-college, the disordered universe of men living alone?

Would it feel as though he'd dashed out for a haircut, or for dish soap, and could return at any moment? Or would the house have the aura of the abandoned, like a woman whose husband runs out to gas up the car and forgets to come home?

The house was hers, on paper.

Funny how death did that—made things yours.

It was a few years after Flora and her mother moved out, after they who had needed only one house suddenly needed two, after all that had gone wrong, that her father had finally left the President's House and come here to this house he owned, giving up one of his worlds, the world of industrial stoves, and Betsy coming to work every day, a world where you had to dial 9 to get an outside line, as though it were an office, which of course it also was, a world of life-size paintings of dead men and grand chandeliers and fire escapes, to return to the life of the full-time academic—the word *full-time* in this case meaning you had to show up four times a week for approximately two hours a pop. He'd loved it right away, his old farmhouse. "I like a house that tells you how it feels," he said of its creaks and moans. In winter there was a fire always burning, in summer the windows thrown open. "I'm embowered," he said in spring, the yellow green of leaves and buds filling every view. In high school, Flora had stayed there with him Tuesday nights, that old habit outlasting its necessity, her mother completely analyzed, for better or worse, and no longer fleeing Darwin weekly for the city. Her father's house. A place she visited—if she visited—with a packed bag.

Inside, all appeared tidy. She dropped her bag in the kitchen, waiting.

"Hello?" she called, to disturb the silence. *There you are,* her father would say if he were there. "Here I am."

She started with his study, surveying—no need to linger now. Off the kitchen, browns and grays, a blend of woods, snug. Books on shelves like rows of crooked teeth. On the desk, tall piles of papers. But no reading glasses lying, arms crossed in wait, on the table by the Shaker chair. No forgotten encrusted cereal bowl. She skimmed her fingers across the old Smith Corona portable with its round green keys. Nothing. Entering the homes of other people was something Flora did for a living—or had done. She was adept at moving through other people's spaces, taking inventory. A professional snoop.

Back through the kitchen. No cottony coating of dust on the banister. Upstairs, the bed made, the duvet new and crisp and hotel-like. Not a single sock on the wide-planked floor. No bath mat on the terracotta tiles of the bathroom floor, but folded and hung neatly on the side of the tub like a coat hung over an arm. No unearthly blue toothpaste smudges on the sink, only gleaming porcelain. Had her father even lived there? Had anyone? In her job, she'd had to orchestrate the removal of the personal for photo shoots: She'd scoured living rooms for family snapshots, reclaimed refrigerators from the collage of a child's artwork. Here, her work had been done for her.

The fridge, she thought. Back downstairs. She opened it and stared into cavernous whiteness—still more nothing. Had he stopped eating? He had looked a little thinner, maybe, when she saw him last. The neatness was disappointing—to have nothing to scrub, to fix, to set right. Then she saw the note, fixed to the refrigerator door with a magnetic college mascot, the Darwin Dodo: "Dear Flora, Stopped by and straightened up a bit. I have Larks. I'm so sorry. Mrs. J."

Larks, her father's dog, short for Larkin, named for the poet. Flora had completely forgotten him. Were it not for Mrs. J., the dog, too, would be dead. Of course Mrs. J. would have thought to clean out the fridge and straighten up the house and feed and care for the dog, and the cloying neatness surrounding Flora was not a sign of her father's life, just more proof of his death. Evidence kept piling up. For a moment, she resented Mrs. J.'s thoughtfulness, her thoroughness. What if in her cleaning she had erased some sign her father left behind, some communiqué from the beyond he'd intended just for her?

Her father hadn't died in the house—a small relief. He'd gone to his old office to say hello and pick up some mail. While there, he'd cut short a conversation with Pat Jenkins, the English Department secretary, and gone into the bathroom abruptly. It was so uncharacteristic of him, cutting short a good chat like that, and when he didn't reemerge after fifteen minutes, Pat sent Jed Schwartz, an associate professor, in after him. Jed found him lying on the floor, bleeding from a gash on his forehead. It looked as though he'd passed out and hit his head on the sink. A horrible place to die, a bathroom—an embarrassing venue for such an important moment. He wouldn't have liked that, wouldn't have written it that way. When Flora heard the details, she had tried to clarify, tried to undo: "You're absolutely certain it was in the bathroom?" She'd gotten stuck on it for days, until her mother said, "Jesus, Flora, of all things to worry about." But where mattered, just like when mattered, and how mattered.

The how he would have liked better. No humiliating, protracted illness. No slow, relentless degeneration. A colossal bang, a candle snuff. *Sudden death*—an expression from the world of sports. One day life being life and the next day it being something else. Flora would not have admitted it to herself before, but she'd long expected that if her father died, he would die in a car crash. He had loved driving and made long, senseless drives—to the shore for a great lobster roll, to a neighboring state for a book he couldn't find in town, to the city to take her to lunch—back and forth all in a day, speeding like a bandit. Plenty of traffic tickets, even a course for delinquent drivers, but no fiery crash, only an internal inferno; Flora wrong again, her ability to know the future as inadequate as her understanding of the past.

When Pat Jenkins called Flora from the hospital pay phone and said the words *heart attack,* words that had always sounded not physical but emotional—like a particularly acute heartbreak or an overabundance of fellow feeling, *an attack of heart*—she'd first been confused: car attack? Such things happened now, but on the news, not near home. But then Pat said it again, *heart attack,* and stressed how unexpected it was, how sudden, and the complete physicality struck Flora, the seizing, the constricting, the gasping, the collapsing. It struck her the way the ground struck her when, at age nine, she fell from the high branch on the apple tree in her backyard, "the break-your-nose branch," as she and her best friend Georgia had called it.

Had Pat tried to reach her first at work? How did she have the number? In another life, with a different family, her mother would have been the one to break the news to Flora—to smash it, really, to cream the news. In this world, though, it was loyal Pat, the only person in the English Department her father could abide, the only one he went to talk to.

"He must have known something was wrong but didn't want to upset anyone, so he went off to be by himself," Pat said. "He was a gentleman till the end."

What was he, an animal going off to die alone? A gentlemanly heart attack. A courteous coronary. How civilized. Gentlemanly. That was one word for it, Flora thought, standing in the immaculate kitchen in her childlike costume. Gentlemanly, proud, stupid, selfish—suicidal even. It bothered her that she hadn't known at the precise moment of his death, hadn't felt it. She liked to think of herself as someone who really knew people, a watcher, a noticer of others—particularly her parents. She knew them better than they knew themselves (better, maybe, than she knew herself). In her fantasy of herself, she would have felt his absence. She would have experienced the sudden seizing just then, been gripped by a stabbing pain in her head. She would have tripped at least, fallen and scraped a knee.

Instead, if you worked out the times, you'd find her in her apartment, inert before afternoon TV, watching an inspirational story about a woman who'd forgiven the man who viciously attacked her and left her for dead, claimed now even to love him, just as her father's heart attacked him. The woman called the whole disaster "a real learning experience," and whenever anyone called a disaster a learning experience, Flora wanted to stick her finger in her mouth and pretend to shoot her brains out. What did one learn from disaster? What worth learning anyway? Perhaps at the very moment of his attack Flora made her life-mocking gesture, or lifted her mug of lukewarm coffee to her lips, debating whether it was worth another sip. She'd called in sick to the magazine again that day, the second time in three weeks. But Flora wasn't sick, just tired, rising from her bed at eleven-thirty, sleep-drunk. "If it's not done by noon," her father, who woke at dawn, had always said, "then to hell with it."

She'd read about the parents of marines who died at war waiting to receive their son's or daughter's luggage, and when it finally arrived, rushing to unzip it, yearning for the scent of him or her, only to meet with the oily perfume of clean laundry, the heartbreak of erasure. It was marine policy to wash all clothes before returning them. Was that what she had done—returned to Darwin to smell her father's smell? If so, Mrs. J. had, marine-like, washed the man right out of his house. Or had she? Flora remembered clasping her arms around his neck, long ago, in that other house in Darwin; he had just returned from playing tennis, and smelled sweetly of sweat, and of orange juice. But the only trace of citrus in the house today came from the toxic lemon of cleaning solvents, a faint note of tea leaves sneaking out from underneath. Or maybe the smell of tea was a hallucination, a wish gone haywire in the brain.

It was teatime, wasn't it? Had she come up to Darwin to visit her father, he would have put the kettle on in anticipation of her arrival. A manic, cheerful, boiling whistle might have welcomed her as she walked through the door. There would be milk in the fridge, and he would have prepared the mugs with a thin layer of it, two teaspoons of sugar for him and three-quarters of one for her. He'd liked his tea sweet, the way she had as a child, but outgrew. He'd had a boyish love of sweets, his excitement at the prospect of a slice of cake uncommon in an adult. Had she come when he was alive, he would have made a plate of cookies—dark chocolate on shortbread biscuits, his favorites. Why had she not come to see him? Would he have lived longer if she had come?

The answering machine on the counter blinked the number 3 at her. Calls to her father; calls to the dead. *I'm sorry, he can't come to the phone right now—could he get back to you never? Actually, he's deceased at the moment—would you like to leave a message?* Flora picked up the small white box and held it in the bowl of her hands. About the size of her father's heart—this thought accosted her. When she allowed herself to consider what had happened to him, she felt like fainting—a dissonant ring in her ears, a clouding overcrowding her eyes, a sickening yanking of the crown of her head toward the ground. She yanked the cord out of the wall and threw the machine in the trash. She would regret that later. But then, she was in the regret business these days.

She had bought the machine for him years ago as a Christmas present. Exactly the wrong gift for him, but he had made himself a message, reluctantly asking callers he'd been lucky enough to miss to tell him who they were and what they wanted.

"You don't have to use it," she'd told him, seeing his good manners dueling it out with his lust for solitude, the two impulses equal and extreme.

"No, no," he'd said. "It'll be good for me. Important to keep oneself gently tethered to the outside world."

But was that true? Maybe it was time to untether. To hell with good manners and the outside world.

Flora stood in the shadow-darkening kitchen, still in her coat, her hands against the smooth butcher block of her father's counter. She felt winded, and brittle. Her fingers were twigs; they could be snapped off. Her nails were as thin as paper. If only they could have been left behind, too. She could have scattered a trail of fingers and toes and other breakable bits and pieces out the window of the cab, like Hansel and Gretel hoping against hope to find their way back home.

As a child, Flora hated to be told to go to bed; to be expected to sleep while others sucked more life from the day was the height of unfairness. Now she longed for someone to send her to sleep. Sleep, she would sleep. But where? She couldn't sleep in the master bedroom, her father's bed. There was a double bed in the little guest room on the ground floor, off the living room, but she couldn't sleep in the guest room. She'd stay where she always stayed—if she stayed—in the room called "hers," sleep in the narrow twin bed under the yellowing blanket that had once been new, and near perfect.

She left the body bag where it lay, and took herself up the narrow back stairs, her fatigue the fatigue of the old, stepping, leaning, pausing, up to the small, neat room of dresser, desk, and bed, all the surfaces bare and buffed and signless. The lone ornamental object, a palm-size silver clock, read five-twenty-five. She opened the closet. It, too, was bare but for one small box she'd left behind years before. Flora was not a keeper of notes exchanged in long-ago classrooms. Her childhood bedrooms—there were multiple—had not been preserved shrine-like, like those of some of her friends, friends with families like time capsules; you checked on them ten years later and nothing had changed.

She pulled her feet out of her sneakers and let her coat slip to the ground, and she climbed into the tightly tucked sheets of the bed with her fraying clothing still on. She pushed her fragile hands between the safety of her knees. It was a canopy bed, the bed she'd dreamt of as a little girl and one day gotten. The canopy had long since disappeared, and now it was just a large boxy metal frame, the blueprint of a tomb. She closed her eyes. The sharp, shrill blare of the telephone (*ring* wasn't the right word, was it?) startled her. Flora did not like to answer its assault. She never had, but now even less. The phone rang, with no machine to interrupt it, on and on, and then stopped—almost violently, the sound vanishing, leaving behind the ghost of noise.

———

On the day they moved to Darwin, Flora's mother went shopping. She bought a rough-wooled cardigan and a white bumpy bed-spread. She bought them, not liking them, because it's easier to focus on disliking small, specific things than your life in general. The pattern of the sweater imitated panes of stained glass—cool and dark—and it went for many years unworn. Finally, she passed it off to a friend, or a garbage can. The bedspread did find use, in Flora's parents' bedroom, one of the few rooms in the institutional house whose furnishings fell under her mother's jurisdiction, and she kept it until the day she and Flora left the house ten months later, when she burned it in one of the living room fireplaces, though it was nearly summer, and hot, and she had to cut it up into small pieces first to do so.

The movers were huge, the largest men Flora, who was eight, had ever seen. One made a muscle and let her hang from it, swinging her around. Another pulled her braids and told her how in grade school he'd once cut off a girl's pigtails, *snip, snip*, while she sat in front of him in class. He seemed to still find it funny, but from then on, for a long while, Flora feared that at any moment someone might sneak behind her and snip her braids sheer off.

A job had brought them there, to Darwin, to the house. Her father had liked his job in the city, but how could he turn down an offer like that—to be *president*? The president of Darwin College.

"He always goes where he's asked," Flora's mother told her.

But then, she never said "Don't." In his new contract with Darwin, he'd arranged to teach his Hardy seminar every spring in addition to his administrative duties, so he felt he really wasn't giving anything up. "It's the best of both worlds," he said.

"You have two?" her mother observed. "I've got zip."

In memory, Flora saw that first house in Darwin—the big house—as though under a magnifying glass. The red Formica counters in the kitchen, the scratchy gray industrial rug on the third floor and along the back staircase, the teal-and-brown paisley wallpaper in her bedroom, which she knew to be ugly but loved anyway—all the materials enlarged and vivid, as though directly in front of her nose. She saw the redbrick facade of the house that way, so close she could almost feel its grainy roughness pressing against her palm. They called it "the house," not "home," the way, after the divorce, her father called her mother "your mom," never just "Mom." The fact that it was a house, a freestanding house, was in itself remarkable. Coming from the city, they found internal staircases the height of luxury; upstairs meant rich. For a long time after Flora left the house, every dream she had was set inside it, no matter what the subject, or who the cast of characters, as though her unconscious couldn't afford a change of scenery. The setting of dreams, it was dreamlike, like something in a story someone else had told her.

The President's House. A borrowed mansion. The house came with the job, and left with it, too. Darwin owned it, and furnished it, and repainted it when it needed repainting, and scheduled parties to be held in it. And they lived there—Flora, and her mother, and her father. They lived in a house that was like a hotel. It employed a support staff—a full-time housekeeper and a cleaning woman and two gardeners to manicure the elaborate grounds, and a crew of waiters and waitresses who worked the parties. There were two formal guest rooms, the blue room and the gold room (which was really yellow), each with its own bathroom, where trustees of the college and their wives stayed several times a year. Each guest room had two twin poster beds, as though it were out of the fifties, and sometimes Flora and Georgia slept in one of them, for a little variety. There were two velvet-swaddled living rooms that stood back to back, ignoring each other, one with a baby-grand piano, and each with a fireplace, and a library with walls of bookshelves filled with books that weren't theirs, that were really nobody's, and there was a veranda—not a porch, a veranda—painted moss green and populated with white wicker furniture, and in the dining room, there was a table so long, it seemed impractical, made for sitting on, not at, long enough for Flora and Georgia to cartwheel across.

Flora first met Georgia at her father's inauguration, an event she resented deeply because she was required to wear a stiff, scratchy dress. Beyond the discomfort, the dress was hideous: a busy mauve-ish brown print, with deeper mauve-brown ribbons edging the sleeves and girthing her middle, gouging her flesh and making her fidget. The worst kind of little-girl dress. Her mother had picked it out, saying, "This is the first time in your whole life I've told you what you had to wear."

"Maybe if you'd done it before, you'd be better at it," Flora told her.

There was a small triumph in the matter of footwear: She could wear her black patent-leather shoes, which she wore as often as possible.

"They don't go with the dress," her mother pointed out.

"Thank God," Flora said.

But it seemed a bad omen: Darwin meant itchy, ugly dresses; Darwin meant you didn't get to choose.

The night before, she'd fallen asleep to the sound of her father's slow, thoughtful footsteps pacing the long hall outside her bedroom door. This was how he wrote his speeches, in his head, walking back and forth, back and forth, like words on a page, and only going to his typewriter when the thing was composed and whole. His footsteps paused now and then, and she could imagine him looking off into the air around him, poised in place by an idea. He did this in conversation; if they were walking down the street together and he came to a good point in his story, he would stop and stand still, and Flora would stop, too, to listen, both of them recognizing that some stories needed one's full attention, that some words deserved stillness.

At the inauguration, he led a parade of the faculty and trustees to the tinny music of the brass band, the ominous melodies of momentous occasions—not "Pomp and Circumstance," but its first or second cousin. "Pompous Circumstance" was how Flora had heard the name as a very little girl, and it had become the family's term for these events. Those in the processional wore their long robes with their richly colored velvet hoods—the costume getting fancier as the degree got harder. The plan had been to process into the quad, but the day went wet and gray, so the world of Darwin assembled instead inside the old gymnasium with its shiny, squeaky wooden floors and its smell of sneakers. Her father gave his long speech. Her mother smiled and shook hands and laughed and nodded, but you could see the strain in her eyes—you could always see things in her eyes, like when she had been crying, or when she'd had too much to drink. Flora tried to read her eyes like a barometer, to see what was on the horizon, what was coming her way.

Georgia, whose mother was a neuroscientist on the Darwin faculty, had been to many such Darwinian celebrations and wore a weary expression of knowingness.

"Why did they name you Georgia?" Flora asked her. "Why not Mississippi?"

"Because of all the famous women Georges," she said, as though it should be obvious. "My mom thought it would be auspicious."

"Oh," Flora said, not knowing any women named George. Did *auspicious* mean suspicious?

"I guess George used to be a woman's name. You know George Eliot, right?"

Flora nodded. She hated not knowing things. Her mother would say, "You're not supposed to know everything automatically—we all start out not knowing." But the not knowing made her feel alone and ashamed. She was forever looking up words in the dictionary so as not to have to ask anyone what they meant. She would look them up nervously, furtively, scouting over her shoulder, straining to hear if someone was coming up behind, not wanting to get caught in the act of discovery. It seemed unfair of life to start you out with nothing, to leave it all up to you. And so many times one mystery would lead to another, the definition as confounding as the word itself, like the time she heard someone say "blow job," and looked it up, only to be confronted with *fellatio*.

"Why did they name you Flora?" Georgia asked.

"I don't know. They liked it, I guess."

"Flora," Georgia repeated, looking thoughtful and scholarly. "Better than being called Fauna, I think."

Flora eyed her skeptically. Had she just been insulted?

"I'm precocious," Georgia explained.

They sat under their chairs on the floor, crouched, fake-whispering. It was rude, and Flora waited for her mother to scold them, but she didn't. Georgia taught Flora the folk songs they sang at the school she went to—the school Flora would be going to in a week: "The Sloop John B," "The Titanic," "The Golden Vanity." This was life in the country; this was new—singing songs about boats.

Later, walking to the new house with her mother in the light rain while her father lingered with his new colleagues, Flora waited for her to say something, and finally she said, "I saw you made a friend."

"I guess. What does *precocious* mean?" Her mother was the one person Flora could admit ignorance to, the one person she trusted with her questions, though her mother's answers were often confusing and possibly unreliable.

"It means pain in the ass," her mother said.

It was the twilight of the day, the twilight of the season, a late-August twilight. That time of day in that season, the blurring of the blue day into the blue night, the blending of earth and air, made things bigger, fuller. Life froze; paused to revel in itself.

"What did you think of the inauguration?" Flora asked, the new word unwieldy in her mouth.

"A good show. They sure know how to put on a show."

"Pompous Circumstance?"

Her mother just smiled at her as though from far away.

"Did you meet any new friends?"

"Ah, Flo," her mother said. "The wife of the boss never has friends."

2

Paris, Athens, Rome, Darwin

SHE WOKE UP ravenous and disoriented. She'd eaten nothing but broth in days, her insides aslosh in briny liquids. Had she eaten at all yesterday? Her dreams had been someone else's. His, maybe. Dreams full of people she didn't know, weather she'd never encountered. Even lying down she was light-headed, her jaw stiff and sore as an old man's joints from a busy night of clenching. Where was she? So many times Flora had wished to run away, to leave everyone she knew, everything but her own skin behind—even her own skin if she could—but she had never managed it, unless you counted the time nearly twenty years ago when she and Georgia ran away from school, or the time a year later when she did it again, alone, but then she had run away to the house she lived in, and now, if you thought about it, she had done the same thing, run away to her father's house, run away home.

Her house: She was a landowner, a mint member of the landed gentry, a different Flora, financially, than she'd been a month before. In addition to leaving Flora the house—which he owned free and clear—and his pension and savings, minus five thousand dollars, which went to Mrs. J., her father had named her his literary executor: the most formal title ever bestowed on her, a grown-up title. It was all very organized; *he was a gentleman till the end.* But what did it mean to inherit words? All those orphaned words, words she did not want to read. She was their guardian. They were peeking sorrowfully out at her from their manila folder in her suitcase downstairs and from the piles on the study desk, woeing their bad luck in life in ending up with her. His LPs he'd left to Rubie—his best friend, Ira Rubenstein—with the exception of his opera collection, which went to Flora. And most of the books also went to Flora, except his first editions and other rare things, which he'd left to the college.

"Nothing for me, after all those years of service?" her mother had asked, only half a joke.

Flora grabbed her sneakers and coat from their puddle on the floor and went downstairs. From the body bag she extracted fresh shirt and socks. In the downstairs bathroom she doused her face and examined it. Not too deranged. Certainly not for Darwin. She closed the front door without locking it and walked into town.

Darwin in November looked bleak, the streets emptied of life, as though posing for a Hopper. The cursed spot next to the post office, which welcomed a new restaurant of some new ethnicity with every passing season, was in a Burmese incarnation. The art-house movie theater, still playing its obscure Romanian films, as desultory as ever—how was it hanging on? A front, surely. Maybe all the businesses surrounding the town common were mere facades, elaborate stage sets of the cozy academic enclave. One solid push would knock them over. The banner above Pleasant Street advertised an out-of-date anti–Columbus Day rally.

At Gus Simonds's shop, Flora filled a basket with milk and eggs, bread and coffee. Hungry for the first time in days, she couldn't see past breakfast. Her fingers felt more robust in the faded light of morning, but she kept her mittens on inside, in case. Gus's had long been the place to buy basics—the makings of a modest meal, new notebooks for school, greeting cards, Halloween costumes, and green-and-gold Darwin College paraphernalia. Flora's favorite T-shirt growing up had been one that listed PARIS, ATHENS, ROME, DARWIN. Next to each word stood a simple rendering of the iconic structure—Eiffel Tower, Parthenon, Colosseum, and the college library. As with so many Darwinian outputs, it was difficult to read the tone: self-deprecating or self-important?

Gus was a man of indeterminate age. He could pass for fifty, but then again, he might be nearing his seventies. His colorless hair

matched the morning—not quite gray, though no longer blond—
a little like her father's hair. His face had the wide wrinkles of a
man who spent his days outside in the sun. He looked misplaced—
caged, almost—standing behind his register.

"Flora," he said gently, recognizing her as she pulled her hat off.

"Gus," she said back.

"You've come home."

"Here I am," she said.

"I miss your old man," he told her. "Really I do. This town won't
be the same without him. You know, he came in here with Larks for
the paper every morning at seven, like clockwork. Often my first
customer. My first words spoken were to him. We started our days
together." Flora added the local newspaper, *The Daily Darwin
Gazette,* to her pile of groceries. It was nearly eleven. "Where is Larks
anyway?" Gus asked.

"Oh, back at the house." The little lie easier than explaining.

"Sports scores," Gus went on. "We spent a lot of time on that. He
liked to talk games, and to hear them recounted. We filled each
other in on what we'd missed."

Her father had been famous in her family (if one can be famous
among two other people) for the enthusiasm with which he offered
meticulous plot summaries of films and books. The telling often
took longer than the watching or reading. Most of all, he loved to
reveal surprise endings. "Are you planning to see it?" he'd ask. An
answer of "Yes" was clearly wrong—disappointing, and a little rude.

"How long are you staying?" Gus asked.

"Not sure. As long as it all takes, I guess." An evasion, but Gus
nodded.

"You'll let me know if you need anything, I hope." He awkwardly
handed her the bag. "It's on me, Flora."

"Don't be silly—how much do I owe you?"

"No, I mean it. Don't say another word. You know how your dad
always overpaid. When he said 'Keep the change,' too often that
meant change for a twenty off twelve dollars of tennis balls. I
owe him."

"This once," Flora said. "Then we call it even. I pay my way or I stop coming back."

Gus grinned at her. "You'll be back. This is Darwin, Flora. Where else will you go?"

Leaving the shop, Flora thought she saw Esther Moon—a lost friend from high school—parking. Flora recognized the car first— an enormous, old, weirdly symmetrical Chevy, like a child's drawing of a car, the ugliest car ever made, Esther had liked to say. She'd bought it for one dollar from a Darwin historian who'd been desperate to be rid of it. The car couldn't still be alive. It couldn't have outlived her father, was Flora's thought. But then, there was a car seat in the back, with a child inside, a further impossibility. Esther Moon could not be a parent. A friend Flora considered more responsible had gotten pregnant the year before at age twenty-seven, and a part of her had been shocked to find it not a scandal requiring adult intervention and furious gossiping. When had pregnancy, of all things, become acceptable? And even if that mother were Esther, talking to her now, answering questions like "How are you?" was not an option. Flora didn't know how to answer the standard questions anymore: "How are you?" "What are your plans?" "Where do you live?" For the time being, all were stumpers. Easier not to be asked. She'd never understood with those questions anyway how much honesty people wanted in return.

She decided on the long way back, through campus. The air was cool, but fresh. The leaves were down and gone, but the grass on the common clung to the last of its New England green. She could see the tall rhododendron bushes barricading the President's House, but she crossed the street and walked toward the quad instead. An eerily peopleless landscape: Where were the students? Where the professoriat? But what did she want? She dreaded chance encounters with people she'd once known—those warm smiles of recognition homing in on her, missile-like—but then she felt disgruntled if she made it through without being sighted.

In town, in Darwin, she'd always been daughter-of. It was all, when it came to her, relative. A strange thing, recognition by association. At once flattering and diminishing. Teachers taking attendance on the first day of school asking obsequiously, "Are you, by chance, related to *Lewis* Dempsey?" Flora reddening, nodding, conceding: "My dad." The recognition more embarrassing even than those unpronounceable hyphenated names so many of her classmates had been saddled with. "This town won't be the same without him," Gus had offered. Was that true, or something one said? Her father had a prominent place in Darwin as president, and then president emeritus. As scholars went, he'd been known; "a populist critic" he'd been called by admirers and detractors alike. His first book, *Reader as Understander,* tracing the history of how poetry— from Shakespeare to Stevens—was read in its day, sold well, and not just among rivals and graduate students; it won awards and accolades; it had become a book club favorite. At once learned and mass-market. People who did not read poetry had read his book, or at least bought it. Within the confines of the town, her father's life had been quite public, and so his death had been public. A sudden, public death made people vulnerable, aware of the risks of living. No one liked that kind of awareness, or the people who provided it. Who knew, they might be contagious. Perhaps the town was relieved he was gone, the last of the Dempseys finally purged— though there she was, another one popping up like a rogue mushroom that refuses to be rooted out. Or was all that just narcissism? Again: self-important or self-deprecating? Was the notion of being reviled more palatable than the thought of being, like so much in life, simply tolerated? To most people who had known her father, his death was likely like any other—a cause for sadness, but sadness on the normal scale. The town would be the same for them.

It had been over a year since she'd returned to Darwin, though weeks ago she'd come close, as far as the hospital outside of town, with her mother, to see the body. She had needed to see him, needed to see that he was really dead. Her nerves jittered, like she didn't know the etiquette. Hysterics seemed appropriate, but didn't arrive. As her mother stood beside her, she tried to remember the last time the three of them had been alone in a room together. A long time ago, another life. It was uncomfortable—it had long been—to have the two of them in the same place, and she didn't like her mother to see her father not looking well. Perverse, but that was her thought. His body, to his neck, was covered with a half-blanket, half-tarp, and his neck and earlobes were ruddy from—the recognition impossible to avoid—freezer burn. But it was her mother who had touched him first, who put her hand on his hair in an affectionate way and said, "Oh, Lew," as if he'd gone and done something truly unreasonable, and so Flora saw that she could press her mouth to his forehead and feel the terrible coldness of his changing skin and not regret not having done it.

"Do you want to be alone with him?" her mother had asked, and Flora told her no, and then she asked, "Do you want to cut a piece of his hair?" and the thought of asking the staff for scissors filled Flora with worry, as if they might suspect her of some barbaric act, but it turned out her mother had a tiny pair in her purse, and she cut the hair, which was a soft gray that moved toward a yellowish white, and still wavy—her mother said that, "Still wavy," and Flora had been thinking the same thing, though why *still*, why would death have straightened his hair out? And Flora had signed the papers she needed to sign and they had turned back around, back to the city, away from Darwin.

There was the Darwin College chapel—an imposing stone fortress, its delicate white steeple like an ill-fitting cap—where in a matter of weeks his memorial would be held. The same chapel her parents had brought her to as a child to hear the undergraduate a cappella groups perform their wildly harmonized renditions of "Yesterday" and "I Heard It Through the Grapevine." The same chapel that held the annual holiday Vespers, in which celebration Flora, a self-declared agnostic from the age of six, had once read a short excerpt from the Gospel of Luke. The same chapel where her father had hosted academic forums on "The Poet as Prose Artist," and "The Fin de Siècle." *Fantasy Echo,* she had misheard at the time, and assumed that was an important term of poetry: the fantasy echo. Like a chorus or refrain, but more mysterious and ghostly. The same chapel where he had mourned other dead scholars over the years—and yet not the same: those memories long layered there less convincing now the eulogizer was to be eulogized. Had it really been he who'd done such things, who'd been there all along?

He'd been a wonderful speaker. Witty and canny, with the easy appearance (though a false one) of off-the-cuffness. He always prepared. "He could work a room," her mother would put it. But that was unfair. He was the same with everyone he met, and this authenticity radiated, and pulled people in toward him. Flora felt herself so changeable, and found that quality in him miraculous. She even felt she looked different from day to day: Something about her face hadn't yet gelled; her self hadn't gelled. To be so constant, so reliably oneself, what would that feel like? Was yourself something you became? Had he been like that—himself—even at her age?

Flora wound her way around the two oldest dorms, built in the early 1800s, North and South ("Here" and "There," her mother had called them), humble redbrick twins, and down to College Hill, which offered the best views of the mountains and, in winter, the best sledding. A dip at the foot sent you flying above your sled and then, at the moment of reunion, thudding painfully back to earth. As a child, the pain had been part of the fun, falling under the category of pain/pleasure, like a loose tooth you trouble with your tongue, or like the time she and Georgia had given themselves paper cuts, tracing the lines on their palms and fingers till they were red and raw.

Her father had been a mountains man when it came to views—Flora went more in for oceans. He'd loved this hilltop and walked here with Larks most mornings. The range ringing the valley that was Darwin was densely wooded with bands of late-fall orange amid swaths of evergreens. Flora was struck by its ruggedness, its wildness. Even cushy Darwin could seem remote. Going to the country was like going back in time, seeing how the world looked before it changed.

A windbreakered father and daughter appeared beside her, he with a camera strapped around his neck, she with the eager expression of a college hopeful. He asked if Flora would take their picture before the view.

"Are you a student here?" the father asked as they posed together, inches of green and orange visible between them.

"I love it," Flora said, lowering the camera.

"A beautiful campus," he said. "And quiet. Everyone busy studying, I guess."

"Or sleeping off their hangovers," Flora said.

The girl released a nervous, knowing laugh. The father reached for his camera.

Down the hill, on the old clay tennis courts, two well-bundled men Flora identified as assistant professors were hitting stiffly back and forth in the chill, as if their primary goal were to move in the smallest radius possible. What day was it? She was losing track already—not hard to do in Darwin. On the other side of the courts was the small wooded area with the path running through called the Bird Sanctuary, where she had gone on gloomy walks with her father as a girl, and on the other side of the Bird Sanctuary stood the small house she had shared with her mother after they left the President's House. A grim walking tour it was. The assistant professors waved—not necessarily out of recognition, but because waving was the done thing. She felt a sudden urge to perform for them—to do a cartwheel, or to lift her clothing and flash her breasts, to shock, to make a fool of herself. But she'd exhausted suddenness. She simply returned the wave and then turned and followed the road back toward her father's house, a walk her father had taken countless times on his way to and from the courts, until his knees betrayed him a few years back and he'd had to stop playing. She could see him in his ancient sweats, the racket held at his side, rising every so often to map out a stroke. It was as if she had done nothing her whole life but make a study of his movements: her father shaking hands—a slow, graceful greeting, not at all the firm spasm meant to convey power; throwing his head back in laughter as he tried to get through a joke he loved; reading while walking from car to house, anticipating when the slate steps began and reaching for the handrail without lowering his book; listening to music—choral, orchestral, surging—holding his hand up as if to draw her attention to the surge, transported, nearly tearful; staring at her mother in overt contempt. And now here they were, the images, reminding her of all she'd learned. What she had to show for the long work of growing up.

At the side of her father's house stood a woman, tall and thin, peering in the kitchen window. She turned at the sound of Flora's footsteps. She was well into middle age, sixty maybe, with sharp features and veins of gray in the red hair that hung around her shoulders, wearing a green scarf, a purple vest, and sensible-looking Mary Janes. Had a five-year-old dressed her?

"Flora?" the woman said, approaching.

"Yes?"

"I'm Cynthia Reynolds. A friend of your father. I heard I might find you here—I ran into Mrs. J. I'd left a message yesterday, but then thought I'd just stop by."

A message. In the garbage can. There had been three messages.

"The machine broke," Flora said. "Finally. The thing was a relic—I'd given it to him years ago and—"

"It's really so lovely to meet you," Cynthia said. She wasn't interested in the machine. She was searching Flora's eyes, searching for him, maybe. But she wouldn't find him there. It appeared she might cry. She looked down at her feet and said, as if by explanation, "I only just arrived."

"How do you do," Flora said, and shook her hand, as Cynthia's eyes moved past her, into the house. "Won't you come in?"

"Please."

Cynthia hung her vest on one of the hooks along the wall by the door, next to one of Flora's father's well-worn Darwin College sweatshirts: a familiar, almost proprietary act. To get to the kitchen they each had to step first over the body bag, rather rudely unzipped in the middle of the floor. Her father's manuscript poked out of the opening, and Flora threw her coat down over it and kicked the suitcase out of the way.

"I was just going to make some coffee," Flora said.

"That sounds lovely." Cynthia moved to the kitchen table and sat down, unbidden. But of course he had friends. Friends who spent time here. He had a life. A life with other people in it.

"You also teach at Darwin?" Flora asked as she filled the kettle with water. Someone had to speak, and it was a safe starting point. Almost everyone who lived in Darwin taught at the college, or that was how it felt. It was like Hollywood, a one-industry town, though less glamorous, and possibly meaner.

"Yes, art history, nineteenth-century European," Cynthia said. "You look so like him, you know?"

"No," Flora said. She wished she had bathed. Did she still smell of bus and sleep? "Actually, I look like my maternal grandmother. The family joke was that all her genes were dominant, like everything else about her."

"Oh, I see a strong resemblance."

"I think you're the first."

"Modiglianiesque," Cynthia said, undeterred, smiling warmly. Her teeth were even, and small, and stained. "Long-necked, long-bodied. I always thought he was, and you certainly are." *Always?* She *always* thought? Cynthia followed this bold observation by turning shyly to stare out the window, apparently down to the flower beds below, where moments before she had stood outside, looking in. As comfortable as she made herself in the house, her movements were nervous. She fussed with her hands, which Flora noticed wore no rings. She stood up. "Can I help?" she asked, and sat down again when Flora told her no. She did not want help. Though Flora wasn't sure with her father's coffeepot—a retro hourglass beaker, waist cinched in a stylish belt of wood and leather—how much coffee was enough, how much was too much. She erred on the side of undrinkably strong, piling the grinds high into the filter.

Cynthia Reynolds watched. Flora was sure she'd never heard the name. *Sin-thee-ya.* It didn't sound like the name of an academic. It was the name of a flight attendant, or a soap-opera star. Perhaps she was a Reynolds of foil fame. An heiress.

"I'm so sorry," she was saying, her voice shaky. "This must be such a difficult time for you. It's a difficult time for everyone who knew your father."

"Yes, thank you." Was she suggesting they had equal claims to grief?

"He spoke so lovingly of you. He adored you, as I'm sure you know. He told me he thought you were his best work. He quoted that old Ben Jonson poem where he calls his son his 'best piece of poetry.'"

"Better even than his introduction to *The Complete Poems of Thomas Hardy*?" Flora joked, though it came out wrong—bitter and ungrateful. It was her turn to fidget. She grabbed the milk from her bag of groceries and found the sugar bowl in the cabinet. By not returning to Darwin, not visiting her father, she'd stripped him of all context. He'd existed only in her world, an irregular weather pattern that passed through her neighborhood every now and then, a rare mood. Of course she hadn't known when he died; she hadn't really known when he did anything. When had he had the house painted? And when had Cynthia sat at that table across from him?

The kettle whistled, and Flora turned off the stove and reached for the handle.

"Fuck," she yelled, recoiling. It was a copper kettle, a copper handle, and scalding, requiring a pot holder to lift.

Cynthia was beside her in moments, the cold water on and Flora's hand being led toward it. A pot holder retrieved from the nearest drawer. The coffee beaker filled with water. Every gesture smooth and efficient and oozing knowing, and only when her tasks were complete did she say, "That must have hurt."

"I'm fine," Flora said, though a blister was forming on the soft pillows of her fingers. Ha! Her fingers *were* vulnerable. She'd just been wrong about the how. She would not cry in front of this woman, this stranger who knew where everything was. "It's a new kettle. I didn't know."

"Yes, I'm sorry," Cynthia said, as if it were she who had burned her. Cynthia opened the cabinet and pulled down two mugs and a little blue pitcher. She poured the milk Flora had bought at Gus's into the pitcher, poured the coffee into the mugs, then took the mugs over to the table and sat down.

"Were you and my father close?" Flora asked above the rush of the faucet.

"We'd begun spending time together." Cynthia squinted at Flora, examining her.

Did that mean dating? Did that mean sleeping together? "Were you romantically involved?" The stiff euphemism of a sentence the simplest to say.

Cynthia paused. "We were very much in love." The words burst out of her, as though she were a child with a secret, as though not saying them right then would have been impossible.

Flora smacked the faucet off and joined Cynthia at the table. She hoped her face looked as though her surprise were only very slight.

"But for how long?" she asked.

"Nearly a year."

Flora inspected her burn. That wasn't possible. That much she would have known. That he would have told her. Why wouldn't he? It hadn't gone well with his girlfriends in the past, but Flora was an adult now, allegedly, where she hadn't been then. She hadn't then been capable of civility. Now, for the most part, she was. Then, none of the women he'd introduced her to had seemed serious or plausible. This one was clearly different. One of the others had hung lace underpants like ornaments from doorknobs, and sprinkled nude photographs of herself alluringly throughout the house. On an overnight visit, Flora had stumbled upon one tucked into a hand towel.

"Is it hurting you?" Cynthia asked. "Your hand?"

"I think I'll live," Flora said. She sipped her coffee. It was undrinkable.

"You're surprised," Cynthia said. "I really didn't mean to drop this on you."

"No?"

"Of course, I realize I have dropped it on you," Cynthia stammered. "I just want to know you, Flora. That's why I'm here. I thought you might have suspected he was—"

"Very much in love?"

"Maybe I should go. Give you some time. We could talk later."

"You know, he never mentioned you," Flora said.

"He was waiting for the right time."

Flora laughed a short, harsh laugh that made her throat burn. "Yes, well. What a good plan."

"I think he would have wanted you to know, wanted us to know each other."

"It's hard to know what he would have wanted, isn't it?" Flora stood and picked up her coffee with her good hand and dumped it in the sink.

Cynthia winced, again almost tearful. "I'm hurting, too," she said.

"I've been rude," Flora said. "It's just—who knew my father was such a man of secrets?"

"He was protecting you."

"From what, you?"

"He felt you were unhappy, going through something."

"Did he?" She hated to think of her unhappiness discussed, and pitied. Cynthia, the expert, who had known so much, while she knew nothing.

"Do you need any help, Flora? Can't I help you? With the house, or anything?"

"The house?"

"I spent a lot of time here over the last year, and I know how much work an old house can be. The roof was starting to leak. Your dad was planning—"

"No, really, I'm fine."

"You're doing everything alone?"

"Not entirely."

"I'm not sure if this is the best time for me to ask—or if there even is a best time—but I know you must be in the thick of planning his memorial service, and I've been thinking I might like to read something, if you wouldn't mind too much, if you felt there was room for me. I was thinking one of Hardy's poems of 1912 and '13. You know, those hauntingly beautiful, haunted poems about the death of his first wife. Your father loved those poems. He loved reading them aloud. He even mentioned wanting them as part of his funeral. You know that funeral-planning predilection of his."

"Yes, I know," Flora said. "Ira Rubenstein is reading Hardy." She lied, without deciding first to lie; she had no idea what Ira would read. "You know Ira, I suppose?"

"Yes, I know Ira. That makes sense. Hardy is the natural choice, of course. Do you know which one he's reading?"

"I can't remember. I can find out and let you know."

"Well, if it's not the one I was thinking of . . ."

"It would be difficult to move things around at this point." This suggested firm plans were in place. Cynthia's input would no doubt be useful, make Flora's life easier. Sharing often made life easier.

"If there ends up being anything I can do, please, Flora, you'll let me know, won't you?" Cynthia stood up to leave. "You're staying here, in town, for a while?"

All her questions were phrased as demands.

"Yes. For now," Flora said.

"Oh, good. I hope we'll see each other again soon."

Flora tried to smile.

"We could talk. We have so much to talk about."

Just that morning, there had been no Cynthia Reynolds, no other woman; her father had sent her a communiqué from the beyond after all. "Yes," Flora said finally. "I'm sure that we do."

Cynthia left, walking herself to the door and closing it behind her, and as she did, Flora moved to the garbage can and retrieved the answering machine, wiping it off with a dishrag, though it was quite clean—there was nothing else in the trash. She plugged it back into the wall. She was afraid unplugging it might have erased the messages, but there it was, the number 3, appearing to her like a beacon. All three messages were from her, from Cynthia. The first warm, eager, loving: *Lewis, I thought we were meeting at six-fifteen. Did we get our signals crossed? Call me, love.* In the second, the voice lifting to a crescendo of concern: *Darling, it's quarter past seven. I'm worried now. You're never late. Please call as soon as you get this.* The third introducing a new, tentative voice, less fond: *Hello, Flora? This is Cynthia Reynolds. I'm a friend—I was a friend of your father. I just wanted to say hello, and to see if I could stop by the house and offer my condolences. . . . I'll try again later.*

Flora unplugged the machine and returned it to the trash can. Was that what she had done, offer condolences? It hadn't quite felt like it. Flora needed air. She opened windows, one-handed, to let the cool air into the house. She needed to call her mother, who would be worried by now. She needed to read; there was so much reading to do. Her father had left her an assignment, she'd inherited homework—his essays and reviews, his new, secret poems. Well, thanks, Dad. Just what I wanted. How could he not have told her? Was she a child, best kept in the dark? She'd been too depressed to withstand his happiness? It seemed unlikely; she doubted thoughtfulness had been the true root of his withholding.

She grabbed the thick green woolen blanket from the back of the couch and went outside and climbed into the hammock, which hung on the edge of the yard between two tall, near-leafless maples. She cocooned herself in the blanket. The irregular fall moon sat low in the sky, pale and sheepish at its early arrival. A breeze came up and sent the fallen leaves panicking across the lawn. When she was little, Flora never understood how a hammock could be relaxing. It seemed vulnerable, on the verge of collapse—foolish. She hadn't then been afraid of heights, or dares, or other things she should have been afraid of, but she'd been afraid of hammocks. Now, as she let her body sink down, she felt herself floating up, untethered. At the very least, she'd progressed on the hammock front.

Cynthia Reynolds, her father's girlfriend. Or, what word did one use at their age? *Partner? Lover?* How revolting. Though there had been the occasional other person, neither of her parents had remarried (or not that she was aware of). "Your mother cured me of marriage," her father had told her once, long ago, a pithy little phrase she tried to unhear, to unremember. In life, he had not wanted his daughter and his lover to know one another. So how could Cynthia say that in death his mind would change? And it was nervy, wasn't it, insinuating herself into the funeral planning—"You know that predilection of his," she'd said smugly. He'd never mentioned those Hardy poems to Flora. Though it was true that her father had planned his own funeral—casually mentioning over a meal a particular piece of music he'd like played, or whom he would or would not like to speak. When years back a famous pianist received an honorary degree from Darwin, her father cheerfully announced, "We hit it off. I'm sure he'd be willing to play for me. When I go, try to track him down." Though the man had been older. Why had her father assumed he would be the first to die? And, as it turned out, the pianist was busy, booked already on that date in December when the memorial would be held, a concert in Berlin, though terribly sorry to miss it. Her father was an exceptional man, et cetera, et cetera. Making the arrangements was now an act of recall. Which Beethoven trio had her father preferred? What was it he said about the dean of students? Why had she not taken notes? Worse, she had tried not to listen. She'd said, "Dad, can we please talk about something else?"

It was her mother who remembered—though Flora worried her information was out-of-date. It was the *Archduke* Trio. And it must be performed live. The conductor of the student orchestra could recommend the best players. The dean of students should be discouraged from eulogizing. Ira Rubenstein would be too distraught to read his own words, but he could choose some other text. The idea of her mother planning her father's funeral was wrong; he wouldn't like it. But Flora did need help, and she didn't want Cynthia's. Who else had known him so well? And her mother wouldn't sabotage his funeral, would she? Or would she? The brilliant final act of revenge: the wrong music, the wrong words.

What had life been like, in the city, before Georgia? Flora could not remember life before.

"They're in love," Flora heard her mother say to Georgia's mother, Madeleine, in a laughing voice, a mocking voice.

"I know," Madeleine said. "It's the sweetest thing."

But it was true; Flora loved Georgia with the full ferocity of her eight-year-old feelings. Georgia, an only child, too, accustomed to occupying long hours alone—reading, inventing homework assignments for herself, tending to the small furry creatures whose aquariums lined the walls of her bedroom—accepted Flora's ardor gratefully. She slept over at the President's House most weekends, the bottom bunk of Flora's new bunk beds quickly hers. They spelled out their names in glow-in-the-dark star stickers across their respective headboards—labeling, claiming—FLORA and GEORGIA.

"Like sisters," everyone said.

But they weren't sisters—for starters, they looked nothing alike: Georgia with her bark brown bob, her warm smudgy eyes, her roundness of face, and Flora, even then angular, her ever-darkening blond hair in braids nearly to her waist, her mother having decided the experience of forcing her to trim them was one not worth repeating. Yes, Flora and Georgia were both only children, but the similarities between their families ended there. Georgia called her mother Madeleine and her father Ray and they all had the same last name, McNair-Wallach, each parent taking a small but essential part of the other as their own. Hyphenated last names were big in Darwin, like tofu, and recycling, and Flora found their collective hyphenate—the outward manifestation of the mutuality of their merging—annoying. Flora's mother had taken her father's name, but he had not taken hers, and she liked to say, seeing her full name in print, that it made her feel like an imposter. "Who is that woman?" she'd ask coyly, examining an envelope addressed to her. "Have we met?"

Flora and Georgia were not sisters: They were better than sisters; they were partners in crime; they were spies contriving ways into the neighbors' houses; they were invincible and indivisible. The President's House—the setting of their romance—invited games-manship and danger. A mansion invites make-believe, makes pre-tense and delusion easy. Living there, Flora imagined she was a princess, with almost no effort. And just as effortlessly she imag-ined she was an orphan, and a runaway, and a prisoner. She and Georgia played hide-and-seek, of course, and Pollyanna, a game loosely modeled on the Hayley Mills movie, in which Flora was a paralyzed saint and Georgia her devoted nurse, pushing her around the long hallways on the large red leather desk chair with its sticky wheels, their roles always the same—Flora the brave invalid, Georgia the patient caregiver. With the Ghost Game, they created a complicated world, in which the giant portraits in the foyer of Darwin alumni of minor historical note came alive at night and the girls became tour guides, shuttling big groups of no one through the house as though it were a ghost museum, inventing and narrating the biographies of the men in the paintings, what they had done in life and what they did when they returned from the dead. One of the paintings, above the staircase, a life-size, full-body portrait of an officer in the Civil War, with an elaborate uni-form and a sword taller than Flora, wandered around murmuring, "Have you seen my horse?" The staircase itself, with its darkly gleaming mahogany banister and a landing as long as a hallway, invited jumping contests. They would jump down, four, five, six steps at a time, hurling their bodies onto the itchy beige carpet below, Flora pushing—"Just one more"—and Georgia hesitating—"Maybe we've gone high enough for today."

When they tired of contests, they invented rides. Flora's bed-room had two doors, one leading to the hallway, the other to her father's study, and she and Georgia would each climb onto the doorknobs, hoist themselves up to the tops, and sit there and swing back and forth, each on her respective door, talking for hours until they heard the footsteps of approaching adults, and they would throw themselves to the ground, bruising, scuffing, laughing. Many of Flora's childhood memories involved hitting the ground hard—hitting the ground was one of life's daily realities. Rug burns standard; scabs eternal. Jumping from stairs, doors, trees, bicycles. Looking back, one's childhood body seemed so resilient and catlike, bendable and unbreakable—or almost so.

Together, they played Annie. They were orphans escaping from the orphanage and the tyrannical Miss Hannigan. They climbed out the window on the third floor to the ladder that ran along the side of the house—the old fire escape Flora's mother had declared off-limits, barring any actual emergency. Gripping the metal rungs, the chipping black paint scratching their palms, they climbed down, slowly, carefully, hand under hand, tentative foot below foot, all the way to the ground, and then they climbed back up, into the sky, and then down again, and up, and again, and again, as though they were rewinding a tape, each time risking anew discovery, and capture, and death.

3

Literary Executioners

THE CROSS COLLEGE LIBRARY was named for the wealthy Darwin alumnus who financed its building in the 1960s, but it was often mistaken for some sort of religious institution at the center of campus, and once, in the '90s, protested by a group of Jewish students who refused to study in a shrine to Christian iconography. This was where her father's first editions and rarer books would be moving as soon as Flora went through and packed them up. She remembered visiting the library as a child in that first year in Darwin, and looking up her father's name in the most recent volume of *Who's Who in America*. There he was, listed and defined in the encyclopedia of Americans. Her father was a Who. He existed not only in the world but, indelibly, in print. Important people existed in books.

Now she was there for him again, this time to research literary executors, the elite fellowship to which she had newly been appointed. Research, in Darwin, had to be done elsewhere. The house was not equipped. Her father lived without technology, and so Flora lived without technology. He had never even had an e-mail account, or at least not one he checked. He'd been loyal to his Smith Corona portable, shunning the computer with impressive tenacity. A cell phone was as preposterous to him as a handheld refrigerator. "Why bring the inside outside?" had been his line on people listening to music while jogging or walking their dogs, back in the early days of the Walkman.

Though Flora hadn't visited him, her father had come to the city every few months. He'd stay with Rubie, who lived nearby, meeting Flora for eggs and bacon at the diner near her office before she went to work, and taking her to dinner and sometimes the opera after (always the Italians was his rule, and preferably Verdi), these occasions strangely datelike—the heightened excitement of a special occasion, the dressing up, the one-on-oneness. The post-divorce romance one has with one's parents. "We haven't put a foot wrong," he'd tell her, patting her hand, as they waited for the curtain to rise, "not a foot wrong, my Flora-Girl."

It was on the last visit that he'd given her his poems over breakfast.

"Appallingly rough," he'd told her before handing her the folder agape with words he had written. "Some good bits, though, I think."

She'd asked if anyone else had read them yet, and he'd shaken his head.

"You're the reader I trust most."

A flattering phrase she repeated in the privacy of her mind.

It was enjoyable, being in a library. It had been a while. The design was universally acclaimed: dark wooden beams punctuating tall, thick walls of glass—at night it was said to glow like a paper lantern. Libraries often smelled of ignored dust and generations of book crumbs, but this one had a pleasing air of sterility. A few stoop-shouldered students read nearby, foreheads folding into books as though study were an act of osmosis, while Flora trolled the Internet for stories, many of which seemed more the stuff of fiction than of life and death. She read of Ted Hughes's zany spinster sister, who'd built a fortress around her brother and Plath's poems; of the obsessive and controlling Joyce heir, bane of scholars and Bloomsday fanatics alike—a professional ruiner of all Joyce-related fun; of J. R. R. Tolkien's kin, still writing his father's books; and of Dmitri Nabokov, with his jaunty conversations with ghost dad. Apparently, good old ghost dad thought his son should publish, and profit.

Were they all crazy before they filled the role of executor, or was it the post-death nomination that had unfurled, flaglike, the full neuroses of those familial relations? *Executor*—it sounded much like *executioner*. I am his Literary Executioner, Flora thought. The Lord High Literary Executioner.

It was a paradoxical position: at once powerful and subservient, generous and greedy. To control someone else's free expression—a power one should never hold. How muddled protectiveness and professional jealousy could become. Was it better to share everything, or was that slatternly? The impossible requirement of reading, among many, many other things, the mind of the dead—what would he want? Writers wanted readers, no? That was why they wrote. But what sorts of readers did they want, and at what point?

There was the added problem that Flora had never read her father's work. Not the influential *Reader as Understander*, or his later scholarly books; not his regular reviews in *The New Republic*; not even the poems that he had months ago given just to her—the reader he trusted most really the least trustworthy. Had he assumed that she, along with all children of Darwin, was well versed in the Dempsey canon? Or had she somehow duped him into thinking she was reliable and literate?

She heard the strains of talking-whispers and turned. It was Madeleine McNair-Wallach, arguing with the librarian. How many years had it been? She'd cut her hair pixie-short and gone gray, her shoulders gently stooped. Funny, the genericness of aging—bodies that start out so rich and varied resembling one another more and more. Though even the blurring of time could do nothing to diminish Madeleine's substantial breasts, covered now by a thick green sweater she had probably knit herself. The librarian moved to answer a phone, and Madeleine scanned the high-ceilinged, lofted space.

Would they be happy to see each other? Flora waited for Madeleine's reaction before releasing one of her own, but she could see from across the room Madeleine suddenly beaming, with surprise and that particular brand of happiness adults display upon seeing those they knew when small.

"Flora Dempsey!" she called out, and then covered her mouth, remembering where she was. The librarian flashed her a look she didn't notice.

Madeleine was approaching and Flora stood and they held out their arms in unison and then the excruciation of each going for a different cheek and the resulting mid-embrace adjustment.

Flora pulled back. "So nice to see you, Madeleine."

"Flora Dempsey," Madeleine said again, the freckles on her nose scrunching, her green eyes darting back and forth as they'd always done when she was absorbed in thought. The constancy of facial expressions—it was reassuring.

"How are you? How are all of you?" Flora asked.

"We're all all right. I've been thinking of you, Flora. Since I heard about your dad. I've been trying to find a way to get in touch, but I could only find your mother's address—I actually sent her a note, hoping she'd pass it on. I didn't know you were back in town."

"I didn't know I'd be here, either. I haven't been back long. That was sweet of you—to write."

"What a blow this must be. I know your relationship with him wasn't always easy, but a man like your father—even when he's not your father—takes up a lot of space, doesn't he? His is a large absence, I'd imagine."

Flora clutched her fingers with her other fingers and looked around, as if sizing up the extent of his absence. How to respond, and what to? This was why she was on the lam from the aggressive condolers. Anything apart from the comforting clichés seemed to Flora almost horrible. "Yes," she made herself say. "What's Georgia up to these days?"

"In Mongolia interviewing nomads. It sounds like a punch line every time I say it, but you know Georgia. She's an anthropologist, finishing her Ph.D. She lives in a yurt. She could do without all the mutton stew, and the various digestive challenges, but other than that, she's completely at home. I thought Ray and I were pretty intrepid, pretty low-maintenance, but she's taken it to a new level." Madeleine spoke with a distant admiration, as if describing a public figure, and not her own child. "You know Georgia," she said again. "How she throws herself into things."

"Yes," Flora said, apparently the highlight of her conversational repertoire. And she felt she knew Georgia. But of course she didn't anymore. "I can picture her doing that," she added. "Not that I have an accurate picture—or any real picture—of what Mongolia looks like."

"Are you picturing sheep? Because if so, I think you're on the right track."

"Okay," Flora said. "I think I see it."

They both smiled, and their smiles lingered till it seemed they'd run out of things to say.

"I was just using the computer," Flora said, though Madeleine had seen her sitting there not five minutes before.

"I'm teaching a Freud seminar. It's the first time I've taught it, and of course every conceivable thing has gone wrong with the readings." Madeleine glanced back at the librarian. Then she leaned in conspiratorially. "That woman is torturing me," she whispered. "Ray says I killed her cat in a former life."

Flora wished they could sit. The thought of what she'd done to Madeleine in a former life was stifling in its presence. "How is Ray?" she asked.

"Good, good. He'd love to see you, Flora. It really is amazing to see you after all these years. You look good. I'm sure you're not—how could you be? But you look it."

"Well." Flora, shy-struck and miserable, gestured again to the computer. "It's really good to see you, too."

"Maybe you'd come over sometime for dinner? Ray would love it. We both would. I want to hear all about your life."

"Oh, no, really? I'd love to come, but only if you promise we won't have to talk about that."

Madeleine pinched Flora's shoulder. "Hang in there, kiddo."

"Okay," Flora said, tears she hoped were invisible pushing their way up.

"I'll be in touch," Madeleine said, leaving her.

Flora sat back down at the computer, staring without sight at the glow of the page. That was it, then. A friendly reunion, old wounds just benign hazy scars whose origins had been forgotten. Or maybe she had suffered enough, finally, to be forgiven. To be welcomed back into the bosom of their perfect family. Darwin's flawed orphaned daughter—they were ready for her now.

———

In school, they spent all their time together. They talked constantly. There was so much to talk about. Georgia knew everything. She'd read the encyclopedia, volumes *A* through *S,* though that was a secret only Flora knew. In private, Georgia was proud of that fact, but in public she would be humiliated by it. This was often the way things were then. While they chatted together, their third-grade teacher, Lynn, kind and young, would look at them pleadingly, and then separate them. They were always being separated. This school was different from Flora's school in the city, where there were only girls, and teachers were called Mister and Missus, and students wore thick maroon uniforms—uniforms Flora had despised and her mother adored, as they meant no more morning arguments over wardrobe. Flora had been taught that last names were polite, but now in Darwin, where everyone insisted on first names, they'd begun to seem rude. This school had no uniforms, no Mister or Missus, and was different in every way.

For one thing, recess was outside, grassy and dirty, whereas back in the city it had been in the sky, on the roof of the school building. At recess in Darwin, Flora loved playing games with the boys, kickball and tetherball, and most of all a game called Swedish, which involved pegging other people with the red rubber ball. The rule was whoever got to the field first could choose the game of the day. Flora and Georgia always ran to the field, ran so fast their throats burned and their chests hurt and they couldn't talk. They almost always got there first. The boys called them Flo-Geo, like the sprinter, and they liked that, having one shared identity.

Third grade meant studying Greek mythology, making togas

and bas-relief clay tiles depicting scenes of the pantheon of gods. They were staging a production of *Prometheus Bound*. Georgia was outraged that she couldn't play Prometheus simply because she was a girl. She deserved the leading role because she was the only one who could remember the lines accurately, who would be true to Aeschylus's vision of the tragedy. Instead, they were both cast in the chorus. Flora didn't mind; after all, the chorus got to be onstage the whole time, and wasn't that the point? But Georgia wrote a letter to Lynn, describing how unfair, and possibly sexist, she found the casting decisions, and so it was decided that Alex Tillman could be Prometheus in the first performance, Georgia in the second. After that, being in the chorus didn't seem quite as good to Flora.

One day during rehearsals, they got to the field first at recess and announced that the game would be Swedish, as usual. But the gym teacher, Peggy, who was short and mean and whom nobody liked anyway, intervened. "You've played Swedish every day this week," she said. "I think your classmates would appreciate a change."

When Flora protested, Peggy rolled her eyes. "It's not up for discussion," she said. "We'll play Wiffle ball today."

Sarah Feldman and the other prissy girls clapped. They didn't like Swedish. But Flora hated Wiffle ball. Even the name was stupid, and made you sound like you had a lisp. She and Georgia walked off the field. They couldn't tolerate such blatant flouting of the system. They walked in the direction of the cargo net. They could play in there instead. When they got there, though, it looked boring, hanging listlessly, a giant useless cobweb. Georgia was annoyed, but Flora was furious.

"The rule is whoever gets there first chooses," she said. "That's the rule."

"I know," Georgia said.

"This is worse than the Prometheus casting. What's wrong with this place?"

"I'm not sure it's worse," Georgia said. "Just as bad, maybe."

Flora was adamant. "We should get to choose."

They came to the edge of the school's driveway and could hear in the distance the sounds of their classmates cheering someone round the bases.

"We have to leave," she said.

"Leave school?" Georgia asked.

"Yes."

"And go where?"

"Anywhere. We have to show them we won't stand for this unfairness."

"Really? By leaving?"

"Yes, really."

"Okay," Georgia said, but Flora could see she didn't like the idea.

"Okay," Flora said anyway.

The President's House was a mile away and they walked in that direction. There was a chance that Betsy, the housekeeper, would be there. Flora could see Georgia was hoping she would be, that she wanted them to get caught. Flora had never walked so far without a grown-up and she wanted to run and tear leaves and sing all her favorite songs. But they walked in silence. At the house, there was a long row of tall, dense bushes along the side, protecting it from the street like a living fence, and Flora could climb up into the first one and then crawl to the next and the next, inside, unseen. She'd emerge from the other end, shin-scraped and triumphant. They could play in there. But when they got to the house, Georgia said she needed a glass of water, and when the two of them went inside, there in the kitchen was Betsy, who had already received a call from the school. She shuffled them into her El Camino, stuffing them into the front seat together, and they were back and in the headmaster's office in minutes, their protest squashed, their powerlessness confirmed.

The headmaster and Lynn told Flora and Georgia how disappointed they were. The school functioned according to an honor system, and they had broken that trust. Flora didn't point out that it was the school that had broken their trust first. She didn't make eye contact with Georgia, who never said "It was Flora's idea." Lynn said if they were angry or upset, they should talk to someone about it, but not run away, never just run away. It was the first time girls at the school had been sent to talk to the headmaster, and Flora thought they should be proud; her mother talked about feminist milestones, and that's what they had done—achieved a kind of feminist milestone.

But at the end of the day, Madeleine picked Georgia up from school and Georgia started to cry, as though she regretted everything, and her mother put her arm around her and bent down to kiss the top of her head, as though Georgia had done nothing wrong, and the two of them walked to their car, Georgia tucked safely into the crook of Madeleine's arm, nestled against her huge maternal breasts.

Betsy was in the El Camino, idling in the school's driveway. "Your parents are going to be pissed, Flo," she said.

They were both out, but later that evening Flora went into the kitchen, where her mother was making dinner. She was heating oil and chopping onions and listening to talk radio and not looking at Flora. Where was her father? Work for him often meant dinner these days; dinner meant meetings. Her mother had already learned to hate the big industrial stove, with its eight burners and two ovens and a broiler above one of the ovens. She'd singed her eyebrows lighting the broiler while making dinner for the first time in the big house—the acrid smell of burned hair lingering for days—and now whenever she cooked, Flora felt nervous. Flora leaned against the counter and pressed her palms into the sharp edge of the red Formica and she made herself cry. She didn't regret anything, but it had worked for Georgia.

Her mother looked up and saw the tears. She paused, and for a moment Flora thought she would put down her knife and come to her and hold her. Her eyes seemed to be watering, too. But then she just shook her head. "Don't give me that shit," she said, and returned to her chopping.

The next day at school, while Georgia—bound to the cardboard rock with cardboard chains—rehearsed one of her scenes, Flora leaned over to Alex Tillman.

"You want to know what Georgia does in her spare time?" she whispered in his ear. "She reads the encyclopedia."

4

Nighttimes

IN FLORA'S LITTLE APARTMENT in the city, there were two ways in: the thick front door bejeweled with chain and bolt, and the metal-gated window that led to the fire escape. People called the country safe, but in her father's house, every thin pane of glass on each of the ground-floor windows asked to be broken with a casually thrown rock, and every door to the outside (three total) looked a formality, a token gesture to security. Even the exterior walls felt meager, insubstantial boundaries between inside and out. The house was built in the 1860s and spoke the language of creaks and moans that all old houses speak. When the heat came on, the hot water rushing through the pipes, the house made a great fuss, letting one know how taxing one's selfish need for warmth was on its old bones. "I like a house that tells you how it feels," her father told her when she'd complained on a visit. "It's letting us know it's still with us." But the noises were ominous. Flora heard the whispers of voices in the pipes—a steady murmuring, like a cocktail party next door she tried to ignore. Where was the line exactly between loneliness and insanity? And how would she know if—when—she transgressed?

With the lights out, the house was impenetrable, so dark it almost ceased to exist. With the lights on, it was a giant aquarium—Flora a bottom-dwelling flounder, perfectly visible to the outside world, which was perfectly invisible to her. Anyone might be peering in, or no one, watching her as she made herself a dinner of fried eggs. That had been breakfast, and lunch, too. That was life for the time being: fried eggs.

Soon Mrs. J. would be stopping by with Larks. Flora had called her to say she'd be happy to take him now, after she'd awakened in the night several times badly needing to pee but too terrified to leave bed. Larks was no fearsome guard dog; he was a wet-nosed tail wagger. But he was alive, another creature, a witness.

In the country, in her father's house newly hers, Flora felt aware of being alive to an uncomfortable degree. When people said something made them feel *so alive,* they seemed to mean it was a desirable state to find oneself in, a source of elation. But for Flora, feeling so conscious of her beingness was lonely, and a little gross. Being *so alive* was morbid; it was near death.

"I'm having a near-death experience," she told her mother over the phone, and it was true; death was near all right—it was her housemate. She'd called from the kitchen phone to have a little company while she ate her eggs, but the short tether of the cord reached only as far as the counter, so she ate standing up.

As a child, she loved to play a simple word game with her mother. Her mother would say, "I'm me, and you're you." And then Flora would say, "No! *I'm* me, and *you're* you." Her mother: "Sorry, Flo. I'm me, and you're you." Flora: "Nooo! I'm me, and you're you." And so on, the game continuing indefinitely and hilariously, with no hope of resolution, Flora's laughter increasingly hysterical. How could they both be right? Were they both me? Were they both you? Now it seemed more poignant than funny: a parent and child negotiating the murky territory between them—that border loosely patrolled, and regularly trespassed. In her father's house, back in Darwin, who was who exactly?

"What are you going to do up there all by yourself?" her mother asked. "I still don't understand this plan."

"Plan," Flora said. "That's a nice word for it."

"I thought so."

"I'm going to have Larks. I won't be all by myself."

"In that case. What are you and the dog going to do up there all by yourselves?"

Rude questions. Also bewildering.

"Your friends are calling here daily, Flo. They're trying to track you down. They say your cell phone isn't working."

Flora had imagined her father's life in Darwin as romantic and solitary; she'd been right only on the romance. But now, if she wanted, she could live out that fantasy of romantic solitude. She hadn't told friends in the city where to find her, because she didn't know what to tell them. And she liked that no one knew where she was; she liked that her cell phone was no longer accepting messages. The comfort lay in the easy explanation she had for her mood: death, a justification; a death-justified hooky from the world. It reminded her of the first time she lied to her parents about where she was going, of running away from school—the complete liberation in letting others down. Still, she feared for herself the way she might fear for another person. Her life might not work out. It seemed more than a possibility.

"Everyone's worried. They want to know how you are."

"They want credit for calling," Flora said. "They want their concern noted."

"That's a little low, isn't it? You really don't think your friends love you and want to know how you are?"

"I suppose both impulses could be in play." Was that low, or was it true? Was she right, or just depressed? Her thoughts appeared clear, and lucid—she could see through everyone. But perhaps what she was seeing was her own foul mood reflected back like lights in a mirror. "What do you tell them?"

"I say you're not quite up for talking, but that it means a lot to you that they're checking in and that you'll be in touch soon. You will be in touch soon, won't you? Otherwise, maybe you could cut a small portion from your large inheritance for your poor old social secretary here in the city?"

"You're shameless."

"On the vulgar matter of coin, and the matter of your father, I suppose I am."

"Have I lost my mind, is that what's going on here?"

"You're doing fine," her mother said.

"You don't sound quite convinced."

"One day at a time, Flo—like the alcoholics."

"I'm glad you brought that up—I'm seriously considering it, alcoholism. Seems a logical next step, doesn't it? The New England way—stoical self-destruction."

"Don't go Protestant on me, Flora. That I can't take. And don't make me come up to Darwin and rescue you."

"No, no. No interventions needed yet." Mrs. J.'s sedan glided into the pool of light that was the driveway. "I've got to go, Mom. The dog's here."

"Tell Mrs. J. hello from me. Tell her I still use that ironing-board cover she made me all those years ago."

"But you don't. As far as I know, you don't even own an iron."

"I most certainly do. You really are a revolting child. Who brought you up?"

"Good-bye, Mom."

She watched through the kitchen window as Larks, released, bounded toward the door, his black-and-white body frantic, his excitement uncomfortable. He could not keep all four paws on the ground. He knew better than to bark—her father never stood for that—but he let out an almost squeal. It seemed cruel to open the door, to meet such anticipation with the disappointment that was herself. But Larks was happy to see her. She squatted down, the screen door against her back, and he burrowed his cool nose into her hair, her hand, her lap.

"Larks," she said, holding his two plush ears in her hands like ponytails. "Hello, Larks."

When she'd first met the new puppy, she'd asked her father, "Isn't it pretentious to name your dog after a poet—and such a depressive one at that?" She'd told him, "He looks more like a Fred to me."

"Are you kidding?" her father had said. "This dog has the soul of a poet. This dog understands the vicissitudes of the human condition."

"Boy, is he happy to be home," said Mrs. J. She sagged with shopping bags. Flora stood quickly to help and the dog ran into the house, tail wagging, in search.

"So good to see you," Flora said, taking two bags and kissing Mrs. J. on the cheek. She smelled of breath mints. The plumpness of her skin was peach-soft. She was in her sixties, around the same age as Flora's father, but had always seemed both younger and older than he—less worn, but of another generation. Only the hair around her temples had truly grayed, and her small roundness gave her an air of permanence, of invulnerability. "You haven't aged in however many years since I saw you last," Flora told her. "Really, Mrs. J., your DNA ought to be studied."

"Almost two years now," Mrs. J. said. "You look just the same, too, Flora. Just as you did as a little girl. Your dad always said that."

"I'm not sure it's a compliment at this point."

"Oh, it's a compliment. You're still too young to know it, but it's a compliment."

Mrs. J., short for Jankowitz, had cleaned house for Flora's family, or for her father, for two decades, since they first moved to Darwin. She'd been there, through it all, straightening up. They held the doors open for each other and dumped their bags by the fridge. Flora cleared her dinner dishes to the sink. It was suddenly embarrassing to be eating breakfast at night.

"What's all this?" she asked of the bags.

"Some food for Larks. A few little things for you. I made beef stew. I remembered how much you loved my beef stew back when I used to babysit. Remember that? I put it in a few containers—you can freeze them. Have them as you like."

Flora's eyes stung; her throat stabbed. Kindness took its toll on the body. She nodded, and they silently loaded the containers into the freezer.

"And noodles. I got a few packages—it's good with these egg noodles."

Mrs. J. had bought three big bags of dog food, which she carried one by one over to the pantry closet. Larks had returned, expectant, and stood watching his food as it moved across the room.

"You've done too much," Flora said.

Mrs. J. stopped and stared at her. "Please, Flora," she said.

"He gets one scoop in the morning, and a scoop and half a can of wet food at night," she went on. "Do you want me to write it down for you?"

"No, no," Flora said, but she did anyway.

"I guess I should be getting back," Mrs. J. said. "Told Mr. J. I'd be back in a flash. But I'll be stopping by. To see you, Flora, and Larks."

In all the years, Flora had never met Mr. J., though she'd seen pictures and knew he existed. The family theory had been that he'd struck upon some undeserved good luck when Mrs. J. agreed to have him, though Flora couldn't now remember why.

Flora walked her outside. The sky was quilted with star cover. "You're the best," she said, and she bent to embrace this almost grandmother, this woman she'd once known so well.

"Flora—your father. He was so good to me. So good. They don't make men like him anymore. I hate to say it, but they don't."

Flora tucked her hands into the sleeves of her sweatshirt and hugged her arms around herself.

"That girlfriend of his," Mrs. J. continued. "That Cynthia. I have to tell you, I don't care for her. From the beginning, I didn't trust her. I didn't like it when she was alone in the house. I felt she was after something, from him, from your dad. Can't say what it was— his money, maybe, the house?"

"My dad seems an unlikely target for a gold digger," Flora said. "A bronze digger, maybe."

"I'm telling you, Flora, I don't care for her at all."

It was one thing for Flora to dislike her father's girlfriend. But Mrs. J.? Was Cynthia actually unlikable? "I just met her, so it's hard for me to say."

"I know, I know. And I don't like to trouble you with any more than what you've got on your plate already. But I thought you should know. Just keep your eyes open."

"Okay," Flora said. "Thanks." She was suddenly exhausted. *Leave me alone,* she wanted to say, she almost said. *Leave me.*

"Like I said, I'll be stopping by, checking in, seeing if you all need anything."

"Thanks again, Mrs. J.," Flora said. She felt she needed to say more. "It's a comfort to know you're nearby," she added.

"I know it is, sweetie. I know."

Back inside, Flora headed for the guest room. Her father's television was nearly as old as she was, and if there had ever been a remote, it had long since vanished, so flipping the channels required standing by the box and stooping to press the tiny up or down button. Flora stooped; she pressed. America was obsessed with rejection. On one channel, there was a show where, one by one, girls were rejected from a career in modeling. In another show, each week a new family got the ax for not having quite a miserable-enough life—almost, but not quite. In a third show, young women were gradually and systematically rejected by a man they had just met who did not, it turned out, want to marry them.

Did Flora share in the national fervor? She had rejected her father, not visiting him in Darwin, and then not reading his manuscript of poems when first he gave it to her over breakfast at the diner—wandering the papers, instead, around the desert of her apartment, from bedside table to desk to drawer, simultaneously fussing and neglecting, handling them like a fetish she must be cured of. Even now, she rejected him by not wanting to read them, exiling them to the body bag, rejecting her role as his chosen reader, the one he trusted, his executioner. She'd rejected her mother, and her friends, and her work—everything she left behind in the city so hastily, as if she'd been waiting for the chance to leave them all along. And now she'd rejected Cynthia, whom she had just met, regardless of whether she could be trusted or not, by saying no, there was no room for her in the memorial service, or her father's house, no room for her in life or death.

On the shows, the moment of rejection was stretched out to the most awkward extent possible and saved for the very last minute of programming, as though it were a reward held out to viewers for getting through all the optimism and pluck of the previous hour. The rejected one usually cried, his or her face crumpling into wrin-

kles of injury and despair, but so did the ones who had been nar-
rowly spared from rejection for one more week—whether out of
malice or relief, empathy, love, or fury, it was hard to tell.

Flora, watching, cried, too. She had a hard time not crying when
she saw other people cry, as if her face were a mirror. Was that all
she was? The thought was troubling. But then, it was a relief to cry,
to in fact weep. To sit on the floor beneath the blue daze of the television and weep. "Did you cry?" her father had once asked her after
some insignificant childhood mishap, some bike or tree unfooting.
"Did I cry? I weeped!" Flora had told him indignantly. It had
become a family story. She did not cry; she weeped. She cried so
hard, her mouth grew dry, her tongue hurt. She cried as she'd cried
as a child, alone in her room at the President's House, making
ugly, desperate noises, her face hot and wet, the dog standing above
her, slowly wagging his tail, watching her with interest, head atilt,
waiting.

Later, sapped and waterlogged, she retreated to her little room with
the cordless telephone and the phone book—her links to other
human beings, but also, each in its own way, a reasonable weapon
against the skull of an intruder, should the need arise. Her city
cell phone, now permanently off, received spotty service in her
father's house anyway—service was spotty in Darwin in general,
a metaphor for its disconnection from the larger world. If the
would-be intruder thought to cut the phone lines, she'd have no
way to call for help. She and Larks would be on their own.

What Flora needed was expert advice. Her fellow literary execu-
tioners and Plath and Joyce were of no practical use. Her father
was not Plath or Joyce. But even when an early Plath poem had
lately been discovered by some graduate student rousing long-
slumbering manuscripts, it had birthed only limited curiosity.
Flora knew because she'd read about the incident in the library.
There was no such thing as a poem heard around the world. But
still, her father had been a prominent scholar, of the Harold Bloom
and Helen Vendler crowd—the triumvirate of pop poetry criticism,

could there be said to be such a thing. It was not unthinkable that Lewis Dempsey's poems could prompt limited attention, too, whether they were any good or not.

She needed to consult someone who knew things. Paul something—something Welsh, or Scottish—that was her father's lawyer; he had drawn up the will. He'd put everything in order, officially documenting and organizing her father's death. A former student was as much as she knew. A Darwin English major turned attorney. She opened the phone book to the business pages in the back. The last name started with a *B*, or a *D*. In the *D*'s she found "Davies, Paul, Esq." It was nearly midnight, but she would just call the office while no one was there and leave a message, while she was thinking of it. But a man answered on the first ring.

"Oh," she said. "I must have dialed the wrong number."

She was about to hang up when she heard the man say, "Who are you trying to reach?"

"A lawyer. I'm sorry if I woke you. I thought I was calling an office. I was going to leave a message."

"Is this an emergency?"

"No, no, I was just hoping to make an appointment. Please accept my apol—"

"You have called a lawyer. This is my office."

"Who is this?" she asked.

"Who is this calling?"

Had she stumbled upon some pervert who now wanted to play late-night phone games with her? "Listen, I really am sorry to have disturbed you. I'm going to hang up."

"This is one of the stranger phone calls I've ever received," the man said. "Let's start over. Hello, this is Paul Davies."

"Really? That's whom I was calling. I was assuming no one would be there, I was going to—"

"Yes, leave a message, but here I am. Who is this?"

"This is Flora Dempsey. My father—"

"Sure, Lew Dempsey. One of my favorite clients. One of my favorite teachers. I'm so sorry for your loss."

"Was he? Thank you." Almost no one called her father Lew—her mother, Ira Rubenstein. In the mouth of this stranger, it sounded overly intimate, intrusive, crass.

"A great guy—a legend in town." He paused. "What can I do for you today, Ms. Dempsey?"

Today? Was it even, officially, one day or another? Was the lawyer always this preemptory? Was he working against a major deadline? Or had she caught him mid-tryst? "Flora, please," she said. She was not prepared; she was in her pajamas. "Why don't we make an appointment for another time. I'm just hoping to ask your advice on a few details of the will."

"What sort of details?"

"*Details* maybe isn't the right word. More overview, I guess."

"All right, overview of what?"

"These things I've inherited—the house, the writing. Mostly the writing. I'm not sure what to do. But it's late, and I feel I must be keeping you from something important."

"It's pretty straightforward. And you've caught me now. Why don't I run through what I'd tell you if you came in for an appointment."

"If it's no trouble—"

"As literary executor, essentially you are a stand-in for your father vis-à-vis his work. So, in that capacity, you may be asked to sign contracts or grant permission, or you may choose to edit a piece of his writing in anticipation of publication. But the extent of your involvement is entirely up to you." He paused, as though waiting for confirmation that she was following. She muttered in compliance. "It's presumed by the designation that your interests will be in line with his—with what he would have wanted for the work."

"Is it?"

"That's the assumption, yes."

Her interests primarily concerned not reading her father's work. How would that have squared with his? Surely there were former students like this know-it-all on the line—worshipful, ambitious, and far more capable—her father might have appointed to the job. When had he first chosen her from among all the possible literary executors? When had he said, *Flora, it must be Flora*? Had he said anything to Paul Davies about why he wanted her? She wanted to stop him now and ask him. But Paul was still explaining—a barrage of legalese, and not what she wanted from him. She wanted him to tell her that her father had said how wonderful she was, how sensitive, how she was such a good reader, and a good daughter. She wanted him to say that her father had left behind detailed instructions enumerating his expectations. She wanted him to say she didn't have to do anything, that there was a caveat in the will, or a mistake. She wanted him to say that as it turned out, her father wasn't dead after all. She watched the hands of the clock on the bedside table meet as though in prayer, pointing at the ceiling.

"The biggest hassles for a literary executor usually occur when there is a separate heir—the heir's and the executor's interests may be at odds, financially speaking," he was saying. "But since you're both executor and heir, your situation is relatively simple."

Was that supposed to be reassuring? He'd said it so cheerfully. Executor and heir. Both. Her new, symbiotic, bipolar identity. Why had she admitted ignorance to the lawyer? Why had she even bothered asking? She was old enough to know not to make phone calls in her dead father's house in the middle of the night.

"It's like the estate," he blazed on, an assault of information and analogy. "You're in charge of the house now, and in that capacity you can choose to remodel or leave it sitting empty, or you can put it on the market to sell. As I said, it's entirely up to you."

Was he patronizing her? Would he have said the same, with such perfunctory pep, to Ted Hughes had he called for a consultation on Sylvia's poems? "It's that easy?" she asked him.

"Legally speaking, yes."

Legally speaking, financially speaking. She knew his type. She could easily picture this man—he sounded young and undeservingly self-confident—a bully in his khakis, his white monogrammed pressed shirt now untucked as the single concession to the hour. Everything was neat to guys like him, the perfect soul-killing jargon holstered and at the ready. Life a series of logical legalities, spread out before him like an illuminated path to heaven. A man who comforted himself with his old, annotated paperbacks of Beat poets, who at cocktail parties with other lawyers talked about how *Naked Lunch* had changed his life. Had her father really trusted this man with his will, with his death? *Will*—it was a funny word. *This is my will. I will it to be so.*

Now all she had to do, according to this legal expert, was guess the most private hopes her father might have had *vis-à-vis* a stack of poems he wrote in the last year of his life without ever showing or telling anyone other than her. The *relatively simple* task before her a mere matter of deciding whether they were ready for publication, and, if not, how to make them so. And then, of course, there was the correspondence, the early drafts, the speeches from his presidency, the essays from his forty-year career, the whole of his life in letters, now, impossibly, hers. Executor and heir. She had it all.

"Ms. Dempsey, are you still there?"

She was, but she didn't want to be. So she did something she hadn't done since high school, in a fight with her boyfriend or her mother, the abruptness as satisfying as the sharp smash of a slammed door: She hung up.

———

They were always in different rooms: Flora's father reading the paper in his study, her mother reading Laura Ingalls Wilder to her downstairs in the library; him falling asleep in front of some game on the television in their bedroom, her smoking her Marlboro reds in front of a murder mystery on the other television on the third floor. The excesses of the President's House welcomed such separations. Her parents were the sun and the moon, only rarely inhabiting the same sky, and when it happened, the feeling eclipse-like—exhilarating, and unnerving. But he could make her laugh the way no one else could, the way Flora never could. Flora's grandmother had told her mother, "Marry the man who makes you laugh—they all make you cry," and she had taken the advice literally.

Her job now was to be the wife of the president of Darwin, and even Flora could see that she had decided not to do it well. She was certainly determined not to look the part. Her hair turned an alarming shade of purple overnight, and it was discovered she'd experimented with Manic Panic, a company whose target customer attended junior high school. She bought a pair of black combat boots and wore them around town unlaced. To complete the adolescent goth look, it could only be assumed, she, who never wore eye makeup, had her eyelashes dyed black. Her new eyes made her look depressed. And she left them every Tuesday night, Flora and her father, to return to the city and flee Darwin, back to her old life, the life she had never wanted to leave in the first place and still refused to give up, to see her friends and her analyst.

"Doesn't everyone's mother have an analyst?" Flora asked Georgia.

Georgia, who loved to be consulted on all matters of human behavior, paused to consider before answering. "Many do, but not all" was her assessment.

Abandoned, Flora and her father developed a Tuesday-night routine of their own. Dinner at Ponzu, a Japanese restaurant on an ugly commercial strip just out of town, with huge grills on the tables where the chefs cooked in front of you and did tricks like flipping a shrimp in the air and catching it in their pockets. They were beloved guests because they came every week and because her father tipped exorbitantly. The hostess insisted on bringing them, on the house, a soda for Flora, and for her father, plum wine, which he found cloyingly sweet but drank out of politeness. He was a man who cleaned his plate, even if he didn't like something, and this annoyed Flora's mother, who felt his manners missed the point. "I'd rather have you leave some food and listen to me when I talk to you instead," she'd say, as if one had a choice about that kind of thing.

Sometimes Georgia came with them to dinner. Flora's father called Georgia "the Wizard," for Georgia's love of science and magic, and because the tops of her ears came to the gentlest of points. "It's the Wild Wizard!" he'd say to her in greeting, and they would both look delighted.

"Like sisters," the staff at Ponzu said.

Over dinner, there were competitions. "Let the competitions commence" was her father's rallying cry. "Who can make the best cow sound?" And the three of them mooed, one at a time, her father announcing, "I won that one," and they would shriek with laughter at the corruption of the judging system. "I'm sorr-ry," he'd say, exaggerating the word to show he wasn't a bit sorry. "Even the Lithuanian judge gave mine a nine-point-eight. You two squeaked by with an eight-point-two."

Back at the house, her father made Flora sweet, milky tea, and then he would read to her, picking up wherever her mother had left off the night before. Flora would offer a synopsis of what he'd missed, but he never seemed to mind that these weekly sessions meant he only ever heard one-seventh of a story. One month he started to read to her from a different book, a book of his choosing, one he had loved growing up and bought for her in town at Finch's Books: *Swallows and Amazons*. But Flora had found it boring and they'd quit halfway through. It was years later, remembering her father's hopefulness upon presenting her with the hardbound volume with a simple line drawing of a canoe or some other member of the boat family across its cover, that it occurred to her that in rejecting the story, she might have hurt his feelings—learning she had the power to wound her parents a long, slow lesson for her.

Just before nine o'clock, her father always found a stopping place and closed the book, and the two of them went upstairs and turned on the television. Together, they watched a show her mother would never have watched, where things blew up and people jumped out of planes and punched one another. It was terrible, a fact both Flora and her father freely acknowledged, but they loved it. The show was funny, both intentionally and unintentionally, and they shouted at the television as they watched.

"Not everyone can appreciate the subtle genius of this show," he told her. "But you and I, we've grasped the secret of its stealthy power, haven't we?"

And Flora loved the exclusivity of it all—of the show and Ponzu, that they were hers and her father's and only sometimes Georgia's. There was no need to share with others. Tuesdays were theirs, and no one else's.

Before bed, Flora's mother called to check in. Her voice from the city sounded different, lighter. It was her old voice, temporarily restored, though often she sounded tired from her drive, or all the analyzing, and Flora, wide-awake, tried to make her voice sound tired, too. But Flora wasn't much for talking on the phone, and after a few minutes she would pass it off to her father and brush her teeth and get ready for bed while her parents talked. When her father hung up, she could see the pull of work and other matters on his face—he, who had been hers all night, no longer hers. He tucked her in quickly, rushing a little, pulling the blankets up around her ears and telling her she was "the best of all possible Flos," and then he turned out the light and went next door, into his study, and she listened for the sounds of his worries—papers whispering against one another, books slipping away from the shelf, the sigh of leather as he adjusted himself in his chair.

It was then, staring at the light from his study as it sneaked beneath her door, that Flora began to miss her mother, her stomach suddenly a little queasy. She lay on her side, and the sound of her own heartbeat in her ear worried her, and she played the game she played when she couldn't sleep, trying to scare herself to sleep. There was a witch walking up the long, formal staircase, moving slowly, step by step, each heartbeat another step. Now she was at the last step Flora and Georgia could jump off of; now she was on the landing; now she was admiring the chandelier. Flora had to be asleep by the time the witch got to the doorway of her room, or else. On other nights, her parents inhabited their separate spheres throughout the house, but they were both there. Flora could find them if she needed to; she knew where they were, the world less precarious, quieter.

Still other nights, they both were gone. Her father traveled for work—he was out wooing fat cats, a funny image—and would bring her T-shirts from the cities he visited: CLEVELAND—YOU'VE GOTTA BE TOUGH; ITHACA IS GORGES. Flora treasured them, as if they were thoughtful gifts. Sometimes her mother went along. Once, they were invited to the president's house in Washington, D.C. They both had voted against the president, but it was only Joan who wondered if she could bear to sit in the same room with him. She bought a floor-length shimmering blue dress that made her blue-gray eyes shine like icy water. She had never looked more beautiful, though she complained it had been a mistake, it wasn't her, she felt like an imposter.

"Maybe it's okay if it's not you," Flora said. "That way you can pretend you're someone else when you have to meet the president. Someone who likes him more."

"I'm getting tired of being someone else," her mother said.

Mrs. J. came and stayed with Flora and made her beef stew and they played gin rummy on the red Formica of the kitchen counter and drank soda, and Flora didn't miss her parents at all. Mrs. J. told her stories. The previous president of Darwin had killed himself. Not in the house, but after. He'd been a good man, Mrs. J. said, but he'd had a hard time of it.

"Some people are too good for this world," she said—a chastening dictum that seemed to rewrite the universe, and Flora's place in it.

Her parents had probably not told Flora this on purpose. It would be a story she would cling to, or one that clung to her. A story she knew without them knowing, that she knew in spite of them. Some people were too good for this world, and some people weren't.

A few weeks after the trip, a photograph arrived in the mail. It was of Joan Dempsey shaking hands with the president in the receiving line, signed to her across the bottom, "With kind regards," from him.

"What am I supposed to do with this? Frame it and hang it on my wall?"

"I'll keep it," Flora said.

But instead, her mother signed it, too, across the top, "With kind regards, Joan Dempsey," and she mailed it right back to the White House.

It was embarrassing, like when her mother made a scene in a restaurant about the food not being warm or the plates arriving at different times. But it was also exciting. It was exciting when people misbehaved. Flora's father, though, wasn't excited.

"What an infantile thing to do," he accused. "Was it really necessary?"

"When did you become such a coward?" her mother said, her voice as icy as her eyes.

5

Rearrangements

THE LIVING ROOM FURNITURE in her father's house was all wrong. When you entered the room, you were met with the back of the couch, rudely blocking your path. The best spot for reading—the faded gold armchair with its supplicant ottoman—was lampless. And the round wooden coffee table was simply too big for the space, an oversize hamburger bun in the center of the room. Flora pushed the couch out of the way and dragged the bun out of the room and into the kitchen. It was heavy, like dragging a fat corpse by the arms. She tried not to scuff the floors as she dragged, the attempt more theoretical than practical—moving furniture alone, there was no way not to scuff.

Now, if she moved the couch ninety degrees to the right, it would block the windows and the old door to the street. Ninety degrees to the left and it would block the fireplace. The only choice was to move the couch to its exact opposite position in the room, so it could look at where it once stood and face the world that had existed only behind it. Was it loneliness that created this compulsion to animate? Post-divorce, her mother had taken to furniture rearrangement as if it were a useful hobby, as she'd picked up other hobbies over the years, like hair dying, or clipping newspaper articles. On many days, returning from school to the small house they shared, Flora found that the living room and the dining room had switched places. A week later, they might have switched again. After months of this, she'd pretended not to notice; though carrying her dinner plate out from the kitchen, she would often find herself in the wrong room.

But she'd inherited the trait, the furniture-rearranging gene passed down from mother to daughter, along with the crooked row of bottom teeth, the circumflex eyebrows, the narrow feet. Flora loved rearranging her tiny one-bedroom apartment in the city, and in hotel rooms, or the homes of friends, or her boss's office, she had to stop herself from moving things around. She could enter a room and see why it was wrong, and how to make it right, and this was one of the reasons she'd been good at her job. If only, she'd said in response to compliments, such problem-solving skills extended to other parts of life. But it had gotten her into trouble, too. Some people didn't warm to the implication that what they had could be improved upon.

Back in that previous life that now seemed another person's, weeks ago when she had a life that more nearly resembled the lives of her friends, Flora worked at a magazine for the domestically obsessive and organically minded, editing stories on other people's houses. She wrote copy on subjects such as organizing your pantry, the best nontoxic paints, and biodynamic gardening. She'd liked gardening best: Having never actually done it herself, she found it closest to fiction. She liked dreaming up the exact adjective a green thumb might use for soil or trowels (*lush, loamy; ergonomic, essential*). Orchids—the gardener of her mind was rugged and practical, moved by beautiful things but alarmed by fussiness—where would he stand on orchids? Where would he stand on Flora? He'd approve of the rearranging—it was, after all, a version of thrift, a chance to make changes without paying for them.

As soon as the couch reversed its position in the room, the gold chair could take its place. The gold chair: where her father had read in the evenings, and on weekends, the upholstery worn thin by the sedentary pleasures he took in life. She moved the chair so it was closest to the fireplace. She would make a fire, and sit in the chair, and finally read her father's manuscript. The wood was out behind the garage. She made four trips—who knew how long this reading would take. She loved tending fires, prodding them into fuller life, but she'd never been good at starting them. Her father's trick had been to incinerate an entire newspaper and begin with a great blaze that wore itself away in moments. He'd had wasteful habits, and this had seemed to her one of them. She used three sheets of newspaper, balled tightly, and built a pyramid of small logs and kindling around them. To her surprise, it caught on the first match. Smoke seeped into the house. It took her a moment to realize this was wrong and why. In the President's House, the flue was perpetually open, her father having forgotten to close it, and bats had used it as a private entrance. She could see her parents standing in the industrial kitchen in their bathrobes, clutching badminton rackets, swatting at one terrified creature turned demonic, furry shuttlecock. It was tiny at rest, and large and looming in flight. When Flora had started to cry, her mother promised they would not hurt the bat.

"If we happen to hurt the little fucker, so be it," her father had said. He was enjoying himself, into the sport of it. Afterward, once the winged rodent had been released unscathed, Flora had made him swear that he hadn't been serious, that he'd meant the animal no harm. He had been unable to say so without grinning.

The flames were just low enough that she could reach in and lift the flue out of the way, but the room was invaded. She opened the old door to let the air change places. She retrieved the manuscript from where it lay buried in the body bag. She made a pot of tea. The living room was then cold, the fire dismal. She closed the door and placed two small logs on, easing them into perfect position with the tongs, which left the smell of metal on her hands. She poured the tea. She collected the papers and her mug and sat down in the gold chair. With the new configuration, there was nowhere to put her tea except the floor, and Larks came and lapped out of the cup before she could push him away.

"Okay, Larks," Flora said. "You have that one." Her father had made the dog tea—sweet, milky tea, as he'd made it for Flora when she was small—every afternoon.

She went back into the kitchen and poured herself another cup. She sat cross-legged in the gold chair, the manuscript on her lap. "I'm not performing for anyone anymore, just writing for myself," her father had told her on his last visit. "Appallingly rough," he'd said, resting the palm of his hand gently on the folder of poems. "Some good bits though, I think."

The fire was suddenly impressive. She felt a childish pride looking at it. I did that, she thought, all by myself. But she could not make herself turn past the title page. Her father's handwriting, neat and illegible:

In Darwin's Gardens
POEMS

By Lewis Dempsey

The ink on the page was jet-black, the paper ivory and unlined. The stack of papers was the apotheosis of manuscript—so manuscriptlike, it looked a caricature, a prop designed by an expert. *Manu-script*. Funny the feminists hadn't had their way with that one yet. So intimate—the handwritten word. The letters breathed on the page; the manuscript seemed to her alive. She didn't like to be alone with it. It was as if writing were something one died of, like cancer or cholesterol. She imagined the words whispered in the pretend hush of gossip: "It wasn't until he died that they found out—he had *poems*."

The words might have been written in another language, the shape of the letters exotic, except for the word *POEMS*, which her father had written all in capitals. She imagined him making each stroke slowly, smiling slightly in satisfaction. How one knew and recognized handwriting, as one knew and recognized a voice in the distance, or on the other end of a phone. These details of personhood we learned and memorized, as if access to that information meant we knew and understood one another. We felt a sense of ownership knowing such things. But the voice died with the person, absent a recording—and she'd thrown away the answering machine. The handwriting survived, though, particularly if writing had been something one did. Journals and manuscripts, but in subtler manifestations, too—notes in margins, and "LD," his initials, written into each of his books, alongside the date at which it had been read, and often numerous dates, numerous rereadings: "April '64," "June '73," "December '89." His full initials were really LSD, which Flora in middle school had teased him about, serenading him with "Lucy in the Sky with Diamonds," though he had certainly never tried the drug or any drug stronger than aspirin. He'd been a bit of a square; intellectually daring, but in many ways a square.

He had wanted to be the poet, and not the poet's ideal reader, but had taken the safer route. And had been dissatisfied all those years on the wrong side of the words. Not surprising, that; she knew well his disappointments. She'd just never thought he'd do anything to quell them. He understood his poets—"the Hardy Boys," he called them, and Hardy most of all—knew them better, maybe, than they'd known themselves (or than he'd known himself), and though that hadn't been enough, the scantness was more acceptable than the thought of failure. The whole thing very *Chariots of Fire—I won't run if I can't win*, and all that. Until the end. Had he guessed it was the end? In his final months, he'd reversed and risked himself, trading interpretation for invention, and started writing, and, from the look of the stack of poems, written a lot. And then he had given them to her, and left her alone with them, leaving her in the very position he had resented in his own life, the academic position, and now she had to be his perfect reader, the perfect understander, living not in her own imagination, but in his.

No one knew the poems existed. Her father had given them only to her. They could easily disappear. Manuscripts had disappeared before. Manuscript and fire—as linked in the literary imagination as tuberculosis and undiscovered genius. Max Brod, Kafka's literary executor, had famously not burned his friend's papers, and all the literati considered him a hero for it. Having never read Kafka, Flora could imagine a world without him; her world *was* without him. She had read about the posthumous act of defiance at the Cross Library while doing her executioner research. Defiant, and dishonest, wasn't it? Brod had what she wanted: instructions in a will. And ignored them.

A violent act: throwing a book on a fire. Irreversible, like death. And a bit Victorian—manuscripts weren't burned anymore; they were lost in the wilds of hard drives, they crashed, or were mistakenly trashed. Something romantic and old-fashioned, then, in throwing papers on a fire. Also anti-intellectual, repressive, and selfish. What Republicans did, or geniuses overcome by madness. Her father had told her the story of Dante Gabriel Rossetti burying his manuscript with his muse, only to regret the move years later and have the body and papers disinterred. There were many acts more brutal than incineration.

What would it look like to incinerate a manuscript? How long to turn to ash and ember? Most of her father's work Flora regarded with equal parts tedium and fascination. But the poems were a special case. It was flattering to be the only one he had trusted with them, as though he had left her, in addition to the house and the money, a piece of his mind, his most private self. Still, she did not want to read them. Reader's block—a mutation of the old, familiar literary neurosis. She'd read poetry, but never seriously, and mostly at her father's suggestion. "Pay particular attention to the third stanza," he'd instruct. "That's where he begins to make the language work for him." "Don't bother with Stevens yet," he'd told her once when she picked a volume off his shelves in high school. "If you read him now, you won't love him. Don't deny yourself that falling in love." But had she ever fallen in love with a poet, or a poem? When she was little, she asked her father in tears, "What if I don't like poetry when I grow up?" fearing this would be the end for them. "Of course you'll like poetry," he told her, and she'd believed him. And she did like poetry. But she felt she didn't love poetry as she ought to. What if she couldn't love his poems?

Looking at the fire, and the possibilities it presented, she became aware of her pulse. The thrill of a bad idea. One's body telling one to act. Fight or flight. But how to know which action it was recommending? Childhood had been so ripe with opportunities for disobedience. What opportunities had the past seven years of her life—her trial adulthood—presented? A gradual diminution in photocopying responsibilities, an ever-fluctuating stream of anxi-

ety and anxiety medication, a haze of cigarette hangovers and hair-
cuts she couldn't afford, afternoons spent in Laundromats reading
Susan Sontag at the recommendation of some boy with only mini-
mal comprehension, sex without foreplay and urinary-tract infec-
tions, air-shaft apartments with bathroom doors painted over so
many times they wouldn't shut. Was this, the loss of her father, the
means of escape she'd been wishing for, a new opportunity to dis-
obey, her own act of defiance in the making? She'd packed her
party dress, for Christ's sake. Her twenties, now, had something of
a narrative arc: My father died, and everything changed.

She'd had violent fantasies before—tripping, shoving, plate
shattering—but they'd remained fantasies. Having no siblings,
Flora had never hit or been hit. She pulled back the screen. She
could throw one page, one poem, on the fire and see how it felt.
Once she'd pinched Georgia hard on the arm, and her fingertips
had left a dark purple welt that so appalled her, she didn't speak to
Georgia for a full day, as if she had been the one responsible. Just
the title page, perhaps. Nothing of substance would be lost.

"Some good bits, though," her father had said, handing her his
poems over breakfast, asking for her opinion. The last time she saw
him. "But be kind to your old dad. Don't give me the full editorial
treatment. Big picture. Favorite and least favorite lines. Triumphs
and disasters. That sort of thing. But I hope you like them, Flora-
Girl, I really do."

She threw her tea on the fire. It released an unsatisfying hiss,
then a sputter, then nothing. There would be no incinerating, no
disinterring. She was not a deranged genius; she was no book
burner; there were limits, even, to her selfishness. She turned the
page and faced the first poem.

———

It was a Tuesday evening, after dinner at Ponzu, that her father told
Flora without her mother, breaking with the standard practice, the
recommended protocol of both parents presenting a united front,
a last hurrah of togetherness, an encore. He said afterward, when it

had become another thing for them to fight over, that he'd felt he had to; something Flora said had made him think she knew. Flora didn't know what that was, what it could have been. She knew nothing. How could she have known? Her father took the tea and English muffin up to her mother in bed every morning—he always did this, up until the very end. Then he and Flora ate their breakfasts together in the big kitchen, on the tall white stools, resting their elbows on the red Formica countertop, and then he'd make her lunch and take her to school. Every day, like that, just the same.

When he told her, he said, "Your mother and I have reached an end," as though there were many possible ends and they had arrived at one by chance, as though it were a board game, or a choose-your-own-adventure story, and she said, "I don't know what you mean," though she was crying. She was sitting on the ground on the rough gray industrial carpet on the third floor, once the maids' quarters, now the family area, and she was crying and sweating a little, and she said, "I don't know what you mean," and he said, "We're filing for divorce." And she cried, sitting on the floor, with her father in a chair above her, and she didn't want him to come near her, to comfort her, and he didn't try to, as if he knew, or didn't care. She wanted to run away and throw herself down the stairs, down all the stairs in one great leap, to smash her body into the floor below.

Once she knew what they had known for a few months, there was no need for pretense, no need for civility. She wanted to not know, to unknow. Before, they had spoken in French so she wouldn't understand, laughing exotic secrets to each other. Now they fought in French when they remembered or cared that she could hear them. Her mother cried and ate Reese's peanut butter cups. "Your father is such a prick," she told Flora as she braided her hair tightly for school. Her father moved into the guest room and had a private phone line installed. "Your mother is a sick woman," he said, buttering Flora's English muffin.

The house, in its institutional grandeur, was impervious to them, untroubled by their misery. It easily accommodated her father's move, and the new private phone line. He disappeared into the gold room. Flora rarely saw him, except at breakfast, which was weirdly normal, their routines impervious to them as well. When she saw him in the evenings, he was on his phone, already tethered to another person, another life. He hired Jimmy Mills, a local sleazebag, as his divorce lawyer. "Dark Satanic Mills," her mother called him. Flora didn't get the joke. The only one who got the joke was her father, and he pretended it wasn't funny. They'd reached a stalemate in the financial agreement. They would all live together—the three of them in the President's House, all in separate bedrooms, as if it were a dormitory—until the divorce was final, the contract signed.

"It's my only leverage," her mother said. "He wants us out of here so badly."

"Mom says you're trying to evict us," Flora told him one morning as he drove her to school.

"No, sweetheart," her father assured her. "Not you, never you."

But they all knew, without discussing it, that she would live with her mother, that when she went, Flora would go, too.

6

Revolts

DAWN, AND A DAMP SPOT nestled beside Flora in the twin bed, spooning her. Above the canopy frame a brown ring, the paint bubbling sinisterly. The house was in revolt against her: She hadn't read the poems.

"Fuck," she said, realizing what had happened. "Fuck this stupid fucking house."

The roof had given way, with God-like precision, to the arkworthy rains overnight. Cynthia had warned of—or perhaps willed into being—such an event. Who did one call when it started raining indoors? There was no super, or father to call; Flora was in charge. She needed to know about things like poetry and leaking roofs. But she couldn't face the morning, or the mess. She found a plastic basin under the sink in the bathroom and placed it on the sheet below the leak, then slinked down the hall to her father's room. The thought of someone seeing, or explaining the move to her mother, embarrassed her. It looked bad. Damn Freud! Couldn't a grown woman sleep in her father's bed in peace?

Larks watched, the black caterpillars of fur above his eyes lifting, ears poised.

"Lie down, Larks," she said, and he settled into his spot at the foot of the bed with a sigh.

Larks was still in mourning, or, more accurately, in patient wait. Maybe that was what mourning was—waiting. Larks was a sweet, affectionate dog who liked everyone well enough, but he'd regarded Flora's father with an undignified level of devotion, and his days were now devoted to the kitchen window, where he could gaze at the slate steps for hours. His anticipation constant, his optimism irritating.

"He's not coming back, Larks," she'd told him in a hard voice, and then felt hard. She'd scratched around his soft ears. "You know he never would have left you by choice. His plan was to outlive you," she'd said, the way her father had spoken to the dog—in complete sentences, as though talking to a person.

Being in a proper bed, a bed big enough for two, was a thrill. She could sprawl; she could stretch; she could span. At a certain age, twin beds became ridiculous, demeaning even, sad, and she had reached that age. His mattress was extremely comfortable, the sheets silken and expensive to the touch. New? Flora liked interiors. Hence the job. Hence the rearranging. She liked making a space her own. She liked being in a space she had made. But did she like her father's interior? The whole house was very comfortable, if imperfectly arranged, well stuffed and clean. Her father liked good wood—cherry above all—and simple Shaker lines. He liked paintings of barns or broken wooden fences, leather boxes with motley mementos stuffed inside—a postcard she'd sent from Mexico, an arrowhead, a hand-carved spoon, a photograph of Larks as a puppy. It was all tasteful, easy, with ample storage space. A strange setting for a lone twenty-something girl. What would become of her living in the midst of this throw-pillowed, subzeroed existence? Would she skip her thirties and suddenly emerge middle-aged?

This room was much nicer than hers, with an extra window, better light. There was even a working fireplace and a larger closet. There was no need to preserve the room as some kind of shrine, was there, or to leave it lying fallow? The door to the closet hung open, offering a glimpse inside, as though her father's shirts and pants, his shoes and his ties were stunned by, and monitoring closely, this new move. He was a man who even in his presidential years owned only two suits, which he referred to as "the suit" and "the other suit." But for someone who cared so little about clothes, he'd worn them well, relaxed and elegant, if a little rumpled. Like a colonial Raj—at home in the world, his world, confident and at ease.

He was never going to wear any of those shirts again. He would not come home, annoyed to find himself displaced, a refugee in his own home. He would not take back his house, his manuscript. He could not revoke her literary executorship, her control of the estate. He would never know her secrets from him, or what she had learned of his from her. Such revelations kept striking, mallet-like—he will not be there to throw tennis balls for Larks tomorrow; if I answer the telephone, he will not be on the other end—each a fresh, wounding surprise. The permanence of death a continual surprise. Like Larks, she waited. She listened for his footsteps on the slate.

The yawning maw of the closet accused her. She got up and closed the door. If she slept in her father's room, she would do so clothed. There was no need to be naked in there. The whole house was hers. She'd use her old bedroom as a dressing room, keep her things in there for now. But God, if she stayed in his house, would she never have sex again?

She sank into sleep but was awakened by the phone—who on earth? It was still "sparrow fart," as her father called the early morning. She didn't answer. It would not be him on the other end. She was not a call screener, as that implied there were people whose calls she would receive. She just didn't answer. She listened to the rain, an aural cliché of relaxation and coziness, but in this case a reminder of the hole in the roof, the burgeoning decay above. Again, the phone. Either an emergency or an asshole. She answered.

It was Cynthia Reynolds, her father's friend.

"Yes, Cynthia, of course I remember," Flora said, sitting up. As if she would have forgotten. In her father's bed, her father's lover in her ear, she felt newly self-conscious, as though Cynthia could see her there; as if Cynthia had a greater claim to that bed than she did and knew it.

"Am I calling too early?" Cynthia said. "I see it's just gone eight o'clock. I never know when it becomes acceptable to phone. You see, I'm a terrifically early riser—like your father. I guess I'm used to dialing his number at odd hours."

"No, it's fine. I'm up."

"I called a few minutes ago, but there was no machine, so I was worried I'd dialed wrong. But now it occurs to me you told me the machine had broken. . . . How are you?"

Flora debated mentioning the leak. Cynthia might know a roofer, know a number to call. "I'm fine," she said instead. This had been her default reply to such inquiries since childhood, regardless of circumstance, misery and joy reduced to the same monosyllable. Though in Flora's case, she stretched the word out over two syllables, raising her pitch slightly at the end: *Fi-ine.* "How are you?"

"I'm sure you have plans for Thanksgiving," Cynthia said. "But I'm having a few people over and we're going to eat late. I was hoping you might be able to stop by for dessert and coffee in the evening."

"Sure." The curt word out before Flora thought to say no.

Thanksgiving: the great feast of familial gratitude; the onslaught of the season of good cheer. It was a week—or was it days?—away. Flora already had two Thanksgivings planned. The first a brief visit with Georgia's parents—Madeleine had called to invite her after their reunion at the library, perhaps out of pity, because that was what one did when someone's father died. The second was dinner with her mother, who was coming to Darwin to check on her, a preemptive intervention, though she would stay not with Flora, but with friends in town. "It would be too weird to sleep in that house, your father's house," she'd insisted.

"Oh, that's wonderful." Cynthia spoke too enthusiastically, with exaggerated warmth. "About nine, then?"

"Yes." Flora wrote down the address, which was nearby, as everything was in Darwin—inescapably convenient.

"Oh, I'm so pleased you can make it."

"Can I bring anything?"

"Oh, no, just yourself."

Did the woman start every sentence with the word *Oh*? And what other, truer words did it leave unsaid?

"Thanks for the invitation," Flora said. "See you then."

And Cynthia hung up without saying good-bye.

Mrs. J. had described her as "after something." Was she now *after Flora*? Was she wooing the daughter, as she'd wooed the father? Or was Mrs. J. right that it was the house she wanted? Flora's father's bedroom had been sprinkled with some unmistakably feminine touches—a gratuitous glass bottle on the dresser, what looked like a vintage silk scarf, red and floral, laid like a runner across the mantel. Cynthia had certainly spent more time there than Flora over the last year. It had probably come to feel like her house as she gradually, month by month, began to make herself more at home in it, as one does at a boyfriend's place, slowly colonizing the maleness—a new bath mat here, a ceramic coaster there—seeping in, claiming, detail by detail.

"But, technically, it's my house now, not his," Flora had reasoned against her mother's objection to sleeping over. "What if I decide to live here for the rest of my life? Will you never come visit me?"

"God, Flo," her mother had said. "You're not seriously considering that, are you?"

Her mother had fled from Darwin as soon as Flora graduated from high school, and talked about the town as if it were below Chernobyl on the list of places one might want to live. She had no use at all for nature—city parks presented too much greenery for her taste—and so Darwin's bucolic charms, such as they were, were another strike against, rather than for. She still talked about the move to Darwin as though Flora's father had brought her to the most backward of backwaters against her will.

Back in Darwin, Flora felt a sharp longing, like the quick thrill of a bitten tongue, to go back in time, to protect her younger self from what was to come. But then, she was going back, wasn't she? The word *move* suggested action, suggested progress. But the move to Darwin, if that's what it was, the move into her father's house, and now his bedroom. What was she doing? She heard her mother's voice, her disapproval: *Flora, what exactly is going on with you?*

———

Divorce—it was a glamorous word, a fancy word. Flora liked to say it like two separate words, stretching out the syllables: *Deee-voarse.*

"When you get a deee-voarse," she explained to Georgia, "you stop loving one another."

"Isn't it the other way around?" Georgia—a stickler—asked.

"You can't understand because it hasn't happened to you," Flora said.

Her friend's face fell. Georgia made a point of understanding everything. Flora had wounded her, but Georgia pretended otherwise, picking her face back up, and Flora pretended she hadn't noticed. Flora was getting good at pretending not to notice.

She started subscribing to bridal magazines. She was doing research. She stole her mother's checkbook and Georgia forged her signature. Georgia had grown-up handwriting. When Flora's mother found the magazines in her room, she accused Flora of shoplifting.

"I'm no thief," Flora said, though it occurred to her that what she had done might not be better than stealing. That, in fact, it was stealing, just a different sort. She waited for her punishment.

"Do they make you feel better—the magazines?" her mother asked.

"No," she admitted. "They're really boring." It was true—big white cakes, and dresses that looked like the cakes, checklists, and *I Do*s and *I Don't*s, cold feet and karats and cuts, and Flora began to wonder, was there a divorce magazine? Maybe that would be more useful.

Her mother told her the story of their wedding, her parents' wedding, a story she'd heard before, an unromantic story, a City Hall wedding on the vernal equinox, the start of all that should be spring, with four guests, half of whom were required by law as witnesses, and the bride, who never wore suits, in a suit—a brown woolen suit.

"I didn't feel like myself," her mother said.

"You're making me feel worse," Flora said. She grabbed her mother's hand. "We can move back," she said. "To the city. Pretend this never happened. Forget Darwin."

"You like Darwin, don't you, baby?" her mother asked.

"I can like other places just as much. Maybe more."

"What's happening to your father and me, it's not Darwin's fault."

"We were happy before. Things were fine. Remember?" Why couldn't she see it? Why wouldn't she fix it?

Flora sought refuge at Georgia's house, sleepover upon sleepover, leaving the FLORA and GEORGIA bunk beds behind, even sometimes on school nights, something not permitted before, but now encouraged—with divorce, it seemed, came leniency. But it bothered her: What made it work for Madeleine and Ray, Georgia's parents, and not for hers? Was it the hyphenated last name? Or all the first names? Was that a possible clue? Should she start calling her parents Lewis and Joan? There was more research to be done. She enlisted Georgia as her assistant.

They started slowly, hesitantly. Ears pressed tentatively to doors, hands shyly navigating the corners of a desk drawer. Ray and Madeleine were the control group, Flora's parents the focus of the study. There were infinite variables. Everything from college major to hair color had to be factored in. They organized systems; they prepared—scientific discovery could lead to terrifying results.

They bought supplies in town at Gus Simonds's shop: five spiral-ringed, college-ruled notebooks, two pads of graph paper (Georgia, convinced their study could one day be valuable, insisted upon charts and graphs, telling Flora with passion, "Cold, hard fact comes alive in its visual representation"), thumbtacks, four highlighters (pink, green, yellow, blue), a package of ballpoint pens, ten number-two pencils with superior erasers, and a battery-operated pencil sharpener. Georgia's purple bedroom became their lab. With its considerable caged rodent population and all the encyclopedias, it felt like a lab. They pinned paper upon paper containing list upon list all over the yellow walls of her closet, for the sake of discretion. Each list had a heading, such as "Things They Fight About," with a line down the middle of the page separating the data into two columns. Ray and Madeleine fought about compost and recycling (one category), politics, money, and the car (she hated it; he loved it). Flora's parents fought about money, his interrupting her, his plagiarizing her good lines, her unhappiness, her coldness. It didn't take a genius to interpret the findings: Georgia's parents wanted to change things about each other; Flora's parents wanted each other to be different people. And everyone fought about money.

"The more we learn, the more hopeless I feel," she told Georgia.

"That's the way it is," Georgia said. "Understanding doesn't bring happiness. Ask anyone at Darwin."

"What does it bring?"

Georgia thought for a moment. "Understanding," she said.

Georgia's intellectual interest in the project soon waned. She didn't like spying on her parents. She said she never found anything, but Flora could tell she wasn't trying. Georgia would say encouragingly, "They had another fight this morning—over the compost," but her words were hollow with eagerness. Flora made her go along, go further than she wanted. As in their games, hurling their small bodies from one height or another—stairs, tree branches, bedroom doors—as in running away from school, Flora pushed.

"If you don't want to help me, that's fine. I'll do it myself," Flora told her. But of course Georgia wanted to help. Georgia wouldn't let her do it alone.

Once Flora started spying, she couldn't stop. She stuck her hands into her mother's shoes, wore her long dresses over her own clothing, and she was not careful to put them back as she'd found them. She opened her mother's lipsticks just to smell them, to breathe in the strange chemical sweetness, the chalky smell of color. Looking through her mother's things, Flora became her. They were united in her father's rejection. She combed through her dresser in the afternoons—always the top drawer, the top drawer was the one with secrets. Pushing the panty hose, the underwear and the bras, the socks with holes and the socks without mates off to the side, Flora examined the delicate silk satchels that held her mother's favorite jewelry—the cameo pin, the silver cuff bracelet, the jade ring—none of it from her father. She touched each thing as though it were a museum piece, and touching was illicit and punishable. It all held a mysterious power over her, like the items in her mother's purse, which would be tossed into the backseat on long car trips to silence her when her boredom reached desperation.

Searching in the drawer, in a little box, she found something round and rubber, which she knew to be sexual in some way, but not quite how, and she wondered if it was a good sign that her mother still had it, whatever it was. Maybe things weren't as final as they seemed. But she also found the white ghosts of pills in translucent bottles—"May cause drowsiness," the label said. "Do not operate heavy machinery"—with the name of her mother's analyst stamped across the top. Why was the analyst drugging her mother? Flora waited to be accused, waited for her mother to say, "I know what you're doing," but she never said anything.

In her father's room, Flora was more tentative. She didn't open drawers. She didn't touch anything. She stood, she hovered, a forensic detective taking pains not to disturb a crime scene. She saw a phone number on a piece of paper on the table by the new phone with its new private line, and when she found it, she knew there was no need to look any further. She didn't take the piece of paper, but carefully copied the seven digits into one of the spiral notebooks. She didn't show it to Georgia.

When she dialed the number a few days later, her fingers shaking as they turned the rotary dial, a woman answered, and Flora said, "Who is this?"

And the woman said, "Who is this?"

And then Flora hung up.

7

Other People Are a Wall

FLORA DECIDED SHE WOULD DRESS UP to meet Paul Davies. So few opportunities to remove one's sneakers presented themselves in Darwin; one had to act.

He had called a few days after their bizarre midnight encounter to apologize. "I shouldn't have insisted we have that conversation in the middle of the night," he said. "I'm trying to cut back on the coffee—it turns me into a bulldozer. I'm sorry about that."

"Really?" Flora hated apologizing, had always hated it, but she liked being apologized to. Better to blame and forgive than to be blamed and repent. *Whose fault is it?* A question she often asked her parents, a refrain of childhood, but just as often they lacked a satisfactory answer—no one was officially to blame. "I'd been meaning to call back," she lied. "I was on a cordless and the battery died and—"

"Why don't you come in to the office and we can run through it all. You can ask the questions you didn't get to ask."

"I'm pretty sure you covered it."

"I scared you off," he said.

"No, you answered all my questions."

"I can be an insensitive lawyerly prick sometimes. I really am sorry we got off on the wrong foot."

It was a neat equation: The more the lawyer apologized, the more attractive he became.

"Your father was such a great guy. I'd hate for you to have this idea of me."

"I don't, truly. Absolutely no ideas."

"Come by the office, I can show you some documents I have in your father's file, and then I'll buy you a drink to make it up to you."

A drink? With her father's lawyer? She had furniture to re-arrange, fires to stoke, a house to colonize. Poems to not read. "It's sweet of you to offer, but it's not necessary. This is a no-fault state, isn't it?"

"Even in a no-fault state, somebody has to pay. C'mon. Let me do this."

Had her father shown him a picture of her? But no, this was about him—her father—not her. Not a date, but a duty. As with Mrs. J. and Gus, Flora was the beneficiary of generosity owed her father. She'd inherited, along with the house and the money and the words, the goodwill of these people. "I owe him," Gus had said. Still, the word *documents* was alluring. What documents might be lingering in her father's file? *Posthumous Me: The Complete User's Manual? A Letter to My Dearest Flora-Girl?*

She longed to wear the inappropriate-for-every-occasion dress, which had been wasting in the body bag, but she couldn't. It was too much, or, more precisely, too little. She put on her green A-line skirt with the soft pink cardigan, the effect tulipesque, and out of step with the seasons, but not so much as to appear crazy. Or so she hoped.

Once, at the magazine, Flora had been asked to do a TV spot for a morning show on spring bulbs. At the studio, the producers had fitted her with a little earpiece, and as she spoke to the host about when exactly to plant different bulbs in the various hardiness zones and the most desirable soil conditions for doing so, a voice inside her head barked instructions: "Don't pick up the narcissus!" it commanded. "Look at camera two! No, the other one!" and "Wrap it up! Ten seconds!" She'd felt deranged and scared and as though her words came to her five seconds slower than normal. But later, when she watched the tape, she was amazed to see how com-posed she looked, how fluidly her words seemed to come, how she appeared to be speaking into the right camera the whole time. She hoped the same was true now—that what was going on inside her mind remained invisible to other people. That things looked better from the outside.

To counter the pastel daintiness of her clothing—and to indulge herself—she strapped on the four-inch stilettos. In difficult social situations, it was good to be distracted by your footwear. Instead of thinking about what she and the lawyer might talk about, she could focus on the encroaching numbness in her left pinkie toe. Her plan was to walk into town, despite the discomfort. Flora had lived long enough in the city to regard driving the way other people did air travel—dangerous and best reserved for longer trips. But out on the sidewalk, so tall and fancy in her finery, she felt like a gangly flamingo, the subject of a nature documentary. *Look at the strange behavior of the displaced city girl!* Her legs were cold and skinny and vulnerable. And as she slowly made her way, a station wagon pulled alongside her.

"Flora Dempsey! Do you need a lift?" It was Janet Rosen, the director of admissions. She'd thought it was her, heard she was back in town.

Flora leaned down and called into the open passenger window, "I'm fine, thanks. Not going far. Nice to see you."

Was she going to a party? No, no, just felt like dressing up a little. Anyway, it was great to see her out, and doing so well.

Was that what heels in Darwin meant? Doing well?

Paul's office was on the third floor of a three-story building in town, directly above the office of the shrink her parents had sent her to when they were splitting up, Dr. Berry. Flora hoped she wouldn't run into her, but one ran into everyone in Darwin eventually, and Flora, as they all insisted on telling her, looked just as she had as a young girl and was instantly recognizable—long, straight dirty-blond hair (though no longer worn in two braids, Laura Ingalls–style), long-toothed, long-bodied, skinny, and wolfish, with narrow features and light eyes. "Modiglianiesque," Cynthia had said. Like her father.

Her outfit, at the lawyer's half-open door, was ridiculous. She was desperate; she was a fool. She felt like a hick, a rube. The only

thing missing was the French twist and the hair spray. She was trying too hard. She was deranged. But it was too late to turn around
and run away, as she'd had to buzz from downstairs to get in. He
knew she was there. There was nothing to do but push the door
open and reveal her ridiculousness.

The office was empty and impersonal and ugly, with big naked
windows too low on the walls, looking out onto the common, a
view she remembered from her sessions with Dr. Berry. What furniture there was was bloated, and clearly secondhand: a swollen desk,
a bruised metal filing cabinet, three unmatched leather chairs. On
the desk, the incongruity of a complicated violet orchid. Unimaginable that the lawyer had bought the flower for himself.

"Nice orchid," she said, not knowing what else to observe.

He looked up. "A thank-you gift," he said. "Though I think I'm
killing it."

When he stood to shake her hand, he proved himself not at all
the lawyer of her mind: no khakis, no loafers, no starchy monogrammed shirt. Instead, a soft gray flannel, worn corduroys, and
serious-looking hiking boots. Overplaying the whole country
lawyer thing perhaps, but this, she saw, was part of why her father
had chosen Paul. He would have liked the lack of overt lawyerliness;
the woodsy aesthetic would have appealed to him. Her immediate
impression was: too tall for Darwin. Most men in Darwin were
short and runty, their wives towering over them imperiously. Her
mother had noticed it first. And almost everyone in town had
asthma. Something in the water, maybe—something growth stunt-
ing and lung shrinking. Though her father had been tall. She liked
the lawyer's nose. A good, prominent nose, bony and a little
crooked. The nose saved him from the rest of his features, which
were attempting to make him adorable. Thanks to the nose, he
looked smart. Why was it that beaky noses made people look
smarter? Was it one of those myths, like the big hand/big penis
myth—if that was even a myth? As her mind raced and landed on
the word *penis,* Flora felt like a bystander—a guilty bystander—
observing the erratic behavior of another person. What did people

do in public under normal circumstances? How was it, again, one communicated with another human being?

"What's a guy like you doing in a town like Darwin?" she said by way of introduction. No, that wasn't right. It sounded like a line in a Humphrey Bogart movie, a line involving a cigarette and a match, something that no one would utter in real life, and certainly not post-1955. But then Paul's nut brown eyes lit up when she said it. A *Bambi boy*—Flora's mother's term: "You always like those smudgy-eyed Bambi boys."

"It's not so bad here, is it?" Paul asked, smiling. He had one dimple, but again, the cuteness was redeemed by the odd placement, high on his left cheek.

"Pretty bad," she said. "I almost had to wear my Orphan Annie wig coming here—I was afraid of running into my old shrink." Jesus, really? Mentioning the shrink in the first minute of conversation? She mistrusted strangers who spoke intimately of their therapists or their treatments, who disclosed too much too soon. Cynthia's words—"We were very much in love"—flashed across her brain. Had the days alone in her father's house made her into one of those people? Being alone, it was difficult to judge your own mood. Other people were a wall you could bounce yourself off of and see how you came back.

But Paul seemed unfazed. "Dr. Berry?" he said. "She's hilarious. I love that woman."

"Hilarious. That's not exactly how I remember her."

"It probably depends on the context." He gestured to one of the dwarfing chairs, and Flora sat. "Anyway, it's really nice to meet you. I was a huge fan of your dad. He was such a great guy."

"Really? What makes you say that?"

He looked at her as though he hadn't heard.

"What in particular? Because, don't people always say that? When someone dies? Without meaning anything?" The editing function in her brain had short-circuited. "I mean, yes, he was great. I think so. But why do you?"

"Let's see." Paul tapped his fingertips together, reasoning with a temperamental child. "He was a natural storyteller, your dad. Everything with him was an opportunity for an anecdote. What an incredible memory. In class and in conversation, he was the best free-associator I've ever met, making these effortless connections to some yarn about Byron or Winston Churchill or being at Yale in the sixties."

Some yarn? Who said *yarn?* "Yes. What else?"

"We all loved him, all his students loved him because he was brilliant—he taught me to read poetry in a whole new way, he taught me to *love* poetry—and because he always let class out ten minutes early."

"That sounds right. What else?"

"He was an original. I used to see him walking with Larks around town all the time—no leash, of course—and once I heard him tell Gus Simonds that when they played catch, your dad could just say, 'That's quite enough of that,' and the dog would pick up the ball and head toward home."

"That's true," Flora said. "He used to say the dog had a vocabulary of over one hundred words." She looked out the window. It was nearly dark. It was chronic sundown in November in Darwin. Her father had a good throwing arm; he could throw a tennis ball to Larks clear across the common. But there were no dogs playing catch with their owners tonight. Just one solitary student in a woolly hat, sitting in the cold near dark, a guitar on his lap. Darwin was a folk-song-singing kind of town. Flora had sung them all at her elementary school, and with Georgia, lying on the floor in the big house. "The Sloop John B." That was a sad one. "I feel so broke up, I want to go home." They were all sad, but that one was really sad.

"Is there anything I can do for you today, Flora?" Paul asked. He said her name gently, and she remembered how it had felt as a teenager when some boy she had a crush on would say her name for the first time—how intimate it felt, how strangely flattering.

"You mentioned some documents?"

He handed her a file and pointed to key clauses, but it was nothing of interest, no manual or idiot's guide to death. Tax returns, a

copy of the deed to the house. Grown-up papers. Boring and terrifying. Something about the chair in his name at the college; something about his pension; something about royalties from his first
book, on Victorian poetry, which was still used in courses. Small
print punctuated by the scrawl of her father's signature. It was
warm in the lawyer's office, ugly but comfortable, and she looked
through the papers slowly. He watched her patiently.

"I'm not sure what to make of any of this," she admitted.

"It's overwhelming," he said.

"Yes." She felt the sudden heat of tears.

"Nothing has to be decided today."

"I certainly hope not."

"Ready for that drink?"

Paul suggested they walk over to the Beagle Inn, the only hotel in
town. It presided over the north end of the common, across from
his office. Flora had been there for weddings, and, toward the end
of her parents' marriage, for depressing, silent family dinners, but
never for drinks, never as an adult. It had been named, of course,
for Darwin's boat. Such nomenclature was not unique to that
establishment. Businesses throughout the town had embraced the
Darwinian theme—Galapagos Islands (selling kitchen supplies),
Charles's (a bar frequented by underage college students), Evolu-
tions (a salon), Finch's Books, and, of course, the health-food store,
Natural Selections.

"This place never changes," she said.

Paul pointed out a few things that had changed. A wine bar, trying to look urban with menacing metallics. A new coffee shop,
which he swore sold delicious pastries baked with local wheat and
butter. A store devoted to recycled and reclaimed objects—picture
frames made from old mantels, bowls made from paper clips.

"Even the stores lecture you," Flora said.

Paul's dimple approved. "Your father's daughter, I see."

In the hotel bar, he ordered a beer, Flora bourbon on the rocks.
He looked tired. It had been a long week. She'd almost forgotten
that other people still had jobs, that they worked for a living; that
they lived for a living.

"So what kept you at your office till all hours this week?" she asked.

"The usual—real estate, divorce."

"What else is there?" she said. "In life, I mean."

"That covers it, I guess. A shocking number of divorces. I help some couple close on a house and a few years later I help sort out who keeps it. Even Darwin's not immune to national trends."

"I think Darwin likes to imagine it is immune to the rest of the country. I remember when I was in high school, the default banner above Pleasant Street read 'Spay or Neuter Your Pet.' As if that were the most pressing civic issue."

"That's still a favorite. That and 'Darwin: A Nuclear-Free Zone.'"

"Oh God," Flora groaned. "I'd forgotten."

"The problems of the elite. Imagine if that energy were turned out rather than in—toward the intractable joblessness twenty miles away, say."

"It would be a different history of the world if the elite looked out rather than in—hell, if the human race as a whole did."

"Dark," Paul said. "I like dark."

"Who wouldn't?" Flora said. "It's delightful."

She looked away from Paul and around the room. The decor of the Beagle was faux gentlemen's club: resiny wood, green leather, bookcases stuffed with hardbound books that might not open— the hollow shells of books. They could hear the clink and clatter of dishes and silver coming from the restaurant, but they were the only two people sitting at the bar.

"Do you know any roofers? Someone who works on roofs?" she asked. The dullest possible question, but also the most urgent, and all she could think to say.

"I know a contractor in town. He might know someone. You've got a leaky roof?"

"Right," she said. "It would be great if I could get his number from you."

"Sure, no problem."

"Great, thanks. I wasn't sure who to ask."

"No problem at all," he said again. "Just remind me later."

Flora wished she could crawl behind the bar and hide. She drank. Paul coughed.

Finally, he said, "What was it like growing up here, in Darwin?"

"You know, the usual—part wonderful, part terrible."

"Which part won out?"

"It depended on the year." She didn't want to talk about herself, didn't feel like talking. Why had she come? Who was this man? She heaved the talk away from herself: "What about you? Where did you grow up?"

"Not too far. Not far geographically. Culturally, a world away. In one of the old mill towns. Home of the intractable joblessness."

"How was that for you?"

"Lots of exploring in the old abandoned factories. Lots of tetanus shots. My sisters and I pretended we were archaeologists, exploring a lost civilization. We'd bring old toothbrushes to carefully dust our findings—the ancient relics of beer bottles and spools of thread."

"How many sisters?"

"Two—one older, one younger."

"Ah, the middle child."

"You say that so ominously. What about you—the only child?"

"Yes," she said. "It's just me."

Paul made conversation with the bartender, a gaunt-faced man with two rogue hairs fighting their way from the tip of his pointy nose. It was not Paul's first time at the Beagle Bar. They each ordered another drink.

"What have you been doing since you've been back?" Paul asked.

"Good question," Flora said. "These days, I feel like all I do is make coffee and clean out the coffeepot. I mean, that's life. That's it."

"Good coffee at least, I hope."

"Pretty mediocre, actually."

"When my mother died," Paul said, "everyone in my family gave something up." He traced a line along the foggy edge of his glass, not quite looking at her, maybe not even talking to her. It seemed the saddest thing she'd ever heard.

"What did you give up?"

"Academic aspirations. My friends and I, at Darwin—your father called us 'the Apostles,' after Lytton Strachey and the Cambridge Bloomsbury lot—we were all headed that way. Now they've settled into tenure-track positions, or jobs at publishing houses and literary magazines. None had debts to pay. Salary was seen as distinctly secondary to integrity—a distinction I couldn't afford. I had loans. And my dad had given up his sobriety. I couldn't leave my sisters to take care of him."

"How did it happen?"

It had been breast cancer. Caught too late. She never went to the doctor, never liked to make a fuss. He'd had a fellowship to Princeton. Instead, after he graduated from college, he lived at home for two years, tending bar at the local pub. Law school had seemed the easiest way out, and Darwin, ultimately, the compromise—close enough to be of use, but far enough that his father didn't call him at one in the morning for a ride home from the pub, or, at least, didn't call him first.

Listening, Flora felt sympathy mixed with the sinister tingle of excitement that comes from news of other people's hard luck. It was a relief to remember other people had sad stories, that other people's parents died. When you suffered some misfortune, other people wanted to tell you theirs; impossible, at the sight of a cast, not to show off one's own scars, or share stories of shattered limbs. What was that? Commiseration? Competitiveness? Or was it just that life offered too few opportunities for such complaints, so when one came along, like dressing up in Darwin, you had to seize it?

"What a cheerful evening," Paul observed. "I bet you're wishing you'd stayed at home with your coffeepot." Flora watched his face close like a curtain, diffidence where openness had been.

They moved toward easier topics—favorite spots in Darwin; the girls' high school basketball team, which the year before had won the state championships; his younger sister, who lived near Flora in the city. They ordered a third round. There was nothing to eat but the infinite bowl of pretzels the bartender kept replenishing. The saltiness was making her ill, but Flora kept eating them. Such abundance of the stuff you didn't want. Between the salt and the bourbon, she felt parched. Also drunk.

"Do you still think about it? The academic life?" she asked him.

"In another life, I'm a writer, and a scholar—like your dad."

"Dangerous work, that. You're better off with the real estate divorces."

"You think so?"

"Sometimes I feel I'm *in* my other life. I'm in the parallel universe and my real life is going on smoothly without me somewhere completely inaccessible."

"So what's it doing—your real life?"

"These friends I have from college, their parents exposed them to so many experiences growing up. You know, a sabbatical in Alexandria, or Beijing. A kibbutz here, a New Zealand sheep farm there. They've collected all these life experiences and now they're experience junkies—professional excursionists. That's what my real life is doing—it's out there collecting experiences, international ones. Harvesting grapes in Sicily as we speak."

Paul did not respond. She had stopped aiming for sense, or appropriate behavior. She was inappropriate for every occasion, like her shoes.

"Where do you stand on poetry?" she asked him.

"On the whole, I think I'm in favor of it."

"Yes, yes, of course. But do you read it?"

"In college I did. As I think I said earlier, your dad made me see poetry in a whole new way. Now I don't read as much as I should."

"But why 'should'? Why does one feel so obligated in the face of poetry?"

"I'm surprised to hear you, of all people, say that. With your dad's brilliant writing on the subject—his brilliant talking. You were lucky enough to grow up in that milieu, steeped in the literary culture. *Reader as Understander* changed my life. Temporarily at least, it really did."

"You know, he wrote his own poetry, too." It was the first time she'd said the words out loud, acknowledged the existence of the poems to anyone. She hadn't liked Paul's tone—"you, of all people"—patronizing, superior. What did he know of her luck? She'd wanted to awe him, to make clear where exactly each of them stood in regard to her father. It worked.

Paul sat back in his chair. "I didn't realize that," he said. "I thought it was just the criticism."

"No, no one does. Only me," she bragged. She couldn't help herself. "He gave me the manuscript—a full collection. Just months ago."

"That's amazing. How are they?"

"It's hard to say. Difficult to describe."

"Amazing." Paul shook his head. "I'd love to read them."

Her taunt had been an error. Interactions were pipped with errors; solitude and silence safer. "They're unfinished," she said. "Some of them. I don't think he was ready to share them with the *world*." She emphasized the word *world* to convey Paul's very slight part in the one that was her father's.

"I was confused when you called that night," he said, "why you were making such a big deal of the literary executorship. I assumed you were asking about already published work. Now I see. Do you know if he planned to publish them?"

"We hadn't discussed it. I was actually hoping there might be some revelatory document in his file."

"And you say no one else knows. Even Cynthia Reynolds?"

"You know Cynthia?" Paul had seemed so benign and handsome before; her attraction now trumped by an urge to accidentally spill the dregs of her drink in his lap.

"I know of her," he said. "I'd heard through the Darwin rumor mill that she'd shacked up with your dad."

"'Shacked up'?"

"Moved in with him."

The bar had decided to orbit. That was misinformation. Flora stood. "I think I need to eat something," she said.

"Are you all right?" He gestured to the bartender for the check.

"Fine."

"Let me drive you home, Flora," Paul said, handsome again. "I doubt if you're up for the walk back in those shoes."

She was so happy he'd noticed that she kissed him on the cheek, her frivolous self flooding gleefully to the surface. He paid the bill and drove her home in his flimsy, clean two-door, and they sat in the car, in the driveway, chatting for a minute. She remembered her parents doing this when she was little, when they came home from a party. She would look out the window of the big house and watch them, parked in the big circular driveway, talking, and wonder what it was they were talking about, and beg Mrs. J., who babysat for her, to let her go out and join them, and Mrs. J. would say, "Oh, Flora, do you have to be a part of every little thing?" And Flora would think, What a stupid question. And sometimes she would run past Mrs. J., run right outside in her pajamas and climb into the backseat and demand to know what they were talking about, what could possibly be keeping them from rushing in to see her. They would look at her, annoyed by the interruption, but fond and forgiving, and they would all get out of the car together and her father would pick her up because she was barefoot and carry her back into the house. How nice it would be to take off her shoes, which were hurting now, and to have Paul pick her up, to let him carry her inside. To let him take care of things a little—Cynthia, the roof, the poems. He seemed so capable. No taste, and possibly a jerk, but grown-up in a way she wasn't. "I like a man who knows how to tip the concierge," her mother said, and in all the ways Paul might not make sense, he and her father shared that competence. Was that male, that knowing how to function in the world? Or was she sexist? Or just terribly immature?

She kissed him again on the cheek. "I had a good time," she told him, unsure if it was a lie.

She didn't wait for him to reply, but opened the car door, stepped out, and walked herself up the short path to her father's house.

———

Flora's were not the only crimes. One night while the three of them still lived in the big house together but on the brink of apart, Flora's mother stole the license plates from her father's car, drove her own car twenty miles out of town, and threw his plates into the river. Her mother was handy with a screwdriver; she was good at repairs, and now they were all discovering she was equally adept at disrepair.

Flora knew this because her mother told her the next morning as she drove her to school in the car that she always drove, the one she would be driving to the city later that day, as she did every Tuesday.

"There's a problem with the other car, your father's car. You'll have to get a lift with Georgia tomorrow." Her mother's eyelashes had finally faded to a color that appeared in nature. From the neck up, she looked almost like a mom. But she was wide-awake and excited. She was usually groggy and in bed when Flora left for school with her dad.

"What happened?"

"Vandalism, it looks like."

"Scratches?"

"No, worse. The license plates have been stolen. You know, you can't drive without a license plate."

"Why would someone do that? Steal a license plate?"

"It's a major inconvenience. Makes life more difficult. Could be some kind of college prank."

"You think students did it?"

"Who knows. Your father has his share of enemies in town. I'm sure there are plenty of people who wouldn't mind inconveniencing him."

"But isn't it kind of an inconvenient thing to steal? It must be a lot of work."

"You're right." Joan looked happier than she had in weeks. "A lot of trouble to go to."

"Does this mean Dad and I can't go to Ponzu tonight?"

"Oh, Flo, I hadn't thought of that." No one spoke as the inadvertent confession filled the station wagon, crowding out the earnest voices of public radio. Her mother pulled to the side of the road and stopped the car.

"I don't want to upset you," she said. "I'm sorry if I have."

"You have." Though Flora didn't exactly feel upset. She felt nervous.

"I don't expect you to understand. It was just something I had to do."

"You had to steal Dad's license plates?"

"I'm sure that doesn't make sense to you. I don't want it to make sense to you. I'm fine. I don't want you to take care of me. I'm fine." Her mother began to cry. Flora watched her cry. "Your father holds all the cards—he has the money, the job, the house. I had to do something to make me feel less powerless. It was between the license plates and shredding all the clothes in his closet. I felt the license plates were subtler."

"Were you scared, doing it?"

"No. It was so dark, and so quiet. Darwin is quite beautiful at night, with no other people around."

Flora could see her mother dressed all in black, walking on the tips of her toes, like the woman in some old movie her parents had shown her, a cat burglar. She saw her standing on the bank of the river, skimming the metal rectangles into the water one after the other, as though skipping oversize stones.

"What if you had gotten caught?" Flora asked.

"There's no sense worrying about what might have happened. I didn't get caught. I'm here. I'm fine."

She didn't seem fine. "It would have been embarrassing. You could have been arrested or something." Darwin was a gossiping town; everyone knew what was happening to her family. Flora felt their knowing on her skin when they looked at her.

"Maybe Ponzu will deliver?" her mother suggested. "You could eat it at home."

"The whole point is that you go there and watch them cook right in front of you. That's the whole point of Ponzu."

"You could order Chinese. Or walk somewhere in town. Anyway, I'm sure everything will be resolved by next Tuesday. You'll be back at Ponzu in a week."

Her mother had chosen this night of all nights, her night with her father, to leave them stranded. She had done it not just to him but also to Flora. What if they needed to escape town in a hurry? They had never not gone to Ponzu on a Tuesday since they first discovered the place. Would the cooks think they had abandoned them? Would their free drinks sit sweating, waiting for them on the bar all night?

"I hate to ask you to keep secrets from your father."

"You know I won't tell him."

What had become of them in the months since the move? What had Darwin done to them? Flora now the spy, and her mother the thief. But what about her father? Was he, too, adopting a life of crime? Or did he not care enough about them to deceive them? Instead, he was plotting their removal, their eviction and elimination from the house and his life. He was retreating into the gold room with his separate line to the outside world, into the part of him that was Lewis Dempsey, and not Dad. She could see him moving further and further away, growing smaller and smaller, a flea dancing on the horizon. What would her mother do next? Whatever it was, she would end up in jail, and her father would not bail her out and they would never go to Ponzu again and Flora's life would be ruined and everyone would know.

"It's just a license plate, baby," her mother told her. "Right? Nobody got hurt."

8

The Good Parents

It wasn't Flora's first Thanksgiving without her father. Since her parents' divorce, she'd spent the holiday with her mother's family. Christmas she had alternated year to year, one his, the next hers, at first with a strict fairness, which slid into haphazardry. When was her last Christmas in Darwin? And yet of course it was the first Thanksgiving without him. Death, like birth, like love, opened up a world of firsts. The first Sunday, the first week, the first November, the first winter.

Flora had dreaded the day so thoroughly this year, she'd lost track. She woke that Thursday convinced it was Friday, that she'd succeeded in missing it all together. She called the operator and asked for the date, and then had to clarify: "No, I meant day of the week."

The operator's voice revealed no consternation, such desperate isolation old hat in her profession. "Happy Thanksgiving, miss," she said blandly before disconnecting.

Flora would have to drive to make it between her many celebrations, and she hated driving. In fact, it was her first time in her father's car. The car, a gray Volvo, was new and safe and did not smell of him. She clutched the wheel, and hit the brakes in spasms. She tried to calm herself—she was only stopping in to say hello to Georgia's parents before she went to meet her mother for dinner at the Beagle Inn. What a place to become a regular. *But what did she expect in Darwin?* her mother might ask. Flora hadn't spoken to Paul since their evening there together. She tried to imagine him at home in his hiking boots with his two sisters and his drunk father. Was he trying to imagine her?

Her last time in the McNair-Wallach house she was nine, and spying on her parents as if it were a job, and life without Georgia was unimaginable. It had been almost home, better than home. Conjuring its smell—ripe with nostalgia—in the innocuous sterility of the station wagon sent Flora's brain careening into childhood. Then, Georgia, the budding scientist, had kept a small army of rodents—gerbils, mice, and a lone dwarf Russian hamster—and a trace of the sawdusty shavings that made their bedding germed the air. But mostly the smell was a mixture of wood, fresh paint, vanilla, and an inkling of marijuana, from the joints Georgia's father, Ray, sneaked on the back porch. It was one of those open family secrets—Madeleine pretending not to notice the scent on his clothing and in his beard, and, in return, Ray pretending not to notice when she raided his stash and threw his pot down the garbage disposal a few times a year. In this way, the McNair-Wallachs were united, even by their secrets from one another. Then, Flora had resented Georgia her good luck in parents. Sometimes, amazingly, she still felt that way, jealous of Georgia. She kept waiting for the moment she'd be done with those feelings, move on, grow up, but the moment never arrived. Adulthood, it turned out, didn't strike the way adolescence once had, in an unmistakable spree of new angles and attitudes.

Their house was beautiful, and little changed. For Flora, this was rare. Most of the settings of her childhood were gone or off-limits; there were few material places she could return to, to remember and compare. Ray, a carpenter, had designed and built it himself with wonderful woods, and Madeleine had chosen a crushed peach pink paint for the exterior, a color Georgia had loved, and found mortifying.

Flora knocked, and when no one answered, she let herself in.

"Hello?" she said.

The decor was what she liked to think of as "futon-chic," the dominant aesthetic in Darwin—low to the floor, unfussy, comfortable but not luxurious—the furniture equivalent of a station wagon. Though the uniqueness of color extended within the house. Madeleine had majored in art in college and was a great weaver, and her rugs of brilliant greens and yellows punctuated the blond maple of the floors.

In the living room, in front of the small television, sat Ray's ancient mother, Betty, and her friend from the nursing home, Hal, the football game on, though irrelevant. Ray and Madeleine were in the kitchen.

"In here," they called out, as if she were a regular visitor who came and went with ease.

Madeleine was trimming brussels sprouts over the old aqua sink, reclaimed from a 1950s farmhouse Ray had remodeled; Ray, the cook of the family, was manning the various burners on the stove. To find them there in the same space, as if they hadn't moved an inch, as if their life were a diorama, frozen all these almost twenty years, and yet no longer the young parents of Flora's youth, was strange. Ray's beard had grown grayer, and both sparser and wilder, his glasses bigger, the lenses thicker.

He shook his head as if he couldn't quite believe what he was seeing. Then he wrapped his arms around Flora and said into her hair, "You're still a wisp of a girl, aren't you? Got to fatten you up for the New England winter. You're staying awhile, in Darwin, aren't you?"

It was so normal, so familiar. Madeleine hugged Flora tightly and quickly, then released her. This was how feeling came from Madeleine, in emphatic bursts. She could be affectionate, but only in short, strong doses. Georgia had been this way, too, a half-hearted, one-armed hugger—she hugged because one was expected to in certain instances. But hugging was not the way she demonstrated her affection. Flora had sometimes hugged her just to torture her, chanting, "I won't let you go, I won't let you go," and Georgia would shriek with hysterical laughter, as though she were being tickled.

Madeleine handed Flora a mug of mulled wine. "The only thing to do during these family occasions is to start drinking as early as possible."

Ray hunched over the oven, admiring his work. He looked up at Flora and beamed, proud, and happy to see her.

"That's some turkey, Ray," Flora said. She moved closer to admire.

"We're calling him Alfred, for Alfred Russel Wallace—the man who nearly scooped Darwin," he told her. Naming the turkey was a Thanksgiving tradition Georgia had started—the namesakes always scientists. The only one Flora knew in memory was Marie. "Alfred weighed in at eighteen pounds," Ray said.

Betty had likely reached the stage of life where she chewed and chewed but ate little, and Hal, frail as a greyhound, looked as though he, too, would offer slim help in getting through the feast Ray was preparing.

"Did you stop being a vegetarian?" Flora asked Madeleine.

"Nope." She rolled her eyes fondly at her husband's excesses.

"More leftovers for the carnivores. You'll have to come over for sandwiches, Flor," Ray said. "Anyway, Madeleine always cheats on Thanksgiving. She can't resist my bird."

"Sit down, sit down," Madeleine said, pointing to the kitchen chairs. "Tell us everything." Madeleine's old command. She liked to hear the details you left out for other people—when you woke up, what you ate for breakfast, which route you took when you left the house. Flora's mother had a phobia of logistics, as if life were attempting to kill her with sheer dullness, but for Madeleine, the marginalia, the smallnesses, the scraps and bits—that was the stuff she craved and gathered like an avid collector.

So this was how it would be. They would not ask for an apology, nor would they apologize to Flora or in any way dispute their own blamelessness. No disputes, no forgiveness. Just the small things you'd forgotten returning—or reappearing, as if they'd been there all along but the view had been blocked. Or were they small things? Maybe these were the things that mattered: the gestures, the habits, the clues to the self. Maybe the events, which took up so much room—the view blockers—were really insignificant.

They looked at her, Madeleine sitting, Ray pausing where he stood, stirring flour into the gravy, waiting.

Flora obliged, sticking to recent history, telling them about quitting her job, her sudden need to return. She talked about Larks and her father's house and her plans for the memorial. When they seemed to still want more, she decided to seek her own scraps: "Do you know someone in Art History named Cynthia Reynolds?" she asked.

"Sure, we know Cynthia," Madeleine said.

"You know her? Well?"

"No, not well. From committees and that sort of thing."

"She was my dad's girlfriend. We just met."

Ray looked at Madeleine.

"You knew?" Flora asked.

"Yes," Ray said.

"Why didn't I know?"

"Why didn't he tell you, your father, you mean," Madeleine said gently.

Flora drank her wine.

"Anyway, we didn't really know. We never saw your father, especially once he retired. It was the usual Darwinian gossip, and you can never be sure about that. You know how it is around here."

That Flora did know. "Worse than a group of teenage girls," her mother liked to say of the Darwin faculty. "Of course they are—much more spare time on their hands. The leisure of the theory class allows for much mischief." During the divorce, she had flirted with the possibility of spreading false rumors about her soon-to-be ex. "It would be so easy," she'd said, finding the idea hilarious. "Nothing too horrible—you know, a narcotic addiction, a doll collection."

But they had known, Ray and Madeleine, who never saw her father, who had, for many years, avoided him. Darwin had known. His own daughter the last to know.

"So, what's she like?" Flora asked.

"Cynthia?" Madeleine smiled a little to herself. "Oh, well, you know."

The phrase was irksome. "No, I don't know—that's the whole

thing," Flora said, her petulant child self surprising her as it emerged.

"She's fine," Ray called out. "She's nice."

"That's great, Ray, what a vivid description," Madeleine said. "Don't you feel you know her a little better already, Flo?" But with Ray, one knew he said it out of kindness, not vagueness. He picked up a brussels sprout from the bowl beside him, threatening to throw it at his wife.

"I met her only briefly," Flora explained. "She came by the house. She was dressed in this ridiculous outfit. She looked like a giant toddler."

Madeleine laughed with pleasure, wrinkling the freckles on her cheeks and nose. "She's very popular with the students," she said. "She teaches a lecture, on . . . oh, I can't remember. Not Impressionists, but some movement, and there's always full enrollment. Lord knows, she's one of the only women on the Darwin faculty to teach a lecture course."

"Okay, so she's successful," Flora said. "But, Madeleine, I want to know what you really think. Mrs. J. said she didn't trust her."

Madeleine stared at Flora, her eyes darting. "The whole breathless, wide-eyed thing. I mean, you said it, the big toddler. I don't buy it. Overcompensating, I would say."

"For what?"

"You know Madeleine," Ray said, rubbing his beard in mock psychoanalytic posture. "She thinks everyone is overcompensating for something. Overcompensating, projecting, transferring, sublimating. They're all very big around here."

"It's not as though I'm saying something awful, Ray," Madeleine said. "Don't get so nervous." She turned to Flora. "I think she's hungry, ambitious. If she wants something, she works her ass off to get it. That's all."

Hungry, ambitious. That was all. It sounded ominous. *Ambitious* was almost a dirty word in Flora's family. Not that they didn't have ambition, but they paired it with a neurotic dose of self-sabotage.

"Speaking of hungry," Ray said, "Flora, come here and taste this stuffing." And talk of the meal took over.

While they finished their preparations, they told her more about Georgia, whom they hadn't seen in six months. They were planning a visit to Mongolia over spring break. They, too, would be sleeping in a yurt. Georgia was living there with her husband, who had been her professor.

"You can probably guess how that news was received," Ray said, eyebrows raised toward his wife.

But they'd come around to him, though they found the closeness of his age to their own disconcerting, and the fact of his two earlier marriages and two children just years younger than Georgia.

"We have children to keep us humble," Madeleine said. "One's own child in many ways a mystery. It's good to remember we're not in control."

"You're not?" Ray asked.

Georgia—a stepmother, another Dr. McNair-Wallach, a proper grown-up with a substantial grown-up life, married to a man old enough to be her father. Flora had many times tried to imagine what Georgia was like now, what she did for a living, how she wore her hair. If ever Flora saw a little girl who looked like Georgia, looked how she had looked then—soft brown smudgy eyes, a button nose, big cheeks, and a thick mane of bark brown hair bobbed around her chin—Flora would ache to sit down and talk to her. *It's me,* she'd want to call out. *It's me.*

Flora remembered in images that came to her like sensations—like a hand plunged into boiling water, so hot it feels cold. She wanted to ask Ray and Madeleine, *Remember? Remember the time she finished her report on the black-capped chickadee so early that she wrote a second one, on the crow? Remember how she made us breakfast in bed? Remember when she organized the books in the living room chronologically?* Weren't they remembering, too? Georgia—whom they, too, longed for, off living her life far away, as children were meant to do.

————

Georgia's house, with Madeleine and Ray, was sanctuary. They waited on Flora, as though she were an invalid or a princess, Georgia waking her with a tray of toast and tea, as Flora's father had for many years done for her mother. They made her lunches of peanut butter and jelly on white bread—her longtime favorite, and a sacrifice for them, as they, like the rest of Darwin, did not believe in white bread. White bread was a near sin in Darwin. Weeks after their arrival in town, another mother had pulled Joan Dempsey aside in the school parking lot to ask if she knew how harmful processed foods could be for a growing child, and suggested she buy wheat instead.

"My daughter would rather die than eat whole-wheat bread," Joan had replied. "From what I gather, starvation is more harmful to a growing child than junky bread." She'd been irate for days, disproportionately so, complaining to Flora's father that he had moved them to the kingdom of granola, that she didn't know how much longer she could take it. "In the city, a person would have a moment's hesitation before intervening in a case of actual child abuse. In Darwin, lack of whole grains constitutes abuse. Clearly," she concluded, "these people have not suffered enough."

So Flora continued to eat white bread, and peanut butter so smooth its natural state could not be traced, and jelly sweet as dessert; she was getting too old for such unsophisticated fare, but sophistication, when it came to lunch, was gross. Weekends at the McNair-Wallachs', Ray would cut her sandwich in half diagonally, not horizontally, the way her parents did, and he would make one for himself, too, and some other kind of sandwich with greens and sprouts for Madeleine and Georgia, and the four of them would all sit down at the table to eat.

"Delish if not nutrish," Ray would say, eating one of his halves in three bites.

Sometimes they would bring the gerbils and mice down to the kitchen from Georgia's room and eat to the sound of the turning of the tiny rodent wheel, the squeaks and roots of rodent life. Flora helped Georgia build obstacle courses from toilet paper rolls and shoe boxes, but she never really liked the animals or wanted to touch them. You picked them up by their stringy tails, which seemed mean and risky—would the tail hold? "Squirming fur balls," her mother called them, and the description stayed with Flora. Still, she lifted the lid of each cage one by one, dutifully, somberly, holding by turns Mozart and Scherzo, Archibald and Reginald, their jumpy hearts pushing into her palm.

And then they'd go on outings—a trip to a nearby farm to pet sheep, an afternoon collecting and boiling sap into their very own maple syrup at a sugar shack, a visit to Ray's woodworking studio, where he would teach Flora and Georgia how to use the tools and machines, the lathe and the sander, surrounded by the seared smells of man-madeness. In Flora's family, conversation was the primary activity, what you did with other people: You talked about ideas; you made witty, surprising remarks; you said something rude, but accurate, devastating in a good way—during a meal, or a journey, over the top of your newspaper or a book. But conversation had let them down. Madeleine and Ray were right to have found other things. Their life was not so flimsy, so breakable. For them, Flora even started to eat wheat bread, though she didn't tell her mother and still ate white at home.

One day at the studio, they made a picture frame out of a beautiful mottled wood. You could see in it the subtle dark veins; you could see how the wood had once been alive. When Flora got back to the house, she presented it to her mother, but her mother was distracted, working on one of her projects that led to nowhere, clippings spread on the floor in a ring around her, the room stale, her ashtray full.

"Hey, nice. What are you going to do with that?" she asked.

"Put a picture in it."

"Good."

"Maybe a picture of me and Ray and Madeleine. Since we made it together."

"Ummm. Okay."

"I love Ray and Madeleine," Flora announced. "They're my good parents."

A line never quite undone.

9

The Living

FLORA HAD KEPT HER MOTHER WAITING at the Beagle Inn, and her mother didn't like to wait. She'd been born prickly, and her prickliness was sharpening with age. She'd never felt she fit in Darwin, and still she didn't. Both of Flora's parents were large people—and not only in her own mind. Her mother, in heels, was well over six feet tall. When she'd yelled at Flora over some childhood infraction, she'd grown to giantess proportions, and Flora had once thrown herself on the ground, feigning death, in order to avoid being killed—a sensible strategy, at which her mother had laughed and called her "my little Sarah Bernhardt." It seemed impossible she would ever begin to shrink. She colored her hair an icy blond (graduating from Manic Panic purples when she graduated from the President's House), but the Darwinian norm was a more natural fading. Her clothing was expensive and tailored, and, whenever possible, black. She was sitting at the back of the restaurant. Now, in restaurants, she had to sit with her back to the wall, gangster-like, to avoid being bumped. Being bumped could ruin her whole evening, as could plates arriving at different times. Restaurants were land mines of disappointments and mix-ups. But it was Thanksgiving, and Flora's father had died, and so she was to be excused for her lateness, mostly. The evening was yet to be ruined.

Flora apologized but did not explain. Her mother could hold a grudge, too, like a mafioso, her memory for wrongs—perceived or actual—done to her or Flora elephantine, and she would not approve of the return to the McNair-Wallach household.

They hadn't seen each other in nearly a month—a long time for them. Her mother, a chronically bad sleeper, had dark circles around her eyes that looked in Darwin darker and deeper. Why was everyone getting so old? This was annoying. Flora didn't have it in her at the moment to worry about the fact that her mother had stopped sleeping and would one day die. Still, Joan was a remarkable-looking woman, though she insisted looks had never been her thing. "I was never beautiful," she'd told Flora when she was little. When Flora found pictures at her grandparents' house, she'd felt betrayed: Why had her mother lied to her?

Joan Dempsey, who'd kept her ex-husband's name because she thought he wouldn't like it, had had many careers both pre- and post-Darwin, not roosting anywhere. Currently, she was working for a small nonprofit, doing investigations on prisoners' rights in the United States. She read the newspaper meticulously, as though she were going to be tested on it the next day, cutting out articles and making rune-like notations on the clippings before stashing them away in her imposing filing cabinet. She'd been a freelance journalist for a few years, after the divorce, and that was when the newspaper habit had reached its zenith. As a child, Flora thought she, too, would read the paper that way once she became an adult, just like she thought she would start rising early, as her father did, as soon as she grew up, taking her parents' behavior to be the norm and pinnacle of adulthood. Her parents were so thoroughly themselves, so definite.

Her mother was incensed about the state of the country. Incensed was one of her primary modes of being. She was incensed about recent court rulings systematically eroding *Roe v. Wade*. She was incensed about "Bible-thumpers" sprouting up all over the country in the guise of politicians, "like a plague of idiots." She was incensed about statements the White House had made, casting evolution as a crackpot fringe theory supported only by extremists.

"Every day there's some new denialist denying the existence of some atrocity—there never was a Holocaust, no Armenian genocide, HIV doesn't cause AIDS, there's no such thing as global warming. Have you noticed this? If it doesn't work for your agenda, say it never happened. Fantasy policy."

"Right," Flora said. She had not read about these international developments, or any developments in the outside world, and so sat silently as possible as her mother offered her commentary, not wanting to bring attention to her ignorance.

"Sure, we'd all like to live in a world where bad things never happen, but how do you take that next step of actually believing the whopper—denying history, denying science?"

How did she summon so much energy, such indignation in the presence of turkey so dry and cranberries so shocking as to be nearly fluorescent?

"Zealots," her mother said. "Trying to bring the apocalypse down upon us."

"Is that what this is?" A joke, and Flora smiled as she made it.

Her mother leaned in across the table. "Are you okay, Flo? You're awfully quiet."

"No, I'm fine," Flora said, answering the question both ways.

"You must be missing Dad."

"Really, Mom, I'm interested in what you're saying."

And her mother kept talking, telling her about the blog she had started—The Responsible Anarchist—from which she launched her secular leftist missives. It had attracted a healthy group of readers, some of them, admittedly, insane—who else was Googling the word *anarchist*? But what Flora was interested in, really, was the next stop on her itinerary. What would she say to Cynthia Reynolds? Would they talk about her father? Would they have anything to say? *Hungry, ambitious.* Madeleine's words ran in a loop in her brain, tailing that other line, *We were very much in love.* Had her father liked that about Cynthia? Her hunger? Had he, too, become hungry and ambitious? Did that explain the sudden arrival of poetry?

Sitting at the little table for two in the dark dining room, facing her mother over the simulacrum of Thanksgiving dinner, Flora felt her life shrinking. The smallness of the table provided a good metaphor. No room for other people. Soon her life would cease to be a table; it wouldn't even be a cocktail table. It would be a solitary chair, hard-backed and wooden, much like the chair she was sitting on now. She comforted herself that the waiters, college-aged and no doubt far from home, were having a worse Thanksgiving than she was.

"Tell me something, Flo," her mother said. "Anything. But something, please."

"There's not much to tell. My life up here has been pretty quiet. You know how it is in Darwin."

Her mother put her silverware down and waited.

"I had drinks with someone," Flora said. "A lawyer in town. He was Dad's lawyer, actually, a Darwin alum. That's how we met. But it was nothing. I'm sure nothing will come of it."

"Why are you so sure? You had a good time?"

"I don't know. Sort of."

"Flora, it's okay to enjoy yourself. You should be nice to yourself."

"Should I?" That had been one of her father's lines. One of his stupider lines.

"I worry about you, sweetheart. You know that. Throwing yourself into Darwin, this precipitous move on the heels of your father's death. I'm not sure what to make of it all. You've given up your job. You won't speak to any of your friends."

"What was so great about my job anyway? Telling people that for a more fulfilling existence they ought to buy cork flooring and use organic household sprays? How could I have walked away from all that? And yes, I've spoken to people, or I will soon. But I don't want to get into this with you right now, Mom. It's Thanksgiving, remember?"

"I thought you liked your job."

"I was lucky they hadn't fired me yet. I was a terrible employee, totally unreliable. I was looking for a way out."

"Have you thought about volunteering somewhere, while you're up here?"

"Have I thought about volunteering somewhere?" Flora repeated.

"It might be good for you to have something to focus on. Something outside yourself," her mother added. "To provide some structure."

"How wonderfully helpful, Mom. How sage." Joan's own father had died when she was at the vulnerable age of forty-six, and it had undone her. She knew nothing of Flora's life. Never had known, never would know.

"Don't get cross. I'm not allowed to tell you what I think?"

"I'm a little tired," Flora said.

A wedge of gelatinous pumpkin pie arrived, quivering on a single plate. They watched it quiver.

"Have some dessert," her mother coaxed.

"No thank you."

"I suggest that you volunteer somewhere, and it derails the whole evening? Am I allowed to be a participant in a conversation about your life? To offer my opinion? Or maybe it's safer for you to provide me with a script ahead of time, so that way, if and when you decide to tell me anything, you won't find my reactions so disappointing."

"Please, don't act like I'm being unreasonable. You may recall my father died a few weeks ago."

"Hey, slow down, okay? You've had a hell of a month, Flo. A terrible, difficult few weeks. I just want you to make the best decisions for yourself, not the ones you feel like you have to make for whatever reason. And maybe you're getting mad at me now because you have your own hesitations about being back here."

"That is so classic. I'm getting mad at you because of myself. Right. It has nothing to do with you and your behavior. Nothing at all. You're perfect. It's all me."

"No, c'mon, that's not fair. I know I'm deficient in all sorts of ways." Her mother's voice was cracking. It always came as a surprise how easily she cried—the impossible fragility within the toughness. "I really do want what's best for you, Flo, though it's hard to tell what that is these days. But of course I want to help you. Whatever you need, or want, just let me know."

Flora liked it better when her mother was being unreasonable.

She was not going to feel sorry for her; that wasn't her job. "Fine, I'll let you know," she said.

There was a silence. "I'm sorry I didn't say the right thing," her mother said.

"You know what, Mom? You can save that kind of apology. Really, no thanks."

"Flora, I'm trying."

It was true: Her mother was trying. She'd risen to the dispiriting occasion with the yeast of animated conversation, filled the emptiness of the holiday with the sound of her opinions. She had canceled plans to spend the day with her sisters to be with Flora in Darwin instead. Maybe things would be better if her mother tried a little less. Flora wished for the millionth time her mother had someone else in her life to worry over and be wounded by. Or did she wish it? Her father had found that for himself, and it, too, presented problems. Here she was, waiting for the moment she could sneak away from her mother for a tryst with her father's girlfriend. She hadn't been so secretive since she was a teenager. *I'm me, and you're you.* Secrets were one way to test the boundary, to assert your own impenetrable selfhood. She was regressing, moving backward, growing down, like tree roots, and not up, like normal people her age who had boyfriends they lived with, or husbands even, and assistants at work, or fieldwork in Mongolia, and read the paper daily, and never slept till noon, and no longer lied to their parents.

"You're right. I'm sorry," Flora said. "I'm rotten company right now."

"No, you're not. Difficult and infuriating, but not rotten." Her mother took her hand. "I know I told you I wouldn't sleep in that house, but I will if you'd like me to."

"No, no, that's okay," Flora said quickly, queasy with the guilt and irritation that come from lying. "I'm just going to fall into bed." She did not say "into Dad's bed."

Her mother signed the bill and they walked together out to the parking lot.

"Come back to the city with me," she said. "Tomorrow. For a few days. Take a break from all this, from your father, from Darwin."

"I can't," Flora said. "Not right now. I'm not sure why, but I can't."

Her mother put her hands on either side of Flora's face. It was a fond gesture, but the expression that accompanied it was critical, her eyes heavy-lidded and harsh. "You can't live his life for him, Flo. You know that. You can't rewrite the past, redo Darwin."

Flora heard the premonition of a yell. *You never could fucking understand, could you?* Tears pooled in her eyes, but she did not storm away, shouting over her shoulder as she might have done a month before. Both her parents were—or had been—yellers, and Flora, who came by it naturally, could yell, too. With a good yell, there came that sudden release, narcotic but short-lived. What followed was hangover-like, your body depleted, your mood stiff, achy, and repentant. No more yelling. Let it be the end of that. Be done with something. She wiped her cheeks dry with the back of her hand.

"Mom," she said, returning the gesture of hands on face, "good night."

And she hugged her, and thanked her for coming, and she kissed her on the cheek, and climbed right into her father's station wagon and pulled away.

The dead left you alone, but it was the living who filled you up with loneliness.

10

Poems

CYNTHIA'S GUESTS HAD LEFT by the time Flora arrived, and Cynthia was in the kitchen, wearing a vintage apron—the kind that tied, impractically, around the waist, a half skirt—washing up.

"I'm sorry it's late," Flora said. "I couldn't get away any earlier." She wasn't that late, was she? Had there even been any guests to begin with?

"Not at all," Cynthia said. "It's nicer this way. We'll get a chance to talk."

She untied her apron and led Flora into the living room. The furniture was scarlet-hued, dainty, skinny-ankled, and Victorian, made for a time when people were smaller. Two longhaired, owl-faced white cats sat plumply on twin burgundy chairs, their paws tucked under them, like steeping kettles.

"Andy and Pablo," Cynthia said. "Complete prima donnas, as you might expect."

The walls were covered with art, like a giant collage, painting and painting upon drawing and drawing. The effect was oppressive and beautiful. Landscapes and portraits, and Flora thought she recognized one of her father's watercolors among the mayhem— a blur of copper fox dashing through wintry birches. She tried to picture her father sitting amid all this. Was this a room he'd enjoyed spending time in? Where had they spent most of their time together? Here? Or at his house, where Paul said they'd "shacked up"? Flora's curiosity was uncomfortable—an almost perverted urge to riffle through all of Cynthia's belongings, to ransack the place.

"Do you mind if I use the bathroom?" she asked.

"Well, of course not." Cynthia pointed down the hall. "First door on your left."

Well, of course it would be the first door, the trip there offering no new insights. And the bathroom itself was a great disappointment—only toilet, sink, and mirror. No medicine cabinet. The full bath no doubt upstairs with all the other areas of interest. The wallpaper of the little room was bright and blooming, rife with obscene pink peonies. And on the marble sink, beside the delicate china soap dish, was a single bottle of perfume. Flora removed the cap and breathed in. Yes, that was what Cynthia smelled like. Slightly musky, powdery, and sweet. Flora's mother had never worn perfume—scents of all sorts gave her headaches. Flora had to stop herself from dotting some onto her wrist. She made herself flush the toilet and wash her hands and return to the living room and sit beside Cynthia on the love seat. On the round glass coffee table before them, in a dove gray ceramic pot, a blood-red orchid displayed its private parts.

"It's a lovely house," Flora said. Perhaps that would incite a tour.

"Oh, it's nice enough. A bit dark for my taste. The ceilings a little low. I know I should be grateful, living in subsidized housing, but at my age it makes one feel vulnerable to have one's roof contingent on one's employment."

That's right—it was a Darwin faculty house. Flora thought she remembered someone else living there, some friend of her mother, when she was younger. Home ownership in a town like Darwin, a college town, extravagant, like travel by private jet or elective surgeries. When her father had bought his house, it had come as a surprise, a sign that life had changed again. Professors didn't buy; they rented from the college at a discount. It was the Darwin way—the landlessness of the intelligentsia, the feudalism of academia, keeping the serfs dependent and bound to the manor, always within walking distance.

"Anyway, enough complaints. How *are* you?" Cynthia asked, as though they were dear old friends in need of a catch-up.

"I'm fine."

"Good. I've always loved Thanksgiving, since my girlhood. I was the eldest of five, so it was a huge affair."

The eldest of five. As an only child, Flora regarded the idea of siblings with fascination, in the way she found mythical creatures fascinating—as though they occurred only in art, or other cultures. Growing up, Flora often fantasized about having a sister—part rival, part ally. A sister would be nice right now, today. If she had a sister, one of them could keep Cynthia distracted while the other searched the house.

"What was that like?"

"Oh, the family? Noisy," Cynthia said. "Complete chaos."

But Flora could see she did not want to go back in memory, or not that far. "Were you and my father planning to celebrate the holiday together?" She was an investigative reporter, trying to uncover, to verify, to retrace.

"We hadn't talked about it, but I'd assumed we were, since he said that you would be with your mother." Flora watched as Cynthia's eyes filled with tears. "I miss him terribly," she said.

Was this openness, as Madeleine had suggested, an act, a cover? Was it a ploy to get at what she was after? Or were they all too guarded, too closed to recognize a certain kind of innocence when they encountered it? Flora wondered if she should reach out to Cynthia, put her hand on her arm or shoulder, say something kind.

"I know," she said. It was the best she could do, but it was quite enough for Cynthia.

"I'd never been married, never had children," she said. "I'd lived my whole adult life alone and I was used to it, good at it even. But when your father and I . . . He broke me of the habit, and now, here I am in my sixties and suddenly, for the first time, I'm no good at it."

Cynthia, in profile, looked a little like Flora's mother. The Lewis Dempsey type, maybe. Joan would not be caught dead in Cynthia's wardrobe, or in her perfume, and she would say that Cynthia's living room made her feel the walls were closing in on her, but they shared a look—narrow, smooth-skinned faces, boldly featured, light-eyed. Both of them beautiful, but their beauty unexpected, something you didn't notice right away.

"Did you and my dad talk of getting married?"

"Oh, Flora, we hadn't gotten there yet." Cynthia placed her cool hand for just an instant over Flora's hand. "At our age, romantic notions of marriage seem slightly preposterous. Perhaps we would have done it eventually, but then only for practical reasons."

Flora said nothing. She knew enough to know that practical reasons meant money. Was that what Cynthia wanted from her—her father's money? Did she feel she had earned it, that she was owed an inheritance of her own?

"I guess marriage is not in the cards for me. Not now," Cynthia said. "But what about you? Is there someone in your life?"

Is there someone in your life? A terrifying question. "No," Flora said. There was no one in her life, no someone at all.

An awkward silence seeped into the busy room.

"How do you fill your time—since?" Flora asked. This seemed to her the quintessential question, the part of life she hadn't been able to sort out. Filling time. Spending it. How was it done?

"Oh, I'm working on a book, nearing the end. On Turner. And I'm teaching, and students have a way of filling up one's time. I have friends I see. This and that. Most of all, I wish it were spring. I love to garden. In spring and summer, I'm always in the yard, kneeling in the soil. Last summer, I spent a lot of time in your father's garden. I keep feeling all of this would be made a bit easier if I could just spend Sundays in the garden."

Flora's father, Cynthia explained, would read out on the lawn chair or the hammock, and keep her company while she worked, calling out passages when something seized him. To Flora, such scenes had a whiff of servant and master: Cynthia kneeling, digging; her father reclining, edifying. "Didn't he ever help you?" she asked.

"Oh, of course he helped, gathering my weeds and prunings, tidying up after me, and he was always offering to do more, and I would show him how to do certain things. Most of all, he loved learning the names of plants. You know how he felt about proper nouns. But it wasn't work for me, discovering a new garden like that. I didn't mind at all. I loved every minute."

"I was wondering who'd been tending those flower beds," Flora said. "They look like they were lovely."

"But what about you, Flora? What are your plans?"

"I don't know. I don't have any plans."

"That's probably wise. For what it's worth, people keep telling me you shouldn't make any big decisions or life changes in the first year after you lose someone."

Flora hated that phrase. *Lost, passed, passed away*—the passive euphemisms of grief. She hadn't lost anything. Something had been taken, not lost. "It's a little late for me for that advice," she said. "I mean, I'm here. I seem to have left my whole life behind and moved back to Darwin."

"You did what you had to do," Cynthia said quickly. "Your father would call such bromides 'psychobabble' anyway."

"Yes, he would."

Cynthia shook her head. "At moments, certain expressions— you're so like him, it's scary."

Flora blushed with pleasure. Funny how the thought of being like one's parents could be simultaneously a source of dread and delight. "Really?" she asked.

"Yes, really," Cynthia said. "I used to get a little jealous, you know. The way your father spoke of you. The long phone conversations you two would have sometimes after dinner." She seemed to read Flora's expression and paused. "I know how strange it must be for you, that I was there, in the background, through all that."

"He was the only person I liked talking to on the phone," Flora said. "His phone calls were like great letters. You know, notable anecdotes described in careful detail. No *How's the weather*—unless it was relevant to a story—no *Have you taken care of such and such?* Just good stories. *You'll never believe whom I ran into . . .* and he was off." To be able to remember him with someone else who had loved him was rare and new. She smiled at Cynthia for the first time since she'd arrived.

Cynthia stood up abruptly and disappeared down the hall, as though the smile were the signal she'd been waiting for. Her footsteps hurried past the little bathroom. A light went on. Flora could hear a drawer opening, then closing again. When Cynthia returned, she held a stack of papers in her hand. She pushed aside the orchid and placed them on the coffee table in front of Flora.

"I've been dying to talk to you about them," Cynthia said. She was beaming. She looked like the proudest woman on earth. "Aren't they exquisite?"

"I'm sorry," Flora said, staring at her. "What?"

"The poems," Cynthia said. "Your father's poems."

In spite of all the evidence now before her—the papers, Cynthia's face, what she slowly recognized to be an inscription in her father's handwriting across the top of the first page—Flora could not bring herself to believe that Cynthia knew of the poems' existence, that she possessed them, that she had read them. Flora was his one and only reader. She was the one he trusted.

"I know your father gave you a copy," Cynthia said. "He was so eager to know what you thought of them."

A copy? Flora looked more closely at the inscription: "For my darling Cynthia," it read in a twilight blue ink, "without whom these poems never would have been. L."

"What did you think of them?" Cynthia pressed.

"I didn't know," Flora said stupidly. "I'm not sure I'm ready to talk about them with you."

Cynthia looked down, wounded. "No, of course not," she said. "I understand."

"I'm just surprised. I didn't realize."

"I shouldn't have sprung this on you," Cynthia said. "I seem to keep doing that."

Flora wanted to reach for the stack of poems, Cynthia's poems, to touch them, to mess them, to hear that sound fingers make against paper, but she didn't trust herself; she felt as though her hands were shaking. She clasped her fingers together and pressed them into her lap.

"But I should tell you"—Cynthia was beaming again—"I've spo-

ken with an old friend of mine, an editor, and I sent him a small
sample of the poems, and he's quite interested. He thinks they're
eminently publishable—that's what he told me."

Flora stood up. Those were her poems. Her father had left them
to her. "It's late," she said.

"Yes." Cynthia picked up the manuscript. "We've made it
through this holiday. This long, long day." She walked Flora to the
door, clutching the poems to her chest. "He's a wonderful editor.
He'd be so right for your father's work. Truly. I think you'd like him
a great deal. And whenever you're ready to talk, Flora, I'll be here."

"Good night," Flora said.

She drove slowly through the empty streets of Darwin. No one,
it appeared, had anywhere to be but safely ensconced in their snug
country houses, giving silent thanks for their good fortune. Except
for the occasional upstairs light shining optimistically into the
night, most of the houses were dark, her own destination the dark-
est of them all. She went in, and without turning on the lights, she
found her way upstairs, Larks padding after her. In the body bag on
the floor of the room called hers sat the poems. She grabbed the
bag and took it into her father's bedroom. She switched on the
lamp and opened the folder. There was no inscription on her copy,
and looking closer, she noticed what she hadn't seen before, that it
was just that—a copy.

*Gemlike. Subtle and spare. Startlingly original. Timeless. The common-
place rendered miraculous. The miraculous in the commonplace. Aston-
ishing depth. Vividly realized.* The ubiquitous blurbspeak of poetry,
the extravagant clichés, the lexicon like that of wine—silly and
bewildering.

But how to describe a poem? Flora had stayed up all night reading and rereading the poems in her father's bed. Such intimacy in
reading—how closely one attended to the words on the page, more
closely than to the words of troubled intimates. How one felt one
knew a writer when reading—and yet, when one did know the
writer, how distancing the reading could be. How troubling and

infuriating. It had been jealousy, finally, and not loyalty, not love, not even duty, that inspired Flora to read. If Cynthia had read them and knew them, Flora wanted to know them better. There was power in knowing, a loss of power in not knowing. "Who owns this kid?" she'd once yelled to her mother while at the playground in the city, before Darwin, the small offender having gotten in her way. Who owns these poems? That was the question now. "For my darling Cynthia," her father had written, while telling Flora she was the reader he trusted.

We want to know our parents' secrets, their lives before and beyond our own. But then to know can be terrible. To know is to want to not know. After so much worry about how the poems would sound, what they said came as a shock. The content surprised her most of all, and the content was Cynthia. Cynthia was the Eve of Darwin's Garden, though she was not Eve-like at all. She was open and honest, boldly aware of her own nakedness. Her nakedness was described with care—Flora read with interest and shame. One knew one's parents had bodies, used them even, and yet there it was on the page in her father's handwriting, his thoughts about his body and others', thoughts Flora felt she shouldn't know. Certain things children should not know.

It had been his way of telling her—of telling her rather too much—about Cynthia. She might have known about the happy lovers for many months if only she had read the manuscript. No wonder Cynthia had been so unprepared for her surprise, her confusion. For whatever reason, her father had been unable to say, "I'm very much in love," but instead had handed her the fertile product of his romance and asked her to read it. He must have found it rude, or odd, that she never said, "So, who's this woman, Dad?" That she said nothing at all. But then he hadn't asked, or even mentioned the handoff that had occurred that morning at the diner before she went to work. It had been as if it had never happened. And perhaps that had been the point: *If I don't read these poems, or mention them, then maybe they will cease to exist.* But they existed. More than existed. They throbbed unappetizingly with life. This was why

Cynthia loved the poems. Who would not love to see herself so por-
trayed? Cynthia the revelation; Cynthia the rescuer.

In one poem, "The Gardener," he watches her planting bulbs:
"Impossible in her palm in their crinkly tunics." Flora remembered
the word *tunic* from her days on the gardening beat. Of course
he would have found the noun, upon learning it from Cynthia,
irresistible—the very word for the thing and yet possessing an
innate poetry, an innate metaphor. *Crinkly*, too, was winning—one
heard it, like grabbing an onion. When he stuck to the word for the
thing, he was good. But later, with Cynthia, he got into trouble.
Reassuring, almost, to see the self-centered silliness of romance was
not ageist. New love, no matter when, made one see the profound
in the ordinary—*the miraculous in the commonplace*—and not in a
good way.

He imagines the two of them meeting years earlier, when they
were young, when she was still a girl, her body "serpentine, unbit-
ten; the bulb below my ribs not yet ripened." Had he not realized
what was undone under such revisions? For example, Flora? Better
to have Cynthia from the beginning than to have had Flora at all?
And her mother, beyond being erased, became the emblem of all
that had gone wrong, fifteen years of marriage reduced to a regret-
table error corrected only with the second coming of love, the
Edenic Cynthia, the post-apocalyptic redemption of sins past, the
clean slate, o brave new world, the wonder and rightness of it all, at
long bloody last. If her father had lived, these paroxysms might
have come to seem overdone even to him, but he had not lived, and
so their passion was poised and immortalized in the state of per-
fection, in the state of poetry. Surely he would have gone over that
stuff again, cleaned it up—surely he would have. *He would have:* the
tragic conditional. Who knew the man was such a thoroughgoing
narcissist? Poetry as memoir. She'd heard him say so-and-so was
not a novelist because his novels adhered so closely to his life; did
all the self-serving autobiography, then, make her father not a
poet? Or were poets exempt from such distinctions, as they were
from most cares of the world? Flora had been wise not to read the

poems. What good could ever come of having read them? What good to her, that is. Her mother could never read them.

It was not yet nine the next morning when she called Cynthia, but she got the machine, the intrepid gardener already in the loam somewhere.

"Cynthia, hello, this is Flora Dempsey. I'm afraid I'm going to have to say no, as my father's literary executor, to your friend the editor. Please do pass on my regrets. The poems are simply not ready for publication. But thank you so much for the gracious offer to help."

Winter

11

A Man Who Noticed Things

SHE WANTED TO LOOK NICE FOR HIM. Her mother's advice was to wear something she didn't mind never wearing again. That made sense, but then, did it mean wear something ugly? And she still didn't like to defer to her mother's ideas of dress. Flora wanted to wear something beautiful, and serious. She continued to care about clothing. She continued to care about the way she looked. Death had no impact whatsoever upon her vanity.

Days before his memorial, she walked into town, to the shop she'd bought her prom dress in a decade ago, a store filled with floor-length gauzy dresses in a spectrum of colors meant to be ethereal, all in the sorbet family. The dresses were unchanged by the years. It was amazing to reflect on the rainbow of proms—all that virginity lost and alcohol vomited, friends betrayed and parents deceived, all that ordinary high school triumph and disaster—that had kept the store so long in business. Three high school girls were trying on strapless or strappy gowns for the winter formal. As Flora browsed the racks, she met eyes with one of them in the mirror. She was tall and busty, with a swimmer's broad shoulders, and had on a champagne-colored slip dress that suited her long blond ponytail, cut on the bias, and slinky.

"You look great," Flora told her. "Fits like a dream."

The girl flashed a look of shy longing, an almost cringe. "I love it so much. But my mother will never buy it for me."

"Too sexy?"

"Too much money, too little fabric."

Flora laughed. "So often the way."

The idea of wearing any of those dresses to a funeral was absurd and offensive. Feeling a voyeur, she made herself leave, though she had wanted to stay, to talk to the girls, or listen to them talking to one another in their semiprivate language of nicknames and personal jokes. She wanted to sneak them money for that perfect dress, to honor the way one feels at that age that the perfect dress might change your life. Who knew—maybe it could. Other small things had been known to change lives.

The black silk cocktail dress she'd bought years before for a life she thought she was heading toward but somehow missed along the way, that she'd folded into the body bag for her return to Darwin—she would wear that; this was, no doubt, the occasion for which she had packed it. It was Audrey Hepburn-ish, with a high neck and little cupped sleeves, cut just above the knee, with a slight sheen to the dark fabric. Serious, and beautiful. The morning of the memorial, in the dress, Flora tied her hair back and brushed blush on her cheeks, though she rarely wore makeup. She was reminded of the nights at the opera with her father, their dates, as though the memorial were their final date. What was that about, dressing for one's father? Another Freudianism best left unexplored.

At the chapel, a long line of downy winter coats stood quietly in the hush of new snow, waiting to gain entrance. The students were on break, exams ended, but many had stayed behind in Darwin to attend. They sat in cliques in the mezzanine, the young men touching and nervous in their ties, the young girls tearful, as though he had been their father. It seemed the whole faculty, from assistant to emeritus, even Madeleine, with Ray beside her, had come. Her father's editor from *The New Republic* had flown in from Washington. Gus Simonds was there, and Paul Davies, sitting with a group of young men with beards and glasses and ironic, ill-fitting suits—his fellow Apostles. Were Paul's hiking boots lurking down below? A carful of Flora's friends had driven up from the city, as had her old boss. Her friends looked like elegant aliens, slinging their oversize city bags. What were they thinking? What had they missed by

signing on to be here in Darwin? Flora remembered attending the
funeral of the sister of a boy she knew in high school and feeling
all the appropriate sadnesses—weepy, vulnerable, sympathetic. But
also envious. She'd envied the boy the drama of the occasion. He
was so clearly one of the stars of this big event; his life had seemed
bigger than hers. Did her friends now begrudge her this moment?
Flora hated them for feeling what she imagined they felt. She
waved but did not approach.

The pews were crowded to the point of claustrophobia. There
was no way out. Though of course there was a way out: Her father
had taken it. They were all there for him, and yet there was no him
there. She was grateful to have no polished and padded coffin,
which at her grandfather's funeral had struck her as boatlike and
vulgar. Grateful to have no graying face poking sculpturally out of
a painstakingly chosen suit and tie. And yet. Where was he? Her
father could now be stored—in an urn, or a shoe box, or a tightly
sealed mason jar. In an ornamental paisley tin. It was too ridiculous. And horrifying, that one's father, that first and ultimate
model of maleness, could be reduced to something so small, so
portable; could be transformed into something one could run
through a sieve, become another element: from animal to mineral.
Grotesque. She felt faint every time she considered what had
become of him.

The question of whom to sit with was a difficult one. One that
shouldn't be difficult—one sat with family, one was *the* family—but
in her case was. She hovered awkwardly like an uninvited guest; she
waited to be told what to do. Also, there was the question of what
to do with her mother.

"Don't worry about me. I'm here for you," her mother told her,
adding, "If you want me up in the front with you, I'm happy to do
that, but if you'd prefer, I can sit in the back with Steve and Heidi."

Perhaps funerals should have assigned seating, like weddings.
Calligraphied place cards; each row given quirky and idiosyncratic
names. In the end, Flora sat beside Ira Rubenstein and other old
friends of her father, Mrs. J. and Betsy and Pat Jenkins just behind.
Her mother a few rows farther back. Beyond her, Flora thought she

saw Dr. Berry. Her hair had gone a steely gray and grown a few inches longer, from earlobes to chin. Would they have to embrace? It had been years. Embracing might be expected. The thought of hugging her former shrink was appalling. Near her sat the new president of the college, a handsome Brit with a young family. At first, Flora couldn't see Cynthia, but then she spotted her on the other side and inadvertently caught her eye. Had she been staring, waiting to be summoned? She came up and kissed Flora almost on the mouth.

"Come sit with us, Cyn," Ira said as she grasped his hand with both of her hands. "You should be up here with us."

Sin? Flora hadn't realized they were such intimates. Cynthia looked to Flora for approval. It was the first they'd seen of each other since Flora told her no.

"Of course," Flora said.

Out of her brilliant array of colors, Cynthia appeared older, and smaller. She was wearing a blue-gray blazer that looked several sizes too big, like a man's jacket. Was it possible that it was Flora's father's jacket? That was too weird, even for Cynthia, wasn't it? Though it was likely that he'd left things behind at her house, that pieces of his wardrobe still lived in her closet.

The student players took their seats "up at the holy end," as Larkin had written in a poem about a church—she knew this from her father's quoting, not her own reading; this was how she knew most references, her references really his. The mourners stirred and hushed. The seats were uncomfortable, as they were intended to be. Around the sides of the chapel were portraits of all of Darwin's past presidents—gray-haired men in dark robes, impossible to guess the year by the portrait, 1872 and 1972 indistinguishable. Her father's was up in the mezzanine, where she couldn't see it, thankfully. He had hated it, felt the artist had gone a bit Rembrandt on him. "Chiaroscuro up the wazoo," he'd said. "And I can't help feeling he didn't do justice to my nose."

Smothered in black velvet, two women—a violinist and cellist—began to tune their instruments, releasing the mournful wail of

disparate voices blindly trying to find each other. The slow movement of Beethoven's *Archduke* Trio, the notes of the piano quietly
insistent, the thread of the music trading back and forth from
piano to strings. Repetitive, though Flora liked the rolling patches
of piano. She preferred music with words. Opera had been their
compromise. But as she listened, she saw her father, his hand held
up, palm toward her to catch her attention, his eyebrows rising
with the music, his eyes glassing and spilling, and then the slow
shake of his head, his pure appreciation of the skill of the thing.
"The fucker could write," he'd say, slightly embarrassed by his own
emotion. "The fucker could really write."

He had a recording he loved of Pablo Casals playing the piece,
where you could just hear Casals grunting irrepressibly at the good
bits. "Did you hear that?" he'd say, his wet eyes breaking into smile.
"Did you hear it?"

Ira read from Hardy, as Flora had suggested he do. Not one of
the Emma poems, as had been Cynthia's hope (poems to a dead
estranged wife were wrong for this occasion, weren't they?), but
"Afterwards," of wanting to be remembered as "a man who used to
notice such things." Flora avoided Cynthia's gaze, which she could
feel pointed at her, as he read.

"Yes, Lew, we do remember you that way," Ira said, his voice
straining at his friend's name.

James Wood talked about his scholarship, his brilliance as a
reader: "Harold Bloom has written at length about 'strong mis-
readings.' But Dempsey was interested above all in strong readings." Bloom was himself in attendance, so Wood did not say that
Dempsey had referred to the former's famous book as *The Anxiety
of Flatulence.* "Dempsey's book *Reader as Understander,*" Wood went
on, "moved readers away from narcissism. Books were not mirrors,
he argued, but windows. One ought not read to understand one's
own place in the world, or the world in abstract, but to understand
the individual experience of another. And even more, to understand the individual force and resonance of words. 'Who owns
these words?' he often asked of books he read, of Hardy's novels in

particular. He better understood the intricacies of point of view than anyone. Many talk of close reading, but what interested him was close writing."

He called her father "vatic," his writing "plangent," and offered other words for which Flora required a dictionary. Even death could not dampen a scholar's erudition; even death an opportunity to edify and exclude.

"Those of you who knew my father well know that he surely imagined the words to be spoken on this very occasion," she began her eulogy, releasing a nervous laugh. "And any of you who had the pleasure of hearing him speak know what a daunting task I have before me in trying to live up to his version."

It had taken so long to write the words on the papers before her, but all she wanted to do, up there like a bride abandoned at the altar, was sing the songs he had written for her when she was small, to share his secret words. Her father, the great nicknamer, was also an inveterate lexicographer, compiling their own private family dictionary. It had taken Flora a long time to learn that these words were not in common parlance, that other families did not say "birfus" for *birthday,* or "I'm having an attack of the fondines" when they felt crazy about someone. Still other words were actual words, though rare—one gave the dog a *sop,* not a treat or bite; one woke not at dawn but at *sparrow fart,* and wore not party clothes but *finery.* Now it was like speaking Yiddish, or some other dying language; soon there would be nobody around to talk to. All families, she suspected—unhappy or otherwise—spoke their own dying languages. Or maybe they didn't. Maybe her family—her father—really was remarkable.

But she followed her script and told the crush of mourners that she had never asked him the meaning of a word he couldn't define, that it seemed he knew every word ever made, and as a child she assumed that was a prerequisite of parenthood—knowing all the definitions. She told stories about summer vacations on the shore, his enthusiasm for the simple pleasures of good days—a nice sandwich, a long walk, a book, a swim, a fire. Writing the words she would speak, she had found herself again and again going back in time, to her childhood, her earliest memories, to the years before Darwin, as if those years had been real life, and afterwards something else entirely, a wrong turn, an anomaly overrunning a working system.

She talked about his tastes. How he applauded the low as much as the high, how he could narrate a commercial he loved with such relish, nearly equal to his relish for talking Larkin. How he had such confidence in his own views ("So-and-so is only partly right in thinking . . ."), how she often had to remind herself that what he was offering was an opinion, and that she was entitled to disagree, and, in fact, he loved it when she did. Where did that come from, that academic certainty about ideas, the total lack of intimidation in the land of thought? She had written too much, and almost wanted to skip a page, but she read to the end, and when she sat down, Ira nodded at her with what looked like approbation, and Cynthia's cheeks were wet and shining and she squeezed Flora's hand with her damp hand. But Flora felt embarrassed and exhausted and miserable—had she talked for too long, and too much about herself? Had she simply indulged her inexhaustible appetite for sentimental childhood memories, remarkable only for their very commonness? Would her father have been disappointed that she was not herself more scholarly, more vatic? She had put a foot wrong—many, many feet wrong.

The old bricks of the rounded ceiling of the chapel had begun letting go and one had nearly brained the chaplain, so a gauzy netting had been hung overhead to catch them. It looked insubstantial, like mosquito netting. Why not instead restore the bricks and shore them up? It seemed demoralizingly like Darwin to give in to entropy like that, to let them fall. As the tuxedoed a cappella group Flora had worshiped in the early days took their positions, sounded their pitch pipe, and broke into the old Irish song her father had so loved, "Will you go, lassie, go? And we'll all go together," Flora imagined the bricks releasing themselves in a single God-like gesture, plummeting through the nets, pummeling one and all, death begetting still more death, and when she let out a sob, she surprised herself, and Cynthia reached right up and put her arm around, pulling Flora toward her, cradling her in the crook of her narrow arm and rocking her gently in the surging harmonies.

Then it was over and there were endless arms and hands, holding her, touching her, squeezing and patting, offering what they hoped to be comfort but which made Flora feel soiled and bruised. A blur of weepy faces—why were they all crying? It was her father, for God's sake. Sudden death was not a learning experience; it had not made Flora larger-souled, or kinder. It had made her jumpier, like a feral cat, ears twitching at fresh movements and unseen noises. "Thank you, thank you, thank you so much for coming," she told the hands and arms, the salty cheeks. "You spoke so wonderfully," they told her; "he would have loved it." What was there to say to that? She'd invited it, invoked it, she supposed. "Thank you," she said, "thank you for being here." She'd never been so thankful in all her life. Thank God there was no reception.

Madeleine and Ray presented their unified front, clasping not her but each other.

"You're a hell of a girl, Flora Dempsey," Madeleine said.

What did that mean?

"Not girl, young woman," Ray corrected.

And Flora's eyes spilled over again and her nose would never stop running and she felt small and childlike, crying so freely among the adults, and Madeleine gave her a pack of tissues from her purse and they left.

"I wasn't expecting to see them here," her mother said, appearing behind her. "They've finally forgiven you, after all these years?" Then she added, "How are you holding up? You okay?"

Flora wanted to be alone, alone with her father. She wanted to talk to his coffin, confide in his grave—there were good reasons for these things she lacked. She hadn't yet decided what do with his ashes. She didn't like the idea of spreading them, of scattering him. Who wanted to be scattered or spread thin? She would bury them, one day, if ever the ground thawed, alone, like Antigone burying her brother—another reference she'd learned from him.

"Why didn't you tell me there was a woman in your father's life?" her mother asked, angling her head toward Cynthia. "C'mon Flo, you know how they say the wife always knows? Well, it's true of the ex-wife, too. Even the ex-wife always knows. I could spot your father's type anywhere. Wolfish. I know his type better than I know my own."

Flora was distracted by a batch of students.

"How's Larks?" one asked. Her father, who'd taken the dog to class with him, liked to say, "He's very big on Hardy. Weak on Rossetti, but big on the Hardiness."

"Your father was such a great mentor to me," another claimed.

A third, who insisted they'd met, insinuated himself: "If you need help with anything, anything at all."

"Thanks," she said. Why not just be frank and say "Fuck off"? If ever there was a moment to get away with it.

Her city friends told her she was beautiful, and *so strong*. "I don't think I could have handled that if I were you," one said.

"Call us," said another. "We miss you."

Her mother moved in the direction of Ira and Cynthia. She and Rubie had liked each other a great deal, but her father had gotten him in the divorce. Could he now be her mother's friend, her father gone? They greeted each other with a hesitant kiss on the cheek and fond faces. Ira started to introduce her to Cynthia, and the dean of admissions stepped in and blocked Flora's view.

———

Change came fast once it came. Boxes packed, the rental house found, movers scheduled in days. Flora and her mother were moving five blocks away. Five blocks—an inconsequential, horrifying distance. Their last move, from the city, had happened gradually, every household object contemplated before it was lovingly swaddled in bubble wrap, the choice of what to keep and what to give away deliberated, piles made and analyzed. This move was hurried and careless; things were broken in the process. As her final stand, Flora's mother burned the white bedspread she'd bought on the day of their arrival in the fireplace in the living room, though the June air was sickly sweet and hot. Flora watched the molten strips of cotton drifting toward the chimney as though possessed, and thought, She's going to burn the house down. Don't let her burn it down. Please, let her.

But divorce was not discrete. Divorce kept happening. Her parents didn't love each other. When her mother got mad, Flora would ask, "Do you still love me?" and her mother would say, "I still love you. But I don't like you much at the moment." Flora only returned to the President's House on Tuesdays. Tuesdays were the only day of the week that hadn't changed—Flora and her father back at Ponzu, sometimes with Georgia, her mother in the city being analyzed. All other nights it was her and her mother alone together in the normal-size house, which would have seemed huge a year ago but now seemed small, the two stories furnished sparsely with tables and chairs from the third floor of the big house, a reenactment of their old apartment in the city, which was somehow the place where they'd all lived just a year before. Sometimes Flora imagined that her father had died. That was why she saw so little of him.

If she had to choose between her two parents, whom would she want to die? And between her parents and Georgia? She could not imagine life without her mother. "You don't get to choose—you're not in charge," her mother would tell her if Flora voiced these deliberations, which she tried not to do. "Take it from someone who has spent a lifetime wishing people dead. There's no harm in it, but there's not much of a future, either. You're not that powerful." But Flora feared she was that powerful—more powerful than her mother. If she had not moved to Darwin, what would the world look like? Would her parents still love each other? Would no one ever run away from school? Would the Flora in the city be generally more sophisticated, taller?

That summer, there was terror in unexpected places. In school she'd been going through a literature of atrocities phase. All the girls in her class had gone through it, swapping and devouring the school's little library of Holocaust books. They traded books about young girls paralyzed by drunk drivers, abandoned by parents, abused by older brothers. The terror in these books was their allure.

But in the new house, the books turned sinister. Flora read *I Am the Cheese* and then made her mother read it and swear to her there was no way, under any circumstances, their family would end up in the witness protection program. She saw the movie *The Incredible Shrinking Woman*—a comedy?—and worried that her mother was growing incrementally and imperceptibly smaller, that one day she would fit inside a cage, like one of the gerbils or mice in Georgia's room. How could Flora know which terrors existed within the realm of possibility and which without? Previously unimaginable things had happened in brisk succession. The plausible had ceased to be—if it had ever even been—knowable.

The thing was that life had been hard before. There'd been weeping; there'd been fury. People said, "That's life," when something unfair or unfortunate happened. Did that mean life was bad even when it was good? "Who said life was fair?" her mother had said before when Flora complained about the smallnesses of badness—an early bedtime, a denied play date. Now she also said, "God breaketh not all men's hearts alike," not because she believed in God, but because she believed in heartbreak.

12

Institutional Life

CHRISTMAS MORNING BEGAN WITH SEX. Better, longer the second time around, though less stunning. Flora liked having sex with Paul, but she would have preferred to do it in the afternoon or evening, or at least after she'd had her coffee. She felt incompatible with most men she'd been with for this reason—morning sex. She caught herself missing the sex of her girlhood, which had occurred later in the day. There was something about high school sex. Not skill, of course. And really, she was romanticizing it. She was always doing that, getting the past wrong. But as sex became more competent, more expected, even more pleasurable, it seemed a little less exciting, less dangerous. Gone was the sense of being bad. Where the titillating fear of getting caught? No wonder academics loved adultery (along with the rest of the planet). It saved them from the suffocating appropriateness of the rest of their lives. Growing up, it became harder and harder to feel illicit. So what, you fucked. Big deal, you smoked. Okay, you went on the occasional bender. You were an adult. You knew what you were doing. You used condoms. You understood the risks. You repented with brain-pummeling hangovers.

Flora had decided not to celebrate Christmas. Her mother, who'd grown up just Jewish enough to be deprived of the holiday, had never been very good at it, and didn't seem to mind when Flora announced after the memorial that she would not be observing it this year. The Christmases they shared in the little house had been the most desultory occasions, deliberately gloomy—such gloom could not be arrived at by accident. Two sad presents under the tree, and later, no tree at all. So much trouble. All those dried pine needles. "I'm better at daily life," her mother had offered as an explanation. But her father had excelled at Christmas. He'd loved it with an unabashed glee found more often in people under the age of ten. He used pillowcases for stockings, stuffing them with thoughtful curiosities—a clear plastic stapler where you could watch the interstices at work, a pocket-size kaleidoscope, a hand-carved wooden spoon with a coiled serpent tail for a handle. His cards were watercolors he'd made, with captions running across the top: "Flora-Girl at Work," "Where Is My Flora-Girl?" The first of a small Flora behind a giant desk, the second showing a sad mouse on the phone, looking patiently out a kitchen window. He'd drawn himself as an importuning mouse, rendering her and, before her, her mother as cats. Flora still had a yellowing card he'd made her mother when she was newly pregnant. It showed a round-bellied Rapunzel-like cat, her tail trailing out a window, the humble mouse on the ground, hat in hand. The caption read "From the Mouse Who Loved the Puce So Much He Gave Her Exactly What She Wanted."

Flora had spent Christmas Eve at Paul's apartment so she would not wake on the morning itself in her father's bed. She had called him at his office that night, having no one else to call, and he had sounded as lonely as she was, and when he arrived at her father's house to pick her up, standing there in the kitchen she had felt that if they weren't naked in minutes, she would die. She led him upstairs, though not to her father's bed, but up the back stairs to her old bed, the twin canopy, where she had lost her virginity at fifteen, her father away at a conference and her mother thinking she was staying with him—how much easier parents who did not speak had made a life of deception—and she pulled off his clothes and helped him with hers and they had fucked and she had come in moments. Afterward she was embarrassed and Paul was stunned, and it seemed better not to think too much about it. But the good thing about it was that while lying on his back he noticed she had done nothing to fix the leak, nothing, that is, but duct-tape a garbage bag over the offending area of ceiling, and he had reached for his pants and found his cell phone and called the contractor he knew and soon, right after the holidays, it would be fixed, or at least patched. No longer oozing, or molding. But a new roof would have to wait. Threads and patches would do for now.

Despite the threadbare roof, the niceness of her father's house was awkward. There Flora was, not working, never expected to show up anywhere at any given moment, and living alone in a house big enough for an upper-middle-class family of five, while Paul worked late nights to pay back his student loans and make rent on his one-bedroom in town. And there was the further awkwardness of his knowing the intimacies of her finances—knowing them perhaps better than she herself knew them. While lying post-coitally stunned and staring at the garbage bag where the ceiling should have been, he had asked her if she'd thought of selling the house. The mortgage was paid off; the local market had appreciated in recent years. "You'd make enough to buy something in the city," he said. "More than enough."

But mixing financial and sexual services seemed inadvisable.

"Let's leave, I think," she said.

And they fled with Larks to Paul's apartment, which smelled faintly but persistently of kitchen grease from the Burmese restaurant below. They ordered pizza from a new place and brought it back, and the eating was almost as brief as the fucking, as Paul was determined to get to midnight Mass.

He invited her to join him, and she laughed. When she saw that he wasn't joking, she asked, "Are you religious or something?"

"Or something?" he said.

Who was this Paul? He flinched when she described what they had just done as "fucking." Curse words, he called them, not swears.

"You like cursing, don't you?" he asked her. And maybe he was right—such words curses, sending ill will out into the cosmos like a vulgarized call to prayer.

Flora was a mutt, with generations of intermarrying Catholics and Protestants on her father's side, Catholics and Jews on her mother's. No one really knew what she was, and so she was really nothing. Being nothing, she tended to forget religion was a category for other people; that in other families the Bible was the book, that the Word meant the word of God. When she was little, she had visceral reactions to churches and synagogues, struck suddenly feverish in the midst of a family wedding or bar mitzvah. "Mom," she'd plead, "seriously, I've got to get out of here." Her mother would hand over her purse, as if boredom were the problem, and not God. Now, during pious ceremonies, Flora suffered Tourette's-like fantasies of hurling obscenities at the silent devotees—*fuck*, or even a word she hated, like *cunt*. What would they do if she did? Sometimes she imagined it so vigorously, she worried she had done it.

"I think I'll pass," she told Paul—one service in a chapel already that month more than enough for her—and she climbed into his bed and fell asleep and only woke at his return to ask, "Did you all get Jesus born?"

Either he did not reply or she was asleep again before he could.

In the morning, he made her coffee—after the sex—and brought it to her in bed. This alone seemed a solid foundation on which to build a future, though, she reminded herself, her father had brought tea and an English muffin to her mother's bedside each morning and it had proved not to be enough. Paul was driving to his father's for Christmas dinner, and this time he did not invite her to go with him. He left her a key so she could lock the door behind her, and a note alongside it that read "MERRY CHRIST-MAS?" She crossed out the "MERRY," and amended it to read "WEARY CHRISTMAS! AND A HARPY NEW YEAR!"

Alone and conscious in Paul's apartment for the first time, Flora felt urgeless—no yen to prowl through drawers or otherwise invade his privacy. A bad sign, probably. Though there were things she could see without effort. The place was orderly and ugly, conceived without thought, like his office. Had the man no taste, or simply no money, or both? For midnight Mass, he had doffed his hiking boots for black dress shoes, which now sat stiffly by the closet door, his gray slacks hovering above from a metal hanger on the doorknob.

"You look nice all dressed up," she'd told him, because he did, though it was risky to compliment anomalous behavior, implying as it did a criticism of the norm.

Being in the apartment with Paul, she'd not noticed the bareness of the place. It was willfully unfinished. Nothing on the walls—no family photographs even, or museum prints. No lamps, only the harsh glowering of overhead fixtures. What furniture he had could be taken apart into a hundred pieces, like a puzzle. What he did have were books. A tall, precarious wood-laminate shelving unit cluttered with paperbacks was the apartment's central feature. Which was the novel where the low-class man is killed by toppling books? In the bedroom, next to a stack of solved crossword puzzles (there was no bedside table), a threatening heap of periodicals—*The New Yorker, The New York Review, The New Republic,* and fat glossy journals from every conceivable southern state. Being an educated person took a lot of time, left little space for other activity. No wonder her father had resisted the Internet. He'd had no room in his life for more print, digital and ephemeral though it was. Did one read so religiously for enjoyment, or to be able to respond with a firm and knowing *yes* when asked if one had seen so-and-so's latest piece in such and such? The world small and insular, a self-perpetuating colony, with the same names springing up on tables of contents and mastheads, the cast of characters interchangeable. Of course she was an outsider, excluded from, though related to, the anointed. She often felt with the Darwinians and other, less provincial intellectuals that she was being tested, that they were poking her brain for gaps in learning, seeing if she knew what they had deemed important for her to know. She was jealous, defensive, insecure—she was Holden Caulfield railing against "phonies." Or maybe the whole literary intellectual scene really was a colossal snooze. Maybe her father had nominated her to it as an improving punishment, like doses of prune juice or Bikram yoga: *Finally, in death, I'll make my daughter smart.* Or, by choosing her over someone more qualified—someone like Paul—was he, too, testing her, assuming she'd be unable to meet the rigors of the responsibility with her lazy, flaccid brain?

She grabbed her long black coat, which had absorbed the unappetizing smell of the apartment, threw it on over her shirt and the old pair of plaid flannel pajamas she'd borrowed from Paul, put Larks's leash on, and left. The town was sealed for the holiday, windows along the common dark. On the common, the plastic, lightbulbed menorah stood beside the brown-hued manger in politically correct vulgarity. Where were the Jews? The nonbelievers? In the city, they'd be well on their way to matinees and Chinese food. She could go back to her father's house and order delivery, watch television. How cheery. Or she could drop Larks off and go to a movie—she liked seeing movies by herself. But she found she was walking in the direction of the President's House. It would be decorated like a frenzied Yuletide catalog at this time of year, wreaths and ribbons, poinsettia and holly, and a strapping, showy tree. At the annual Darwin Christmas party, Betsy, who still worked at the house, served suckling pigs that looked like pigs but had apples in their mouths and grapes for eyes, which Flora as a girl found disgusting and wonderful. Her father's half-teasing mantra to Betsy for the endless stream of college events was "Ship 'em in, ship 'em out," but Flora had loved the parties that first year, till the end, and especially the Christmas party—the crowds, the muddle of adult talk, the attention she got from being her father's daughter. One of Darwin's physicists was a near concert pianist, and at the Christmas party he played all the carols and the faculty and families gathered around to sing together. The party was a few days before Christmas, so there would still be plenty of leftovers. A funny thing about institutional living, how protected it was from change, the rules of the calendar guaranteeing a sameness from president to president. The wife (if she could be bothered) might have chosen new colors for the walls, traded out a painting here and there for others from the college museum collection, but no doubt the house looked now much as it had twenty years ago.

Flora walked up the steps through the old rhododendron bushes, Larks pulling, wanting to investigate within, as she had as a child.

"Okay, wild Larks," she whispered, and freed him from the leash. He disappeared into the branches.

Venues of childhood often appear smaller later in life, but the big house was not one of them. It had been a long time, but the house was every bit as big as she remembered. There was a car in the driveway, lights on in the kitchen, but she couldn't see anyone. She walked to the front door but stopped herself from knocking. No one used the front door. They used the side door, which led into the sunporch and the kitchen. The front door was for parties, or strangers. For guests. From where she stood, her hands cupped around her eyes, her face pressed against the window, Flora could see the Christmas tree sparkling with light, just where she remembered it standing, beside the fireplace in the west living room, the refuse of unwrapping scattered across the rug. The wife *had* repainted—the walls looked a pale blue or gray, the room brighter than it had been in her day. Maybe the family had gone out for a walk.

Once, her boss at the magazine had asked if she thought they might photograph the house for a spread on restoring historic homes. She'd said, "Believe me, you don't want to. It's hideous." And maybe it was hideous. She couldn't trust herself to know. What a strange place to live, to grow up. The house made her want to pound her fist against its callous brick. Yet it was still the definitive house for her—when someone said the word, it was what she saw. And it seemed unbelievable that she could not come and go as she pleased, that she was lurking, trespassing.

Watching, Flora became invisible. She could only see; she was only eyes. She was like one of the ghosts in the portraits in the Ghost Game she'd played with Georgia, haunting the house. She longed to go inside, to touch the fabrics, to climb the stairs, to smell the cedar linen closet, to see what had been done to her old room, and for a moment she couldn't stop herself from ringing the bell. "I've got it," a voice called, and a man appeared—the new president, the handsome Brit. He saw her and looked at first confused or worried. In her attire, her hair unbrushed, she might be taken for a demented homeless person, if homeless were a category of person that existed in Darwin. But then she could see the president recognize her, and he held up his hand in greeting, and she turned and ran away like a child, tripping over the long pajama bottoms as she hurried down the stairs.

She heard the door open and called behind her, "I'm sorry. I didn't mean to. Merry Christmas."

She ran back toward her father's house. There was nowhere else to go. Soon she was too winded to run anymore. She hunched over to catch her breath. She pulled up the sagging pajamas and tied the waist tighter. She was old. Being out of breath had once been part of daily life. God, what would the man think? She *was* a demented homeless person. Pretty lucky, as far as demented homeless people went, with better clothing and access to a shower and many more life options; but fundamentally, demented, and without a place she called home.

It was as she walked up the driveway to her father's house that she noticed the limp leash in her hand and remembered that she had left Larks behind, nosing around the presidential grounds.

"Fuck," she said. Should she call over there? Walk back? Would he get hit by a car trying to find his way to her? She stood frozen, panic rising like water poured slowly into a glass. Why wasn't there someone she could ask what to do? Why wasn't there anyone to fucking help her?

And then, as if summoned, a car turned into the driveway. The car she had seen outside the President's House, with the president driving, and Larks in the backseat. For a moment her cheeks flushed with color. But relief surpassed embarrassment.

"Larks!" she called, and she opened the back door and squatted down, and they were both so happy to see each other, Larks's whole shining body wagging—his standard greeting. This was the point of dogs—no blame, no grudges, negligible memory.

"Would you like to come back to the house?" the president asked through his unrolled window. Such an Englishman to simply not mention what had led them to this moment. "Have a look around?"

"Thank you so much. And it's so good of you to ask." She wasn't sure which to make excuses for—her behavior or her aloneness. "But I have company coming."

He nodded. "A first-rate dog," he said. "Your father had one hell of a throwing arm. Walking to the office in the mornings, I'd often see Larks bounding after a tennis ball. They made the post-presidential life look awfully good, the two of them."

"Poor Larks," she said. "Now he has to settle for my pathetic tosses."

"'I'm well out of it, my friend,' he'd say whenever I stopped to chat about the job. He defied that F. Scott Fitzgerald line on no second acts in American life, didn't he, your father? Second, and third, in his case. Always working on something new. But then, people are always quoting that line to disagree with it, to note the exception, aren't they?"

What a kind man, making her feel not a lunatic, but someone worth talking to. Had her father mentioned his newest new work, his latest act, to him? "Maybe it was he, Fitzgerald, who had no second act," Flora said. "'All theory is autobiography'—that's someone else's line, no?"

"Betsy talks of you, fondly and often."

"How's she doing? I owe her a phone call."

"Very well. Still threatening retirement and working hard as ever. I've tried to make her promise she'll stay on till my time is up, but she's not having it. She won't commit, as they say."

It was as if they were distant relatives, with enough common ground (literally) to feel they knew each other—a deceptive intimacy in making your life in the same rooms. Could she ask if his wife was miserable, if his family was on the brink of disaster? No. Not that. And anyway, he looked a happy sort. "The room at the top of the stairs," she said, "across from the chandelier—what is it now?"

"My daughter's room. Painted in stripes, these brilliant striations of color, which she fell passionately in love with. Betsy said you created that look. Sure you won't come see it?"

"Yes, thank you. And thanks so much for bringing Larks back. I can't tell you how grateful I am. And I'm sorry I've disturbed your Christmas."

"Not in the least," he said.

They held their hands up to each other in parting. She waited as he left. Watching a car pull away was a lonely sight. But at least she hadn't killed the dog today. She would order Chinese food and watch TV and cuddle on the couch with Larks, even though in her father's rules, Larks wasn't allowed on the furniture. After all, it was Christmas, and he would never know.

"C'mon, babe," she called, and he nipped at her ankles as they trotted back to the house. On the door hung a huge wreath made from delicate brown twigs with poisonous red leaves, the door aflame with color. On it a note from Cynthia: "My dear Flora—Tidings of Comfort and Joy!"

———

For the annual end-of-summer faculty party, the tipsy launching of the academic year, which Georgia attended with her parents, Flora returned to the President's House on a day other than Tuesday. Tall tents were set up in the garden, and as dusk descended, the professors stopped eating and kept drinking and the din swelled and Flora wondered what her mother was doing alone in the quiet little house down the road.

Before leaving, Flora had stuffed herself into the ugly dress her mother had bought for the inauguration a year ago now, thinking this might cheer her up, but she had seemed not to notice.

"Have a good time," she'd called from her smoky perch on the couch as Flora walked herself out.

Flora could walk the five blocks between her parents alone, though it was strange, walking in her fancy, horrid dress. People would look; people would notice. So she ran and was winded and hot by the time she arrived, like a visitor, like another of the invited guests. Betsy and Mrs. J. made a fuss over her—how pretty she looked, how nice it was to see her. As they came with the house, her father had gotten them in the divorce. Like many things, they were no longer part of daily life.

At the party, there was a woman next to her father, standing just beside him, their arms touching. "You remember Sharon, don't you?" he asked, his hand on Sharon's back. She was curly-haired and smiling, young and athletic.

"No," Flora said.

"It's so nice to see you, Flora. What a beautiful dress," Sharon cooed. Was she an idiot, or did she think Flora was an idiot?

"My mother bought it for me," Flora told her.

She went to find Georgia and the two of them went inside and upstairs, up the grand staircase, which had been such a reliable diversion, the steps they had leapt from so many times. But the big house was a stranger. Her father had left the gold room and moved back into the master bedroom. Her own bedroom had been pillaged, most of her stuff at the other place, her mother's house. What was left was the ghost of a girl's bedroom, with the FLORA and GEORGIA bunk beds and the paisley wallpaper, but the books and stuffed animals and piles of clothing all gone. No one lived there. Flora fiddled with the teal paisleys of the wallpaper, the wallpaper only she loved, but even that no longer hers. She ripped off a small piece.

"Don't do that," Georgia said. "You'll be sad later."

They next tried the third floor, but nowhere was safe. It, too, was barren, with most of the furniture brought from the city now moved into the new house. From so many feet above, the roar of grown-ups was muted as it came in through the open window. Outside the window was the fire escape.

"Let's play Annie," Flora said, though they'd stopped playing games like that a few months ago when the scientific study commenced. They were suddenly too old for such games, but still too young for everything else. "Let's escape from the orphanage."

"No, Flora, in our dresses?" Georgia was wearing a blue sundress with white buttons on the straps and red sandals with shiny buckles.

"Yes. We have to."

"I don't think it's a good idea," Georgia said. "With the party."

"I haven't forgotten about the party. But it's fine. I'll just do it without you." It was a trap. Flora knew Georgia would not let her do it alone, not now, not tonight. Georgia would never do that to her.

They took off their shoes and climbed onto the metal terrace that led to the ladder down the side of the house. The sky was dark, though warm light from the lamps below reflected out onto the grass invitingly. The metal was rough beneath their feet, the paint chipped and worn. From that perch at the top of the house, they could see above the silver outlines of the trees to more trees, and other roofs. The sky was touchable, the ground remote.

"I'll go first," Georgia said, anxious to have it over.

And she started climbing down, and Flora followed after her, and it was hard to see the black-painted metal in the dark night, and when Georgia lost her grip, Flora heard it happen and she stopped, frozen in midair.

13

Women Without Men

SHE HAD AVOIDED THIS ROOM. This room most him. This room of beloved books, this sanctuary for paper and word. Frost, Hardy, Bishop, Pound.

"Does your name have to be a word to be a poet?" she'd asked her father as a child, aware that under such stipulations her first name at least would qualify her; his would not.

All the sacred objects, the ancient talismans and abandoned artifacts. The simple gray-and-black etchings hung above the desk—reeds standing waist-high in marshes, a watering can left behind on an old stone wall. The walnut bookcases. The careful wooden boxes, the chunks of quartz used as bookends. The old record player, the old typewriter. On the desk, densely leaved dark brown pinecones he'd gathered on his walks.

In Flora's job, books had been an aesthetic enemy, stylists forcing shelves into artistic tableaux, color-coded, the monotony of spines interrupted with modish tchotchkes—a sprig of coral, an ironic bobblehead. Once, an editor had even had the inspiration to turn all the books around and make them face the wall—the wordless, neutral uniformity of backward books to her much more appealing.

It was New Year's Eve, though like all who've lived their lives to the rhythms of school, Flora felt the new year came more convincingly in September, the academic calendar trumping the Gregorian. Cold, arid, colorless—how could anything be said to begin under such conditions? Paul had invited her to a party in the city, a gathering of the Apostles. The host now edited some new, important online journal. But Flora did not want to return to the city, and the thought of mingling with Darwin alums, saying, *Yes, I'm his daughter,* and *Thank you, yes, he was,* and *Well, I'm not sure, still working things out,* was so dreadful, she had thanked him and declined. He'd seemed disappointed, though she wasn't sure why. Was Dempsey's daughter the perfect leveler to use against his spoiled friends, who, unlike him, could afford the luxury of their own bookishness? Or did he just like Flora and want to spend time with her?

Cynthia, too, had invited Flora to dinner. She had, with that embrace at the memorial, embraced a maternal role. She'd called Flora numerous times since and, when Flora answered, assaulted her with thoughtfulness: "Just checking in, want to see how you're doing." "Did you like the wreath?" "If there's anything I can do . . ." "I wanted to say what a beautiful service it was, how it so fully captured the spirit of your father." Judging her sincerity was impossible. She seemed determined to like Flora, to know Flora, in spite of Flora. Did she not resent being excluded from the ceremony, or having her plans to publish the poems dismissed? Flora had declined her dinner invitation, too, lying and saying she'd be off with Paul.

So she was alone with Larks, on the Shaker chair in her father's study, listening to the record that had been left on the turntable and eating from a defrosted container of the beef stew Mrs. J. had brought, but thinking of Cynthia, as she'd spent other nights over the years worrying how her mother was spending them. She knew her mother had never really minded being alone on major holidays or any given Saturday, but it was the idea of it, the thought that other people might find it sad, might feel sorry for her—being pitiable far worse than being lonely. Women on their own, women without men, so easy to ridicule, so easy to fear. "I've been without a husband, and I've been without work," her mother liked to tell her, "and I can tell you being without work is worse." Still, it was wrong that the former loves of Lewis Dempsey were each left to pass significant moments alone. "Your mother cured me of mar-

riage," he had told Flora long ago. But perhaps it was he who'd
been the cure for companionship.

The fact of Cynthia had a way of inspiring in Flora filial devotion, her inner literary executrix. Listening to the competing
sounds of Strauss's *Four Last Songs* and the prelude to the ball drop
coming from the television in the other room, Flora began to work.
She cleared the papers off the desk. In one stack she found a collection of Charles Darwin's letters, the date by her father's initials
suggesting it was the last book he'd read, or one of the last. Letters
from the dead. He'd loved reading letters: Keats, Virginia Woolf,
even Emily Dickinson, the bleakly garbed, marmish-haired, vir-
ginal recluse—a feverish and avid correspondent. Her father had
named his collection *In Darwin's Gardens.* For the town, yes, but not
only that. He, too, offered a reimagining of the Garden of Eden—
paradisical and rife with biology and sinning.

There was a file drawer filled with the papers of former students:
"The Role of Walking in *Jude the Obscure*"; "Hardy's Layered Time."
Had they been his favorites? Had he suspected them of plagiarism?
She did not read far enough to ascertain, but piled them into
the recycling bin. Old men had been known to die in a clutter
of papers, having stacked themselves in, maze-like, the way old
women were known to die with their harems of cats. She tossed
minutes from department meetings, catalogs from conferences,
dark-rimmed photocopies of pages from old books. The bin was
quickly filled, drawers thinned. What had he been keeping it all for?
Evidence of his former life? *I did that*, the papers said. *That, too.*
There was a sense of liberation in cleaning out one's own drawers
or closets; a sickening thrill in purging someone else's. Ruthless-
ness lacking even greater ruth.

In the last drawer, the top one—the top drawer always the one of
interest—she found her father's journal. Leather-bound, unruled,
punctuated with the occasional watercolor, the occasional quota-
tion, some of it unreadable, written fast and for himself. His journal, like the house, now hers. She skimmed for her name, for a
"Flora-Girl," or "Flo," or even an "F." Surely he would write about
his decision to name her literary executor, his decision not to men-

tion Cynthia, his decision to lie to her and tell her she was his poems' one and only reader, the one he trusted. But "Flora" appeared only once, followed by two quick mentions of "F." "Must remember to ask Flora about dinners with the Wizard—what was the name of that Japanese restaurant?" And later: "No word from F. She insists I have a message machine and yet never answers a call." And later still, after his last trip to the city: "F. looks tired and sad. Gave her the poems, but I'm afraid they will only be a burden to her."

Many more pages were devoted to Cynthia. "C.'s comments so gentle and generous—exactly what I need when I need it." And: "C.'s garden a marvel. How did I live without so long?" And, toward the end: "We took a trip to the city. C. wanted to show me the Turners. An amazing painter. Apparently an insufferable bore as a teacher, but a great artist. Didn't see anyone, kept to ourselves. The best possible weekend."

So his last trip to the city had not been his last. *Didn't see anyone, kept to ourselves. The best possible weekend.* What if she had run into them at the museum, or on the street? The thought of him avoiding her was painful. A child can avoid her parents, can deceive them and have secret love affairs, but ought not the standards for the parent be higher? More she hadn't known of him, more he hadn't told her. It was starting to seem remarkable he'd told her anything at all, that she could pick his face out in a crowd. Nice to meet you, Lewis, I'm Flora. She'd been erased from his life, she who'd thought herself so important, the perfect reader, little more than a footnote, an aside, another person to avoid. Cynthia was the perfect reader. *So gentle and generous—exactly what I need when I need it.* He could not even remember Ponzu, the setting of their original dates. *What was the name of that Japanese restaurant? F. looks tired and sad. I'm afraid they will only be a burden to her.*

How very right he was. But the burden, apparently, had been mutual. Why was she holding on so tightly to the past—to all the details and the proper nouns—when he had angled his life so firmly toward the future?

She put the journal back in its drawer. The record had stopped.

Larks was asleep. She couldn't tell whether the ball had dropped. Who knew what fucking year it was.

————

After the fact, facts recede. Details emerge blurred. No one blamed Flora. She was a child. Grown-ups should have been paying attention. Her father hadn't been paying attention. Of course, at the party there were distractions. Ray and Madeleine had been there, too, out on the lawn. But even before then. Since the separation. He hadn't noticed Flora. Hadn't seen how desperate she was to have him notice her. He should have been paying attention. The President's House had dangers—dangers he should have known.

No charges would be pressed. No lawsuits. It was an accident. But Flora knew from her mother's analysis that there were no accidents—she'd even heard her mother say that to her father: No such thing. The word itself was a fake, a lie. Flora loved Georgia. She hadn't wanted her to get hurt. But she was hurt, badly. Bones broken, insides injured. Flora, too, had internal injuries, but she wasn't in the hospital like Georgia. Flora could not imagine life without Georgia, and yet there she was, living it. Madeleine and Ray had told her parents Flora was not to visit. Georgia did not want to see her.

It wasn't her fault. If it was anyone's fault, it was her father's. Flora couldn't look him in the eye. She couldn't bear to be near him, though that night he had held her, once the paramedics had coaxed her down the fire escape to the second-floor window and wrapped her in a thick blanket, he had held her, and rocked her back and forth, and whispered over and over like an incantation, "You're fine, you're fine, my love. I'm with you. You're fine."

But now Flora was not with him, though once in town she saw her mother go to him and put her hand on his arm, the first time they'd touched in so many months, and when Flora saw that, she thought maybe it was the end of the end, that the only thing left for them was reunion. That some good could come from disaster.

Instead, her parents sent her to Dr. Berry.

The idea of forty-five minutes had never seemed so long. Flora didn't like doctors of any kind, but her mother assured her she would not have to change out of her clothes and into a nightgown that didn't close properly. She would not be weighed or measured or needled. Her glands would not be strangled, and no one would prod inside her ears or down her throat. Still, she had trouble not squirming in the office, which looked more like a living room. There were plushy, padded pastel armchairs and hard books like encyclopedias on the walls. Flora wanted to sit down on the floor, on what looked like a soft, clean rug, with big green-and-white flowers, like the outside inside. She couldn't stop herself from wanting to do a somersault.

Dr. Berry was a small woman, with dark hair cut just below her earlobes. She was about the same age as Flora's mother, and not as pretty, but looked as though she took better care of herself. Her arms strong, her teeth white. Probably she didn't smoke Marlboro reds like it was her full-time job. Probably she didn't eat chocolate and peanut butter for lunch, or for breakfast.

Flora remembered Dr. Berry observing, "You've had a pretty hard year," and thinking that maybe her parents had told her everything already and she need only agree or disagree with the doctor's assessments. Or maybe Dr. Berry just knew, without having to be told. Darwin knew, and everywhere Flora went people watched. Invitations from friends slowed, then ceased. When she was around, mothers hovered near.

From a cabinet below the bookshelves Dr. Berry extracted a box with a picture on the cover of a night sky swirling over a sleeping village.

"Is that supposed to be Darwin?" Flora asked, and then she felt stupid when Dr. Berry replied, "Vincent van Gogh. It's a famous painting." She should have known; she knew that Georgia would have known, even if she hadn't yet gotten to the letter *V.*

The sky swirled like a storm, but it was clear enough to see the moon.

"Now it's a jigsaw puzzle, too. A really hard puzzle, actually—so much blue." Dr. Berry poured the pieces out on the small table beside her and then Flora did slide off her chair and onto the rug, which was every bit as soft as she'd imagined, and over to the table. She examined the painting, and the hundreds of pieces that would add up to it.

"I love you to pieces" was what her mother said to her before bed, a phrase that, like books, had turned sinister. People said, "My life is in pieces," when things were really a mess. Her mother also said, "God breaketh not all men's hearts alike." Broken was the standard. But there were better and worse breaks, like with bones.

"Was he a lunatic—Vincent?" Flora asked. The sky in the painting was scary, mad. *Lunatic* was one of her mother's favorite words. Sometimes she used it affectionately, about Flora, when she expressed some silly worry like the one about the witness protection program: "My little lunatic." Other times she used it unaffectionately, about various Darwinians: "That man is a fucking lunatic."

Dr. Berry laughed, a big, friendly laugh. Flora liked making her laugh.

"Actually, he was. A major loon."

They set to work in silent collaboration. Surely there was talking, and still later, there'd be crying, but that first day there was the puzzle of small pieces that could be put together in only one way, and once they were, the whole could reveal something miraculous, like a storm on a clear night.

14

Lifelong Learner

THE STUDENTS WERE RETURNING TO DARWIN, rugged, fleece-clad mountaineers, their gear strapped to their backs. Steps behind, devoted parental Sherpas stooped under several months of clean laundry. Round two, the spring semester, that midyear clean slate academia offered, the chance to be disappointed and disappoint anew.

Flora had decided to audit a class: Modern Poetry, a survey course, taught by her father's archrival in the department, Sidney Carpenter. But what choice did she have? In an English department, weren't they all rivals of varying degrees? And in her role as her father's literary executor, his chosen reader, shouldn't she learn some of the things he had known by heart? (That old phrase now taking on new meaning, his own valve having proved itself so unreliable.) Yes, she should know, she should learn, for him. But that was how academia worked—what began as an act of loyalty transformed into a betrayal. You were helpless in the face of your good intentions. Not that her father had been so loyal, or trustworthy. While Flora made the arrangements with Pat Jenkins in the department, she could see Pat—the messenger, the news breaker—judging her, thinking, Some daughter she is. Or was that just the way she looked—rather stern in her dun-colored blazer and turtleneck, her short hair seal smooth, her only approximation of jewelry the plastic chain from which her glasses hung. There was something of the 1970s about her and the whole English Department. Darwin had a big endowment for a small college, but English lagged a few decades behind the rest. Paint chipped. Interoffice envelopes abounded. Paper yellowed. From down the hall, the men's bathroom menaced.

But the class was something to do, or to tell people she was doing if they asked how she was keeping busy. And Flora wanted to know more about poetry. In college, she'd avoided such classes, feeling the form somehow her father's. As if people could be said to own entire genres or disciplines. This semester, she would rent poetry and see how she liked it.

Sidney Carpenter was a few years older than her father, somewhere solidly in his seventies. He was short, with a round gut that echoed the roundness of his shiny, hairless dome of a head. Bespectacled and tweeded, and surprisingly agile as he moved to the chalkboard to jot down his office hours. Not instantly identifiable as a nemesis, at any rate. He was famous on campus for his glasses—thick-framed tortoiseshell circles tinged the slightest bit pink. The glasses most of all marked his complete liberation from Idaho. Without his glasses, Carpenter would be far less Carpenterial; he wouldn't look the part. Also without his peculiar style of speech. He spoke slowly, head tilted back, his words projecting in the direction of the ceiling. He was one of those Americans who'd turned European somewhere along the way and affected enough accent to make people wonder where exactly he'd been imported from.

The class was a lecture, the wooden rows of seats fanning out around the room, bolted to the floor and one another. It was that fan-shaped configuration that saved the seats from being pewlike, that gentle semicircle the subtle, crucial difference between college and church. Flora, at twenty-eight, did not feel ten years older than the students assembled around her—from the looks of it, mostly freshmen and sophomores. Though what age did one ever feel? "For many years I was twenty-six," her mother had told her. "Until I was well into my thirties, I was twenty-six." Twenty-six, the age at which her mother married her father, once the pinnacle of adulthood, the unreachable future, now two years behind Flora, the unreachable past. Flora looked like one of them, like a student, in her thick gray sweater and dark blue jeans, her hair pulled back in a loose bun. Better rested, but like them still. "Not a day over sixteen, my Flora-Girl," as her father would tell her, the pitch of his voice raised a note or two higher than normal, the voice he used with small children, never patronizing, only fond. But the students, if they heard her age, would begin to feel mildly sorry for her, that for whatever reason her life hadn't worked out, forcing her back in time, back to school. As an undergraduate, she and her friends had regarded the older community members who returned to the university lectures—the "lifelong learners," as they were called—uncharitably, with scorn. Now here she was, a lifelong learner herself.

One of the strangenesses of Darwin: It was defined, hourglass-like, by what passed through. Those promising young scholars, on their way to so much more. The whiteness of the room surprised Flora—both in the sense of race and in the sense of paleness. Were they all unwell? Though a few had clearly just returned from ski vacations in Aspen and the like, with those sinister and ridiculous goggle tan lines. Rich and white and young, with near-perfect SAT scores and dazzling extracurriculars: the world their world. So well-rounded, they had no edges at all. Good at everything and with no shred of personal taste that might get in the way of general excellence. And yet, that wasn't fair. You couldn't dismiss everyone you envied as an asshole, could you? You couldn't write off an entire classroom because they had the audacity to be younger than you, and higher-achieving. And Flora felt a charge being there with them; the room was charged with their eagerness, their longing to please, to succeed, to think thoughts no one had ever thought before. And there it was, floating above the hard-backed almost pews—the excitement of the first day of school. The new notebooks, the distribution of the syllabus still warm from the photocopier, the litany of titles, books you still have every intention of reading, authors who might change your life. The sense of potential, raw and pungent, like gingerroot. The room tense, and lusty. She remembered that—the cool surveying of your fellow classmates to see who you will while the long minutes away imagining you are kissing, who will become your friend, who might be smarter than you, who, thank God, stupider. The boys looked not only younger but smaller than the girls, a vaguely fetal look about many of them, their skin too thin, their nerve endings exposed. They were out-numbered, too. Growing up in her household, Flora had regarded poetry as a male profession, but judging by the class, reading poetry, at least, was a woman's game.

"A blowhard," her father had said of Sid Carpenter. "A voice like a tuba."

And he wasn't wrong. And yet there was something winning about the man, in the extremity of his professorialness, in the oper-atic tilt of his head, in his tweed jacket and pink glasses. Carpenter was telling stories, free-associating as her favorite teachers and talk-ers always did. "The best free-associator," Paul had called her father. Carpenter was handing out copies of Auden's poem on the death of Yeats.

He said: "In a censorious mode, Philip Larkin wrote a piece called 'What's Become of Wystan?' in essence arguing that post-1940 Auden wasn't worth reading. That he'd gone from a cheeky insouciance toward the past—mocking the holy trinity of Dante, Goethe, and Shakespeare with Joyce's 'Daunty, Gouty and Shopkeeper'—to being a drippy eulogizer. He claimed Auden had 'become a reader rather than a writer,' as though the two were mutually exclusive—an absurd suggestion. It won't come as a shock to any of you that we're all trying to sort out our relations with our forebears—to say nothing of our contemporaries. And more often than not, our views ripen and soften. And they should soften. Youth looks soft but is hard really."

What had been the source of her father's animosity, her father's hardness? Some well-preserved jamlike grievance—a vestige of the presidency perhaps, the fallout of one committee or another, a feud played out in the rancorous world of scholarship. Maybe he would have softened had he lived a few years longer. But her father had not lived long enough to learn to like Sidney Carpenter. They were old men by most standards, certainly by their students', but too young for death, or forgiveness. "The hairy knot of anxiety doesn't dissolve till thirty"—that was one of her father's lines, or Ira's; she couldn't now remember. But what of the hairy knot of competition, or professional jealousy? Those more fetid, mangier, and harder to untangle.

Carpenter read: " 'The words of a dead man / Are modified in the guts of the living.' " Well, fuck. That was apropos of everything. Her father still everywhere, the narcissism of loss like the narcissism of love. He did own poetry, after all.

"He's an inferior mind," she'd heard him say of Carpenter more than once.

Though Carpenter's mind seemed quite fine to Flora. He was warm; he had charm. He was self-deprecating; he was self-taught.

"An autodidact," her father had said, his voice heavy with snobbery; in anyone else he would have found the trait admirable. "With all the bizarreness and unevenness of thought that entails."

Carpenter had not been to Oxford, or even to Yale. He'd been to some small college in the West, and a state university for his Ph.D. Like Carpenter, Flora had not gone to a school like Darwin. Growing up in Darwin as she had, she could almost imagine she'd been a student there, but she hadn't the grades. Her parents had insisted if she wanted to, if she really tried, she could be a great student. She had the brain but not the will. But that was a wish on their part, or at least a guess. It was an untested hypothesis. Once, as a child, Flora said to her mother that she wished she lived in Victorian times, when there was no expectation that women would work. Her mother had looked at first indignant, then amused. "You wicked girl," she said, pulling a braid. "What a revolting thing to say." She had laughed, and Flora heard her repeat the anecdote to friends as though it were charming. Was it charming, Flora's naked lack of ambition? Or was there ambition—only to be unambitious? Was she willfully unexceptional?

People often talked about parents envying a child. But it was possible, too, to envy a parent. Her father's had been the kind of accomplishment Flora resented in people her own age. Had her father been her contemporary, she might have written him off as a summa cum laude asshole. A golden boy, whose hair had at one time actually been rather golden. Perhaps Carpenter had resented him on similar grounds. Flora had friends from college who were now architects. She saw them only if they hosted parties attended largely by other architects. She had friends who were artists and hung out with other "creative" people who "made art." No one she knew in her generation was doing anything to make the world better—she leading the charge of helping nobody. The one doctor she knew was a dermatologist, saving humanity from the indignity of acne, one adolescent at a time. But maybe she just knew the wrong people.

Carpenter told the class a story against himself of "discovering Auden" at a used-book store in his college town, a battered, early volume, thinking he'd happened upon some unknown, unappreciated genius, as he'd never heard the name.

"None of you would make that mistake," he said. "But oh, the things I did not know." He shook his head, his expression between embarrassment and awe. "What is the saying—'It could fill a book'? And then some. A bookstore, I suppose, in my case. Though I was not entirely wrong—he was undiscovered, at least by me. Every reader has to discover the writers who move him or her most, and in those discoveries we make the writer new again. Every silent revelation, every moment of recognition that takes place on the page between reader and writer is a renewal and a rebirth. You have all that still ahead of you." He paused and looked theatrically around the room. "I do not mean to say there was no Auden before I 'discovered' him. And yet. If you are hoping to engage in postcolonialist examinations of the word *discovery,* or any other word, for that matter, I'm afraid you've come to the wrong place. If theory is what you're after—poststructuralist, deconstructionist (why so many building metaphors, have critics suddenly become engineers?)—if you are in the market for Marxist or Lacanian interpretations or any kind of 'critical lens,' please, go down the hall to Professor Das's seminar. She will be delighted to have you. What we will be doing in here is simply reading. Some call it *close reading,* a term I must say has always struck me as redundant and boorish—as if there could be any other kind. How does one read without attending closely to the words on the page? Not very fashionable these days, I'm afraid. New Criticism is, of course, anything but."

He filled the time allotted, the full seventy-five minutes—something her father would never have dreamt of doing on the first day—reading aloud for long stretches, rocking back on his heels as though the force of the words might tip him right over, his passion so much at odds with the apathy of his audience—spacey mouth breathers, twitchy watch checkers, bemused text messagers asserting their opposable-thumbness. But the performer seemed unaware of the ingratitude displayed before him—there it was, the revelation between reader and writer, the pure appreciation of craft, of word, of gift. The poems of old men undid him. At one point, his eyes watered and he had to remove his glasses to wipe the tears away on his sleeve. Was there anyone in Carpenter's life, anyone living and present, about whom he felt this way, or anything near to it? Was that the burden readers faced—beyond the world of print, no one quite measured up?

We readily accepted that there were no perfect fathers or daughters or lovers. But we persisted in thinking history might give a writer in the fullness of time a perfect reader; or, on the other side, the scholar's fantasy that he could understand, see, know a book, a poem, as all others had failed to see before. We saw so little, so wrongly, with the people in front of us, and yet with words on a page, we fooled ourselves that we could get it right. If Flora knew anyone, it was her parents. She had studied them in that academic way children learn their parents. She was the world's living expert on her father. Ready with the footnotes, a thoroughly cross-referenced index: the boarding school years, the Yale years, the Rhodes years, the city interlude, and the Darwin recapitulation and coda. And yet, did such scrutiny and research make her his perfect reader? Looking closely did not mean seeing truly. In fact, it might mean reading wrongly—magnifying glasses distort—everything writ large. And then there was all she did not know, all he'd kept from her. How little she had factored in. She, his own daughter. Barely a footnote in his journal.

At the end of class, Flora waited till the last backpacks had floated out the door, then approached the professor, a nervousness in her stomach, as if she were a real student. "I wanted to introduce myself, or reintroduce myself," she said. "I'm Flora Dempsey."

"Of course you are!" Carpenter rocked back on his heels, pointing his chin upward, a wolf baying at the moon. "How lovely to see you. Pat mentioned you'd be sitting in on the class. You look very well."

"Thank you."

"I remember seeing you walking across the campus with your father when you were as tall as this desk," he said, laying his hand upon the desk and leaning against it. He smiled at the memory, as if it were special. "Are you thinking of following in your father's footsteps? Does academe lie lurking in your future?"

"No," she said quickly. "Not for me. No, I don't think so. The class just sounded interesting."

"'Interesting'? I don't recall what you've been doing to keep yourself busy—you graduated more than a few years ago, if I'm not mistaken."

"I've been working. In the city. At a magazine."

"Ah, a journalist!" Everything he said implied an exclamation point.

"That's rather a grandiose term for what I was. It was a magazine for the home and garden."

"I've always admired the domestic arts," Carpenter said. Was he trying to make her feel bad or better? "I'm a disastrous housekeeper myself. Can never find a thing."

"It's not really about housekeeping—the magazine," Flora couldn't help saying. "More about design, style, a holistic approach to living."

"Of course."

"But I've left my job, and I'm not sure what comes next. But no, no graduate school for me. I don't think so."

"You know, I was reading something about you."

"About me? Or my father?"

"No, no, I did not misspeak. About you. Well, both of you. That he was working on a great new project before the end. And that you have been named his literary executor and hold the reins." Carpenter had the faded eyes of the old, an eerily translucent liquid blue that lit up greedily as he announced this information. He was a beaming, radiant nemesis. "The scholarly world now awaits your next move!"

"Did Cynthia Reynolds say something to you?" She could see his interest stirred.

"No, I've not spoken about the matter with Ms. Reynolds."

"Where did you say you read this?" Had Cynthia's editor friend told someone?

"Some online journal, I think. Don't look so surprised, my dear. I am well aware of the Internet, and perfectly capable of browsing the latest literary gossip. An odd verb choice—*browsing*. Suggests all research is basically shopping, no?"

"Did they mention what he was working on?"

"Well, Ms. Dempsey, I'm sure you know more about it than I. A far cry from your material at the magazine, hmm?"

The snobbery stung.

"They just said he was moving in a new direction," Carpenter crowed. "I'd be curious to read Lewis Dempsey's new material, certainly. Always intriguing when the critic is bold enough to face a jury of his peers."

"I'm afraid I have to run. But I'm really so looking forward to this semester." Flora gestured to the syllabus in her hand, speaking with exaggerated warmth, as one does when lying. She shook Carpenter's hand, and escaped the cloister of the classroom. She ran across the quad to the Cross Library. At the computer, she typed "Flora Dempsey poems publication," feeling self-conscious, as one does when researching oneself—the feeling not unlike that of being caught in the act of examining one's own reflection. Nothing. She tried "Lewis Dempsey poems" and "Lewis Dempsey literary executor" and "Dempsey Darwin death poetry." A photograph of her father from his inauguration appeared and with it an archived article from Darwin's alumni magazine that described a small child— her—running out and hugging her father as he led the processional into the gymnasium. She hadn't remembered doing that. But she could not find the story of his new material, of literary anticipation. Was it possible Carpenter had invented it? But then, how would he know of the new project in the first place?

Another story came to her—one her father had told her about Sidney Carpenter. He'd been so disgruntled with the college a few years back that he'd become a Deep Throat for *The Darwin Witness,* the student newspaper, leaking bits of administrative gossip to the reporters, enumerating the excruciating minutiae of the endless faculty meetings, telling them who exactly had been the dissenting vote at some beloved associate professor's tenure decision. How had a man who so loved words, a man so enamored of the subject of his work, come to feel such an equally exquisite loathing for the institution that supported his devotion? What was wrong with this place—this corrosive, embittering bastion of enlightenment?

Flora counted and dreaded down the days to fourth grade. The counting made it come quicker, and the dread. School resuming—the ostensible, official return to normal life. But Georgia would not be there. Georgia was home from the hospital but still in bed. Flora pictured her in her purple room plastered into a full-body cast covered in marker—loving notes of encouragement, none from her. Almost everyone from school had visited Georgia—everyone but Flora. The class made her a giant "Get Well Soon" card, and while the other girls scrawled how terribly they missed her, Flora simply signed her name, "FLORA," as if they hardly knew each other.

Flora loved her new teacher, Kate, who was slow to smile, but when she did, when you made her, it made you feel important. Flora's life was thickly populated by adults now—Kate, her mother, and occasionally her father, Betsy, who picked her up from school some days and brought her back to her mother's house, and Dr. Berry. Even Robert Frost and Emily Dickinson—in class they were studying poetry—were grown-ups, and the author of that year's play, too, Shakespeare. The play was *Macbeth,* or at least *Macbeth's* greatest hits: the witches boiling and toiling, Lady Macbeth out, outing, and Flora, as Macbeth himself, performing the soliloquy of "Tomorrow and tomorrow and tomorrow." Was Kate being nice to her in assigning her the role, or trying to keep her busy, or was the consensus that she, of all the nine-year-olds, could most relate to the material? Of course you couldn't call it *Macbeth* anywhere near the stage. You called it "the Scottish play." If you called it *Macbeth,* bad things might happen. Everyone was very strict about it, especially Sarah Feldman, the tallest, prissiest girl in their grade.

"It doesn't work that way. A word can't control the universe," Flora told her.

"Just don't say it, okay?" Sarah said, as though trying to be patient.

There was no Georgia, but there was a new student in Flora's class, a boy named Ezekiel. No nicknames, only Ezekiel. He was the only black student in their class of eighteen. He was not as smart as Georgia, but then, no one was. But he was very smart and had lived in England and, before that, Nigeria, and he had a wonderful accent that made everything sound surprising. He played Banquo, and Banquo's ghost, to Flora's Macbeth.

In the evenings, her mother helped her memorize her lines, Flora reading them again and again and again, and then reciting them as her mother, patiently at first, then less so, read along. "And all our yesterdays have lighted fools the way to dusty death." Why was death dusty? Flora didn't like that part. "Do I have to say that?" she asked.

"Yes," her mother said. "That's the whole point. He wrote it, you speak it. You don't get to write it, too."

"I don't think I want to be an actress," Flora observed. Though she still liked sneaking through her mother's things, and trying on her life. She still liked spying in other people's windows, and drawers, though now she did it alone. But she drew the line at other people's words.

At the performance, Flora tried not to look at her father, but it was impossible not to look at him. He had come in as the show was beginning and stood off to the side, leaning against the wall in his tan suit, his tie off. She thought she could see his eyes watering; he looked the way he did when he listened to music he loved. When she got through to the end of the soliloquy without making a mistake, he let out a strong "Yes" and clapped, loudly and slowly, and then Flora's eyes watered, too.

"*Macbeth, Macbeth, Macbeth,*" she whispered as she walked offstage.

No one in school said an unkind word to Flora. The girls in her class simply withdrew from her and banded together around Sarah Feldman. They seemed to like one another more than they once had. Mistrust of Flora united them. Over lunch, they talked loudly about Georgia, how brave she was, how she itched under her cast, how they loved to feed her gerbils for her. One day, they all came to school wearing skirts, a perfectly synchronized fashion attack, Flora the only girl in shorts. Flora noticed but hoped no one else would—acknowledgment worse than the thing itself. But Kate did notice, and she pulled Flora aside and apologized. She said she'd talked to the girls about excluding people, and it wouldn't happen again. Flora wondered if they'd been sent to the headmaster, as she and Georgia had, if many girls had faced what had once been their groundbreaking punishment.

"It doesn't matter," Flora told Kate, though she cried to her mother that night and begged her to let them move. Her mother had hated Darwin before, and now she refused to leave. But from then on, she referred to Sarah Feldman as "that little bitch."

The next day, Flora went to school with safety pins in the holes in her ears, where earrings used to be. She looked like her mom with purple hair. Her ears said other people didn't matter. At lunch, Kate pulled her aside again and asked her to take them out.

"They look like you're trying to hurt yourself," she said.

"I'm not," Flora said. "They don't hurt at all."

Ezekiel did not try to befriend Flora, though they were the only two to sit alone at lunch. He seemed not to need friends, and this made Flora want to know him more. How did one do that, not need company? Flora watched him and he didn't notice her. Like Flora in the beginning, he had a hard time calling the teachers by their first names. Instead, he called them "Excuse me." His posture

was impeccable, his neck a foot long. Every day he wore a knit vest
over a pressed white shirt, as though the school had a uniform,
which it didn't, which was one of the best things about the school.

"Why do you dress like that?" she asked him. "You don't have to,
you know. T-shirts are fine here."

He didn't answer, denying her even his accent.

Flora asked him, "Which do you like better, Africa or England?"

He was silent, and Flora couldn't tell if he was thinking or ignoring her.

"I've been to England," she told him, because her family had
once, a few summers back, gone to London and stayed in a flat
where the living room walls were painted black, which her mother
found lugubrious, Flora glamorous. Her father had taken her to
Laura Ashley immediately upon their arrival from the airport to
buy a white petticoated dress with a scarlet pinafore; the perfect
outfit, what Laura Ingalls would call her "Sunday best," her "finery," as her father called it. "I like the punks on the King's Road,"
she said.

Ezekiel said, "Africa is a continent. England is a country. You
can't compare them."

"I know that," she snapped. They hadn't studied Africa yet—that
was fifth grade—but she wasn't an idiot. "I'm not asking you to
compare them. I'm asking for your opinion, which you like more."

But he had no opinions, or none he was willing to share.

Finally, one day weeks into school, she trapped him in the cargo
net at recess and asked what she'd wanted to ask, what she'd suspected all along. "Was your family happier before you moved here,
before you came to Darwin?"

"No," he said without a glimmer of doubt. "We are happier now.
We are very lucky to live in Darwin. Darwin is an ideal place to
grow up."

That finished Ezekiel for Flora. There was nothing she could
learn from him.

15

New Routines

THE WINDOWS OF THE SPOTTED SALAMANDER, the bakery in town, had been painted in frosty shades of white by local schoolchildren with snowmen and snowflakes, sleighs and secular stars. Two decades ago, Flora had been one of them. The Spotted Salamander was so named in honor of Darwin's Springtime Salamander Crossing, an event in which roads in town were blocked off to make way for the amphibians' annual migration to their mating grounds. Though not actually grounds—they mated in pools of water, a fact that Flora and Georgia had, with the silly prurience of youth, found endlessly amusing, conjuring as it did steaming hot tubs and salamanders with towels around the waist. A movement had long been afoot in Darwin to dig little tunnels along the salamanders' desired route to provide them even safer passage. How the Darwinians cherished the lower members of the animal kingdom.

Flora was becoming a Spotted Salamander regular, having decided she needed new routines for the new year, or at least some semblance of routine, period, and her breakfasts there were not unlike the old Tuesday-night dinners at the unmemorable Ponzu in their neat, formulaic construction—though lonelier—and this time currant scones and overpriced coffees in large saucerless mugs instead of scorched shrimp, cold soda, and plum wine, the college kid behind the counter flirting with her, stamping her free-coffee card extravagantly, winkingly, six times for every one so that every other week hers would be on the house—the cheap perks of monotony. Though today she was not alone.

She had called Cynthia and suggested they meet. Cynthia was the star of her father's journals—the "gentle and generous" C., C. the "marvel." Cynthia possessed the poems, had what appeared to be the original manuscript. She had an inscription, a dedication, a claim. She had an interested editor. Cynthia would not disappear, move across the country, or die anytime soon. But Flora was the executor; her father had left her in charge. If he had lived longer, perhaps all that would have changed, but he hadn't. If mutual adoration was unlikely, perhaps a bland apathy could be achieved, an enduring emotional stalemate arrived at in the place of mutual understanding.

"I was *so* happy that you called, Flora," Cynthia said, emphasizing the emphatic word *so* to the point that Flora pictured it as she had written it in letters as a child with a long string of *o*'s. "I was so hoping this moment would come, when you would be ready to sit down and talk about your father's work. I'm so glad it's here."

"Yes, me too," Flora said.

"Do you have a favorite?" Cynthia homed. "My favorite is always changing. I'm always discovering some new miracle in his words."

"Hmmm, yes," Flora answered, vagueness her only weapon against Cynthia's enthusiasms. She admired her scone. "I know what you mean." But Flora did have a favorite, the one she returned to, trying to make sense of it, the one that stood out from the others as a work not of self-reflection or narcissistic adoration, but of imagination and empathy, that on her first night of reading she'd put aside to think about later, the one poem she felt sure Cynthia would never mention, but which Flora could now recite: the one called "The Wizard."

"How would you describe his style?" Cynthia asked.

"What a good question," Flora said, looking deeply into her paper napkin.

"Lyrical, certainly. Scholarly, steeped in the English tradition," Cynthia offered. The bakery was overheated, but she wore a long knit scarf coiled around her, this one an orgy of magentas—too many days in gardens had chilled her blood.

"Umm," Flora said. "Yes."

"But how would you put it?"

"I was surprised by them, I think."

"Really? I think of them as being so entirely, so fully him."

"I wasn't expecting them to be so . . . so steamy."

"Oh." Cynthia smiled more to herself than at Flora. "Some of them are steamy."

"I guess you never expect to gain access to your father's erotic mind in that way."

"No, you don't," Cynthia said. "I hadn't thought of that."

Flora watched as Cynthia considered this new perspective, her perspective. The moment didn't last long.

"But they were also richer than I expected them to be," Flora went on, the sudden lift, the pleasure in talking about him. "His writing, it's musical—or, more specifically, it strikes me as choral, with many voices singing different parts. He used to listen to this ancient choral music. I forget the composer and the exact era, but it had forty-seven different parts or something, dozens of singers singing in their own voices, each part small, but the cumulative effect huge, grand. His work reminds me of that. He was so good at voices—literally, at creating different voices. He was a good mimic. There was a famous family story of him reading *The Wind in the Willows* to my mother early in their courtship and doing all the voices." Flora looked to see how this news was received, but Cynthia, a great nodder, was nodding at almost every word Flora said. What was that, agreement? "When I read the poems, I can see him hearing them, if that makes sense. The writing is more aural than visual. Meant to be engaged with the ear and not the eye."

"We must host a reading of them!" Cynthia burst out, as though the nods had propelled the words from deep within her.

Flora had shared too much. Stupidly, she'd told Cynthia what she thought. Her brief openness an error. The call had been a bad idea. The thing to do was toss the phone in the trash, to send it off to the landfill with its brother the answering machine.

Cynthia pushed: "I was just so taken with what you were saying, with the rightness of it. It made me want to hear them aloud. Wouldn't that be lovely?"

The point was not to hear other voices reading them, but to hear *his*. Reading the poems to herself, alone in the house, Flora heard his voice. The poems were hers. They made her squirm, they made her mad, but they were *hers*. What would Cynthia do, distribute the manuscript to everyone in town? Perhaps she already had. She'd admitted to sending some pages to the editor. Likely, there were multiple copies afloat. She was handing them out on street corners. "Here, take them, take them," she'd call out, her head bobbing like a buoy in agreement with herself. "Read these exquisite poems all about me!"

"It might be something to think about, Flora. We could get a group of his friends and colleagues—Ira, and a few others from Darwin's English Department, and maybe Wood would come down—and they could each read one, perhaps they could each even choose the one they wanted to read. Oh, it would be wonderful."

"He was so private about them. Do you think he'd really want that?"

"I think so. Don't you? Something to consider—a precursor to publication. Whet the public appetite! A wonderful idea," Cynthia said, as if Flora had come up with it.

"Maybe at some point. But not now, I don't think." A precursor to publication? How many different ways would she have to say no to this woman? Her indefatigability was irritating. Her hopefulness refused crushing.

"What's the story with Paul?" Cynthia asked, a tactical change of subject. "How was New Year's Eve? Is it love?"

That seemed so like Cynthia, making a good thing seem less so by introducing the one thing it was definitely not.

"No, it's not love," Flora said. "Less than love, more than lust."

"What a wonderful title for a country song." Cynthia repeated Flora's words back to her in a smoky twang.

That was annoying, too. Just as Flora succeeded in disliking her, Cynthia insisted on making herself likable. "A possible profession. Maybe I'll look into that—country music," Flora said.

"You're not interested in going back to the magazine?"

"I just sort of ended up there. I was interested in houses, in rooms, in the way things looked. Working with words was the only way to make my parents not think it too frivolous."

"Don't you think your father wanted you to do what you wanted, no matter what?"

"I mean, they wouldn't be wrong. It is frivolous. My father cared about books, my mother cared about justice. They wanted me to care about something beyond rooms."

"Oh, I don't know. What's so bad about frivolous? Anyway, I'm not sure it is. What could be more important to our daily lives than rooms? Think of Virginia Woolf's great book on women writers—no small emphasis put on rooms there. And caring about the way things look or sound—paintings, gardens, furniture, sentences—it's all aesthetics when you get down to it. Prettiness is an oft-slighted virtue, but why?"

"Did you ever want to be something else? A painter, or an artist of some sort?"

"Oh, you mean like your father's wanting to be a poet? Your father was always a poet—that's what he naturally was, and what he should have been in the world all along. I'm just grateful he found out before it was too late." A silence as Cynthia looked away. Flora felt like an exhausted mother with her newborn, or how she imagined that felt—the constant anxiety that this strange creature before her was going to dissolve into hysterics. "But no, for me, not at all. No hidden easels in my house. No works on paper tucked away in a drawer. You know, so many academics, so many of my colleagues, have this defensive posture toward their work—apologetic, almost hostile to their own research—in response, I suppose, to all the malicious maxims of the 'Those who can't, teach' variety. It's such a derisive profession—the derision directed both inside and out. But I never felt that particular worry. I've always believed that the interpretive and analytical arts are just that—arts—and every bit as rich as the generative ones. At root, it's all about seeing differently, about looking at the world in a new way, finding something no one else has quite struck upon before—noticing."

A man who used to notice—the Hardy poem Ira read.

"The poems, my father's poems," Flora said. She wanted to

make Cynthia see her way of looking. "They're so personal. If there was a reading, or some other public forum, they could make everyone close to him feel . . . exposed. I don't know, maybe it would be different or easier if they were paintings. Something other than poems."

"But what about poor Madame X, who had her reputation ruined by Sargent's famous painting? It's not only the written word that can expose or impugn. Artists often make people uncomfortable, but is that the worst thing in the world?"

"Not for the artist."

Cynthia laughed. "Your father and I had conversations of this sort all the time, about the responsibility of the artist, and that of the audience. I'd never known anyone to have such a strong sense of the role of the reader, or viewer. For him, observing was not at all a passive act. He felt one could read rightly only if one read selflessly, he saw true reading as a selfless act. He hated the book clubification of American culture—even if it meant more people reading. The 'What in your own life does this remind you of?' approach to books appalled him. 'Method reading,' he called it. But then, you know all this from *Reader as Understander.*"

It didn't seem the moment to mention she'd never read his famous book. It was Flora's turn to turn the talk. "How was it, again, you two got to know each other?"

Cynthia smiled warmly, her eyes squinting as if she could watch the memory play out before her. "Through Turner and Hardy, really. They were our matchmakers, for which I'll be eternally grateful. We'd known each other for years, in passing, as one does on a small campus, and liked and respected each other. But it was when your father was organizing the biannual Hardy at Darwin conference and he wanted someone to lecture on Turner, Hardy's favorite artist, and I was already at work on the book. So he called on me. Our research had brought us to the same place at more or less the same time—looking at the English landscape in the nineteenth century—but we came at it from different angles. 'Different fields, same farm,' we used to say. We immediately had so much to talk about. We could talk for hours. I'd never felt I had so much to say and so much I wanted to hear from anyone ever before in my life. In our early conversations, I always left thinking, Oh, but we've only just begun!"

There was the royal *we,* the editorial *we,* and, here, the exclusive *we,* suggesting Cynthia and her father were one, not two, a collective, two hearts that beat as one, one is the loneliest number. Had Flora ever had that kind of bond with anyone? Since Georgia? But it was false, such unity a fantasy, wasn't it? Once Cynthia was off on the tales of their incomparable we-dom, she could not be stopped. *Relish,* that was the word. She didn't seem to notice much, but she *relished* things. In her, Lewis Dempsey had found a rare thing to his breed—their breed—someone who loved life, who was good at it. She did not have to live in opposition to her moods, or in spite of them; no, her temperament allowed, abetted, encouraged life. She was hungry for it. As Flora listened to the stories of truly startling like-mindedness, and learned, through Cynthia, of this new, other father, she comforted herself by imagining she was pulling ever so gently on the two separate ends of Cynthia's long magenta scarf.

"The poems helped, too, of course," Cynthia added, circling back, winding down. "He wooed me with some of those poems. Not that I needed wooing. I fell for him fast."

He had wooed her with his poems; she'd known of them for over a year.

"By the way," Cynthia said. "I brought along this card. It's the editor I mentioned, Bill Curtis, his contact information. I haven't heard from him in a while, so it might be worth reaching out. I'm not pushing, Flora. But in case you change your mind, or decide you want another opinion."

Not pushing, no. She slid the card across the table.

———

Tuesdays had ceased to be Tuesdays. Her mother had stopped going to the city and so Flora had stopped staying at the President's House with her father. Or was it the other way around? Flora couldn't go back to the house and everyone knew without her saying. It was like the house had disappeared from her life along with Georgia. Except it hadn't disappeared, and her father still had to live in it, and be alone in it every night. Or maybe he wasn't alone. And her mother wasn't alone, either. She'd made new friends and now had dinner parties to host or attend at least twice a week. Maybe she'd been right about the loneliness of being the boss's wife, or maybe she had made it so.

Her mother was daily life, her primary parent; her father a supporting staff member brought in for special events. He didn't make the rules or know when she broke them. Flora was a messenger. "Will you tell your father I really need him to sign those papers?" "Will you give this check to your mother?" "Do you know if he's finalized his holiday plans? It would be nice if I could make some of my own." "She needs to change the addresses on her accounts—her bills keep coming here."

As a replacement for Tuesdays at Ponzu, she and her father started taking weekly Sunday-afternoon walks in the changing autumn leaves of the Bird Sanctuary. A path in the woods, nothing remarkable about it, just the usual Darwinian fare when it came to birds—jays and chickadees, cardinals and the occasional goldfinch. The walks were quiet, Flora sullen, her father wedging questions under the tight lid of her withholding. Never important questions, they talked around it, talked about the horseback-riding lessons Flora was taking, lots of questions about horses: Did she prefer palomino or pinto? How were they groomed? What did they eat? How high could she jump? Horseback riding was one thing her parents had promised she could do when they first moved to Darwin, and now she was doing it. She was going to do it with Georgia, but now she did it alone. But what her father did not know, because she didn't tell him and her mother didn't speak to him, was that though Flora went to the stable every week, and went to the tack room to retrieve the saddle and bridle, and led her horse, Sandy, from the pasture in his halter, and learned to groom him with the hoof pick and the currycomb, and was taught where to place the saddle pad on his haunches and how to tighten the girth and to coax the bit into his mouth with her fingers, she never rode. During class she stood outside the ring, leaning into the white wooden fence, which left imprints on her skinny arms, and she watched. No amount of coaxing by her mother or Tim, who owned the farm, could convince her to get on the horse. Tim even offered her mother her money back, but Flora liked being there; she didn't care what the other girls thought, or not that much.

"You look sad, Flora-Girl," her father told her, the stupidest possible thing to say.

"That's the way I look."

"You should be nice to yourself. Be nice to yourself, Flora-Girl."

Was her father being nice to himself? Perhaps too nice. Perhaps it was he who should be *less* nice, less forgiving of himself. He was studying trees, learning all the names, and he loved to touch the leaves, and smell them, and feel the bark—"See how smooth the old beech is? No wrinkles to speak of"—and try to make her guess how old a given tree was, and tell her how one knew a fallen maple leaf from an oak—"Look how much narrower the oak is, as if the fat maple leaf had been stretched on a rack"—stretching his face long and making a funny noise. Flora didn't laugh. Trees were trees, weren't they? Shady, buggy, sticky with sap; good for climbing or not, terrifying or vulnerable. Their walks were boring.

"Sometimes," Dr. Berry told her, "boredom is a mask for other, less comfortable feelings."

But Flora saw nothing comfortable in boredom. She was often bored in the new house, her new bedroom (itself a telling anagram for boredom), with no paisley wallpaper, and instead painted a purple she had matched to Georgia's bedroom walls so they could pretend they were in the same room even when they weren't; bored to the point of death. Boredom was a kind of murder. If she died, her parents could be held responsible. So Flora went on the walk every week, never told him no, she didn't want to go, and she passed messages between her parents like a spy, or a carrier pigeon, and their new routine carried them along, and she could only imagine her father found their outings as miserable as she did, but they never mentioned it.

16

Visitations

WEEKENDS THAT WINTER, Flora stayed at Paul's, stuffing her schoolbag with underwear, her toothbrush, a fresh shirt or two, another pair of shoes, maybe. It reminded her of packing for her father's after the divorce, as though Paul and her father's house now shared custody of her. One never had the right things. Something critical always left behind. Larks went, too, though you could tell he was reluctant to be so long away from his post by the kitchen window—what if *he* came home, after all this time, and Larks wasn't there to greet him? But Larks had little choice in the matter.

Weekdays, Flora spent alone. Paul worked long hours, and she had grown to like her time on her own in her father's house. She now knew the creaks and moans. She'd become expert at building fires and preparing simple, tasty meals for one, which she'd never mastered living in the city, that mecca of plastic and delivery. Fried eggs, sole sustenance of the fall, no longer sufficed. She made stir-fries and soups, salads and the occasional fillet. She spent her evenings reading before the fire on the gold chair, or in the study on the Shaker chair, reading her way across her father's bookshelves, retracing the silences of his life. How many hours had he spent alone here with Thomas Hardy or Philip Larkin? More than he had with her—his fellow poets a more reliable presence in his life than his own blood. Flora learned she loved Elizabeth Bishop—the poems, the paintings, the letters, the stories; she learned to love the wicked grimness of Larkin. Hardy, though, she couldn't quite get— why the great appeal? Hardy was still his.

In spite of the weekend visitations, Cynthia's question remained: What *was* the story with Paul? Something more serious between them had seemed to begin with the new year, when he was away in the city visiting the Apostles and his sister. He had called to tell her she was on his mind—but which part of her exactly? And in what capacity? The vagueness of his endearments left too much room for invention, and doubt. But what did she want from him anyway? She barely knew him. Flora hated people who said things like "I met him and I just knew." Maybe some days you just knew you'd want him forever; other days you just knew what a colossal schmuck he'd turn out to be.

A few times they went out to dinner and to the movies at the desultory, popcorn-grimed art-house cinema in town, but mostly they stayed in bed, ordering food from the Burmese place downstairs—green-tea noodles and mango salads. Was this to save money, or to stave off the public humiliation of being caught together, or was it simply hard to beat the pairing of sex and Burmese food? Flora wasn't sure. But it contributed to the unreality of their relationship—if that's what it was—as if it were a play staged weekly in Paul's apartment, in which they were both actors and audience.

Flora slept better the nights she slept in her father's bed, but there was still the awkwardness of the house's niceness, and after that first time she never invited Paul back. But Paul did not sleep well in his own bed, either—a double bed his feet hung off of, a lumpen futon couch rendered perpetually prostrate. One night she woke and found him in the other room, with a book in his hands, a finished crossword puzzle in his lap, his eyes strained and tired in the weak overhead light.

"What's keeping you up?" she asked him, and he smiled as though she'd made a raunchy joke, but then looked suddenly serious.

"Waiting for the phone to ring," he said. "Waiting for my dad."

And she climbed onto the chair with him, the crossword puzzle crinkling beneath her, and kissed him. Kissing Paul was one of life's great pleasures. They could kiss for hours; they were

Olympian kissers. When they kissed, what was happening between them made sense.

His sleeplessness made sense, too, when later the phone did ring, waking them both, the bartender from the pub where Paul had worked years before asking him to come pick up his father and take him home. Flora could hear his voice through the phone. Paul's father was in no condition to drive, in no condition to be alone.

"Yup" was all Paul said, and he threw on his clothes without switching on the light—an expert.

"Do you want me to come with you?" Flora asked him.

He left without answering.

In the grayness of the early morning when he returned, she could feel the sharp prod of his resentment against her skin, his silent accusations as he slid into bed beside her, his long body rigid, forbidding. Why did she not have a job? Was all she'd done that week read and take the dog for walks?

"What are you thinking?" she asked him, hoping he would tell her he was thinking about breakfast or some such mundanity, but he said, "Your dad."

He could not understand her secrecy. Why did she want no one to know of the poems? Why wait? If there was an editor, if Cynthia had already done the work of finding him, and he was smart enough and legit and willing to pay money to bring her father's work to the literary world, why say no?

"Isn't it nearly impossible to sell a collection of poems?" he asked rhetorically.

He pressed: "What do the poems reveal? What makes them so awful?"

And he was further baffled when she assured him that they revealed little beyond the way her father had felt about his own life. No lifelong habit of closeted relations with male students. No presidential embezzlement of college funds. No Internet pornography ring. No extramarital shenanigans. It would almost be easier if they did contain some shocking revelation, some specific humiliation she could point to and say, *There, see that? That's why.*

Paul didn't ask directly if he could read them, but wondered aloud whether it was useful to have multiple readers—readers who could be more objective. He mentioned the fellowship he had received from Princeton but could not accept, and referred again to his friend the Apostle with the online journal, who would jump at the chance to get his hands on the Dempsey poems.

"You didn't say anything, did you?" she asked him.

"No, of course not," he said.

She didn't like the bragging, the name-dropping, the eagerness. Why was everyone so fucking eager, everyone she'd inherited from her father—Larks, Cynthia, Paul, and Carpenter—rendered droolsome, slavering, and toothy at the thought of all that was Lewis Dempsey. Like predators to bones. Obsequious piranhas.

"How's your father doing?" she asked, anticipating rightly it would be the end of any conversation between them.

As winters went, this one turned strange, with stretches of days of sun and balm, days of sweaters and no jackets. The months were mixed up—February a lamb—and Flora let Paul convince her to buy a bicycle. And so they left the black-box theater of his apartment and went to the cluttered local shop where her parents had bought her bikes as a child. She bought an old white Peugeot that made her feel old-fashioned, and she bought a dark brown basket that hooked to the handlebars with leather straps, its very own purse. It was the first item she'd bought for herself in months; life in Darwin, if nothing else, cheap. But when Paul suggested they go for a ride, Flora resisted. Weren't Saturdays for pajamas? Or matinees? Once out on her graceful bike, though, the whirring of the wheels below, and the eerily springlike smell in the air, she forgot her sluggishness; she was in the world entirely. The riding brought her back. She had loved biking when she was little, the speed and smoothness, the freedom from adults. She'd taken a pride in her bicycles as physical objects, as certain grown-ups love their cars, and had mourned the passing of each one she outgrew, first the tiny aqua-and-white one, the one she learned on, then the tough-looking quasi mountain bike with its black Velcroed padding on all the bars.

The Darwin bike path—an endless tongue of asphalt lapping up the countryside—ran along the old railroad tracks beside the Bird

Sanctuary, where Flora used to walk with her father. No self-respecting New England town was without one. It had been laid back when she was in high school, and such projects had come into vogue, bourgeois recreation covering up outdated industry. At the time, the transformation of the tracks had seemed a grave improvement, the best spot in town for chain-smoking remade into a place for healthy adult fitness and play. But now it comforted Flora with its reassuring flatness, so reliable—a small part of life to be counted on.

Riding along the path, Flora spotted Esther Moon—her lost friend from high school, Esther of the immortal car—walking a small child along the side. Esther was pointing out some object on the ground to the child, who looked no more than three, and Flora could easily have escaped unseen. She surprised herself by slowing down. Esther Moon, a mom after all. In high school, Esther had been the girl who suffered every known teenage affliction—bulimia, date rape, summer school; she'd been diagnosed with ADD and charged with DUI. At one point she'd become convinced she had repressed memories of her stepbrother molesting her, and had a brief bisexual period. Beyond the drama, though, Esther had been funny and wild and that all-important high school girl attribute, a good listener. Flora had been friends with her, though she'd had a hard time believing Esther's stories; her list of misfortunes had seemed more symptom than cause.

"Esther!" Flora called as she came to a stop and pulled over to the side.

Esther turned, a quiet smile of recognition passing over her face. She looked good, like an architect: in black, with well-chosen boxy-framed glasses, artfully choppy hair. "Oh, hey, Flora," she said, as though they hadn't seen each other in weeks or months rather than years. "Good to see you."

"You, too!" Flora said. With the bike and the child held by the hand and Esther's breezy affect, Flora decided against a hug, but then Esther swooped in and squeezed her.

"This is Lily." She looked down at the child. "Can you say hello to Flora?"

"Hello, Flora," Lily said with alarming politeness.

"Hello there, Lily."

"Hey, you both have flower names, isn't that cool, Lil?" Esther said. The girl nodded a solemn nod. "What are you up to, Flo?"

"I'm just taking a ride with my—" Flora gestured in the direction of the path, but Paul had ridden ahead, so there was no need to explain what exactly he was to her.

"No, I mean in Darwin, in February?"

Flora started to answer, but Esther cut her off again. "No, wait, sorry, whoa. I heard about your father, Flora. I'm really, really so sorry about that. How horrible. Super intense. Are you okay?"

Tears welled in Flora's eyes. Those three short words—"Are you okay?"—were so demolishing. Esther swooped in and hugged her again.

After a moment, Flora pulled away. "I'm okay," she said, sweeping her knuckle below her eye. Esther reached up and brushed away the tears on her other cheek.

"I know you are," she said. "But shit, it sucks. He was such a charmer, your dad."

It would require so much less energy to cry in front of this old friend who'd seen her cry many times before, years ago, in a different life, to let herself weep right there on that path devoted to physical fitness and satisfaction in the natural world, but Flora caught her breath and rubbed her face dry, and Esther didn't take her eyes off her as she did. "What about you, Esther? Tell me about you."

"Me? Yeah, well. I have a kid." She fanned her arms toward Lily in a sweeping game-show-hostess motion. "Wasn't quite banking on that, but you know, shit happens, right? And so I had to move back in with my mom and stepdad—oh joy, right? *You* know how excited I must have been about that. Remember in high school how crazy they made me? And they still do, but things are much better now, I mean, much, *much* better. I guess I've finally grown up a little, I don't know, or maybe they've mellowed with age, but whatever it is, it's totally manageable. And totally necessary because the prick *f-a-t-h-e-r* kind of vanished when we got the news, and I was not up for being the single mom of a newborn, you know? And while I've been here, to prevent myself from completely dying of boredom, I started this nonprofit, kind of a political thing. It just seemed like Darwin was a good place to do it, with all the self-righteous old lefties running about—I mean, look at these people." Esther pointed to the cyclists cruising by. "The whole sanctimonious 'Darwin knows best' thing, I get so tired of it, you know? Sometimes I can't believe I'm really living here again."

Flora watched the Darwinians in their unflattering spandex and conscientious helmets. "God, I know," she said.

"But, yeah, it's going pretty well. And I think I'll be moving out soon. Now that Lily is older, we can hack it alone, right, Lil?" Another solemn nod. "I hope so. Wow, I really hope so."

Flora laughed, giddy, exhausted. "Wow, Esther, it sounds great. So impressive you're doing all that."

"Yeah? Thanks, Flo."

"Really. A big day for me lately is going into town to run errands."

Esther's forehead creased in concern. "I'll keep you in my prayers. I know you're going to get through it."

Was that a joke? But then Flora noticed a delicate gold cross hanging around Esther's neck. Not an architect; a Christian. "It's so good to see you," Flora said.

"You too, you too."

"So what's it called, your organization?"

"Oh, man, I wrestled with that one. It seemed so important, and on the other hand totally trivial. So I'm just calling it Intelligent Darwin. Kind of a play on Intelligent Design, but also that's what it's about, how this place desperately needs to wake up from its liberal elitist hypocrisy and accept that there are other ways of looking at the world. That there is room out there for both ways to be taught, side by side. I'm proselytizing, aren't I? I'm so used to making my pitch, it's hard to turn that mode off. Wow. Who would have thought back in high school, when I was baked out of my brains, smoking those Parliament Lights like it was my life's work, that it would come to this."

"P-Funks," Flora said, their name for the cigarettes.

"I mean, could those things have been any worse for the environment? With those *plastic* filters. Shit. But what did we know, right?"

"So wait," Flora said. She scanned Esther's face. Her sincerity was plain. But then, Esther had met all her wildly divergent phases with smooth-faced earnestness, as if the contradictions were a problem of interpretation. "Your organization is pro–Intelligent Design?"

"Don't look so shocked, Flo." Esther laughed, clapping her hands together, a gesture Lily echoed. "I'm not a leper, just a Christian. I got pregnant, the guy flaked, and I was all set to get an—well, to end it, and then I couldn't. And I began to see things differently. To understand what my parents had been trying to tell me all those years. That they weren't trying to control me, though it really felt like that. But no, they were trying to save me. I know, Flo, you should see your face right now. It must be super weird for you, hearing me talk like this, seeing my conversion. But I'm still the same Esther, just a little less messed up."

Flora felt a hand on her shoulder. It was Paul. She had almost forgotten she had come there with him. It had taken him a while to notice she was gone.

"Hey," he said. "I thought I'd lost you."

"Esther, this is Paul," Flora said. "Esther and I went to high school together."

"How do you know this character?" Esther asked her. "How are ya, Paul?"

"You two know each other?" Flora said.

"I roped Paul into doing some pro bono stuff for me—you know, dealing with some IRS nonsense for I.D., et cetera."

I.D.? Id. Flora waited for Paul to explain their connection. He was smiling widely, dimpling them indiscriminately. Obviously, he found Esther quite amusing. Who was this man? Volunteering his time to the anti-Darwin lobby? She hoped to God Paul and Esther had never had sex.

"Paul was my father's lawyer," she felt she had to say. "He drew up his will. That's how we met."

"That's intense," Esther said. "And now you're—"

"Biking," Paul said. "You can't put it off forever." He nudged Flora with his elbow—a pal-like, brotherly nudge.

"Cool," Esther said, turning from Paul to Flora. "So, Flo, give me your number and I'll call you. I'll ditch the missus"—she nodded toward Lily—"and we'll catch up."

"Good luck with that," Paul said. "She doesn't answer the phone."

"That's not true." How did he know that? She hadn't known he'd noticed.

"Okay, well then, here's my card. I know, weird, I have cards, right? But call me sometime." Across the bottom, below the contact information, ran a single line of Scripture printed in cursive: *And the light shineth in darkness; and the darkness comprehended it not.*

Esther thought herself so different, so far from all the other Darwinians; in truth, they were all seeking illumination, a way out of the darkness through their separate and opposing methodologies. But what was so bad about darkness? And wasn't faith, of any sort, a whole lot of trouble to go to?

Flora slid Esther's card into her back pocket and climbed onto her bike. How did one take leave of a believer? "Peace be with you"? "Take care, Esther," she said, and she pedaled off down the path without waiting for Paul, into the uncomprehending darkness, to which she was accustomed.

———

Her parents might have let life go on as it was, but it was Dr. Berry who said no. A terrible thing had happened, but her father was still her father. She couldn't keep avoiding him and his house; she couldn't keep running away.

"You're a horseback rider, you know the expression—'You have to get back on the horse,'" Dr. Berry said.

That was a metaphor. Studying poetry in school, Flora had learned about metaphors. She'd known about them for a while, but now she understood them, mostly. Dr. Berry wasn't really talking about horses. So it wasn't worth explaining that she had never gotten on the horse in the first place.

"I don't want to get back on," Flora told her. "I didn't like it that much to begin with."

"Didn't like what?"

"The house." That's what they were talking about, wasn't it? "It's not even our house anyway. It's Darwin's house."

"You never liked it? Never liked living there?"

Flora thought it through. "I loved it. But I didn't like it much."

That earned a slight smile. "Is there anything you could do to make you like it more, to make it feel more like your house?"

"No."

"Nothing?"

She did not ever want to see those bunk beds again, with their glow-in-the-dark star stickers spelling out FLORA across the top headboard and GEORGIA across the bottom. She did not want to climb the steps they'd jumped from or see the emptiness of the third floor. "If it looked different, maybe. New furniture, a new wardrobe for the house."

Flora guessed Dr. Berry would laugh, but she said, "Sounds like a good idea."

So the next week, they went shopping, Flora and her father, performing their shrink-certified homework, at a department store in the mall, over an hour away. It was the longest they'd been alone together in months, and soon they exhausted all their topics of conversation.

He told her again how impressed he'd been with her Macbeth, her sense of the language. "It's hard stuff," he said. "But you're a natural. As if you'd been speaking in iambic pentameter from the word *go*. You have poetry in your soul, Flora-Girl."

"Thank you," she said, formal and shy, as if he were someone else's parent.

They were silent for a while and then he asked, "Any word from the Wizard?" and Flora turned and looked out the window at the other cars as they passed them.

"Not yet," she said.

Her mother had gone shopping on the day they moved to Darwin, but she had made mistakes—the point had been to make mistakes. At the mall, in the home department of the windowless store, with its furniture arranged as though in rooms—bedroom after bedroom, den upon den—Flora was careful not to make mistakes. They bought a new rug and a new lamp and a new desk. Best of all, they bought a bed to replace her old bunk beds—a canopy bed, something she'd always coveted now hers, like the bed of a girl in a story. She couldn't quite believe it was hers, strange to have the longing no longer necessary. If you wanted to, you could swing from the thin wrought-iron bars, from which a gauzy white fabric hung, but Flora didn't want to.

The new furniture was delivered and the old given away and the workmen from Darwin Buildings and Grounds came and they pulled up the carpeting and they pulled down the paisley wallpaper, and Flora helped. It was her first afternoon in the house, and she spent it scraping, yanking, tearing, gummy grime embedding itself beneath her fingernails. Destruction felt good, though she saved a small strip of the paisley, folding it into the pocket of her pants and later tucking it into the top drawer of her new dresser. They listened to Top 40 on the radio on a scratchy, paint-flecked boom box, and drank cold soda Betsy brought up for them when it was time to take a break. "The guys," as Betsy called them, teased Flora: *What, was she trying to take away their jobs, working so hard like that? Trying to make them look lazy?* She laughed and shook her head no. That was the thing about the President's House— there were so many people around and it was never boring, never empty. It was her mother who had hated living in the house, not Flora.

A week later, there was newness—the bed where the dresser had been, and the lamp, which was a standing lamp, now by the bed, not on the desk, and the rug blue and pink and fringed, and on the walls they'd painted wide blue and pink stripes and the room looked like wrapping paper; it looked like a present.

The Tuesday after the room was done, she and her father went back to Ponzu for the first time in ages, the last time they would ever go.

The hostess asked, "Where's your sister?"

Flora looked at her father. "It's just us tonight," he said.

On the car ride home, he said, "That Chinese restaurant in town is pretty good."

The next day, Flora told her mother how much she liked the new room, how it was better being in the house than she'd thought it would be, thinking her mother would be glad for her, but what she said was, "Funny. He was so reluctant to change anything when we first moved in." Though Flora could remember her mother saying, "Why bother?"

"Would you rather I hate it there?" Flora asked her.

"No, of course not."

"You don't think I should have a new room?"

"Don't you think you and your father need to talk about all that's happened, too?" her mother said. "Shouldn't you tell him how you're feeling? I don't know that problems can be solved in the long run through furniture."

Then Flora felt a little bad about the new room, too, in addition to loving it so much. She cared about the wrong things. She was materialistic, a bad thing to be in most places, but especially in Darwin. She was not too good for this world, like Georgia, who almost was. No, she was just bad enough for it. But the room was so beautiful—Flora couldn't believe it was hers. It was just how she wanted it. She loved it guiltily, madly.

17

The Underworld

THEN THE SNOW CAME. It formed itself into steep banks with a tough, crusty shell. You walked on top, yards above the earth, until your foot sank through the crust, half your leg suddenly vanishing. Shoveling the front steps became Flora's new vocation, replacing the coffeepot cleaning. A large truck plowed her driveway, the noise of scraping and mechanical heaving that first morning rousing her rudely from bed, but by the time her coat and boots were on, it had scuffed itself away, and days later a bill arrived. This was life in the country. On the sidewalks, salt crunched underfoot. A snowman in professorial regalia appeared on the Darwin quad. But inside her father's house, all was warm and dry. Paul's friend the contractor had stayed the leaking of the roof, the sound of men working, fixing, laughing, filling the house for days.

Other things, like the snowplowing, that her father had set in place before his death still continued. Like Mrs. J. Because Flora's father had left her money, Mrs. J. insisted on coming twice a month to clean, though Flora tried to tell her it seemed silly; she had plenty of time to do it herself, and the house, with just her in it, never got that messy. Or maybe Mrs. J. did not like to leave anyone too long alone in the house—Cynthia, Flora, anyone who wasn't Lewis. Maybe she liked to make sure Flora hadn't fucked anything up too irrevocably—the dog still breathing, the roof still standing.

Also, his subscription to *The New York Review of Books*. The big-headed cartoons unnerved Flora. She read only the classifieds.

She imagined everyone read only the classifieds, with the exception of Paul, whom she'd caught in the act of actually reading other things. But she couldn't get enough of the self-parody of intellectuals: "Deeply moral 50-something MWM seeks discreet and cultured 30-something WF for talks about Foucault and meaningful orgasms." Curious omission of a comma—did that mean talks about meaningful orgasms? How riveting.

At first, it had seemed a novelty that she was permitted by law, even expected, to open another person's mail—her father's mail, like his journal, and his house, hers. The first and last credit-card bill had presented a puzzle. What, specifically, had he bought for $46.82 at Finch's Books? Was it Cynthia he had taken to dinner at that seafood restaurant by the shore he liked so much? Even after she'd contacted everyone, with Paul's help closed accounts and changed names, mail kept arriving for Lewis Dempsey; to the junk mailers of the world, he was still alive. Did he want a gym membership? Was he aware of recent alterations to the state's recycling rules? Had he given up on animal rights? Even Darwin College still sent him the odd invitation: cocktails in honor of the young classicist who'd published a new translation of Thucydides; the Religion Department was hosting a panel of prominent atheists—would he be interested in attending?

On Tuesdays and Thursdays, Flora made her way across snow and salt to class and back again, the rest of her quiet, studious week taking shape around the lectures, which were themselves bookended by her bedridden weekends with Paul. She loved the class, loved hearing Carpenter read aloud from the poems they discussed. She'd forgotten how much she loved being read to. When Carpenter read, he was a young man, lighter, his voice crisper, and less wrinkled. In her reading, Flora knew exactly what she liked, her taste clear and definite, and she loved when Carpenter pointed to the exact moments she had particularly noted and underlined, the feeling both of kinship and of knowing the right answer. She loved watching the relationships between students shift and evolve in the room, who sat with whom, and the sudden burst of noise as the class, released, lifted from their seats. Her favorites were the ones who looked nervous when they raised their hands and blushed when Carpenter approvingly responded. Had Flora wasted all her years in school? Why had she not liked it more then, when it mattered?

After class one day, Carpenter sidelined Flora. "Ms. Dempsey!" he called over the heads and headphones of undergraduates. "How are you finding the course?" His pale eyes through his pink glasses searched for affirmation.

"It's wonderful," she said. "I love being back in the classroom. Though, really, it's all new to me. I've never read Eliot, you know."

"No!" Carpenter sounded breathless with dismay, as though she'd admitted to complete illiteracy. "Your father never encouraged it?"

"He did, some. But he didn't like to press. And I was always more of a prose reader."

"Surely one doesn't have to choose between the two—as a reader or a writer!"

"True. I was just going to stop by the library and take out the edition of *The Waste Land* with Pound's annotations," she told him.

"Borrow mine!"

"That's kind of you to offer."

But Carpenter insisted. "It's right in my office. Have you ever been down to the Darwin tunnels?" he asked. "I despise wearing an overcoat, so when on campus in the winter, I rarely see the light of day." He laughed joyfully at his own idiosyncrasies.

"No, I never have," Flora said.

The tunnels had been built over a century ago, back when winter was really winter, to connect all the original buildings of the school. They'd been closed in the late sixties, during the campus unrest. Now there was only restricted access—for faculty and students with disabilities. But Flora had been in them several times in high school. Her father had a master key—a remnant from the presidency—which she occasionally borrowed for a midnight swim in the college pool in the new gym, or the exploration of a deserted dorm in hot summer. She and Esther had sneaked into the tunnels late at night to get stoned and scare themselves.

"Allow me," Carpenter said, offering the crook of his arm.

How to read his gallantry? Why was he courting her? A post-humous poke at her father? It must be unsatisfying to have your nemesis die midfight and no one win or lose or repent or forgive—a Pyrrhic victory of sorts for Dempsey. The too-soon dead—honorable, tragic—have the distinct advantage of moral superiority. But then, she might also represent a comforting, nebulous zone for him—not a colleague, not a pupil, neither insider nor outsider, in between, and thus safe. And she had sought him out, not the other way around. Chosen his out of all the possible Darwin courses. Maybe he regretted his long animus with her father and was seizing in her arrival a chance to make it up.

The tunnels were like something out of a submarine—or a submarine movie: dark and fetid, mysterious pipes dripping questionable liquid into puddles below, long sections where one had to bow one's head to pass by. Flora remembered, dimly, pretending with Esther to be on the hunt, or hunted, crooking their elbows, hands clenched around imaginary guns, looking behind in the paranoid style. Since that time, she'd learned claustrophobia. As Carpenter wound her through doorways and sudden rights and lefts, she imagined he was leading her to a place from where she could never return. Years later her skeleton would be discovered by a student on crutches, on his way to class.

"I never found the article you mentioned. About my father's work," she told him.

"No?"

"I looked online that afternoon but couldn't find it anywhere."

"The Internet is so labyrinthine, isn't it? Retracing one's circuitous search steps nearly impossible. Someone should write a contemporary adaptation of 'Hansel and Gretel'—lost online, bread-crumb bookmarks pecked away by faulty memory and malicious worms." He looked to her for appreciation.

She smiled. "Yes, true."

It didn't seem quite enough. "I'm sure I don't remember where the article was. It's possible I heard it in conversation, English

Department chatter, that kind of thing. I'm afraid *my* old memory isn't what it used to be."

English Department chatter? Was Carpenter playing games? Or was he just a fond and foolish old man? They walked and crouched in silence, and were on a long stoop-backed stretch when Flora's gaze fell upon Cynthia, walking toward them in her wildly colorful arrangement of vest, scarf, and tights. It was an awkward space to cross paths with anyone. Spotting her, Flora extricated herself from Carpenter's arm.

"Hello, Flora," Cynthia called out in surprise. "How are you, Sidney?"

"We tackled Yeats today—and now we gird ourselves for Eliot." Seeing Cynthia's confusion, he added, "The lovely Ms. Dempsey is auditing my class. Do you know she's never read *The Waste Land*? I have the privilege of introducing her. She's interested in Pound's annotations."

"How nice," Cynthia said. "You're really settling in." She leaned in and kissed Flora stiffly on the cheek.

"Beginning to, I think." Flora couldn't read Cynthia's expression. Wistful? Annoyed? Her thin lips were stretched taut, her eyes gray and distant. Had the happy couple once walked arm in arm together through this very tunnel? Had they kissed in the shadows when they found themselves alone? Was she in the thick of a memory?

"I bought a bicycle," Flora offered, apropos of nothing. "Since I last saw you. Though now with the snow . . ."

It was an uncomfortable threesome, her relationship to each uncertain, and complicated by her father. They were watching her too closely. "This is my first trip down to the tunnels," she said. "Darwin's underworld. I'd thought they were a myth. And really, there is something mythical about them, isn't there?"

Carpenter nodded; Cynthia shrugged. It was not unlike the feeling she'd had growing up, post-divorce, whenever she found herself in the same room as both her parents—the fear that she would somehow make things worse, the nervous silence, the compulsive need for dull talk. Her life was a series of triangles, her father often at the helm. Maybe it came from being an only child, the defining familial structure a threesome. Wasn't that an expression: "Bad things happen in threes"? Flora remembered her mother cautioning her against play dates with two other friends when she was little. "Threes are unstable," she'd said. "Somebody always gets left out." But if her mother believed that to be true, why hadn't she done something to alter the volatile makeup of their family before it was too late?

"You're a difficult woman to reach," Cynthia said. "I've even thought of buying you an answering machine."

"A Luddite in the digital generation—how delightful!" Carpenter was jolliness itself.

"No, not really. The old one broke. I haven't gotten around to buying a new one."

She had disappointed him again. "Do you two see a lot of each other, then?" he asked.

"We're getting to know each other," Cynthia said. "We have her father in common."

"Yes, yes, of course. It's nice that you have each other to lean on during this difficult time." Neither Flora nor Cynthia responded. "I was recently thumbing through *Reader as Understander*," he went on. "Quite good, quite good. It almost deserved its reputation, I think. Dempsey had a way with words, didn't he?" The way Carpenter said the phrase, it sounded not quite a compliment, as though her father were a charlatan, a huckster.

Cynthia stood motionless, her countergesture to the chronic nods of agreement. "He was a brilliant writer," she said.

Carpenter turned to Flora. "You know, I read some drafts of the early chapters when he first came to Darwin. He'd started it before your family arrived, then put it on hold for a few years. But I was an early encourager, telling him he had to get back to it."

"Really," Cynthia said. "No, I didn't know that."

It seemed true, sincere. Had that, then, been the source of the rift—Carpenter's early edits?

"Do you have a minute? Can I show you something?" Cynthia asked Flora, her back to him. "It's just in my office." She pointed back in the direction from which Flora had come. "It's part of the reason I've been trying to reach you."

"Professor Carpenter and I were just—"

"No, no, Ms. Dempsey, this sounds far more urgent. I'll bring the book to our next class."

"If you're sure you don't mind," Flora said, anxious for one of them to be gone. "Thanks so much."

"Right. Yes, well, if you'll excuse me, ladies," he said. "I have office hours to attend to. Nice to see you both." He bowed his head and retreated. They watched him scurry, crablike, away.

"So," Cynthia said as soon as he was out of sight. "You two have become quite chummy." Her disapproval was excessive, as though she'd caught them together in bed. "I'm puzzled, Flora. Your father couldn't stand that man. It strikes me as more than a little odd that you've chosen to study with him."

She said "puzzled," but she meant *pissed*. It was the first time Flora had seen her bite. "We're hardly chummy," she replied. "I thought I should know something more about poetry, for my new role, as my father's literary executor. His was the only poetry lecture available this semester."

Cynthia did not look chagrined, as Flora hoped she might, her expression preoccupied, as if she hadn't been listening. They walked without speaking, ducking in unison to avoid the interstices of the school—the veins and arteries of plumbing and electricity—like navigating the inside of a body, with odors foul and strange, and knots of activity that looked destined to fail. When they emerged in the Art History building, Flora caught a glimpse of pink sky and breathed. The world still existed.

Cynthia's office was a miniature of her living room—charmingly oppressive, the walls lined with images—though more cluttered, the desk suffocating under paper.

"Death by Turner," she explained. "I'm at the stage where the research has completely taken over. It now has a life of its own. But don't worry, I know just where it is." She flung her vest on the burgundy desk chair and unlocked the oak filing cabinet in the corner of the room. From the top drawer she extracted the small leather bag Flora's father had carried to and from campus every day of his academic life, at least since Flora had been paying attention. How had she not missed its absence in the house? The dark brown leather was worn around the edges, the threads of the handle precarious. Distinctly not a briefcase—that bulging, steroidal carryall—this bag was made to hold documents of the standard letter size, a few books, a scholar's day.

"I stole it," Cynthia said before Flora could ask. "The night your father died. I was deranged and I broke into the house—well, not exactly, I had a key—and I took things. I took his toothbrush, I took the navy blue V-neck sweater that he'd worn the day before, which was lying on the bed, I took his fountain pen from his desk, and I took this. I was in a daze, a frantic daze, if such a thing exists. I put the sweater on, and I shoved the pen and the toothbrush into my pockets, but I had no idea what to do with his bag, so I brought it here and locked it in the cabinet. It made a kind of sense at the time."

The story of her derangement made Cynthia human and likable—the stealing something Flora could understand. She recognized her. "What's in it?" she asked. From the way Cynthia held the bag, Flora saw it had greater significance than a toothbrush.

"Drafts and drafts. Drafts with many markings and annotations—some mine, mostly his. These poems didn't come to your father in some hasty and ill-conceived spasm of inspiration, Flora. I want you to know that. He labored over them, he wrote them slowly, and delicately, and with great care, and he revised and revised and revised."

"I don't doubt it," Flora said. Though really she did. She had never known him to go back; he was not that kind of writer. He wrote in his head, pacing and pausing in the hallway, and came to the page almost finished, done as he began.

"You say they're not ready, but you see, *he* was ready. After months and months of fine-tuning, he felt they were finished. He'd been living with many of the poems for a lifetime. I'd read several different versions by the time he gave you the manuscript. So you see, you may not be ready, for whatever reason, but your father was."

What was she, competing? *I saw them first! Marked them with my pen!* With her confession, Cynthia offered a version of herself Flora could like. But it was a false idol. She wasn't confessing because the bag belonged to Flora and it was the right thing to do; she was pushing, furthering her publication campaign. The woman was relentless.

"You had no right to take that," Flora said. "What, were you going to hide them away in here forever? If we'd not happened upon each other in the bowels of the earth?"

"No, I told you, I've been trying to reach you. What I want to say is, if he were alive right now—"

"*If he were alive right now?* We could spend a lifetime on *if he were alive right now.*"

"My point is, the poems would be well on their way toward publication. An editor whom he respected—"

"I understand your point perfectly well. But the whole point is he is most distinctly not alive right now. Which changes things, doesn't it? If he were, I would not be here in Darwin, and most likely I would still be contentedly unaware of your existence, my father having never bothered to introduce us, and my having never read the magnum opus in the first place." Flora hadn't intended to admit to that, but there it was—out.

Cynthia sat as the words sank in. "That's why you were so surprised that day when I showed up at his house. You hadn't read them."

"And why should I have? I am his daughter, his child. Has everyone forgotten that? Did he honestly want my critical feedback, my unprofessional opinion? On his soft-core porn and fantasies of having never met my mother? Did it ever even occur to him—or to you, for that matter—that I might find some of the *content* objectionable? His ecstasies at your naughtiness, and the agonies of his former married life? Was the thought that I should be able to read the poems simply as works of literature?"

"Is that how you read them? I don't read them that way at all—no regrets or revisions. Imagined worlds, perhaps. But they're about acceptance, finally, and forgiveness, and, yes, sex and love. Even in the poem where he imagines we'd met when we were young, he acknowledges there would be loss in that, too, that then he would not touch me now as he could in this world: 'touch in that now no longer new.' That's the brilliance of his work—he's so clear-eyed. 'Rewriting revisionist history,' he says, and he means it."

"Yes, then, we read them differently."

"I'm not your adversary, Flora. We're on the same side. We both loved your father. We only want what's best for him."

"Oh, please. You want what's best for you. You want the Odes to Cynthia Reynolds to get the attention they deserve. You want the world to finally meet the muse."

Flora had not removed her coat, and felt hot. She had raised her voice only just, but infused it with a reduction of sarcasm that seemed to suit the accusation as well. It was a tone she had never taken with someone she did not love.

Cynthia looked stunned. Had no one ever spoken to her that way? Maybe she'd never seen the Dempsey meanness—that, too, unearned in the briefness of their romance. But she said nothing, and Flora wondered if the silence meant she had won. Cynthia pushed the bag across a clear and narrow path on the desk.

"You should have these," she said.

It was unsatisfying to have her not fight back. If it was a victory, it was a cheap one. There were many things Cynthia might accuse her of: She was an absent daughter, never visiting; she was not her father's perfect reader, not the reader as understander, but had read his poems selfishly; she was hoarding the poems, the house, the memorial, keeping everything his to herself.

Flora took the bag.

"I was hoping for a friendship," Cynthia said. "That's what I had wanted for us. I thought we'd both be grown-up enough to do that." There it was, the dig embedded in the endearment. "And yes, Flora, you are his daughter—I'm well aware of that. No one has forgotten that. But you are no longer a child."

In her chair, Cynthia looked small, as though she were hiding behind the papers, worried Flora might throw something at her.

"Thanks for this," Flora said, lifting her father's bag so Cynthia could see it. "If you'd like, I'd be happy to make you a copy."

18

The Science Correspondent

TWO PLANS WERE SLATED FOR EARLY MARCH, Flora and Paul beginning to plan on each other: On Saturday, they would have dinner at Madeleine and Ray's, and the next day they would drive to his father's house for a family luncheon, his sister from the city briefly visiting.

"We want to meet this guy you're spending all this time with!" Madeleine had said.

"I'm not spending that much time with him," Flora argued, but she had agreed and then failed to extend the invitation, which would necessitate telling Paul about Georgia, telling Paul about herself. She'd seen the McNair-Wallachs twice since Thanksgiving, and each time had been lovely—if you didn't count the crowd of unlovely unspeakables these cozy reunions unearthed.

At her old job at the magazine, one of Flora's favorite things had been cutting—an article had been assigned at three thousand words but an ad had fallen out, they'd lost a page, and it needed to run at fifteen hundred. She was often called upon, the other editors finding the task tedious. But it amazed her how so many words proved themselves expendable, that the story could be just as good, better even, when reduced by half. It amazed and depressed her. But the hewing itself was only pleasurable, a puzzle, a word game. If, as her father's literary executor, she could simply cut his poems in half, cut half of them sheer away, her life would now be simpler. Still, there were other ways to cut. Secrets were a kind of cutting, silences another sort. There were many such cuts between her and Paul. She thought of the stories Cynthia had told her—of her father reading aloud while she worked in the garden—the complete image, the fantasy of companionship. It was hard not to envy. Flora did not tell Paul of her fight with Cynthia because she knew whose side he'd take. And when Madeleine asked her to bring him to dinner, it occurred to Flora she had never mentioned them to Paul.

The week before the chosen day, as they lay in his bed, not yet sleeping, she made herself give Paul the pared-down, brutally edited, clause-pruned version.

"When I was nine, after my parents split, there was an accident at the President's House."

Paul put his crossword aside.

"My best friend, Georgia, was badly hurt."

"You never said."

"I know. That's why I'm telling you."

He stared at her.

"She's fine now," Flora added. "In Mongolia, actually."

"What happened?"

"Oh, stupid kids' games. She fell."

"You still don't like to talk about it?"

"Believe me, I've talked about it. I spent years talking about it with Dr. Berry, among other people."

He nodded. "Love that woman." He wouldn't stop looking at her. He had a way of looking at her that made her feel like she couldn't breathe. His gaze vacuumed the air out of the room. She wanted him to say something thoughtful and benign, but he said nothing. Was her mother right that she expected people to adhere to a script? That she was too easily disappointed by what they came up with on their own? But didn't certain announcements presuppose certain responses? Wasn't mind reading, in times like these, a matter of being fucking human?

"I'd been close to her family—they were almost like surrogate parents—and then I wasn't, and now since I've been back in Darwin, we've gotten back in touch, and anyway, they want to meet you," Flora said. "Madeleine and Ray—Georgia's parents. They've invited us to dinner."

Paul's dimple appeared midcheek, in the sudden, magical way that it did. He was smiling at her. "So, this is getting serious?" he said.

"What is?"

"You and me. You're getting serious about me."

"Why, because I told you?"

"Because of this dinner. Taking me to meet the almost parents."

Was he really finding a way to make this about him? But Flora couldn't help it: She laughed; she played along. "Don't get any funny ideas," she said. "I'm just using you for the free legal advice."

"What about my ass?" he said, pulling her on top of him. "I thought you were using me for my finely toned ass?" This was one of their jokes. Paul, one of those lanky men, his long body two parallel lines, a piece of linguine, with no ass to speak of.

"That, too." She reached her hands under him. "Your legal advice, your ass, and your dimple." She kissed him on the dimple.

"Let's face it," he said. "It's a winning combination." He slipped her tank top off her shoulders, then stopped and looked at her again, looked at her like her face was an endless bewilderment. "My sad Flora," he said. "What am I going to do with you?"

As the dinner approached, it loomed, a mistake. A day after she'd invited him, he'd reciprocated, inviting her to meet his dad and sisters, so that was nice. But she'd left too much out. On the drive there, she said, "Please don't mention the accident."

Paul's face flashed irritation. "So many secrets with you," he said. "How could I mention it? I don't know anything about it."

"Just don't," she said. "And maybe don't mention my dad, either."

"Are you sure you want me to come, Flora? Are there any topics I have your permission to broach?"

But she couldn't say, couldn't explain. She tried to smooth the wrinkles between them. "You know Darwin. Where grudges stick to the ribs like porridge."

They pulled into the driveway and Paul bent his head to examine the bright salmon of the house through the windshield. "Weird color," he said.

"I think it's pretty," Flora said, defensive. An inauspicious start to the evening.

She was relieved when Ray announced the cool night warm enough to cook outside. She wanted to talk to Madeleine alone. Grilling was no casual recreation for Ray—natural wood, not charcoal, timing very sensitive. And even in Darwin, gender rules decreed that where there was meat being charred, there were men. Ray and Paul monitored the smoldering briquettes, the steam from their breath the miniature of the smoke from the grill, and in the kitchen Madeleine and Flora chopped mushrooms and peppers, tofu and lamb into neat squares for the brochettes. When Flora went out to bring the men each a glass of wine, they were on the innocuous topic of tennis. Did Paul play tennis? She didn't even know.

"Very cute," Madeleine half-whispered to Flora as she came back in. "And tall. I see why he caught your eye."

"You don't think it's too weird—the way we met? Through my dad's will?"

"Well, of course it's weird, Flora. But who cares? Something about him reminds me of your father, actually. The way he carries his body—that elegant slouchiness."

"Great, Madeleine. There's an image I don't need."

"Hey, these things are important. We're drawn to the familiar. Don't underestimate the value of narcissism."

"Believe me, I don't. But isn't that maladaptive, to be drawn to the familiar? Shouldn't the preservation of the species drive us to look for mates who are completely different from us? You know, to avoid incest?" Flora had been reading Darwin's letters, as her father had months before. Darwin had insinuated himself into her daily life, the way people in books did. Darwin—the most present man in her life these days. Who understood more about species and their survival than anyone around him, and still married his first cousin; who wrestled to reconcile his faith and his science until his beloved daughter Ann died and faith no longer served.

"We shall now hear from our Evolutionary Biology Correspondent," Madeleine said, deepening her voice to sound like a news commentator. She held the eggplant she had been about to slice in front of Flora as though it were a microphone—an old family joke the McNair-Wallachs brought out when anyone waxed authoritative on a subject of which she knew nothing: the Science Correspondent, the Foreign Policy Correspondent, the Ancient Cultures Correspondent.

"That reminds me," Flora said.

"That reminds you?" Madeleine said, eggplant still in place, laughing.

"Yes, I'm serious, listen." Madeleine lowered the eggplant. Flora wanted to tell her everything; she'd wanted to for weeks. Madeleine didn't like Cynthia; Madeleine would be on her side. "Cynthia Reynolds wants to host a reading of my father's work. She's found an editor, and she wants to publish it, too."

"The criticism? The Hardy Boys? Hasn't that already been published?"

Flora smiled, surprised by Madeleine's memory: Her father's name for his main men. "No, there was more, more writing than just the scholarship. There were poems."

Madeleine did not look surprised. She was nodding, as if it made perfect sense. "He'd always wanted to write poetry, hadn't he? And he finally did it. That gives one hope for the future, doesn't it?"

"Does it?"

"Oh, it doesn't?"

"No, it does, it does. Only they're complicated—the poems. Beyond autobiographical, they're intensely private. They're hard."

"So you don't want to have a reading. You don't want an editor."

"It's not that. I do, I think. I just don't want to do it now. I need more time."

"And Cynthia understands that?"

"I wish there were no Cynthia."

Madeleine's face scrunched into a smile. She ate a bite of yellow pepper. "Your father had a good life, Flora. He accomplished a lot. It shouldn't be a child's job to make sure a parent gets all he wanted out of life in death. That's not your job."

Flora skewered a lump of tofu. "But isn't it? As his literary executor."

"If you want to know what I think, I think it was selfish of him to appoint you. You're young, and still sorting out what to do with your own professional life—you shouldn't have to sort his out, too. It makes it impossible for you to move on, and ultimately that's what you need to do."

Flora had asked for this, known what she was getting. She felt disloyal. Also grateful. There was one thing more she wanted to ask Madeleine, about the poem "The Wizard," but she stopped herself. It belonged to the forbidden past. "You don't think I'm avoiding the inevitable?" she asked instead.

"So what if you are? Speaking of evolutionary traits. Avoidance has served a range of species admirably for millennia. Avoidance often starts out adaptive. Only later does it become neurotic."

Flora rested her head on Madeleine's shoulder. The firmness of the shoulder, the softness of the arm, for a second it was home. How much easier would it be if this really were her family, if she were the daughter bringing her boyfriend home to meet Mom and Dad? Madeleine gave her arm a quick squeeze. The men called out, the grill was ready. Flora lifted her head and relinquished Madeleine from the moment.

At the table, Madeleine told them about a student in her Freud seminar she was convinced had come to class stoned three times in a row. "My question is," she said, emphasizing each word, "why bother coming? It's insulting. Does he think I don't know what being high on dope looks like? Does he think I'm that old and out of it? Or does he think it's okay, it's cool, it's so like whatever, dude?"

Ray focused on his food. Flora feigned shock. "I'm sorry—did you just say 'like whatever, dude'?"

A reformed hippie, Madeleine had become rather strict. She explained that the same thing happened every semester—some student who riled her with his or her rudeness, or the slovenliness of his or her work, or a more general pattern of childishness. Previous years' infractions included baseball cap wearing, lack of teeth brushing and all varieties of limited hygiene, inappropriate cleavage bearing, lateness, and a phantom vibrating cell phone. "I'm not their mother," she said. "Why are they always looking for a mommy? I bet they don't pull this stuff with their male professors."

"Maybe their male professors aren't watching them like hawks," Ray said. He winked at Paul, who received the comment with excessive pleasure.

"Maybe the kid's just sleepy," Flora offered in defense of the most recent case.

"That's what Ray said." Madeleine glared at her husband. "You guys are such softies."

"Or," Flora added, "maybe he has some terrible debilitating illness and it's medical marijuana. Maybe he has to smoke to deal with the pain."

Madeleine jerked her head back, as if to get a better look at who the hell Flora really was. "Cheerful, Flo. Now I have to stop feeling annoyed at the kid and start feeling sorry for him?"

"Or, maybe . . . ," Flora teased.

"Enough! Enough! I see I'm not going to get any sympathy from you."

"For a stoned freshman? No, I don't think so."

Ray changed the subject: "Has Madeleine told you what I've been working on, with your alma mater, Flo, Darwin Regional High. The school, that is?"

"No, what is it?"

"A meditation course. I'm helping to organize it." In recent years, Ray had become a dedicated student of meditation. The way some analysts could trace their lineage back to Freud, Ray's teacher at the Darwin Transcendental Meditation Center was only two steps removed from the Maharishi—one of the many things, Ray said, connecting him to John Lennon. "It's going to be offered in

the cafeteria after school, once a week. Meditation, yoga, prana-
yama. There's a lot of interest in the school system. In the wake of
school shootings and rising dropout rates. There's a lot of activism
in reducing stress, and violence."

"Interesting that sort of thing is allowed, and yet someone raises
the notion of school prayer, which might accomplish similar goals,
and everyone goes berserk," Paul said. He'd been quiet throughout
the meal, busily chewing, and the three of them paused in their eating and stared at him.

"You think there should be mandatory school prayer?" Flora
said. "But which prayer? Whose prayer?"

"But Paul does have a point," Madeleine said. "Where does one
draw the line between traditional spirituality and spirituality in
this nebulous 'healing' form, between 'mindfulness' and prayer?"

"Madeleine thinks it's all hooey," Ray said.

"I don't think it's hooey. Or what I think is hooey is not the act
itself but the notion that one can solve the problem of school
shootings with heavy breathing. That's a fantasy. An understandable one. But a fantasy nonetheless."

"At God, I think. One draws the line at God," Flora said. She
waited for Paul to defend himself. He refused. "That's the difference between what Ray is doing and school prayer."

"Anyway, it's going well," Ray said.

"All this talk of reducing stress and violence. It's so American,
isn't it?" Madeleine said. "Do other cultures talk about these
things?"

"We have a different kind of violence here. It's a real problem,"
Paul said.

"Do people 'go postal' abroad? Or is that coinage and pathology
ours alone?"

"Sometimes violence seems like an excellent way to reduce
stress," Flora said.

"You don't mean that," Paul scolded.

"I'm afraid she does," Madeleine said lightly. "Don't let that
sweet face fool you."

"Everything's delicious," Paul said.

"It's the grill," Ray said, happy to talk food. "Works like a charm. Thanks for your help out there."

The dining room light fixture was an upside-down colander Georgia had painted during her Bloomsbury phase. Paul, Apostle though he was, seemed not to notice. The tablecloth of layered ivories, Madeleine had woven in college. The transporting thinginess of things. Flora felt herself reach the moment of too much wine. She met the moment, and surpassed it. The plates were cleared, and they moved to the futons in the living room for dessert—homemade lemon bars and espresso. Flora stuck with wine.

Madeleine asked Paul about his practice, how he found the legal woes of Darwinians.

"It's mostly divorces, a depressing number of divorces," he said, as was his line. "Divorce and real estate."

"That pretty much sums up my life," Flora said. Everyone ignored her. Did he not believe in divorce, this Paul? Did he believe in the sanctity of marital misery and all that? School prayer? Good Christ. Was he a hypocrite for all the premarital sex? Was every ejaculation not a release but an agony of guilt? What variety of believer was he? And Esther Moon, too, with her out-of-wedlock baby and her sexy gold cross, like a hand gesturing toward her breasts. Was Christianity in Darwin another twenty-first-century trend, a regressive rebellion like the kind enacted by stay-at-home moms?

Paul asked Ray and Madeleine where they liked to hike. They told him about their favorite spot, out by the reservoir, where sometimes in winter they went cross-country skiing at night. They talked headlamps. Talk of headlamps led to talk of camping. They talked tents.

"I bet this one has never so much as set foot inside a tent," Paul said, flirting, oblivious.

"Zipping myself into my room for the night?" Flora said. "No thank you."

After dessert, she followed Ray upstairs while Paul helped wash up. A transaction had been discussed ahead of time. He gave her a plastic bag with three finely rolled joints. "This stuff is smooth," he told her. "I got it from the number two dealer in the state. I met him at the center."

"Who's the number one dealer?"

"I could tell you. But then I'd have to get you stoned so you'd forget about it."

She kissed him on the cheek. She loved his corniness. They were standing side by side in Georgia's old room, where he kept his stash, now an appliance hospital, a vestigial, ruptured room, with Madeleine's broken loom, a neglected treadmill, a dusty radio, unplugged, a vacuum cleaner, a few half-filled boxes. From the top of one, an old rodent aquarium jutted. Dim light came in from the hall. Flora could not see the color of the walls.

"Can you believe that school prayer business?" she asked him.

"Don't be so hard on the guy, Flo. People think differently. But it doesn't make them idiots. He's had such a different life experience from yours."

"What's next? Book banning?"

"Is he really saying anything so extreme? He seems like a nice guy to me, a smart guy. Why don't you talk to him first, then make up your mind. You've always been so quick, so definite."

Had she? Sluggish and vague seemed more accurate. It was surprising, foreign when people described you to yourself. One deceived constantly, with no intention of deceit.

A reasonable suggestion, Ray's—talk first, then get mad. But in the car, on the way not home, as there was no home, but back to Paul's rank apartment, Flora turned mean. Maybe it was the wine. But they had all been so unfailingly polite, so politic when Paul voiced his opinion, which now struck her as ludicrous. It had started drizzling, and she began to sing: "I don't care if it rains or freezes, long as I got my plastic Jesus sitting on the dashboard of my car." She put her feet up on Paul's dashboard. He looked at her and shook his head. "I don't care about bad behavior, long as I got my plastic Savior. . . ."

"You're in a pleasant mood," he observed.

"Do you actually believe," she said, "and by 'you' I mean all of you, that if I don't accept Jesus Christ as my personal Savior, I will burn for all eternity in the fires of hell? Is that it? The nuts and bolts, so to speak?"

"What are you talking about?"

"That my father currently burns there now?"

"We can't know what he believed right at the end, can we?" So like the lawyer to ignore the larger point and zero in on the technicality. The matter of what the dead believed was not one worth arguing.

"I mean, is that the kind of believer you are?" she asked. "What is the point of believing in such a punitive God?"

"Flora, are you listening to yourself? Why don't we talk about this tomorrow, when you're a little less hostile."

"I'm not hostile. I'm hoodwinked. I was sleeping with an evangelical without knowing it. I think I had a right to know." That was the thing. You didn't know anyone, other people constantly revealing themselves to be aliens.

"You make it sound like evangelical Protestantism might as well be syphilis."

"Yes, quite—a spiritually transmitted disease." She felt extremely articulate, anger rendering her smooth and sharp and silver-tongued.

"I'm not a fundamentalist, Flora. Not that I have to defend myself to you. I believe in God, but not only in God. My sister is gay and I love her and accept her."

"How large-souled of you! And who are you, exactly, to accept her?"

"I'm saying it's not an issue for me—I'd think you'd know that. I'm not as narrow-minded as you're suggesting. Really, I'm not as narrow-minded as you are. You realize you're who people have in mind when they complain of the liberal elite?" He turned from the rain-stippled windshield to look at her accusingly. "You Darwinians who preach tolerance to families of any and all configurations. Transgender, fine, wonderful. But Christian, God forbid."

"It's just such bullshit. School prayer? What's next? Intelligent fucking design? You and nutty fucking Esther Moon, putting the evil back in evolution. I mean, what exactly are you doing for her, or with her? Anti-intellectual mumbo jumbo, insidious, culty bull-shit. Did my father know about this secret passion of yours, your mission to convert the schools of Darwin?"

The light in town was red and Paul came to a stop. "One thing I loved about your dad was he was not a snob," he said. "He had no need for snobbery. I think it came from his sureness in himself. My friends at Darwin and other professors regarded religiosity, when not practiced in a purely academic way—*the Bible as literature* and all that—as low-class, a little embarrassing. A bar mitzvah on the Upper West Side, that was one thing, that was cultural. Going to church every Sunday, that was comical. But your dad had an openness to ideas—liberal in the true sense of the word. You like to talk about all you inherited. Well, some things you didn't get from him."

The comparison cut. "The light is green," she said. "So I'm a snob for disavowing school prayer?"

"My mother told this story—the three-martini fight. A couple goes to a party and the man has too much to drink and acts like a jerk. When they get home, the wife says, 'You know, you acted like a jerk tonight. You shouldn't have had that third martini.' And the husband says, 'I didn't have a third martini, I only had two.' And then they begin to fight about that."

"And I'm the drunk jerk husband here?" Flora asked.

"You do seem to have a tendency to overindulge," he said.

His pomposity was insufferable. "Jesus Christ, Paul, don't twelve-step me."

"You're not mad about this, Flora. I don't know what it is that upset you, and I don't really care. I'm tired and I want to get home and go to sleep. But for the record, I don't want to convert anyone, I was just thinking aloud. I rarely discuss my religion with anyone, for this reason."

"Why? Because we'll see you for the idiot you are?"

She'd gone too far. He'd given her a way out and she'd stayed in. The word *idiot* had lodged in her mind when Ray said it in Paul's defense—"it doesn't make them idiots"—and now there it was, on the dashboard. They arrived at the little parking lot behind Paul's apartment and he got out of the car and slammed the door. It would be satisfying to leave, to storm off, too, but logistically unworkable. Flora followed him up the stairs. He undressed and got in the bed and was asleep in minutes, or pretending to be. She watched him. He had delicate skin and his closed eyelids were tinged a near purple, as though they'd been painted or dyed. He looked vulnerable. Watching him, she felt a sudden bolt of intimacy, *an attack of the fondines*. Was it the threat of loss that made him so appealing?

She went into the other room and sat by the window, looking down to the Darwin street. She cracked the window and lit one of the joints Ray had given her, the smell of pot tampering with the tired food smells slinking from the restaurant below and the damp of the night. Her heart soon raced. Marijuana relaxed other people, but it made her feel she might die—a feeling she liked. Was this what it had felt like for her father at the end? "You can't live his life for him," her mother had said. But whose life was she living? It was unrecognizable, not her life. Studying poetry, fucking a Christian? But Paul was wrong in this: She was not one of them, one of the sanctimonious liberal elites of Darwin. He was sanctimonious. It was he who was like them—the moral superiority of Christians not unlike the moral superiority of academics. The ostentatious decency, the constant scolding. The absence of doubt. Flora had yet to experience anything she did not meet with some degree of doubt. To be able to look at the world and assess with utter confidence—yes or no. Or was Paul that way? She knew so little of him; he had not tried to make himself known, but she had not tried to know him, either.

And Cynthia—how had she let things sour so with this most important person in her father's life? Her life had gone wrong when first she moved to Darwin, and it was going wrong again. Where had the Flora of leaps and boldnesses gone? "Quick and definite," Ray said. Maybe she'd been more herself at the age of eight than she was now. But what did it mean to be oneself? People said, "She doesn't seem quite herself," as if selfhood were a state one drifted in and out of, the self a semipermeable membrane. She'd been sleeping through her twenties, often literally. And now she was back in Darwin, where there was no future, only past. This is no country for young women. Why had she returned? To bring it all back, or to bury it?

She fell asleep on the chair in the living room and woke in ashy daylight to a pulsing in her head, steady as a metronome, as though her heart and brain had swapped places. She made her way to water, then to the bed. Paul and his hiking boots were gone. The plan had been today she would meet his family. But the invitation was, it seemed, implicitly rescinded. Paul would remain for Flora—in a way that Flora for the rest of her long life would never manage to see herself as being—fatherless.

Spring

19

The End of School

SPRING WAS DARWIN'S PLEASANTEST and briefest season, a breezy layover between the cold damp of winter and the hot damp of summer, though spring this year had come in winter and seemed unlikely now to fully flourish. March 21, the equinox, in a parallel universe Flora's parents' wedding anniversary. Anniversaries, birthdays, all the little holidays—how relentlessly and routinely we mark time; revenge, perhaps, for all the ways time marks us. But in this universe, the date marked only the end of spring break, and the fast approach of an academic deadline, the first Flora had suffered in years. The assignment was to write an imitation of one of the poets they'd read in the first half of the semester, and even though she was auditing the class, Carpenter had urged her, in his patronizing, jolly way, to give it a stab. Couldn't she give him a stab instead? But no, she'd said she would try. So she sat at her father's typewriter, trying. But the phone was harder than usual to ignore. It harassed and harassed. Finally, she answered.

"Have you seen the *Witness*?" It was Madeleine. They'd been away in Mongolia, visiting Georgia. Flora hadn't known they were back.

"Hey! How are you? What witness?"

"*The Darwin Witness,* the student paper."

"No, why, should I have?"

"I'll be right over."

"Christ. Breaking news? Have they admitted a Republican?"

"Just hold on. I'll be there in ten minutes."

She was there in less—the first time, Flora guessed, Madeleine had ever been inside her father's house. She entered without knocking, placed the paper down on the butcher block, and smacked her hand against the offending article, which lay in the bottom right corner of the front page, below a story on disputes with the town over the proposed building of a new auditorium.

Dempsey's Posthumous Contribution to World of Poetry

President emeritus and Sterling Professor of the Humanities Lewis Dempsey was renowned for his scholarly contributions to the study of poetry. But according to a source close to the family, the author of the popular works of criticism *Reader as Understander* and *Beyond Tess,* who died suddenly this October of a heart attack, had in the last year of his life completed a collection of poems.

The fate of the manuscript is uncertain. Professor Dempsey's only daughter, Flora Dempsey, was named his literary executor and apparently has no plans for publication.

"There was interest from a publisher, but Ms. Dempsey declined," the source, who asked not to be named, told the *Witness.* Her reasons for declining are unclear.

"It's sad, really," the source said. "Those poems are the only hold she has on her father."

Professor of art history and theory Cynthia Reynolds also has a stake in the posthumous collection. She is allegedly in possession of the original manuscript, a handwritten document, and was the one to seek out the prospective publisher. Dr. Reynolds did not return a phone call requesting comment. Ms. Dempsey could not be reached.

Flora read it twice. Was this, really, her life? Who knew of the poems? Cynthia, of course, who did not return a call, and Paul, bound by legal codes of confidentiality, if nothing else. Madeleine, but here she was, practically dewy with intrigue and surprise and with the impenetrable alibi of Mongolia. And then there was Carpenter, with all his Internet innuendo, who clearly knew something—back now to his Deep Throating?

"That prick," Flora said.

"Which prick?"

"Sidney Carpenter. I know he's done this sort of anonymous-sourcing bullshit for the *Witness* before. My father used to complain about it."

"But he's hardly 'a source close to the family,'" Madeleine said.

"Fuck. I was actually starting to like him a little." Flora ripped the page out of the paper and stuck it to the fridge with the Darwin Dodo magnet. *Ms. Dempsey declined; Ms. Dempsey could not be reached.* She did not like the headline: DEMPSEY'S POSTHUMOUS CONTRIBUTION. As though he'd made his contributions after death. Like reading his obituary in the real paper: LEWIS DEMPSEY, PRESIDENT EMERITUS OF DARWIN COLLEGE, IS DEAD AT 68. *Is* dead. The shock of the present tense—that eternal present. The immediacy of it. And grammatically awkward to the ear.

"*It's sad, really,*" Flora mocked. "Please. He doesn't think it's sad. He's pleased as punch at the thought of some Dempsey familial feud. And he always insisted on calling me, rather officiously, *Ms. Dempsey,* as he does here."

"Couldn't it have been someone else?" Madeleine asked. "Someone other than Sid Carpenter?"

"Who, Madeleine? I can see you're thinking of someone in particular."

"What about Dr. Reynolds?"

"Cynthia?"

"You said she kept pressing you. And how would Carpenter know she had the original manuscript, or that it was a 'handwritten document'?"

As much as she wanted not to like Cynthia, Flora didn't believe she'd deliberately wound her, not with the memory of her father hanging over them so nearly. "And writing that she didn't return a call, what's that—ruse, cover-up? A whole lot of subterfuge for a little college paper, isn't it?"

"That's just it—the trouble they go to over trifles. You know the famous line on academia: 'The battles are so bitterly fought because the stakes are so small.'" Madeleine's green eyes vibrated with excitement. She was alive with the thought of Cynthia's betrayal. She'd been critical from the start. "Hungry and ambitious," she'd said. Maybe Madeleine was projecting, or transferring, sublimating her own antipathy. Or was Cynthia that sneaky, that hungry?

The phone rang again. "Are you going to get that?" Madeleine asked.

"I hate the telephone," Flora said, peevish, childish. "Go to hell," she yelled toward the receiver. "I wish I'd been born in Victorian times." It rang itself out.

"You sure? No Tampax, no birth control?"

"Why do people always go to those examples? As though the tampon were the sine qua non of the twentieth-century woman."

"You want other examples? Do you enjoy the right to vote, or inherit property?"

They both moved their eyes around the room.

"Fine," Flora said. "I wish I'd been born a man in Victorian times."

"Cold damp houses, bad teeth."

"Okay—a rich man with many servants to tend the fires in Victorian times. I've never cared much for perfect teeth anyway."

"I remember your dressing up in that red velvet bonnet and brown calico dress your mother made you when you were in the thick of your Laura Ingalls Wilder obsession. You were always making everyone else play poor blind Mary, or some other less desirable part. You always got to be Laura, no matter what." Of course by "everyone else," Madeleine meant Georgia. It was the closest they'd come to their brief shared life. "All little girls, I imagine, play dress up, but for you it wasn't play. It was serious."

"Am I still like that?" Flora heard herself ask. "Am I the same as I was then?"

"You seem pretty grown up to me," Madeleine said.

"My dad said I looked young—'not a day over sixteen, little Flora-Girl.'"

"You think he was right about everything? Maybe he had his own reasons for keeping you young."

There were so many versions of oneself and others to keep track of. The perspectives positively Cubist. Madeleine's version of her father, and Carpenter's, Cynthia's, and her own. There was the version of Flora standing in her father's kitchen, the one pinned to the refrigerator, the one making Georgia play poor blind Mary.

"I wonder where that calico dress is," Flora said. "Probably my mom tossed it in one of the moves. I remember I had a miniature chalkboard, too—that was my 'slate' for my 'lessons'—and paddock boots, and the pigtails, of course. All the accoutrements. Very important to have the proper accessories. As though through the objects I might channel the person." Funny the things you didn't know you knew about yourself. She could not have said that to her mother, who would hold it against her, would shake her head and make some clever remark.

"We all have our magical ways of channeling the past," Madeleine said.

We do? Flora wanted to say. *What are yours?* But such questions would intrude. Without saying anything Madeleine made it clear the personal was inaccessible. A great well of reserve moated her, and raised Flora's own reserve. She did not ask about "The Wizard," ask whether what her father described in that poem had occurred, or whether it was just a fantasy, another alteration of the long-dead past. She did not tell her things with Paul were likely ruined or at least finished when Madeleine asked after him and said what a nice time they'd had at dinner.

"Yes" was all Flora said. "You guys are the best." Then she asked, "How was Mongolia?"

Madeleine's eyes darted and filled and she turned her head away from Flora. "Good," she said, knuckling under her eyes. "Truly, it was. But a mother never stops worrying. I wish she were a little closer. I wish her life were a little easier."

Flora knew it was not her fault, that she was no longer the cause of Madeleine's worries over Georgia, that the long drop from the side of the President's House did not end in a yurt on the Mongolian steppes. Or did it? She wished Madeleine could reassure her, exonerate her, tell her that they'd told Georgia all about her, that when Georia's fieldwork was complete and she returned they would all have dinner together as though the past were not the past.

Larks had watched the conversation attentively and now Madeleine knelt down and consented to a face licking.

"It's good to have something small to take care of, isn't it?" she said. "It keeps you soft."

Flora watched their mutual happiness. "Or it forces you to see your lack of softness," she said.

"What will you do now?" Madeleine asked as she left. "Confront the enemy wheresoever she may lie?"

"He," Flora corrected, letting the screen door slam shut.

She returned to her father's typewriter. She could write her imitation as a fuck off to Carpenter: *They fuck you up, your professors. They really mean to, and they do.* But what was the use of highbrow tell-offs? Poetry—so thick and fast with hints and murmurs, allusion and illusion (she used to confuse the two). She preferred the free, direct style. Say what you mean, she sometimes felt when reading a poem. Better to tell it plain than slant. "I'm puzzled, Flora," Cynthia had said, when what she meant was "I'm furious," or "I don't like you much." *It's sad, really,* the source who asked not to be named sneered.

"Dear Professor Carpenter," she typed. The round keys clanked. One had to push, to mean it—none of the neurotic sensitivity of the computer keypad. Flora was not a touch typist like her mother—who liked to say it was the thing she did best in the world—but neither did she rely solely on her index fingers as her father had his. She was somewhere in between.

She wrote:

I had begun to assume that the grievance between you and my father had been utterly petty, or at least a problem of his own making. But by exposing to public scrutiny in the pages of the

Witness a personal family matter of significance mainly to me and others who loved my father, you have proved that his mistrust of you was not ill-founded. It was wrong of me, and perhaps disloyal, to have reached out to you this semester. Please consider this notice a formal withdrawal from your class.

Flora Dempsey

She sealed it in an envelope, addressed to his office in the English Department, and walked toward campus with Larks. She would slide it under his door, rendering it irretrievable. She did not want tact or restraint to curb this impulse, which seemed the first good one she'd had in months. Perhaps she had signed up with Carpenter as a way to stick it to her father. Perhaps Carpenter was right: The poems were the only hold she had left on him. Perhaps none of it mattered.

Outside, it was warmer than she'd expected, one of those early days when winter has broken and everyone is young. She took off her coat and tied it around her waist. Larks rioted in the emergence of new smells. College Hill was budding with undergraduates, listening to music, talking, laughing, sitting on the still-damp ground in groups, wearing fewer articles of clothing than the weather allowed. Flora had channeled the appropriate righteous indignation for her letter, her moral and wounded objection to behavior unfair and mean-spirited. But weaving her way through the nests of students, panting her way to the top of the steep incline, she felt as she had when walking back to the President's House with Georgia in the middle of the day, the injustice of school behind them, the freedom of betrayal and adventure in front. She wanted to listen to her own music, to strip down like the undergrads and stay up late.

She had not lost her nerve when she was intercepted at the door to the English Department by Pat Jenkins. Was Pat perpetually disapproving, or was it only Flora, imperfect daughter of a perfect gentleman, of whom she disapproved?

"Everything all right, Flora?" she asked. "We don't usually see you here on Mondays." Had she seen the article? Her worst thoughts confirmed? Was Flora now barred from the premises?

"I'm fine, thanks," Flora said. "And you?"

"Can I do something for you?"

"I was just going to leave this for Professor Carpenter."

"I'll give it to him." Pat held out her hand and took the letter. She gave Larks a perfunctory cuddle and they were dismissed. "Nice to see you both," she said.

Flora walked quickly back. She was not wanted on campus, nor did she want to be there. She was done with Darwin College. What was it to her? Her father's employer; her family's former land-lord; the setting of her childhood. A collective of disappointed peo-ple burying themselves under ideas. Who *privileged* (their word) thought above all else. Ambitious thinkers, grasping, striving, while trying to look contemplative, nonchalant, and depressed. And reading, reading, reading. Infinite reading. Always ready with the right reference, the counterargument, the dazzling associative leap. They had what looked to the rest of the world like the most outrageous gig—you barely had to be there; you were an expert; you walked to work. And yet there was something wrong with all of them. Cynthia the only contented academic Flora had ever met.

It was like the last day of school. She almost ran. She almost sang.

"Larks!" she yelled as they approached the tennis courts. "Find a ball." And Larks ran off into the bushes, on assignment, and emerged in seconds yellow-mouthed.

Flora's throwing arm had grown stronger, her technique smoother. She still could not throw as far as her father, but she had improved. She threw till Larks's pink tongue hung as though pulled by weights. "Quite enough of that," she called, and they headed toward home.

Back in her old room, she pulled out from the closet the solitary box of adolescent stuff, the physical past: the black leggings with the lace bottoms, the plastic charm necklace and the bright gummy bracelets, the marblelized glass pipe in its quilted pouch, the assortment of mix tapes arranged by former friends and boyfriends—people she no longer knew. How she'd loved those objects; how unmistakably hers they'd once been. Unlike the relics of her father's former life, none of hers were made from words. She'd never kept a journal. She'd tossed the old letters, the school essays. She grabbed a tape Esther Moon had made their junior year. On one side it read "The Wild Side"; on the other, "The Mild Side." Her father still had a cassette player in his stereo in the study—the one place on earth the tape deck was not yet obsolete.

Flora put in "The Wild Side." The first song: Led Zeppelin, "D'yer Mak'er." "When I read the letter you wrote me . . ." She played it loud. It had been a while. She started dancing, and she remembered dancing, alone in one of her rooms, getting ready to go out. Alone, but with the promise of change. She danced like hell. She swayed and twisted. Darwin knew. The secret was shared. His words a little less hers, his life a little more theirs.

———

The beginning of the end of school came with Georgia's return. Flora had thought that when Georgia returned to school, life would slowly go back to normal. Georgia would be well, and they would be friends again—how could they not be? They were FLORA and GEORGIA, like sisters. They were Flo-Geo, like the sprinter. Though Georgia would not be sprinting anytime soon. She was still on crutches, one of her legs locked in a massive cast, heavy as a safe, and graffitied with other girls' pastel words. Those other girls took turns carrying things for her—her backpack, her notebooks, her lunch—as though it were an honor, a compliment paid them. Flora tried not to think of the two of them playing Pollyanna, of Georgia the soothing nurse pushing Flora the plucky cripple through the long halls of the President's House in her father's leather desk chair. She tried not to remember any of it.

Georgia's first day back, Flora waited. She would let Georgia come to her. Georgia hadn't wanted to see her, but when she did see her, it would be okay. They would apologize and forgive each other.

Or they would talk about other subjects. There was so much to talk about. Maybe Georgia had finished reading the encyclopedia while she was at home. Maybe she was even smarter, and knew all there was to know about xylophones and zebras.

And at lunch, while Flora ate alone, Georgia did come up to her, as Sarah Feldman whispered ferociously with the other girls.

"Hi," Georgia said. She stood above Flora, leaning on her crutches. Georgia's face looked the same, her cheeks and hair the same, but she was not the same. She had always seemed more grown-up, without being older; now she seemed older, too.

"Hi." Flora wondered if she should get up, or help Georgia down, but she sat still, as though paralyzed, her peanut butter and jelly sandwich hovering stupidly in her hand. "How is your leg?" Flora asked. "Does it hurt?"

"They say I might never recover the full use of it," Georgia said, doctor-like.

"Oh," Flora said, trying not to cry. "Otherwise are you okay?"

Georgia looked away. "I had three surgeries, Flora."

"But you're okay now. You look okay."

Georgia tried to stand up straighter, but she couldn't.

"Are you free sometime this week?" Flora asked. "We could do something."

"No," Georgia said.

"You're not free?"

"No."

"Maybe later, next week?" Flora said.

"I don't know," Georgia said. "I might have plans. With Sarah."

"I thought you said she was a priss," Flora said.

"That was before. She's a really good friend."

Flora hadn't known Georgia could be mean. Was that somehow Flora's fault, Georgia's meanness? It was like they were strangers—strangers who once spent every day together, and talked about everything. For months, Flora had been trying to imagine what life would be like if she hadn't moved to Darwin, how the world might look different, and better, and still it was crushing that Georgia had been imagining the same thing. If she could undo the last year, she would. It was an easy choice, a nonchoice. No Flora.

Flora said nothing, but she was crying now, not out of sadness, but fury. Georgia wasn't the only one whom bad things had happened to. What about all that had happened to Flora? Had Georgia forgotten about that? Flora stood, dropping her lunch. She wanted to push Georgia, to shake her, to steal her crutches and run away.

"Good-bye, Flora," Georgia said. She looked a little nervous, as though she knew Flora's thoughts. "Good luck with everything," she said, as if she were a cruel adult.

And Flora walked away, away from Georgia and the rest of the school, down the driveway, and no one came after her, even as she walked all the way to her mother's house. Her mother was at home, and she ran to Flora and caught her in her arms when she walked in the door, and this time she didn't have to turn right around and go back, but instead her mother called the school and explained that she had picked Flora up, that Flora wasn't feeling well, and with her mother's permission, Flora started not feeling well once a week, hooky from school becoming as reliable a routine as the Ponzu dinners had once been. But this routine she did not share with her father. Another secret, another silence. She knew he wouldn't approve, so she never told him. School, after all, was his business.

20

Number One Criminal

THE NEXT DAY, *The Daily Darwin Gazette,* the slightly more grown-up paper in town, had joined the conversation on the lately discovered late Dempsey poems, the letters and editorial pages devoting themselves to the pitiably contemptible figure of Flora Dempsey, Literary Executioner. In a town where salamander fatalities and white bread were cause for alarm, clearly there was a shortage of news.

"I see you're none too popular these days," Gus teased her when she went in with Larks to buy the *Gazette* and milk that morning. "I do love to see the Darwinians tie themselves in knots over some sonnet. Endless books about other books—did Shakespeare write those plays or did he not? That kills me. Can't they leave the poor guy alone?"

"The old man would be proud," Gus went on. "He took a kind of pride in his enemies, didn't he? Maybe a little too much pride." That was a new perspective: Her father would be proud. "'I'm going to take a lot of people down with me, Gus,' he liked to say. You know. One of those funny lines of his."

Flora hurried from the store. It was the second time she'd made the Darwin news, and though the first time, her parents had tried to conceal it from her, she had seen the photos of the fire escape, the headlines warning citizens of DEMPSEY'S DAUGHTER'S DANGEROUS GAMES. This time around, the commentators thoughtfully wondered whether Flora was "fighting the patriarchal establishment of conventional modes of publication," and suggested "the work be released into a 'creative commons' where it could be shared—altered, even—by all Lewis Dempsey's literary admirers." Another argued she, "like the burgeoning movement of evangelicals in town, stood to poison their community of openness and tolerance with the arsenic of artistic censorship." A third psychologized that "with her troubled childhood," it should come as no surprise "that she is not a capable steward of her father's legacy." Others speculated on the legacy itself: Dempsey had written an epic, a modern-day *Iliad*, or an homage to Thomas Hardy in verse.

Who were these people, these experts? Her mother's line had been that they hadn't suffered enough, but maybe it was the opposite; maybe their petty obsessions were a balm for their daily suffering. Flora had stopped on the common to read about herself, the slanderous paper spread awkwardly on the grass before her, Larks moaning with stoical patience, and when Flora finally looked up, she saw Paul Davies leaving his office. Was he coming toward her? She did not want to find out. She did not want to be scolded, or asked to apologize. She folded the paper messily and pulled Larks back toward home. Larks stared, unbudging, in a state of disbelief—first gratuitous outdoor paper reading, and now they were not going on their full walk around the campus?

"Not today," she said. "If you have a complaint, Larks, you'll have to get in line. The complaints department is closed."

At the house, an envelope had been slid beneath the door. Flora paused before bending to pick it up. A death threat from some Darwinian crazy? A petition to release the poems? But then she recognized Carpenter's twirling handwriting from his chalkboard notes. She opened it and read:

Dear Ms. Dempsey,

It was with great regret that I read your letter of March 21, regarding the article in *The Darwin Witness* and your withdrawal from Modern Poetry. Though I don't in the least begrudge you your assumptions, I would like to take this opportunity to clear the air, if I may.

My rivalry with your father—if one can call it that—is no source of pride for me, nor have I any interest in pursuing it into the grave. Nor do I in any way extend some ancient ill will to you, his daughter. I have, in fact, enjoyed getting to know you and having your thoughtful presence in my class this semester. That said, your father and I were not friends, and often over the years mere collegiality proved too much for us to muster. But I have never doubted or denied that your father's fine scholarship was, in the course of his career, a tremendous asset to our Darwin community.

As I mentioned to you once, our first encounters were quite pleasant, and we even exchanged drafts of our respective writing in those days—an early version of the first few chapters of what would come to be *Reader as Understander,* and a project I was working on on Yeats, which remains to this day largely unpublished. Though I saw great promise in his book, he rightly saw very little of merit in mine, and our exchanges of material at that point ceased.

As to how our little newspaper may have learned the story of your father's latest work, I would only say to you, Ms. Dempsey, that this is Darwin! If we tried to account for all the wrongs done us, we'd have time for little else. I do wish you the best, and hope our paths may cross again one day, if not as friends, then at least as friendly acquaintances.

With kind regards,
Sidney Carpenter

So that was it. Far from being a perfect reader, her father had been unkind, a destructive reader for Sidney Carpenter. His meanness the start of the troubles between them. It was possible Carpenter was deceiving her, but it seemed unlikely he would invent a story so disparaging of his own work. It was moving, Carpenter's humility—"he rightly saw very little of merit in mine." Had her father been explicit in his contempt for Carpenter's reading of Yeats, or had it merely been implied in that way intelligent people fool themselves into thinking their transparency is opaque to others less savvy? Had he convinced himself he was doing his rival a favor, preventing the premature publication of such blatantly flawed work?

But if Carpenter was not the *Witness* Deep Throat, who was? Cynthia, as Madeleine suspected? It was so sleazy and desperate, so malicious, leaking a story to a college newspaper, and Cynthia, for all her aggravating enthusiasms and relentless campaigning, had seemed to bear no malice. Perhaps Flora had read her wrong. Or maybe Cynthia was still deranged with grief, still suffering from whatever had compelled her to break into the house and steal her lover's toothbrush that first night. The publication of the poems would be one way to keep Lewis Dempsey alive. There would be readings; there would be discourse! Maybe, in Cynthia's mind, Flora was killing him all over again, or at least insisting he stay dead. Malice, then, would be commensurate with the crime.

Flora would not sit around awaiting the next batch of accusations. Larks was right in bemoaning his indoorness. It was the perfect day for a bike ride: new, breezy, ice blue. She needed to be more active, to take action. Such eagerness, such suddenness was not mania—it was health. First, though, she would need to break into the basement of Paul's apartment building in town to reclaim the old Peugeot—surprisingly easy, it turned out. The building manager even helped her carry the bicycle up the stairs when she assured him it was hers. She looked so innocent, Flora-Girl. She was the perfect thief.

From Paul's, she headed toward campus. She passed the President's House and the well-groomed, well-watered Darwin grounds, and the little house she'd shared with her mother, and her old elementary school. She was moving distinctly in the direction of Cynthia's house. It would be good to talk to Cynthia. Cynthia—the snitch, the anonymous source. Flora needed answers. But Cynthia wasn't home, and she wasn't in the garden, either, Flora discovered after walking around the back of the house. She'd expected something more exuberant, more verdant, and less weeded, and though it was early in the season and the garden might yet spring to life, perhaps she was observing here some significant neglect, evidence Cynthia was depressed or unwell. Had the woman completely lost her mind? Was that the reason behind the betrayal?

The house—small and white, with green-black shutters—wasn't the right house for her. The windows too small, like piggy eyes. And Cynthia was right, it was dark inside, the day's brightness held at bay, Flora observed as she pushed open the back door, which brought her directly into the collage of Cynthia's living room. No locked doors in Darwin. Darwin was perfectly safe. Flora herself the number one criminal.

"Cynthia?" she called out. "Hello?"

The house was empty but for Andy and Pablo. They appeared at the door, circling her, tails at attention. There was something reptilian in their silent slinking.

"Hello, strange cats," Flora said. As she shut the door behind her, the fear nagged of being caught, quite different from the sense of doing wrong. After all, she just wanted to look around. And Cynthia had stolen her father's papers, broken into his house on the day of his death, taken the early drafts and kept them from her for many months. Cynthia had rushed her. Cynthia had said to the Darwin College Woodstein who broke the story, "It's sad, really. Those poems are the only hold she has on her father." Without Cynthia, no poems—her father's chiding inscription. No poems, no transformation to harpy in the local press.

When she'd come for Thanksgiving, Flora had been unable to see the areas of interest—the upstairs. It was a rabbit warren of little rooms. There were three doors off a small hall—one to a bathroom, one to a guest room, and one to Cynthia's bedroom. Her bed was covered by a beautiful antique quilt, the pattern slightly irregular. It was unusual to see things authentically old today—people bought new distressed wood, or denim, the artful appearance of age an added feature like any other, as though time could be contrived in that way, made up on the spot. But Cynthia, like any good WASP with good taste, seemed to have curated her rooms with irreplaceable old objects. Things with stories, and pedigrees. There was a glass of water and a water pitcher by the bed, of the kind of thick glass that distorts, and a stack of books on the side table, which was really a small turquoise chest, the paint chipping to reveal other incarnations below. A new biography of Thomas Hardy, bookmarked, triumphed atop the stack.

In the closet, every color was accounted for, every shoe sensible and heel-less. In the medicine cabinet in the bathroom, a migraine medicine Flora's mother also took. On the wall above the tub, framed pinups from old magazines—of course—and on the sink a red-and-white china pitcher from which fat makeup brushes burst forth, bouquetlike. Under the sink, a basket of pink rollers, of the sort you saw little old ladies walking around in, in the city, doing errands. Flora's grandmother, too, had curled and smoothed the front of her hair with one giant pink roller every morning of her life.

In the guest room, there was a small bookshelf filled with children's books with worn spines, their bold covers faded by the sun or years. Had Cynthia bought them in anticipation of a visit from a friend's child? Or was this where the nieces and nephews stayed? Surely, as one of five siblings, she had many of those. On the top shelf, next to the pea green of *The Secret Garden,* were the *Little House* books, with their yellow covers—nine paperbacks fit snugly into their cardboard case. Flora slid them out, one after another, and flipped through the pages. They were ghosts, the books of one's youth.

She remembered it was back downstairs, past the bathroom, where Cynthia had disappeared so eagerly that night and returned with the manuscript clutched in her arms like some found chunk of Rosetta stone. And indeed, there Flora found the tiny study, filled with grown-up, scholarly books, the tall art books down on the lower shelves, the books losing height as the shelves gained it. On the desk, a dictionary on a wooden pedestal, opened to the *M*'s. The desk was an old sewing table converted now to allow for different sorts of women's work. There were no drawers, everything on display. Nestled into a neat bundle beside the original manuscript were two letters her father had written. Flora fingered them, though she knew better now: She had learned the punishing lesson of reading his most private words. Beneath those was a water-color he had made, with Cynthia depicted as a cat planting bulbs in the garden, himself a Larks-like dog watching her from the hammock, over the top of his book. So he had evolved over the years from mouse to dog, but the women of his life were all hope-lessly feline? Her mother, and Cynthia, and Flora, too, symbolically interchangeable?

One of the real cats—Pablo or Andy, she couldn't tell which—jumped up onto the table next to her, startling her. Was that a car door she heard? She'd stayed too long. She stacked the letters and watercolor more or less as they had been, then picked up the man-uscript with its twilight blue inscription and headed toward the back door. She could slip out there, but stupidly she'd left her bike out front by the driveway. What if someone had seen it? And as she placed the poems into the straw basket of her bicycle, she noticed Cynthia's neighbor noticing her from inside the open garage. Flora waved, as waving was the done thing, and pedaled away.

But as she rode down Cynthia's quiet residential street toward town, the wind picked up, lifting her hair, and first one and then two pages of the manuscript. Three from the end blew off in quick succession. Flora stopped and hurried after them. Another flew away. She chased her father's papers through a meadow by the side of the road. Like a kid chasing butterflies, but clumsier, and less cheerful.

"Goddamn it," she said out loud to herself. "Fuck, fuck, fuck, fuck." It was hard not to ascribe a willfulness to the pages as they eluded her. They were gleeful. They somersaulted and nipped one another's heels. "Come back," she called after them. Her ineptitude was boundless. "Fuck these fucking poems." There had been a quiet dignity in the act of theft she had just committed. Now all was undone. The dignity replaced with absurdity. When did sad-ness simply become absurd? She ran, and tamped down the paper with her feet. She caught every page but one, one Lewis Dempsey original masterpiece lost to Darwin's vernal breezes. The remain-ing pages looked windswept and stepped on, as they had been, the manuscript inscribed now also by the elements.

On the ground by the edge of the road, Flora found a good-size rock and placed it in the basket, pinning the poems down. What was she going to do with the cursed papers? She'd stolen them without thinking, to prove she could, maybe; but what pleasure would keeping them bring? None. She would return them to Cynthia's. Pretend this had never occurred. The elision and the soiling would not go unnoticed, but maybe Cynthia would think it was she who had somehow misplaced the page, it was she who had chased them through a field and trampled them. And if one page was missing, it mattered little to take one more. Flora flipped through till she found the poem "The Wizard." That one she would keep. She folded the page neatly in quarters and tucked it into the back pocket of her jeans. She got on her bike and pedaled back to Cynthia's.

A Darwin Campus Security cruiser was parked in the driveway, a compact uniformed man standing, talking to Cynthia's neighbor. Flora stopped, and the neighbor pointed. She was a large woman, hunched and wide and over eighty, Flora guessed. Still, it seemed unlikely she could outpedal the cruiser on the old Peugeot.

"Excuse me, miss," the officer called over. "Can we have a moment of your time?"

Flora walked her bike toward them.

"Miss . . ."

"Dempsey, Flora Dempsey."

"Any relation to our former President Dempsey?" he asked.

"My father, yes."

"What do you know. Very pleased to meet you, Flora Dempsey." He took off his sunglasses and shook her hand. He did not introduce himself. His eyes were too close together, which made him look either threateningly stupid or benign and lenient. "Mrs. Bianchi here was just telling me she saw a young lady with a bicycle—who may have, in fact, been you—walking around the back of her neighbor's house. Would you know anything about that?"

"She knows about it, because it was her," Mrs. Bianchi contributed. "I recognize her little pink sweater. And she was more sneaking than walking."

"Yes, that was me you saw," Flora said to the woman, who had the musk of near death about her. "Cynthia Reynolds, your neighbor—she and my father . . . she's practically my stepmother. We're practically family." She turned to the Darwin cop. "I was supposed to meet her here to pick something up—these papers—but she was running late and she told me to go ahead in and pick them up. The back door was unlocked, so that's what I did, what I was doing, when Mrs. Bianchi saw me."

Mrs. Bianchi did not look satisfied. "You see someone you don't know snooping around and you worry. You say you're family, but I've never seen you before. We've had burglaries around here. People are foolish not to lock their doors."

"I'm sorry I worried you. But I assure you I'm not a burglar."

"Petty larceny is a problem in the town of Darwin," the officer informed them, hands on belt. "Maybe if we gave Ms. Reynolds a call now, to verify your version of events, Ms. Dempsey, we could put this whole matter to rest." He moved toward his car.

"Flora, please," Flora said calmly. She was Flora-Girl, an innocent, the perfect thief. "And that really is a good idea. But I'm afraid I don't know how to reach her. As I said, she wasn't available to meet me and—"

"She's on faculty, isn't she? It is a faculty house, after all. I'll just call down to the station, find the number of her office, and we'll see if she's there. Put this whole episode to rest so both of you can get on with your day."

There was nothing to be said to that. He got into the cruiser and sat with one leg hanging sloppily out the door, conjuring the obscenity of an unzipped fly. This wouldn't end well. The information was easily attained. In moments, Flora could hear that the officer had Cynthia on the phone.

"This is Doug Daniels, Darwin Campus Security here," he was saying. "I'm sorry to disturb you, ma'am, but I've got a Flora Dempsey here, at your residence 340 Chestnut Lane."

Would Cynthia have her arrested? Did a Darwin Campus Security officer even have the authority to arrest anyone? The editorialists of the *Gazette* would be in fits. She could see the headline in the *Witness:* DEMPSEY DAUGHTER REACHES NEW LOW.

"According to Ms. Dempsey, you two had an appointment you were unable to keep this afternoon," Officer Daniels went on. "This circumstance resulted in you giving her permission to enter the premises at 340 Chestnut to retrieve an item. It appears to be a stack of papers."

A silence. Flora stopped breathing. Mrs. Bianchi's glare orbited from Cynthia's house to the cruiser to Flora's face as she strained to hear.

"Uh-huh," Daniels said. "That's right. Very good. Okay, then. Thanks very much."

He approached them slowly, the highlight of his fucking day. *Guess what happened to me today, boys,* he'd tell his fellow Division Three cops, Darwin's Finest. *Caught the ex-prez's daughter in some petty larceny.* But then he held out his arms in a gesture of understanding and said, "Ms. Reynolds confirms the story. No cause for alarm. We can all be on our way. Though she's lucky to have such a vigilant neighbor, Mrs. Bianchi. We in law enforcement rely a great deal on responsible citizens like yourself."

Was it a trick, a trap? Why was Cynthia being nice? Her way of apologizing for the bad press? Was she claiming the moral high ground, counting on the malleability of a guilty conscience? Or simply planning to use this information to blackmail Flora, to let her know in some noirish way, *The poems see print or I send you to lockup?*

Mrs. Bianchi and the officer were staring at Flora, waiting for her to leave. She could not return the poems to the house. She was stuck holding the evidence against her.

"Okay, thanks a lot," Flora said, and waved good-bye. "Sorry for the misunderstanding." She walked toward her bike. The officer nodded and got back in his car. Mrs. Bianchi edged away, eyeing Flora over her shoulder.

Flora rode away again, free and clear. But there was no surge of relief. After the excitement of the break-in, the malevolent wind act of a bored God, the near arrest, and the benevolent pardoning, she felt very tired. She tried to concentrate on the insect noise the wheels made in spinning, but she could barely push the pedals, or keep a firm grip on the handlebars. She couldn't make the short ride home. She could make it just to town. There was a pay phone by the common; she could call someone to pick her up. But the pay phone cost fifty cents—when had that happened? She had no change and no one to call. She could see the windows of Paul's office, and Dr. Berry's below, but she had no great wish to render herself pathetic to either one of them, no urge to return to that building ever again. She would never return to that building; it was decided. She'd cross a small part of Darwin off the list. Excise something. One fewer place to return to. Enough returning to the scene of the crime. Though it might be a nice gesture to present to Dr. Berry as a parting gift the fact that she'd been sleeping in her father's bed—an irresistible Freudian morsel as an adieu.

She propped the Peugeot against the pay phone and sat on the adjacent bench. She pulled the poem she had intended to keep from her back pocket. With it came two business cards: one rather chaste, with the name Bill Curtis, and the title Editor, which Cynthia had foisted on her over breakfast at the Spotted Salamander; the other bescriptured—*And the light shineth in darkness; and the darkness comprehended it not. John 1:5*—and decreeing Esther Moon, Executive Director and Founder, Intelligent Darwin. Good Lord. How long had it been since she'd washed those jeans? She put the cards back in the pocket and unfolded the poem.

The poem tells of dinners at Ponzu, of watching the two side by side, his daughter "in her day-old braids," and her friend, the Wizard, "neater, stricter." "The first love affair," he writes, "like most won't end well." "She is mine and not my own," the poem goes on, "this other / self I've grown, separates from me, cell-like / and utterly. The truth of Oedipus not Freud's / dirty murder incest romp, but that we / cannot protect our children from their lot." It ends with a conversation between Georgia and Lewis, Georgia young and battered, and Lewis young and battered, too, though in a different way. She claims she is no wizard—how else to explain the fall? No, he counters, it's further proof of wizardry—who else survives such Icarus heights? None of us is unscathed, he says. I was before, she tells him. He tells her, Blame me, if you blame anyone at all; I'm at fault, if someone is. She won't reply but curls her wounded wing around herself and disappears.

"Flora." It was Paul Davies, walking toward her. But he hadn't said it in the nice way, not like the boy you had a crush on acknowledging your presence; he'd been called to the headmaster's office; he'd been caught by the cops. Though it was he who had caught her unprepared.

"Hi, Paul." She tucked the poem away. Was he stalking her?

"Do you have a minute? Do you want to get a cup of coffee?" he asked.

They hadn't spoken since their argument, though as they'd never spoken every day, it was possible to imagine that it was not that they had completely given up on each other, but had simply fallen into a patch of busyness and preoccupation.

He noticed her bike. "So you got that back," he said.

"I'm not in the mood for coffee," Flora said.

"Mind if I sit, then?"

He sat but didn't speak. He looked nervous, and handsome. He played with his hands as if they were some fresh, weird discovery.

"How have you been?" she asked.

"I think I may owe you an apology, Flora."

"For that fight? I don't think so. We both said stupid things. I certainly wish I'd drunk less and said less that night."

"Not for the fight per se."

"Per se?"

"After the fight."

"Not calling? I didn't call, either, Paul. We both behaved childishly. But there's no need to rehash all that. Really."

"I think I may be responsible for the story in the *Witness*, and I guess, by extension, that nonsense in the *Gazette* today."

"You *think*?" She stared at him, but he would not look at her.

"I told someone about your dad's work, and he told someone else, and then that was it. I saw it in the paper."

Flora lowered her head. She would not throw up in front of him, Paul Davies, Esq., though the revelation was nauseating, her stomach empty and metallic. The worst of it was Cynthia's kindness, Cynthia's generosity, Cynthia saying to Officer Daniels of the elite Darwin squad, *Yes, of course she had permission to enter my house. Yes, those papers were hers to take.*

"Please, say something, Flora."

"Why would you do that? You knew I wasn't ready for anyone to know."

"I was so furious, after that fight, I wasn't myself. You seemed so spoiled, so entitled. And your sense of superiority—as if you were trying to control the way I thought. I felt you didn't deserve your father's poetry, that you had no right to be the person in control."

"For an apology, this is shaping up just great," she said.

He had talked to his friend Jim, the Apostle who edited the online journal, and Jim had told a colleague, and eventually the Darwin College intern who worked for Jim, and whose job it was to troll the Web site for the most scurrilous postings and delete them, heard, and told his friend at the *Witness*. "At least I think that's what happened," Paul said.

"And the anonymous source—that quote?" Flora asked.

"It was an approximation of what I'd said to Jim, passed down second- or thirdhand. Not the world's most responsible journalism."

"Or lawyerism, or boyfriendism," Flora said. "Jesus, Paul."

Paul looked at her in his old curious way. "We all do things we're not particularly proud of, because in the short term they make us feel the smallest bit better. Don't we?"

Flora stood up and moved to her bike, her escape vehicle. As someone who hated to apologize, she accepted that. "So much for attorney-client privilege," she said.

"You going to have me disbarred?"

"It's tempting."

"Is there anything I can do?" he asked. "To make amends?"

She was sure she could think of something.

————————

For Thanksgiving that year, Flora and her mother flew south to see her grandparents and soak up a bit of warmth while her father did God knows what in the President's House. They lived in a coral-colored world, as old people often did, faded colors for fading lives, in a narrow two-story condo near the beach. Flora's mother had been closest to her father, but now he was losing himself, every day one further idea or story or proper noun missing or gone. He read excerpts from newspaper articles again and again—always the same sentences from the same stories, his memory failing but his mind remarkably consistent. Each morning, Flora's grandmother helped him to bathe, and to shave, and to dress. After breakfast, she'd say, "I've got to go put my face on"—a creepy expression—before disappearing into the bathroom for what felt like hours. Now it was as if she had to put his face on, too.

It was funny how different Flora's mother and grandmother were, one's parents' parents both mystifying and clarifying. Flora had never known her father's parents—they had died when she was young—and so had never seen what it was for him to be the child. But it was as if Joan Dempsey had formed her womanhood to be her mother's opposite. Unlike her mother, she never wore any makeup except lipstick, staining her already dark lips a deeper red-wine stain. Flora's grandmother wore perfume—she smelled like velvet—and had her nails done, and dressed in colors like lavender and mauve. Her mother found scents suffocating and smelled like Marlboros—a smell Flora also liked—and wore, as much as possible, only black. Their politics were similar—they liked to say they came from anarchist stock—and they both loved old songs by Cole Porter and Stephen Sondheim. But that was about it.

Flora and her mother shared the guest room upstairs, Flora sleeping on the trundle bed that pulled out from under her mother's twin bed. Joan was annoyed because her mother hadn't made the beds, and had made them dash out for groceries as soon as they arrived.

"What a warm welcome," she complained when they were lying side by side in their two small beds. "It's like she wants us to feel like an inconvenience."

"You should be nicer to Nana," Flora said. "She's having a hard time."

"I'm having a hard time, too," her mother said, turning teary. "She should be nicer to me."

And Flora saw how both things were true, and maybe impossible. She loved her grandmother, who was stylish in an old-lady way and had once been a great beauty, and wore perfume and makeup and let Flora prowl through her jewelry box and try on rings and necklaces and brooches and showed her other ways to be a woman. She didn't let Joan smoke in the house, and so her mother sat outside on the steps like a sullen teenager in her pajamas, ashing beside the potted tomato plants Flora's grandmother watered in the mornings.

On Thanksgiving Day, they were going to some friends of her grandmother, and Flora's mother baked an apple pie—the first time she'd done that since before they moved to Darwin. Then she dropped it on the sidewalk on the way to the car and she cried and the day seemed doomed. But her grandmother's friends were two men named Fred and Jon and their house had a pool and Flora and her mother went swimming and had handstand competitions, which her grandmother judged, and on the way home Flora was happily full, her fingertips wrinkled like little brains, and she fell asleep against her mother's shoulder.

When they got back to Darwin and their little house on Sunday afternoon, the key turned, but they couldn't get inside. It was as if the door had been nailed shut, and upon further inspection they saw that it had. An envelope rested against the sealed door with her mother's name written across in her father's cryptic handwriting.

"Maybe you should open that," Flora said. "Maybe it explains something."

Her mother rolled her eyes. "I don't want to deal with his shit right now."

So they went around to the side of the house and let themselves in the other door and saw that the house had been robbed, everything that could be unplugged gone—coffeemaker, toaster, hair dryer, stereo, television. Also Flora's horse fund—a mason jar stuffed with the part of her allowance she'd been saving since they moved so that one day she could buy a horse of her own to never ride. The letter from her father explained there had been a rash of break-ins along the street where they lived and that the postman had discovered their door hanging wide open and reported it to the police and that Darwin Buildings and Grounds would be over on Monday to repair it.

But the letter also said that the television the burglars had stolen had been his—she had taken it from the bedroom of the President's House and not from the third floor and it should never have been in her house in the first place, she was really only supposed to take the things on the third floor, so if she could just send him a check for two hundred dollars, they'd call it even. Her mother tore up the letter and threw the pieces on the ground and, for the third time in four days, grew tearful, lonely, and rageful.

The worst of it was, Flora had been starting to like him again. It was as though her father wanted her to hate him, or at least didn't care one way or the other if she did. So she obliged. She coated herself in anger, hard as a wrinkled walnut shell.

21

Darwin Burning

CYNTHIA HAD PINNED A NOTE to the door: "Flora, Meet me at 280 Main Street. Tomorrow morning, ten o'clock. Please, Flora. Cynthia."

Where was she being summoned? The address was somewhere near town. Some Darwin professor newly rallied to the cause? At the appointed hour, Flora walked, manuscript in hand, and as the numbers descended, she knew just where she was being led. The Margaret Jackson Homestead. The precursor, the first great Darwin poet. The flamboyant eccentric whose posthumous works had long outlived her early critics.

Cynthia was waiting in the garden. It was quite a setting for a scolding. Swaths of tight-fisted greeny-pink buds drooped from long beds. Other, shorter spring blooms sat like schoolchildren at their feet. Of course, Cynthia would know all the names, Linnaean and colloquial.

"Isn't it exquisite?" she said in greeting.

Flora looked up at the house. Redbrick; Georgian. Not unlike the President's House, built no doubt around the same time. The signature moneyed style of Darwin's nineteenth century.

"I mowed the lawn here the summer before I started college," she told Cynthia. She'd almost forgotten that season of self-inflicted degradation in which, under the employment of Darwin College Buildings and Grounds, she mowed, among other things, the lawn of her old house, the president's mansion, in the long shadows of the terrible fire escape, edged by the cobwebby beauty of trembling wisteria. Her mother had tried to talk her out of it, referencing her "perverse punitive streak"; her father, who avoided dispensing any advice that might be deemed overtly parental—preferring the role of playful compadre, or vaguely disapproving teacher—said nothing. From the president's sloping lawn, one had to look up, neck craned, to see the glare of the tall first-floor windows, to see the green and white of the veranda. An *expanse*—that was the word used to describe lazy lawns like these, lawns with tiers and protective hedges, which evoked Henry James and other Americans who'd cultivated their own Europeanness with the zealotry of converts. Flora had at the time recently read *The Great Gatsby,* and with this new perspective on her former residence, it occurred to her that it was Tom and Daisy Buchanan's house—another proud container of misery. Minus the culmination of bay, she'd lived in that very house.

"Really, you?" Cynthia laughed. "I can't see you doing that, Flora."

"I had this notion it would be the perfect summer job—outside in the sun all day. Pruning, weeding, mowing. Letting the mind wander and think its own thoughts." But the reality had resembled the fantasy not at all, her mind refusing to wander. "Instead, I thought, Mowing, mowing, mowing."

"That's what I love about gardening," Cynthia said. "How absorbing it is, the concreteness of the tasks. It's a kind of meditation for me."

"Well, it was a kind of madness for me."

Cynthia's expression changed, as if she were counting to three and making herself say something difficult; the pleasantries were over. "I didn't tell the *Witness* of your father's poems, it wasn't me, Flora. Though I understand why you thought that, and how upset you were about it, and rightly so. And I understand about the house, and the manuscript."

"Please, Cynthia," Flora said. "Stop being so understanding. I don't deserve it." She gave back the manuscript.

Cynthia cradled it in one arm and said, looking down at it, "In that case, then, I must say, I'm glad the story is out. This veil of secrecy surrounding your father's work makes the whole thing silly, and sordid. Now we can each think more clearly, see more clearly." She fixed her eyes on Flora, her planned speech gaining momentum. "Did you know during Jackson's lifetime the only poems she was famous for were those she'd collaborated on with her well-known brother? Her natural rhythms invisible, enjambment thwarted, punctuation made more conventional, in general the work so much less modern. It was only after her death that her sister found the hundreds of poems she'd written on her own sequestered in some padlocked chest. An amazing discovery—this secret world your nearest relative had inhabited alongside you. Apparently, the brother went wild with jealousy and there was a great family brawl over what should be done, the usual possibilities entertained—burning, selling, waiting, changing. Understandable, given the circumstances. The haunting power of marks on paper."

The pedantry of the anecdote, of the grounds, was overmuch. "An instructive parable, Cynthia," Flora said. "That's why you've brought me here? To educate me?"

"Your father was becoming more and more interested in Jackson's work. She was an important influence. What if those poems had never been shared? Think of all the poets—all the writers—she's inspired. Think of the collective loss."

"Do you really think the world would look so different?" Flora said. They were talking of the discovery of poems, not antibiotics.

"What we're dealing with is difficult, Flora, there's no doubt. And we're both doing the best we can. But in the end, it's not about us. It's about your father, the poet."

"We've been through this all before. It is about us. It's about me, and most certainly about you. We're the ones here. We're what's left. And if, as you say, the whole thing is silly, and sordid, why do you care so much?"

"I might ask you the same question."

"Believe me, I ask myself that question every day," Flora said.

Cynthia looked surprised, and then suddenly, splotchy and upset. She grabbed Flora's arm. "They are all I have, Flora. Those poems are all I have from your father. You got everything and I got nothing. And I'm not talking about what I deserve. Lord knows, none of us gets what we truly deserve—really, how can anyone claim to deserve anything? But I lived what was the most important year of my adult life alongside this amazing man—your dad—and now it feels as if that year never happened, as though I invented it. Except for the poems. I can't help feeling he wrote them for me, that he wanted me to have them. You saw the inscription, 'For Cynthia, without whom . . .'" She drifted off and released her grasp to wipe tears from her chin. "Why can't you let me have them, Flora? Why can't you let me have *something*?"

"I don't know," Flora said. She rubbed her arm, marked red from Cynthia's fingers. She wanted to grab the new fists of flowers and tear them from the soil, to uproot the stems until there was only dirt, once hidden, standing where a garden had been. She put her hand around the soft coolness of a bud and squeezed. "I don't know why my father named me his executor, why he left me in charge. Anyone who's paying attention seems to think it was a poor choice. And maybe he would have changed his mind if given more time, or maybe he did it to test me, or to teach me, or to show me something of his world, or maybe it's as clean and simple as the fact that I was his only child and he trusted me to do right by him."

Flora was crying now, too, and she noticed that they were no longer alone in the garden. A bald and taut-skinned middle-aged man, whom she recognized as the head gardener for the college, her former boss, crouched in a chambray shirt and jeans, studiously avoiding looking at them from twenty feet away. "I don't know, Cynthia," she said again. "Maybe you're right. Maybe I should renounce my legal rights and sign the lot over to you and once and for all rid myself of this place."

But Cynthia was already walking away from her, her head bowed, as though contemplating the ground, or her own feet.

Flora waved to the gardener, who either didn't see or pretended politely not to notice. She turned down the steps, through the hedges, and back to the road. The sky had grayed over and a few tentative swollen raindrops fell, leaving dark gumlike stains on the sidewalk.

"Howdy, stranger!" a girl's voice called out. It was Esther Moon, in her massive sagging tank, pulled over across the street. "Need a lift?"

As Flora lowered herself onto the crumbling foam of the seat, it began to pour, the noise on the roof like hysterical popcorn kernels trapped in a pan. For a second, Flora thought of Cynthia, caught in the deluge, and felt a tug of something—protectiveness. But she did not suggest they go in search of her. Perhaps she'd taken shelter at the Spotted Salamander.

"You look like you've been crying," Esther said, and before Flora had to answer, added, "I thought you'd be out of here by now."

Flora hadn't the energy to talk. She twisted to take in the empty car seat. "Where's Lily?" she asked.

"At home with my mom—she babysits most days. You do know it's Wednesday, Flo? A workday, right?"

"Right," Flora said. "Sorry. I must be keeping you from something."

"No, I didn't mean that." The rain relaxed and gave way to the sound of Johnny Cash, sad and throaty. The car still sat on the side of the road. "You okay, Flo? You don't look great."

Flora shook her head. Tears coated her cheeks, slick and hot.

"Oh, Johnny," Esther called out. "Quit it. You're breaking her heart."

Flora tried a laugh.

"Is there somewhere I can take you? Somewhere you want to go?"

"No, no, I'm fine," Flora said. "I can walk from here. Where were you headed?"

"Yeah, Flo, I'm going to let you walk home in this freaking monsoon bawling your eyes out. Right. That sounds like a good idea."

Flora laughed more convincingly.

"Wow, Flo, since when are you such a stoic?"

"A stoic? Hardly. I guess you've heard about the great Dempsey poetry scandal?"

"That, yeah. I heard. This place is so nutty, isn't it? So precious. I mean, really, who gives a shit? No offense or anything, but who cares?"

"None taken."

"You do know it'll blow over, right? Even in Darwin, a nonstory like that can't take hold for too long. Soon they'll be back to passing town ordinances against nuclear power and plastic bags."

"And unplanned animal pregnancies. Don't forget that one."

"Shit, Flo, you know what? Sitting in this car with you, listening to my music, I'm totally craving a cigarette. You always were a bad influence."

"*Moi?*" Flora said, channeling her best Miss Piggy.

"Oh, Miss Innocent. Sneaking into those insane Darwin tunnels. And do you remember the pool? Swimming in our billowing T-shirts alone in that Olympic-size pool in the middle of the night our senior year. That was scary. I still find indoor pools totally terrifying to this day. You should know, I blame you for that. I was so sure I was going to be arrested. You, being your father's daughter, would be instantly pardoned, and I'd be cuffed and read my rights. Although jail would have been preferable to my parents finding out."

Flora had stopped crying. "What about your brief stint as a cosmetics thief?"

Esther pursed her lips in disapproval and adjusted her glasses. "Yes, my shoplifting phase. Not pretty. One of the many not-pretty phases. The saddest part was, I never even used the things I stole. The lipsticks, the cheap drugstore perfumes. I don't think I ever told you that—I never told anyone—but I kept them in their packaging in this box under my bed, and I'd look at them sometimes when I was feeling depressed. Just, you know, hold them, trying to sniff them through the plastic and cardboard. How pathetic is that?"

"Not pathetic at all."

"We were so screwed up," Esther said.

"I guess. Or maybe we were just teenagers."

"C'mon, Flo. You were always trying to get in trouble, to get caught, like you were seeking out punishment, and when you didn't get it, you were disappointed. And me—with all my talk-show self-diagnoses, as if by putting some label on the chaos of my feelings everything would be okay."

They sat silently in the drizzle as Johnny talked more than sang. Things weren't looking so hot, he said.

"I wasn't kidding about the cigarette, though," Esther said.

"Let's go into town and buy some."

"Shit, Flo, do you know how hard it was for me to quit? Patch, pills, that condescending self-help book. No. We can bum some from those kids playing Hacky Sack outside the Spotted Salamander. Then it doesn't count."

"Will they be there, in the rain?"

Esther made a sudden U-turn. "Oh, they'll be there. They're always there."

And there they were, with their sagging pants held precariously by hemp cords and their mysterious ankle agility, unaltered by the passage of a decade since Flora and Esther had been in high school and knew those boys by name. As she demurely asked the white kid with the long dreds if she could borrow two of his cigarettes, and gratefully received them like sacraments from his pack of American Spirits, Flora squinted through the wet window of the Spotted Salamander to see if she could make out Cynthia inside. But she could see only her own reflection, shoulders stooped, hair frizzing with the damp, squinting back at her. She looked either very old or very young.

"Those aren't cloves, are they?" Esther asked as Flora climbed back in. "Those make me ill."

"This day just keeps getting more ridiculous," Flora said.

In her father's driveway, they lit their cigarettes on the car lighter and took them over to the hammock. It was sodden from the cloudburst, and Flora ran inside and grabbed the green blanket. She spread it across the wet ropes. They climbed on, trading the cigarettes back and forth, and lay there side by side, looking skyward, smoking.

"You know what this reminds me of?" Esther said.

"What?"

"Smoking cigarettes with you on your dad's hammock."

They laughed, then drifted back to quiet. The hammock squeaked softly as it rocked in the breeze. Flora felt she could fall asleep. The cigarette was making her stomach queasy, her muscles liquidy. Another teenage pleasure lost. The narrowing that was adulthood, the endless process of elimination. No, not that, not him, not here.

"This place is so great." Esther crooked her neck to see the house and lawn. "You don't need a roommate, do you? No, don't worry—don't look so scared, Flo. Like you need to live with a toddler. Though it might be good for you, to have company." She leaned down and stubbed out her half-smoked cigarette on the ground. Then she leaned back and closed her eyes. "I'm not sure this is right, and maybe it's totally wrong, or totally obvious, but it seems like you've made yourself so alone, at the very moment when it would be good for you to have people around. Do you know what I mean?"

"I haven't been so alone."

Esther's eyes opened and she tried to tilt toward Flora. "Do you mean Paul? Because I wasn't sure I should say anything, but I have some . . . I'm a little wary of him."

"When we first ran into each other on the bike path that day, I wondered if there'd been anything between you two."

"Me and Paul? No, no, no. I'm a celibate monk these days. Since Lily. Really. One might say I learned my lesson. Maybe I'll move to Belgium and make beer and train dogs and shit. I look good in brown. Anyway, no, I really don't know him, Paul, that well, and he's super smart and industrious—you know, the whole self-made-man thing—and he totally looks like that actor, but . . . I'm just not sure he's a good person. That's where I'm going with this. I don't think he's some great scoundrel, I don't mean that. But he's got a chip on his shoulder the size of Alaska, and as much as he loves Darwin and all it represents, I think he hates it a little, too."

"We have that in common," Flora said, wanting, inexplicably, to defend him.

"No, not quite," said Esther. "If you hate Darwin, it's a kind of self-loathing. But to someone like Paul, who feels fundamentally an outsider, you are Darwin, Flora."

"Not at all. I've always felt outside of things here, too. My dad might have been Darwin, but I'm not."

"Then what's going on here?" Esther raised her eyebrows at the house. "I mean, I can understand his bitterness in a lot of ways," she went on. "Living in this town without being part of the college, it's easy to feel superfluous, to feel alien. You say you feel outside of things, but you're so gown, you can't imagine being town. Your dad was mythic in these parts. I remember being in school with you, and teachers taking attendance on the first day, and asking you, all deferential, were you related to *President Dempsey,* and kind of, for like a second, hating you. Of course, it wasn't about you, and, I mean, it was high school and I'm sure there were plenty of times when you hated me. And I'm not saying Paul hates you, and I know he went to Darwin, but what's he still doing here? No one else he went to school with is here anymore. It's almost like he's trying to convince himself that was his life once upon a time, that he still belongs.

"I'm not trying to lecture you or tell you how to live your life, Flo," Esther said, then, catching herself, added, "Well, I guess I am trying to, a little. But only because it seems like no one else is interfering and it seems like your life is kind of crying out for interference right now. And because I think you deserve better."

There was that word again. "How can anyone claim to deserve anything?" Flora said. "Anyway, it's moot. We're not seeing each other anymore."

"Now you tell me, after I've made my whole speech."

"It was a compelling speech."

"Hey, all those years on the debate team were not for nothing."

"You were never on the debate team."

Esther grinned. "I guess I come by it naturally, then."

"Do you think you'll ever leave Darwin?" Flora asked.

"Wow, you know how to hurt a girl, don't you?" Esther paused. "I don't even know if I want to leave. At a certain point you have to forgive your parents, right, and even yourself, for the way your life turned out. For me, it happened when I had Lily. All of a sudden I realized I wanted my life to be more like the life I knew growing up."

"But you were miserable growing up," Flora said. "I was there. I saw it."

"I was miserable because I was expending so much energy trying to resist the world my parents were showing me. As soon as I stopped fighting them, I was shocked to find myself almost at peace."

"Almost?"

"Well, yeah, I'm still me. Can't exactly stop being that, can I? What about you? You staying?"

Flora's cigarette had extinguished itself. She held out her hand. "I'll throw these away," she said.

Esther stood and pulled Flora up from the hammock, and they walked back to Esther's car.

"You bought this car for a dollar, didn't you?" Flora asked.

"Best dollar I ever spent."

"Thanks, Esther, for coming to my rescue today. And for interfering. I really do appreciate it."

"In case this is a real good-bye." Esther wrapped her arms around Flora and gave her a real hug. "Be good, Flo." And then Esther Moon drove away in her immortal ride, leaving behind a trail of Janis Joplin and thick exhaust.

A short, high-pitched bark came from the house. There was Larks, at the kitchen window. His body convulsed into ecstasies of happiness and impatience when Flora looked up at him. The one he was waiting for was her.

―――――――

Weeks before Flora's father left the President's House to move into his farmhouse and his new life, the old college gymnasium, where years back on a rainy summer day his inauguration had been held, burned to the ground.

It was a Tuesday, in the middle of the night, when he got the call—the last Darwin crisis he'd be called upon to manage, or at least observe. He went down the long hall and woke Flora, who would soon be starting high school and was old enough to be left alone. But he did not want her to wake in the dark house and find him gone.

"We're all okay, my love," he said. "But come, something's happened."

She slipped into her clothing from the day before and walked with her father outside and through the rhododendron bushes to the street. She was surprised the sirens hadn't woken her—their road was thick with the red and white and blue of fire trucks and police cars and ambulances—or the smell, or, as they got closer, the dazzling blaze that lit up the sky with an ominous orange halo, or the muggy heat of the night, which seemed as though it, too, had come from the fire. The gym was halfway between her parents' two houses, and the geometry of Darwin's latest calamity seemed to her symbolic. She wished her mother could be there to see it, knew how much she would like watching Darwin burning, even if it was the wrong part.

The police had set up a barricade, but Flora and her father were ushered through. The building could not be saved. Electrical failure of one kind or another. That close, each sense threatened to drown out every other sense—the thick smog of incineration that clung to their skin, and the sighing, popping roar and moaning heaves of falling wooden beams, and the billow of smoke signaling high into the sky. It was like old oil paintings Flora had seen of war—of ships burning at sea, or Houses of Parliament, brilliant as torches.

There had been no one inside—they were as good as certain—and as the paramedics stood uselessly by, leaning into their unfolded stretchers, watching the fire and the hopeless, shimmering sprays of water from the fire hoses, Flora thought of that other night of sirens, when Georgia had fallen and time froze. And her father, maybe thinking of the same thing, held her hand, or maybe he was thinking of how it all began, when the job and the world were new and his marriage was still whole and his daughter was still safe. And they stood beside each other, and there was nothing anyone could do but stand, speechless and amazed—until the morning, when they could begin to rebuild.

22

The Responsible Anarchist

FLORA WOKE to the sound of someone in the kitchen below. Where was Larks? Couldn't he bark a little? Or was it someone he knew? Cynthia? Had she brought Officer Daniels back to finish the job of bringing Flora to justice? Or Mrs. J.? It wasn't her day, was it? Flora put on her father's old gray terry-cloth robe, her housecoat, and went downstairs.

"You don't lock the door?" It was her mother. Looking in the cabinets. And Larks, fearless watchdog, frantically wagging his tail at her.

"I did at first, but then I guess I stopped. Hi, Mom. You don't knock? Or call?"

"Oh, I called. Does your phone even work? It rings and rings like some banal modern Hades. I started to feel I'd go insane if I heard another ring. So, here I am."

"Here you are." She went to give her mother a hug. They withdrew and inspected each other.

"Nice robe," her mother said. "I see Darwin hasn't made you into an early riser. I need a mug. Let's make coffee."

Flora measured the grounds, lit the stove, her movements in the kitchen effortless now. No more burned hands—she'd replaced the copper kettle. She was better at life in Darwin, life in her father's house. Scary, that. A dangerous improvement—mastering someone else's life. Carpenter's assignment had been to write an imitation of a poem, but Flora had done him one better. She'd imitated a poet.

"I was up late," she told her mother. "What time is it anyway? Did you leave the city at dawn?"

"Couldn't sleep? Up with those poems of your dad's you've been squirreling away up here?"

"You heard. Who told you?"

"The only one who *didn't* tell me, Flo, was you. Darwin has been buzzing."

"Really?"

"And not just Darwin. The blogs have been turned on to the story. They're in sadistic ecstasies. Just the kind of literary scandal they love, one with a clear villain."

"The blogs? And I'm the villain, I suppose?"

"See for yourself. You're an Internet sensation." Her mother had printed out pages and pages of postings. On the message boards, Flora was "jealous"; she was "batty and misanthropic"; she was "like a Freudian case study," and "father-obsessed." Descriptions not necessarily inaccurate, but a bit personal, coming, as they did, from people she'd never met, many as anonymous as the *Witness* Deep Throat had been. The ones whose user names sounded like men called her "crazy." The ones she guessed were women called her "selfish." Why were men so quick to call women crazy? And what was so bad about selfishness? In regards to one's parents, it seemed fairly standard. Flora had friends still barely able to ask their parents, "How are you?" As if not convinced there was a *you* there. She recognized Paul's friend the Apostle, Jim, the editor; he, too, had weighed in: The title of his post was "Goneril or Regan?" Someone calling herself LitCritChic was the lone pro-Flora voice amid the vitriol, though even her tolerance was qualified: "Hey, U all R haters. The girl's father just died. Give her a minute."

A sound choice, withdrawing from the world—untethering, not answering—given the world's meanness. That meanness made more so by the advent of the blog.

"It feels so intimate," Flora said. "Why be mean to someone you don't know?"

"You think we should reserve it for our family members, do you?"

Joan said, sly, smiling. "But it's true. The blogs have changed things. A few years ago, all this would have stayed safely within the walls of Darwin—it would have been a very contained frenzy of petty meanness. But the blogosphere loves petty meanness, however local. Anyway, I spent the whole drive crafting my defense," she went on. "I'll post it as soon as we go over it. Do you have high speed?"

"No, no speed. What do you mean? Where are you going to post it?"

"To my blog, Flora. Don't you remember I told you about it over Thanksgiving? But it would help if I knew something about the poems. Are they awful? Utter doggerel?" Her mother opened the refrigerator and stared inside. "This house is nicer than I remembered," she said.

Flora shooed her away. "Sit. I'll do it."

Her mother closed the fridge and leaned against the counter. "My central point is this: Why is virtue always on the side of publication? Hemingway's family, for instance, might have saved him considerable posthumous humiliation if they'd only shown some restraint, as you are doing now."

"You do realize this is my life, Mom, not just a blog entry?"

"Don't lecture me, Flora. I'm here to help you. I'm on your side."

"Right."

"You really are an ungrateful little child," her mother said. "Who raised you?"

Flora laughed. Her mother had a genius for the fond insult. "They're not awful, the poems," Flora told her. "Not doggerel." She poured the coffee and handed her mother a mug. "Some are excellent."

"What's wrong with them, then? What are they about?"

Flora stirred a spoon around. "You don't want to know," she said.

"I do. I'm asking."

"You say that, but you might feel differently if you read them."

"Not a flattering portrait?"

"Distinctly not. Which is why I never told you. One of the reasons."

"It's hard to imagine anything he could say that would wound me at this point," her mother said.

"We both know that's not true."

"Even from the dead he jousts."

"Writers," Flora said.

"It was our anniversary last week. I'm used to not celebrating it with him, of course. I've even gotten used to not acknowledging it to him. But it is strange to have him gone so completely. It was sometimes nice to know he was here."

"I'm glad you're here, Mom," Flora said.

"Good. Me, too."

"But I thought you said it would be too weird to be in this house."

"Be fair—I retracted that, remember? But it is weird. When did your father become such a bourgeois? I think this refrigerator costs more than my car. In our marriage, he made me feel like I was the one who cared too much about money because I tried to put some limit on spending, but it was he who cared, who wanted more. More money, more prestige. Moving us here to Darwin all those years ago for an administrative job that never suited him. What else could that have been about?"

"Mom, please, for the love of God. Let it go."

"Let it go? Me? That's rich, coming from you. Who really lets anything go? No, we store it all away in our greedy, pack-rat-like souls. We don't let go, we hoard."

"A charming philosophy," Flora said. "The soul as chipmunk. I think you may be the anti-Buddha."

"This culture of forgiveness, of acceptance, of living in the present—who needs it? Isn't the very thing that makes us human the fact that we need not live only in the present? That we straddle time with our minds? That we hold on? If there were one word I could strike from the English language, it would be *closure*. What bullshit."

"Just one word to permanently excise and you'd choose *closure*?"

"You put it that way and it's hard to say. So many egregious coinages these days. Nouns shamelessly converted to verbs. But I don't actually consider those words. I liked how you talked about that in the eulogy—about Daddy knowing all the words." At the word *Daddy,* Flora's eyes stung. When was the last time she'd heard her mother refer to her father so sweetly? "We used to play this game—your dad and I. I would randomly select a word from the dictionary, and he would have to define it. He always could. No one could ever say a word against his vocabulary. His personality, yes. But his vocabulary was impeccable." She paused. "Yes, I think for words to delete, I'd choose *closure,* and for phrases, 'pushing the envelope.' Something about that expression makes me want to gag, I don't know why. It's repulsive."

"You're ridiculous," Flora said. "But I know what you mean. 'Very unique' has a similar gag-reflex effect on me—as though there were degrees of uniqueness."

"Yes. Kind of like 'very dead.'"

"Exactly. 'Extremely dead.'"

They fell together into ripples of helpless laughter. They both laughed silently when they laughed hard. They laughed and they sank down to the floor and sat, leaning against the cabinets and each other. Funny how laughter made you weak-kneed, like tears. Every time their eyes met, they were set off again, silently shaking, their eyes watering, trying to catch their breath. When they stopped laughing, they sat there on the floor awhile, depleted, Flora resting against her mother's arm, her mother's arm resting against Flora's bony knee where it poked out from her oversize robe.

They were silent. It was a long silence. Not an uncomfortable one. Her father had talked of learning to like silence, getting better at silence, in the classroom, and elsewhere. Learning to see silence as a manifestation of thought, and not boredom, or indifference. He'd said that one thing about living long was becoming a better teacher. No longer needing to perform, not needing to fill the halls with bombast. Less talking, more listening. More asking.

"Do you believe in self-knowledge, Mom?" Flora said finally. "Unequivocally, I mean? Do you think it does one good? You must, right, after all the analysis?"

"What do you think, self-delusion is better?"

"Maybe, I don't know. Look at all the successful, high-functioning people so blissfully bereft of self-awareness."

"Like who? Who are all these successful dolts?"

"Celebrities, politicians—our president. Never a glimmer of doubt, no curiosity."

"I wouldn't cite them as role models. Are you hoping to become president, Flora?"

"All those bloggers so quick to condemn me—are they really such perfect children to their own parents?"

"Of course not. Much easier to be a critic than a perfect child, or a perfect anything, in my experience."

"What about Dad? Do you think he knew himself?"

"He knew. He was too smart not to. Though often it felt like he didn't. But then this shard of self-awareness would pierce his face, and you knew he knew everything."

"Violent image."

"A brutal business. Not for sissies. What about you, Flo? Pierced by any shards of self-awareness lately?"

"People talk about the death of a child as the worst thing that can happen," Flora said. "And it is. It is the worst thing. But the death of a parent is a loss of self. A loss of history. Who else really remembers your childhood but your parents? It's like you said about the divorce, that it was as if your history had been erased—you put away the youthful pictures because there beside you in the frame was a husband no longer yours, a self no longer yours."

"One thing I remember about you and Georgia from that year," Joan said quietly. "Heartbreaking little-girl knees. Those heartbreaking little-girl legs. Seeing you two walking somewhere together. Never just walking. Skipping, almost running."

The phone began to ring. They ignored it.

"I still remember, Flora. Why don't you let me do some remembering for you? Aren't you due for a sabbatical?"

Flora told her mother of what she'd learned of Georgia, living and working in Mongolia, with her middle-aged husband, how she would one day soon be a professor. She told her about Ray and Madeleine, how they saw one another now and then.

Her mother surprised her by saying, "That's a nice thing that's come out of all this, isn't it?"

The phone rang again. This time, Joan got up to answer it. "I'm sorry," she said. "She's not available." "She has nothing to say on that matter," she said a few minutes later. "Please stop calling." And still later: "Wrong number, I'm afraid." And when the intrepid reporters from *The Darwin Witness* dropped by, she handled them, too—giving them her business card, appealing to their young journalistic egos, convincing them to let her come to their office to use the computer so she could post her defense of Flora to the world on her blog, The Responsible Anarchist.

With her mother gone, the house fell quiet. Flora remembered her aloneness; other people reminded you of that. Without them, it was easy to forget. She read through the printouts again. Was it really she they described, or was it the Joyce heir, the Ted Hughes sister, the Tolkien spawn? She had lived up to the name of Literary Executioner; she had entered the big leagues, joined the ranks of the real crazies. "Goneril or Regan?" A bit much, no? Was he, the Apostle, the Cordelia of sons? Flora thought of Paul going to find his father at the pub, driving him home, helping him to bed in the dark, undressing him, removing his shoes one by one, as his dad had no doubt done for him decades back. Was what she was being asked to do for her father so difficult, so unfair?

The phone rang, and when it stopped, Flora removed it from its cradle. The house was under siege. Even Larks seemed edgy, running between windows, sniffing under doors. She called him upstairs, where it was safer. Clothes might be appropriate for this day. She dressed in her old room, the now closet. She walked down the hall and stripped the sheets from the unmade bed. She fetched clean ones from the linen closet. The freshly made bed looked as it had the day she arrived in Darwin months ago—crisp, hotel-like, as if no one really lived there. She went down to the basement and threw the linens and the robe in the wash. Her mother spoke of the domestic as a trap: A woman could emerge from her household fog and find she'd accomplished nothing but a lifetime of washing and pressing. But Flora found refuge in the domestic, refuge and solace—the tasks so clear and discrete, progress so easily noted. She was a good housewife—a single, orphaned housewife. She had married her dead father. Shared his bed, embraced his community, befriended his dog, taken up his interests. The results of these nuptials had been more or less predictable.

That night, her mother made dinner in her father's kitchen, Flora pointing out where things were and leaning against the butcher block as her mother cooked. The fridge was well stocked, but Joan did not say how shocked she was to find anything more than shriveling limes and flat tonic water—the staples of Flora's city life. She simply looked pleased and eagerly set to work. She would not be staying over in the house, but with friends in town, and driving back to the city in the morning, one night within the Darwin limits still her absolute maximum.

Over dinner, they did not talk of him. Nor did they talk of themselves. They talked of things they'd seen or read or heard. The world beyond. Her mother talked of politics, and Flora talked for the first time of her reading, of what she'd learned in Carpenter's class, of the books she'd read alone at night in her father's house, recounting not whole plots, but exquisite moments, those moments that when you read them, you know you will keep forever.

Her mother did not ask her what all this meant, this sudden reading, or observe that with her father gone she could now do all the things she'd once felt were his. There was no talk of future plans, or of memories of the past.

At the end of the meal, her mother said only, "Thanks for letting me do this for you."

And Flora said, "Anytime."

And then her mother added, "Wherever you go next, Flo, promise me it won't be Mongolia."

And Flora promised. "It won't be Mongolia," she said.

23

Commencement

IT WAS DARWIN'S COMMENCEMENT, the official, academy-sanctioned moment to get on with it, to grow up. The streets in town were clogged with parents, grandparents, and disgruntled siblings, and even as far as Flora's father's street, cars with strange plates and windows smeared with boastful college stickers lined the sidewalks. The banner above Pleasant Street had for the last week congratulated the graduates; REMEMBER, it commanded, THERE'S NO PLACE LIKE DARWIN. Tents bloomed on quads and lawns, the President's House in full entertainment swing, preparing for the forced march that is the end of the academic year—the trustees, the alums, the faculty parties.

Flora was dreaming of the President's House again. Not quite Manderlay, but it did this in phases—took over her unconscious mind, bossy and self-important, such dreams, at least, recognizably her own. The night before, she dreamt she was hosting a party there, the President's House hers to be host in again. Everyone attended: Georgia and her father, her mother and Cynthia, Madeleine and Ray and Dr. Berry, Esther and Paul, Sidney Carpenter, Mrs. J. and Betsy. The party was a success, it hummed with life, and Georgia was a mother, her baby learning to talk, learning to say Flora's name. This was important, and Flora couldn't help wishing the baby would never learn another name, or not for a while. Strangers danced. Flora cried and tried not to cry. She knew it was her last night in the house; she was leaving and this was a good-bye party, though she did not know where she was going. She just knew she was to spend this last night there alone. "Be funny," her parents said, and she knew this meant she was supposed to speak, but she had nothing to say.

"It's sad, leaving," she told Georgia as they said their good-byes, and Georgia said, "It's moving on. It's exciting," and Flora felt annoyed—what did Georgia know about good-byes?

Soon the mansion was empty, and Flora walked from room to room, shutting the lights; there were so many lights in so many rooms, and she was scared and alone with the knowing that no one else quite understood. She was a ghost, like the men in the portraits who came alive in the games she and Georgia played when they were young. And yet she was at the same time proud of her aloneness, the profoundness of her solitude something of an accomplishment.

In the morning, she woke early and called Cynthia and asked if she could swing by after the show was over, once the Pompous Circumstance had exhausted itself. After weeks of logistics, plans were in place.

Cynthia asked, "Is everything okay, Flora? It always seems a major event when you pick up the telephone."

"Everything is fine," Flora said. "I'll see you later."

Flora resisted the pull of the hammock, listless in the cool shade of the old maples, and set to work assembling more boxes, stuffing them as full as she could manage—so many boxes, tidy and awkward. Arriving at her father's house had not been moving. That had been fleeing—running away home. But leaving now was moving—packing not just a body bag but boxes, too. There would be large men, and a large truck. All moves brought back all other moves. She made herself keep working. She'd already gone through and sent the rarer books to the Cross College Library, and she tried not to look through these, her books, as she packed them, tried not to peek inside to see the reliable initials, or when he'd last read *Paradise Lost* or *What Maisie Knew*. She'd have time to linger when she unpacked; she had a lifetime to learn what he had known, or to

choose not to learn. But of course she did look—studying his marginalia, the subtle checks in margins, the occasional exclamation
point or question mark, the mysterious underlinings.

She took her final inventory of the house. There was much she
was leaving behind—her father's clothes still hanging in his closet.
Perhaps she should have given those away. She packed her clothing
into the body bag, the same things going in that had come out, as
if she'd reached the end of a long, thrifty vacation. She closed his
typewriter, the old Smith Corona portable with its round green
keys, into its heavy metal case. It was her last day in Darwin, but she
did not burn anything in the fireplace as her mother had done as
her final protest against the town, against the house and what her
life had become in it. She thought she might bury her father's
ashes in the garden, but the only shovel she could find was the one
she'd used to clear snow from the steps, square-headed, and best
for scraping, not digging. In the garage, she found a neat wooden
box of gardening tools, including a trowel, clean but its wooden
handle well worn—Cynthia's tools. A trowel might work, the soil
soft and damp and smelling of spring, smelling of either life or
death. And one didn't have to dig too deep to bury a tin of ashes.
She could bury them with his manuscript—there was a depraved
poetry in that. As gestures went, though, it would be purely symbolic, her version being only a copy—one, now, of several. Earlier
that week, Flora had gone to the English Department to make four
copies. She needed help, needed professional opinions. When Pat
Jenkins had seen what it was, she'd shaken her head, for the first
time not disapproving, but awed.

A strange practice, burial. Difficult not to feel self-consciously
tragic—Greek, even—at the thought of burying your father's ashes
in his backyard. Would she rend her garments and howl at the
heavens? Gouge out her eyes with the trowel? Months ago, Flora
had been writing gardening stories as though they were works of
fantasy, as though gardening occurred only in the world of fiction,
in her imagination. Now Cynthia's garden was coming to life all
around her—long-eared irises, and tall burgundy and orange tulips
below the pinky milk of the dogwood tree. She thought of her

father's poem, of watching Cynthia planting bulbs. Of his water-color of the image. No, Flora would wait. It was *her* garden, after all. Depriving her father's lover of one memorial would have to be enough.

Cynthia arrived straight from the festivities, her green robe draped over an arm and neat little beads of sweat across her nose.

"What's all this?" she asked, putting her reading glasses on to examine the boxes piled in the kitchen. "Your way of telling me you're leaving town, Flora?"

"Yes, I'm leaving."

"And where will you go?"

"Back to the city for now. Then, I don't know. I have means. I'm able-bodied. Anything might happen. I might buy myself a house, or an apartment, or, who knows?"

"But you're leaving? You're selling this house?"

"Yes, I am. By the way, do you have a dollar?"

"What?"

"A dollar—do you have one on you?"

Cynthia, flustered, fetched her wallet from her bag. "No, just a five. Or—wait, is four quarters all right?"

"Yes, perfect." Flora pointed to the papers on the counter. "Now all I need is your signature."

Cynthia stared at her. She hadn't yet looked down at the papers, but she'd already begun to cry. When she saw the deed, she released a loud sob and covered her eyes with her hands. "It's mine?" she said. She put her hand against the wall and breathed.

"It's yours," Flora said, and she waved her arms overhead and around the room in a buoyant little girl's dance. Paul, with his vast experience of Darwin's real estate divorces, had been helpful. His last act on behalf of her father's estate, his making of amends. "It's all yours," Flora repeated.

Of course, it wasn't what Cynthia wanted most of all. But it was something.

Cynthia was still crying, but her mouth moving toward happiness now, too, dueling weather patterns across her face. She grabbed the pen and signed the papers.

"Except for the gold chair. I'm taking that. And the Shaker chair," Flora added. "And the books. The books are mine. And a few other things. But we can go through all that later." Later there would be many other questions, much to resolve or leave without resolution. "And the roof. You'll need to replace the roof. Sooner rather than later."

Cynthia nodded and laughed, as though it were only more good news. "What about Larks?"

"Larks is coming with me."

On Cynthia's face, a surge of disappointment, or surprise. It would never be enough. "He used to terrorize the cats," she said. "They'll be relieved."

"You can visit him, of course. We can easily arrange that."

"And you'll come visit me, too, won't you, Flora? You'll stay here sometimes, when you come to Darwin?"

"Sure."

"I can keep your room just as it is."

"God no. Please don't," Flora said. "Change the room. Change everything. Do that crazy thing you do to the walls. The living room could use it."

Hers was not a pure benevolence. It was like the time once, on a rainy day in the city, when she'd watched as one young man stole a bag of umbrellas another young man was selling on the street. The salesman yelled out, "Hey! Who took that bag?" And Flora kept walking. How exhilarating for the thief, and how shaming, off to sell the umbrellas he had stolen. She felt both, too, the exhilaration and the shame. What she had wasn't really hers to give. And she was willing to concede it might not work out. It might not work out for any of them. But there was a kind of hopeless optimism in what was happening.

Cynthia threw the pen on the counter and returned the little pirouette. And they stood together in the kitchen, smiling but not quite looking at each other.

Acknowledgments

While there may be in life no perfect readers, I have been very lucky to have had the help of many of the best readers in the world. It is not an exaggeration to say that without their devotion and talents, *In Darwin's Gardens* would not have found its way into the world.

Sidney Carpenter, Ira Rubenstein, and James Wood were three vital and early readers of these poems who knew all the right questions to ask, and, more, could answer any question I put to them along the way. My father's editor, Bill Curtis, believed in the book from the start, promised to do right by it, and kept his word. My mother, Joan Dempsey, offered me bracing support and generosity of spirit as I struggled to do the work I only wish my father could have been alive to do.

Most of all, it is thanks to the boundless energy and sheer heart of Cynthia Reynolds, to whom this collection has been dedicated, that these poems now make their way to the hands of new readers, all perfectly imperfect in their own ways, but I hope and trust, according to the strongest wishes of Lewis Dempsey, each and every one understanders.

Flora Dempsey

AUTHOR'S ACKNOWLEDGMENTS

I owe thanks to many who have lent wisdom and offered comfort throughout the writing of this book. To Jennifer Carlson, insightful, wry, and steadfast, who took a chance on the novel before it was one, read more drafts than is decent, and made the book better every time. To Deborah Garrison, intellectually rigorous, passionate, and sensitive, the editor of my dreams. And to Caroline Zancan, who has made the way smooth. To Rivka Galchen, Ella Georgiades, Alena Graedon, Nellie Hermann, Karen Thompson, and Cora Weimer-Hodes, adored friends, who read earlier versions with generosity, grit, and invaluable intelligence. To my humorous and talented teachers at Columbia's Writing Division, who saw the novel through its awkward stages. To the brilliant Professor Edward Tayler, from whom I borrowed and no doubt bastardized the notion of the reader as understander. To our incomparable critic James Wood, from whom I borrowed several ideas to create the character of James Wood. To Claire Tomalin, whose *Thomas Hardy* helped me to work out who the poet was to Lewis Dempsey. To my family, dazzling and true, for their fierce belief, which at the crucial moment meant everything. And especially to Matt, my home, who has given this book and its author more love and care than either deserved—thank you.

Meet with Interesting People
Enjoy Stimulating Conversation
Discover Wonderful Books